"Brown recognizes that push and pull that drives
families—and drives them crazy. . . . Brown's empathy
for these women who find themselves outcasts is
endearing. . . . A delight."
—*MIAMI HERALD*

"A trip to Paris may be the quickest way for a heroine
to change her life. . . . Warmhearted."
—*THE WASHINGTON POST*

"Fresh, endearing . . . Finely written and absorbing,
and explores the always compelling questions
of how to balance reality and romance,
duty and dreams, family and freedom."
—*MINNEAPOLIS STAR TRIBUNE*

"Plumb[s] the difference between the things in life
that give us joy and the things that we do to stifle that joy.
For all fans of intelligent women's literature."
—*LIBRARY JOURNAL*

"A charming novel about living life on your own
terms that will make you long for the streets of Paris."
—*POPSUGAR.COM*

"Brown conveys the importance of the arts in
creating a life as well as the need to heed
all voices, even those from the past,
in looking to the future."
—*KIRKUS REVIEWS*

Praise for Eleanor Brown

"What a joy to read. What a VOICE. *The Weird Sisters* is family drama dissected by verbal scalpel. If wit and language could protect against growing old, these bewitching sisters might never have to grow up."

—Helen Simonson, bestselling author of *Major Pettigrew's Last Stand*

"At once hilarious, thought-provoking and poignant, this sparkling and devourable debut explores the roles that we play with our siblings, whether we want to or not. *The Weird Sisters* is a tale of the complex family ties that threaten to pull us apart, but sometimes draw us together instead."

—J. Courtney Sullivan, bestselling author of *Commencement*

"Delightful."   —*People*

"A delightful and fascinating book . . . a magnificent tapestry of a tale . . . that beautifully illustrates the pull of family and the ties that bind . . . even when we are about to unravel."   —*The Sacramento Bee*

"This smart, hopeful novel . . . will be the winter's tale for any book lover. . . . A family drama, gracefully costumed in academic garb and lit with warm comedy, 'tis a consummation devoutly to be wished . . . get thee to a bookstore. . . . Brown is such a clever writer, and she's written such an endearing story about sisterly affection and the possibilities of redemption, that it's easy to recommend *The Weird Sisters*. Take Polonius's food advice and 'read on this book.'"

—*The Washington Post*

"A page-turner from the start."   —*Ladies' Home Journal*

"Delightful. . . . That's Brown's gift: She draws you in and makes you believe her weird sisters aren't so weird after all."   —*Miami Herald*

"Even if you don't have a sister, you may feel like you have one after reading this hilarious and utterly winsome novel. Eleanor Brown skillfully ties and then unties the Gordian knot of sisterhood, writing with such knowingness that when the ending came, and the three Andreas sisters—who had slunk home for a rest from themselves only to find to their horror their other two sisters there as well—emerge, I sighed the guilty sigh of pleasure and yes, of recognition."

—Sarah Blake, bestselling author of *The Postmistress*

"[A] likable, gracefully written first novel. . . . This is a story about family, about three sisters finding their separate yet interconnected ways in the world. It's a novel about becoming an adult, at last. Readers who enjoy reading about fraught family relationships, especially among sisters, will find it irresistible."

—*The Boston Globe*

"Here's what I adored about this book: the first person plural narrative voice (I can still hear it in my head), its realistic take on the pleasures and pangs of sisterly relationships, and a cast of complex, three dimensional characters who love reading but find that real life sometimes doesn't fit neatly—or can't be solved—within the pages of a novel."

—Nancy Pearl, author of *Book Lust* and *Book Lust to Go*

"Charming . . . you need not be a Shakespeare scholar to fall in love with this feel-good story—or the bewitching sisters."   —*Woman's Day*

"Lovely . . . This novel should appeal to Shakespeare lovers, bibliophiles, and fans of novels in academic settings and stories of sisterhood. The narration is a creative and original blending of the three *Weird Sisters* as one."   —*Library Journal*

"You don't have to have a sister or be a fan of the Bard to love Brown's bright, literate debut."   —*Publishers Weekly* (starred)

"Genuinely funny . . . buoyant."   —*The New York Times*

Also by Eleanor Brown

The Weird Sisters

THE
LIGHT
OF
PARIS

Eleanor Brown

G. P. Putnam's Sons
New York

PUTNAM

G. P. PUTNAM'S SONS
Publishers Since 1838
An imprint of Penguin Random House LLC
375 Hudson Street
New York, New York 10014

The Library of Congress has catalogued the G. P. Putnam's Sons hardcover edition
as follows:

Names: Brown, Eleanor, author.
Title: The light of Paris / Eleanor Brown.
Description: New York: G. P. Putnam's Sons, [2016]
Identifiers: LCCN 2016009821| ISBN 9780399158919 (hardcover) |
ISBN 9780399573736 (ePub) | ISBN 9780399576980 (international)
Subjects: LCSH: Married women—Fiction. | Self-realization in women—Fiction. |
Self-actualization (Psychology) in women—Fiction. | Paris (France)—Fiction. |
Domestic fiction. | BISAC: FICTION / Contemporary Women. |
FICTION / Literary. | FICTION / Family Life.
Classification: LCC PS3602.R6965 L54 2016 | DDC 813/.6—dc23
LC record available at https://lccn.loc.gov/2016009821
p.   cm.

First G. P. Putnam's Sons hardcover edition / July 2016
First G. P. Putnam's Sons international edition / July 2016
First G. P. Putnam's Sons trade paperback edition / April 2017
G. P. Putnam's Sons trade paperback ISBN: 9780399573729

Printed in the United States of America
1   3   5   7   9   10   8   6   4   2

Book design by Lauren Kolm

For my parents and my grandparents, especially my grandmothers:
Madeline Mercier Brown and Catherine McReynolds Barnes

Paris in the rain is still Paris.

—Catherine Rémine McReynolds,
November 18, 1923

one

MADELEINE
1999

I didn't set out to lose myself. No one does, really. No one purposely swims away from the solid, forgiving anchor of their heart. We simply make the tiniest of compromises, the smallest of decisions, not realizing the way those small changes add up to something larger until we are forced, for better or worse, to face the people we have become.

I had the best of intentions, always: to make my mother happy, to keep the peace, to smooth my rough edges and ease my own way. But in the end, the life I had crafted was like the porcelain figurines that resided in my mother's china cabinets: smooth, ornate, but delicate and hollow. For display only. Do not touch.

Long ago, I might have called myself an artist. As a child, I drew on every blank surface I encountered—including, to my mother's dismay, the walls, deliciously empty front pages of library books, and more than a few freshly ironed tablecloths. In high school, I spent hours in the art room after school, painting until the sun coming through the skylights grew thin and the art teacher would gently put her hand on my shoulder and tell me it was time to go home. Lingering under my Anaïs Anaïs perfume was the smell of paint, and the edges of every textbook I owned were covered with doodles and drawings. On the weekends, I hid from my mother's bottomless disapproval in the basement of our house, where

I had set up an easel, painting until my fingers were stiff and the light had disappeared, rendering the colors I blended on the palette an indiscriminate black.

But I hadn't painted since I had gotten married. Now, I spent hours leading tour groups through the Stabler Art Museum's galleries, pointing out the beautiful blur of the Impressionists, the lush clarity of the Romantics, the lawless color of Abstract Expressionism. As we moved between the rooms, I showed them the progression of the paintings, movement washing into movement like the confluence of rivers, the same medium, the same tools, yet so completely different in appearance, in intent, in heart. No matter how many times I explained it, it seemed beautifully impossible that Monet had been creating his gentle pastorals less than a hundred years before the delicious chaos of Jackson Pollock's murals.

It was almost enough.

Usually Tanis took the older kids; she had four teenage sons and wasn't afraid of anything. But she was out, and the other docents were booked, so the coordinator asked if I would take the group. I had hesitated for a moment—teenagers seemed scary and uncontrolled, all loose limbs and incomprehensible fashion decisions and bad attitudes—and then told him I would. Their teacher would be with us, after all, and she had requested one of my favorite tours, on artists and their influences.

When I met them in the lobby, I asked the kids their names and who their favorite artists were, to which they, predictably, reacted as though I were trying to get them to divulge state secrets. Their teacher, Miss Pine, was young and slender, with hair that fell loose around her shoulders, more knot than curl, as though she wound her fingers in it all the time. I—and most of the women I knew—wore slim sheath dresses with elegant scarves, an acceptably polite pop of color, but Miss Pine was wrapped in a pile of boysenberry-colored fabric that looked less like a dress and more like a collection of handkerchiefs that had been safety-pinned together. She must have been wearing bracelets or bells, because she jingled as she moved. Either that, or she was hiding a number of out-of-season reindeer underneath those swathes of fabric.

"How long have you been teaching?" I asked, making conversation as we headed to the first stop on the tour, followed by our little ducklings, the floors creaking agreeably beneath our feet.

"Almost ten years," Miss Pine said, smiling at me. I must have made a face of horror, because she laughed, a light sound with a rough edge that made me smile just to hear it. "They're not so bad, are they?"

Glancing over my shoulder at the kids, who meandered along in our wake as we climbed the wide marble staircase to the second floor, I laughed too. "Not so bad." The boys were bouncing off each other like pinballs, a couple of the girls walked with their heads bent together in the inimitable intimacy of teenagers, a few others drifted off to the edges of the staircase to look at the paintings that lined the walls or the sculptures on the landing.

"I just have lingering flashbacks to my own experience. I didn't cope so well with high school kids when I was in high school myself. I basically spent four years slinking around, trying to fly under the radar."

Miss Pine waved her hand, setting off her bells again. "We all did. It's much easier from this side of the desk, I promise you. Plus, you get to try to make it a slightly less miserable experience for them than it was for you."

"All right, ladies and gentlemen, first stop," I said when we reached the Renaissance room. I turned to face them, clapping my hands together and then instantly regretting it. I was not an earnest, hand-clapping, Precious Moments stationery–using sort of person. "What do you know about Renaissance art? Lay it on me."

The kids, who had been chattering enthusiastically as we walked, of course chose that moment to fall sullenly silent. Elementary-aged children seemed almost violent in their desire to speak, hurling their entire bodies into the air when they raised their hands, as though they were controlled by marionette strings. But these high schoolers were draped with languid adolescent ease that didn't hide the twitch of their eyes, their anxious fingers worrying their pencils, the edges of their sketch pads. I had thought for sure the Renaissance paintings might get them, all those nudes with their tender, pale skin and tactfully placed hands and leaves, but they seemed only politely interested.

"Come on, people," I said. "I'm getting you out of school for the day. The least you can do is answer my questions."

Miss Pine and a couple of the kids grinned. Eliza, a girl with long brown braids and a T-shirt bearing a faded print of Munch's *The Scream*, raised her hand. She reminded me a little of myself at that age—a spray of pimples across her forehead, curls breaking free of her braids, a thick, sturdy body. She held a paintbrush between her fingers, perhaps in case of an unexpected art emergency, which kind of made me want to give her a hug.

"My savior!" I said. "Pray, my lady, speak."

Eliza flushed a little as her classmates turned to look at her, but when she spoke, her voice was loud and clear and confident. Or at least as confident as a teenage girl could be, her voice lilting up into questions at the end. "They were really interested in, like, Classical art? Like, Greeks?"

"And the Romans, yeah!" I said. I was so excited someone was actually talking that I might have spoken a little too loudly, because a boy named Lam, his black hair swept into a style that made him look as though he were standing in a wind tunnel, actually took a step back. I cleared my throat and tried for something a little less enthusiastic, the reserved voice I used in the rest of my life, where I spent all my time talking about things I didn't care about. "They were fascinated by Greco-Roman culture, and you can see those influences everywhere. Take this painting, for instance," I said, pointing at a piece by an Italian artist. "Do you see these sculptures running along the top of the building in the background?"

The kids leaned forward and I suppressed a grin. So they were interested after all. It was just a matter of breaking through their external cool to find the real people underneath.

Lam spoke up. "It looks like those friezes on the Parthenon."

"It does, doesn't it?" I said. "And that's not an accident. They were trying to revitalize art, so they went looking for the pinnacle of artistic achievement, and they found it in Classical art."

"So they were copying?" a short, slender girl asked. I couldn't remember her name. When she had introduced herself, I was distracted by how small and insubstantial she seemed, as though she were a shadow her owner had left behind.

"It's not copying," a boy named Hunter said, his words dripping with disdain. "It's like, inspiration." The shadow girl dropped her chin, shrinking even further into herself, and I wanted to rush to her rescue. Hunter was good-looking in the irritatingly effortless way some teenage boys have, their features delicate and girlishly pretty, and I could tell from the way the other kids arranged themselves around him that he was the center of their social constellation.

Fortunately, Miss Pine stepped in before I had to. "Dial down the attitude, Hunter," she said mildly, and I watched the kids shift again, Hunter deflating slightly, the shadow girl glancing up from underneath her eyelashes, the others looking somewhat relieved. I gave Miss Pine a mental high five. "It's a fair moral question, given how much you all get harangued about plagiarism."

"And that's really what we're here to talk about today, right? Where artists get their ideas, their techniques, their style," I said.

"From each other," Eliza said, waving her paintbrush at me.

"Exactly," I said. "Why don't we go check out the Neoclassicists and see some more examples?"

Our conversation was livelier in the Neoclassical room, where I managed to engage the kids in a conversation about the Romans, possibly because I mentioned vomitoriums. Proof that no one ever progresses past the age of thirteen, and when nudity fails, gross-out humor is always a good idea.

When the kids had exhausted their (fairly impressive) repertoire of throw-up jokes, I gave them a few minutes to linger in the room. Some of them were sketching wildly, and I felt my fingers itch as I watched them. The self-conscious tightness that had surrounded them fell away, and their inner eager elementary schoolers sprang out. Long ago, that would have been me, so desperate to create I could hardly keep my hands still.

I leaned against the wall, and Miss Pine came to stand beside me. "Anyway," she said, continuing our earlier conversation as though it had never been interrupted, "teaching is really the best way to stay in touch with my own art. If I'm encouraging them to create, I'd feel like a fraud if I didn't do it myself. What about you? Are you an artist?"

"Oh, no. I mean, I took art in school, but that's not, I mean, it wasn't real," I said hurriedly, lest she get the wrong idea.

"Really?" She raised a pale eyebrow. "But you talk about it so passionately. I just assumed . . ."

Tamping down the longing that always emerged when I was talking about art, I shook my head. "I wanted to be a painter, but I just . . . I guess I just grew out of it."

The truth was far too difficult to explain, especially to Miss Pine, with her heart big and warm enough for these kids and their self-conscious eyes, and the earnest chitter of her jewelry. This was the bargain I had made. I knew Phillip had married me partially because he had zero taste and I knew something about art, but I was only allowed to be in contact with it in the most clinical of ways, preferably ones that made him look good. I could visit dealers and haggle over paintings for his office, or for the condo, purchases based more on square footage and their power to impress and/or intimidate the person looking at them than on artistic merit. I could lead tours here, volunteer, but I couldn't make art myself.

"Art isn't something you grow out of just because you're not a teenager anymore. It's not like falling out of love with a teen idol."

I clutched at my heart in fake horror. "Don't even joke about that. Isn't it your job to protect teenage dreams?"

"Not officially, but I suppose I do it anyway. See, if I'd been your teacher, you wouldn't have given up painting."

"Ah, but then who would do the glamorous job of introducing apathetic teenagers to the glories of Rembrandt?" I asked.

"I'm sure someone would step into the breach. Not that I'm mocking what you do. You're a volunteer, right?"

"Right," I said, though I wasn't sure whether volunteering truly made what I did more impressive. The deal was, I worked for free and got to pretend I was altruistic and not just bored to tears with the Chicago Women's Club and the achingly dull business events Phillip insisted I attend with him.

And leading tours brought its own kind of discomfort, the way it boxed me in as surely as any of those other duties. When I talked to tour groups, I spoke about technique, about chiaroscuro and proportion, about brushwork and craquelure with the confidence of a scholar, but I never spoke about the way art made me feel. I never spoke about how seeing a painting for the first time—really seeing it—is a wondrous thing. When I open my eyes to a painting, it is as though everything has changed and will never be the same again. Colors look more vivid, the lines and edges of objects sharper, and I fall in love with the world and all its beauty—the tragedies and love stories on the faces of people walking by, the shine of a wet sidewalk or the way the leaves offer their pale bellies to the wind before a storm. I want to weep for a broken eggshell below a bird's nest, for its jagged edges and the bird inside freed to take flight.

When we finished the tour, Miss Pine let her students spin off where they wanted—to sketch, she told them sternly, not to the gift shop or the café. A few of them wandered back to the Renaissance rooms (I suppose

Venus' bare breasts had been rather too much to turn down after all); a few others lingered with the vibrant beauty of the Impressionists.

"Listen," Miss Pine said, coming over and thrusting a postcard at me, the edges slightly soft and bent from her bag, "if you change your mind and want to get in touch with your inner teenager, I'm teaching a painting class this weekend at a new studio in Bucktown. It starts tonight. You should come."

Staring down at the postcard as though it were the door to Narnia, I pictured it: a bright studio, the smell of paint and canvas, the weight of the brush resting against the curve underneath my thumb, both new and familiar.

"That's very kind of you," I said, slipping back into that smooth, emotionless voice that was my armor, "but I have plans." My presence had been demanded at one of Phillip's dinners that night, and the next day I was leaving to visit my mother. I didn't want to do either of those things, would far rather have spent the weekend at that painting class, but my life was heavy with obligations and light on everything I wanted to do.

She shrugged. "Another time, then. My phone number is right there." She pointed at the bottom of the card, and I saw a smudge of dried paint on the inside of her finger, a sight so familiar it confused me—was it her hand, or mine, a decade ago? "No pressure. Just fun."

"Thank you," I said, knowing I would never reach out to her. I knew it was better to keep that part of myself at bay, but to my surprise, that knowledge felt sharp and raw, as though it were new and not years old.

After Miss Pine and the students left, I ate a handful of cookies in the staff room, shoving them so quickly into my mouth that they scraped against my tongue, then gathered my things and went home. Sometimes I took the long way, in order to pass a string of galleries that always had something deliciously irreverent and exciting on display, but I had to meet Phillip. He was desperately trying to make a deal with a developer named Teddy Stockton, which meant I was doomed to making polite conversation with Teddy's wife, Dimpy, and the other wives all night.

At home, I paused at the front door. Lately I had found myself in a strange, black moment of hope every night, a half wish that my husband would not come home.

I didn't want anything bad to happen to him; I just wished he would go away. He could disappear through a wormhole, or a circle of standing stones. Or maybe one day he would simply decide he'd had enough and move to some Caribbean island without me. I'd wish him well, honestly. I'd pack up his things and send them down to him with a tube of sunscreen and my best wishes. It would be tidy and emotionless and no one would be to blame.

I didn't wonder about the meaning behind these thoughts. I had spent so long swallowing every unpleasant feeling I had that it never occurred to me that having a recurring fantasy in which your husband disappears is probably a sign that something is terribly wrong.

But of course there was no magical circle of stones and no Caribbean island, because when I opened the door, there he was, standing in the kitchen, flipping through the mail. He looked, as he always did, as though he were posing for a catalog photo.

Phillip was older than I was, dancing on the edge of forty, but he would be one of those men who simply became better looking as he aged, less pretty and more handsome, like a movie star, or a newscaster. As I had no interest in plastic surgery, I imagined the gulf between our attractiveness would only continue to widen, until I, wrinkled and tired and gray, would look like the maiden aunt he generously escorted to charity functions.

"You're late," he said as I set down my purse and reached for the sweater I kept in the coat closet. The floor-to-ceiling windows that allowed one to sit on the uncomfortable couch and admire the endless view of Lake Michigan were also, I was fairly sure, the main reason our home was always so chilly. The moment I came home, even during the summer, I slipped on that sweater. I wore socks and slippers at all times and when I stepped out of the shower, I hurried as quickly as possible into a towel and a bathrobe, the water beading into ice on my skin.

"Sorry," I said perfunctorily, walking past him into the living room. We didn't kiss hello or goodbye, not anymore. We had never been a particularly demonstrative couple—Phillip was too concerned with what other people thought, and I was too afraid, even after we were married, of being rejected—but now he didn't even brush his lips across my forehead when he left for the day. The cool exterior we were required to present to the world had swept its way into our private lives, turning us into strangers at a cocktail party who were sure they had met before, giving each other curious glances across the room. *Don't I know you from . . . Didn't we once . . .*

Gathering the mail into a stack, he tapped the pile against the kitchen counter, a smooth, black granite that made it irritatingly impossible to find the dirty spots. "Hurry up. Put on the black dress you wore to the library fundraiser. You look like you ate too much today."

I looked down at the gray dress I had worn to the museum, trying to spot a telltale cookie bump. Maybe I had eaten a few too many, but I couldn't have gained that much weight in an afternoon. Then again, Phillip always seemed to know when I had eaten something I shouldn't have. He was like a well-dressed bloodhound, and if I ate anything other than carrot sticks, he nailed me for it every time, even though I had finally learned to check my shirts for powdered sugar before going home.

"Fine," I said, heading into the bedroom to change into the black dress. Fighting with him wasn't worth the effort—it was easier to eat what he told me to, wear what he wanted me to, act how he thought I should. He was a little like my mother in that way, though in a competition between them, he'd never win. Phillip was used to getting his way, but my mother could kill you with canapés and kindness.

I changed into the assigned dress and slipped on a pair of heels that pinched at my toes. My stomach was tight and painful, but there were no antacids left in the bathroom. After going through a couple of evening bags and the bedside table, I finally found some in my closet and threw them in my mouth, wiping my hands on the hem of my dress as I walked back into the living room.

"I'm ready to go," I announced, hanging my sweater in the closet.

Phillip, who had been flipping impatiently through channels on the television, turned and looked at me. "What is that on your dress?"

I looked down to see the outline of my chalky fingers on the bottom of the skirt. "Oh, you know. I was working a crime scene."

No smile. He sighed and rubbed his eyes. "Just clean up, Madeleine. We're going to be late."

"And I'd hate to miss a moment with Dimpy," I said. I walked over to the kitchen and wet the corner of a towel, dabbing at the dust until it disappeared. Throwing the damp towel onto the counter, I sighed loudly, which was my best passive-aggressive effort at letting Phillip know I didn't want to go to this dinner. I didn't want to pretend to be interested in real estate investment and development, and I didn't want to make conversation with the wives. I hated that we were always on the periphery. And maybe it was worse that night because I knew I could have been with Miss Pine. I could have been painting, and afterward I could have gotten a steak sandwich, which was definitely not on my diet and even more definitely would have been delicious, Phillip's sense of smell be damned.

Instead, we went to Twelve, which was about trendy cocktails, tiny, artfully arranged portions on enormous plates, and waiters so attentive I felt like I had to put my arm protectively around my meager dinner lest they whisk it away if I stopped to take a breath.

"Madeleine, hellllllooooo," Dimpy Stockton brayed at me. We'd seen each other only a few days ago at the Women's Club, and we weren't particular friends, but you might have thought, from the performance she gave, that we were reuniting after the war.

"Hi, Dimpy," I said as she dropped a cool, perfumed kiss on each of my cheeks. She looked exactly like you would expect someone named Dimpy Stockton to look, with a shockingly tight facelift and a pile of cocktail rings more threatening than a set of brass knuckles.

"I thought I might see you at the historical society board meeting today," she said, and there was an odd scolding tone to her voice.

"Oh, on Fridays I read to orphans," I said solemnly.

"Isn't that nice? You're always so community-minded." Dimpy patted me on the hand. I tilted my head at her. How disconnected from reality was she? Life wasn't a production of *Annie*. You couldn't just go to an orphanage and corral unsuspecting children into storytime. But Dimpy was sailing along happily. "You missed the most ghastly argument," she said, tossing her head back and regaling me with a story about the trauma of choosing a theme for the annual gala.

I nodded at whatever Dimpy was saying, watching Phillip glad-handing his way around the table. When he smiled, it was dazzling, and it reminded me of how charming he had been when we first met, how having his attention focused on me had felt rare and precious, had made me into someone else, someone who might have something beautiful and special inside her after all.

Over time, he had treated me less and less that way, focusing his charm on people from whom he still needed something, people who hadn't already sworn to spend their lives with him. Now I could see his charisma was an act, something he turned on and off at will, but I could still recall the way it had felt to be held in the sunlight of his smile, and that only made being out of it colder.

Before Phillip, I had been biding my time until I got married, at which point I assumed my life would really begin. While the girls I had gone to school with found perfect husbands and had perfect babies, I went on blind dates my mother arranged for me with the sons and grandsons of women she knew from the country club. I never managed to retain their

attention for more than a few dates (though, to be fair, they rarely re-
tained mine for more than a few minutes). I had lived alone and worked
in the alumni department of Magnolia Country Day, the same school I
had attended, where I wrote fundraising appeals that managed to be
gracefully desperate, and helped organize an endless parade of events even
I didn't want to go to. I painted, and I read, and the years went by, until
I looked up and I was almost thirty and still no one had chosen me.

Phillip's interest in me had come as a relief. Finally, I would not be
the only single one at class reunions. Finally, my mother would be happy
with me. Finally, I would have proof that someone thought I was beautiful, someone thought I was enough, someone thought I was worth marrying. I wore my engagement ring like a sigil to ward off everyone's
doubt and pity, most of all my own.

My mother, of course, had been thrilled with Phillip's pedigree. His
great-greats of some ordinal or another had made a fortune in real estate,
and now the men of the family continued to make the money and the
women spent it, an arrangement I found incredibly depressing for copi-
ous reasons. I found out after we were married that all was not as smooth
as that—when Phillip's father died, he had left the family's real estate
investment business in crisis, threatening the livelihood of miscellaneous
cousins and brothers-in-law, and it was only through a lot of fist-
clenchingly tough deals and a handful of patient investors, including my
father, that the ship had been righted and everyone could go back to
shopping in blissful ignorance.

Did I ask why he'd never married? Of course I did. I was almost
thirty and single, so basically I might as well have been dead, and Phillip
was thirty-five, which was not as problematic for a man, but was still old
enough to raise some eyebrows. He told me he'd been engaged and she
had broken his heart, and that he had never recovered. Until me, I guess.

But I knew why he had married me. It was because I was so eager to
please, because he would be in control and I would not object when he

told me what to wear or what I could eat or how I should spend my time. And it was because his family's business was in trouble and my father might become an investor if Phillip could only get close enough, and how much closer can you get than to marry a man's spinsterish daughter?

I know. I should have seen it coming. But I had been tired of Sunday night dinners at my parents' house, tired of social events at which I was the only unmarried one, tired of the same job I had held since my college graduation, tied to the endless, thudding repetition of the academic year. And because I thought being married would change things. I thought it would make me someone special. I thought it would mean, at last, that I wasn't wrong and ugly and broken.

So I put aside my misgivings and I married him. I married him and I had the wedding my mother had given up all hope of my having, and I moved to Chicago to be with him, and I told myself this was a sign, a sign that I might be something more than how people had seen me for my entire life. A sign that I might not be as beautiful as my mother wanted me to be, that I might never fit in as easily as everyone around me seemed to, but that someone thought I mattered.

And for a while, that had been enough. Enough for Phillip and me to convince ourselves we were in something that at least resembled love. But it didn't feel that way now. It wasn't enough anymore.

Around me, Dimpy and the other wives kept up a running chatter that I found myself unable to focus on. Most nights I would have suffered through the conversation, distracting myself with other things, but I felt unable to settle down, shifting in my chair, tugging at my dress. Meeting those kids and Miss Pine had reminded me of who I used to be, and now here I sat, squirming in a stylishly aggressive chair, tracing the steps of every tiny decision I had made that had led me away from her.

Swirling around the drain of my emotions, I became angrier and more resentful, wishing I were at that painting class, wishing I were wearing something I could breathe in, wishing I were someone and somewhere else. When the men pushed their chairs back from the table, I shot out of my own seat so quickly I nearly knocked Dimpy, who was leaning forward to hear what one of the other women was saying, on her very pointy chin. As Phillip lingered, I danced my way toward the door, anxious to get in the car, to be in motion.

Phillip's charm must have worked, because as we drove away, he punched the car ceiling and shouted with excitement. Teddy, apparently, had agreed to the deal. I closed my eyes and felt the wheels moving underneath me, pretended I was on a train heading somewhere far away, somewhere I had chosen.

But we only went home, and in the foyer, Phillip stepped up behind me, slipping his arms around my waist so his hands rested on my cookie-swollen belly and kissing the back of my neck. I stepped away with a shiver.

"Come on, Madeleine. I just made a ton of money. Let's celebrate."

"I'm not in the mood."

"You're never in the mood," he said sulkily, and my face went hot with guilt. When we first met, I had found Phillip desperately handsome, but his looks had soon seemed austere and perfect as a marble statue, and his desire something animal and impersonal, completely unrelated to me. He would wake me in the night, pressing himself against me, and I felt not arousal but an offended fury, because his desire came from somewhere else, and there in the darkness, I could have been anyone. "How are we going to have kids if you're never in the mood?"

Phillip began to stalk around the kitchen, opening and closing cabinet doors. Finally, he huffed loudly, dropping a heavy-bottomed tumbler onto the counter so it rattled, and poured himself a drink.

I was still standing in the foyer, which was drafty and cool, and I reached into the closet for my sweater, wrapping myself in its comfortable warmth. I could smell myself on it—perfume, the illicit ice cream I ate when Phillip was out for the evening, NyQuil from my last cold.

"You're not ready to have kids," I said. Children were messy and inconvenient, and Phillip disliked both of those things, and once you had children, you would never be the most important person in the room, and Phillip really disliked that.

"It's the next step. This is what you do. You get married and you have children. Everyone we know has kids. We're the only ones." He took an anxious sip of his drink. Phillip, always so conscious of what everyone else was doing, so worried about being left behind.

"Is that why you married me? Because it was the next step?" I asked. My feet hurt. I slipped out of my shoes, spreading my toes on the cold marble floor, looking for relief.

"Yes. I don't know. It was time. We were both getting older. Both of our families wanted us to."

"Right." I turned and walked into the living room. It was dark inside, but through the windows, I could see the lights of the city stretching off into the distance, and the quiet blackness of the water. Phillip walked into the room behind me and flipped on a light switch, and immediately all I could see was our reflection: me wrapped in my sweater as though I were bracing against a storm, and him standing behind me, a faceless figure wearing an expensive suit and an impatient air.

"What do you want me to say? That's your problem, Madeleine. Nothing is ever good enough for you. You're never happy."

"No," I said, looking at us mirrored in the window as though I were watching a play. "I'm not happy."

"You don't even know how lucky you are." He turned toward me, his mouth pulled down, and leaned back, draining the liquor in a single swallow.

Lucky. I thought of how the days were slipping through my fingers, how empty time went by. It didn't feel lucky to live a life I had chosen but had never wanted. My fists were clenched, and I could feel myself shaking. I had been pushing down my anger, my disappointment, my irritation for years, and it seemed I couldn't keep them inside anymore.

"How am I lucky, Phillip? How? Is it the way I never get do what I want to do? Is it the way you tell me I look fat when I so much as eat a cupcake on my own birthday? Is it that I live in this ugly place where I'm freezing all the time? Is that how I'm lucky?"

I knew I was risking something by speaking so plainly, but with a deep and desperate fervor, I wanted out. I wanted to pick my own clothes and decide my own schedule. I wanted a job and I wanted my own money and I wanted to paint and I wanted a house that didn't feel like a museum, and I wondered how I had gotten to this place, where I had everything and still had nothing that was important to me.

Phillip scoffed, turned, poured himself another drink. "Most women would be thrilled to have a life like this. Expensive dinners, nice clothes, a professionally decorated home, a successful husband."

"I would be thrilled, Phillip, if I cared about those things. But I don't. I don't care about fancy restaurants, or clothes, or interior decorators, and I don't care . . ." I bit off the end of the sentence, my breath coming quickly. I don't know what I would have said at that point; the words were bubbling out of me and I was filled with the kind of helpless, senseless rage that precedes an uncontrollable crying fit and doesn't lend itself to thoughtful discourse.

"Then why," Phillip asked, with a callous detachment, his eyes glittering, "are you still here? Maybe we shouldn't even bother, Madeleine. Maybe we should just get a divorce."

two

MARGIE
1919

My grandmother Margaret (Margie) Pearce was first and foremost a daydreamer, and as soon as she was old enough to write, she began to record the stories she told herself. They were adventure stories sometimes, love stories often. They were stories of escape, of romance, of the future she thought she might have, of the life she wished to live.

And in the same way I thought my life would begin with my wedding, my grandmother thought hers would begin with her debut. She believed her life had been a closed bud until that moment, waiting politely until that rite of passage came to bloom, to bring her all the things she dreamed about—romance and beauty and adventure and art—with the certain cultivated wildness of a rose.

Of course that wasn't the way it worked out. In fact, if Grandmother and I had given it any thought at all, we would have realized debutante balls and weddings were the precise opposite of freedom: a courtly cementing of our futures into the concrete of the families and society in which we had been raised. But at the time, they seemed nothing more than a chance, for once, to be beautiful, and how could either of us turn that away?

Margie made her debut on a blustery, icy December day in Washington, D.C. It was so cold the clouds had been chased away, leaving a clear sky, bright with stars against the darkness. The week before, she had come home from her first semester of college, the months of classes a blur as she dreamed of the moment when she would finally descend the hotel's staircase and make her grand curtsy, when everything would change, everything would begin.

Margie's appetite had all but disappeared in the excitement, so her collarbones stuck out prettily, her cheekbones high, her face flushed. She tried to read, to sew, anything to pass the hours, but she couldn't sit still. Instead, she found herself running to the window again and again, watching people stepping quickly along the sidewalk, their heads bent to break the wind. The weather made everyone hurry, rushing to get back inside, so it looked as though the entire scene had been sped up, the cars hurtling down the street, the tram at the corner buzzing recklessly by. But when she stepped away from the window and looked at the clock again, time had barely moved.

When five o'clock finally came, she rushed upstairs to her room and was already stripping off her day dress and putting on her own corset and petticoat by the time Nellie, the maid, came in.

The gown fell over her head in a rush of silk and the scent of flowers. Nellie had placed rose petals inside the dress while it was hanging, and a few of them fluttered to the floor when Margie slipped her arms into the sleeves. The gown was made with the palest cream silk and had a wide V-neckline. Despite the season, the sleeves were short, and she had a pair of long white gloves sure to make her hands sweat. But the dress's loveliest feature was the delicate pink silk roses crossing the bodice and trailing their way down the skirt, tiny buds of spring pink with green leaves set behind them. To Margie, it looked like a garden come to life.

Other girls, in high school and in college, had suitors, even beaux, though Margie had never thought of such a thing for herself. Her parents would have forbidden it, for one, and for two, who would look at her, with her fat ankles and her broad shoulders, when there were girls like

Elizabeth Tabb or Lucinda Spencer around, delicate little things with the girlish smile of Mary Pickford and dramatic eyes like Gloria Swanson? But that night, listening to the rustle of the silk against her petticoat as she walked slowly down the stairs, her head held high under the unfamiliar weight of a tiara, she thought she might, for once, be worth looking at. This was it, she thought. This was the night her life would begin.

At the hotel, the debutantes waited in an anteroom. Some of their dresses, Margie thought as she looked around, were shockingly modern—casual, even, a loose flow of fabric draping over their bodies without pause, making them look elegantly boyish and square. The dressmaker had offered Margie a similar gown. "It's the newest fashion," the woman had said, showing a dress of thin satin with a lace overlay, loose and flowing.

Margie's mother had been horrified. "You can't even wear a corset under that!"

About the corset, Margie didn't mind, as she was rather fond of breathing, but she did mind that tender afterthought of a dress. It looked so plain compared to the gown she had imagined. And it was all well and good for someone who looked chic in dresses like the one the pleading designer was holding out to her. Those women didn't have broad shoulders or large bosoms or muscular calves like she did. Margie knew well what she would look like in that kind of dress.

But clearly a number of the other girls had been brave enough to take the plunge. Anne Dulaney and Elsie Mills, who had been the first to bob their hair (to their mothers' fury and everyone else's shock), were, of course, wearing those dresses and, of course, being tall and so slender, looked stunning. They were lounging on a pair of fainting couches as though the very thought of the evening exhausted them. Two other girls in shorter dresses huddled together by an open window, smoking (and she was fairly sure the flask they were sharing wasn't lemonade), and another cluster of girls in more traditional gowns stood at the opposite end of the room, pretending to talk while catching admiring glimpses of themselves in the mirror above the fireplace.

Feeling desperate, Margie kept looking for someone she knew well enough to sit with, until she spied Grace Scott and Emily Harrison Palmer, with whom she had gone to school until the ninth grade, when she had left for Abbott Academy and they for Miss Porter's. Their dresses were as formal and old-fashioned as hers, and she felt a sense of relief as she settled down on a sofa beside them, the slight and familiar tremor she had felt upon comparing herself to the others, girls who would always be more beautiful, more fashionable, more *right* than she was, fading.

"Who are they?" Margie whispered, leaning forward and cocking her head toward the smokers.

"Southern," Emily Harrison said, with a touch of haughty contempt, which was rich, considering her parents had come to Washington from Atlanta and her mother had an accent so thick you could have spread it on toast. "But those girls," she said, nodding toward the group at the fireplace, "are European royals. Can you believe it? Minor, of course. Rumor has it they're making the rounds looking for husbands here because their parents are flat broke."

"Don't gossip, Emily Harrison," Grace scolded. Grace had always been overly kind, the sort of girl teachers selected to pal around with the new student, and prone to fits of tears over the tiniest of disappointments. "I'm sure they're perfectly nice."

"I didn't say they weren't perfectly nice, I said they were perfectly broke," Emily Harrison said. She lifted her hands and examined her fingernails. "Everyone in Europe is broke. Everyone here, too, it seems. My mother says there never would have been a ball with this many debutantes in her day."

"They're so glamorous," Margie said dreamily, looking at the Europeans. They faced away from her, a few of them with dresses cut low enough on their backs to reveal skin luminous as snow. Were they princesses? Margie wondered. Two of them wore tiaras, sparkling in the firelight, but Margie wore one herself and she was hardly a princess. It was just that they seemed so graceful, so perfect, every movement of their hands expressive as ballerinas, the curves of their throats, the bones of their faces as though they had been carved from marble. Their spines were stiff, their shoulders straight, and Margie self-consciously pulled herself back from slouching. Even if they weren't princesses, they were royalty, and they would be walking down the steps with her.

"Isn't it exciting?" Margie asked. She couldn't contain herself. She supposed she ought to be blasé, like Anne and Elsie, so languidly aloof on their fainting couches, but she couldn't. The night lay in front of them like a glittering promise, the sparkle of it, the elegance, the mystery of the excitement to come. Oh, Anne and Elsie were old poops, that's all there was to it. She was going to dance with Robert Walsh, the terribly handsome friend of the family who was to be her escort, and drink champagne even if her parents didn't approve, and she was going to enjoy every moment.

"Dreadfully exciting," Grace said, and the sparkle in her eyes matched Margie's, even though Grace was assured of marrying Theo Halloway— their families had arranged it long ago—and might not have bothered coming out at all if her mother hadn't practically run Washington society. "I saw the ballroom on the way in, Margie. It's simply gorgeous. And your gown is really stunning. You look lovely."

"Thank you," Margie said demurely, though inside she fluttered at the compliment.

Her father had said, "You look pretty, kitten," but that was his job, and her mother had said, "Your tiara's on crooked," and then, after she had fixed it, "Nellie didn't do a horrible job with your hair," which was the closest thing to praise Margie had ever gotten from her mother, a tiny, precise woman who had never understood the starry-eyed, lead-footed daughter she had managed to produce.

"You look pretty too," she said to Grace. Under normal circumstances that might have been an exaggeration—it was a good thing Grace was so kind and her parents were so wealthy, because Grace was so plain—but not that night. Grace was dark and the pale yellow of her gown glowed against her skin, and she looked happy, and Margie felt a little rush of sentimental nostalgia for the girls they had once been and the women they were becoming.

"Ladies." Grace's mother, Mrs. Scott, appeared at the doorway. The Southern girls quickly pitched their cigarette ends out the window and Margie saw the flask of not-lemonade disappear into one of their skirts. Mrs. Scott sniffed the air and looked at them disapprovingly. "We are ready to begin."

Margie's last name, Pearce, put her solidly in the middle of the line, right behind Emily Harrison Palmer, but that night she wished it were Robertson, or better yet, Zeigler, so she could savor the anticipation, the shiver in her stomach, the heat in her face. At first all she could see was the hallway and the line of debutantes in front of her, but as Emily Harrison began her slow descent, Margie saw it all laid out before her: the chandelier brilliant above, the pale glow of the girls' dresses, light sparking prisms off hundreds of diamonds, setting the hall aglow. Her breath caught hard in her chest and she didn't breathe, didn't move, holding the moment in her hand like crystal, like snow, terrified it might disappear, shatter and whirl away in the air.

She promised herself she would remember it all, hold on to every moment. But as soon as she set one satin-slippered foot on the stairs, it became nothing more than a lovely blur. She stored away memories of everything she could—the plush carpet beneath her shoes, Robert's hand under hers, the fall of her dress around her knees when she executed her curtsy, graceful and slow as a dancer's plié. The sparkle of champagne on her tongue, and Robert standing beside her, stiff and formal in his white tie, and the kiss her father dropped on her forehead as they waltzed, and the sight of all the debutantes with their escorts, swirling around the enormous dance floor like flowers, like snowdrops, like everything beautiful and bright and enchanted.

When the night was coming to an end, when the tables had been cleared and most of the fathers had left to smoke in the billiard room and the mothers were fluttering around the ballroom, chatting or passing gossip, or sitting at the tables, listening to the orchestra and remembering their own debuts in a more elegant time, a time when there was not so much sadness, when so many young men had not been lost and so many young women were not so bold and strange and unsatisfied, Emily Harrison came to fetch Margie and Grace. They had been standing alone at the edge of the empty dance floor, sighing happily at the music. "Come upstairs," Emily Harrison said. "There's a party."

"This is a party," Margie said, confused. She realized, with a little surprise, that she was somewhat drunk, and with even more surprise, that she rather liked it.

Emily Harrison rolled her eyes. "Not like this. A real party. One of the Europeans has a suite upstairs. Everyone else is gone, didn't you notice? Come on." Margie looked around to see the three of them were the only debutantes left in the ballroom. The rest of the girls had disappeared, as had their escorts. They were, in fact, the youngest women in the room by a good twenty years.

"Oh, I couldn't," Grace demurred, and Emily Harrison huffed impatiently.

"Of course not. Perfect Grace. What about you?" she asked, turning toward Margie, who took a surprised step back. A real party? She didn't know what that meant, but she was sure she'd never been to anything Emily Harrison, who had a tendency to wildness, would have called a real party. But the night was magic and she didn't want it to end. Why shouldn't she go?

"I have to tell my parents," Margie said. "They'll be leaving soon."

"Tell them you're coming home with me. Hurry up already."

Margie found her mother sitting at a table with Anne's and Grace's mothers, their heads bent so close together it looked as though they were eating from a single plate. When Margie approached, they separated slowly, their conversation holding them together like sticky toffee. "Your tiara's crooked again," her mother said. She was wearing a gown of heavy blue velvet that made her eyes burn like sapphires.

Pushing a careless hand up toward her tiara, which didn't feel crooked in the slightest, Margie told her mother she and some of the other girls were going to Emily Harrison's, and she might stay the night there, if that was all right.

It was the biggest lie she had ever told, and she thought, for a moment, as her mother looked piercingly at her, that she had been found out, until her mother's gaze flicked back to Mrs. Dulaney and Mrs. Scott, who hadn't bothered to stop talking for one moment, and she waved Margie off, telling her not to ruin her gown, for goodness' sake, to get Emily Harrison's maid to take care of it and not to forget to pick up the fur she had borrowed from her mother and left at the coat check. Margie promised all these things, and her mother let her go.

Could it have been so simple all along? No wonder girls like Anne and Elsie and Emily Harrison were so wild. How easy it was to slip out from under someone's thumb, if the conditions were right.

The girls left Grace swaying contentedly by herself by the dance floor, like a lily of the valley in a breeze. They took the elevator to the top floor and swished down the hall to a suite whose door was propped open slightly, letting out the sound of music. As Emily Harrison put her hand on the doorknob, there was a shout and a burst of raucous male laughter, and Margie jumped back slightly. She felt a little less drunk now, away from the orchestra and the sparkle of the ballroom, and a little more scared, but Emily Harrison simply hissed at her to come on.

Inside, Margie stood by the door, both terrified and fascinated. Someone put a glass of champagne in her hand and she drank it quickly, the pleasant light-headedness she had felt before rising up again.

One of the Southern girls sat on the sofa, a cigarette burning in one hand and what looked suspiciously like a tumbler of gin in the other. She had taken off the lace overlay of her dress—Margie could see it draped carelessly over the back of a nearby chair—and was sitting there only in the satin chemise, and Margie was certain she didn't have anything on underneath it. A man sat on either side of her, one of them also smoking. Ash had fallen onto the cushions of the cream sofa between them.

In the corner, a phonograph played Al Jolson, and a few of the European girls (and, Margie was shocked to see, Elsie Mills) were dancing with their escorts, who had taken off their ties and tails. It wasn't dancing of the sort she'd learned at cotillion; their bodies were pressed so close together Margie couldn't have gotten a hand in between them. One of the men had dropped cigarette ash on the tallest European's beautiful gown, but no one seemed to notice or care. Elsie and her escort, their eyes half closed, from attraction or liquor, moved more and more slowly, their heads drifting together, and then they began to kiss, at first gently, and then passionately. Margie stared—she had rarely seen anyone kiss, and certainly not with such hunger—and when she finally turned away, her face burned with shame and envy.

The air was hazy with smoke—in addition to the cigarette smokers, a group of escorts was playing cards and smoking cigars in a dining room off the front room. Emily Harrison had disappeared, and Margie felt immediately self-conscious and overheated, her corset pressing too tightly into her stomach. She walked quickly through the room to one of the side doors—*This suite must take the whole floor*, she thought—and opened it to find a couple engaged amorously on a bed. Slamming the door shut, she pressed her hand to her chest. Was this what everyone else had been doing while she and Grace were visiting and performing little plays together or reading on Friday nights? Had this been happening all around her and she had just never been invited until now? Or was this part of the new world that seemed to be trembling around them, ready to break open and swallow them all whole?

She didn't belong here, she thought. But what could she do? She couldn't leave now. Her mother thought she was spending the night at Emily Harrison's, and she didn't even have cab fare.

Taking another few steps away from the blur of the living room, Margie found herself in a hallway lined with rich damask wallpaper in cream and silver. Suddenly, one of the other doors opened, and her escort, Robert Walsh, emerged, straightening his vest, an unlit cigar clamped between his teeth, and she blushed. Margie had always had the worst habit of blushing anytime she was in the company of any boy—or now, man—near her age, especially if he was at all good-looking, which Robert Walsh definitely was. Hearing the sound of a commode flushing behind him, she burned even hotter. "Hey there, are you all right?" he asked. Unable to look at him, she nodded.

"Party rather too much for you, eh?" he asked, and then, accepting her apparently stunned look as a reply, took her by the elbow and steered her away from the living room. "Come on. Let's get you a little fresh air." He led her down the hall to the last door, which opened into an enormous, and blessedly uninhabited, bedroom. Guiding her inside, he closed the door behind them and walked over to a long wall, tugging aside a curtain to reveal a pair of French doors. Margie stepped outside gratefully when he opened them.

The air was icy against her skin, and Margie wished she had gotten her coat from the check after all. Her mother would be furious if she forgot it, especially after she had been reminded. She always complained that Margie was irresponsible and flighty and addle-minded, and most of the time, Margie had to admit, it was true. It was just so easy to get lost in her thoughts, or in a book, or in a story she was writing.

Breathing the air in deep, grateful gulps, Margie felt her heart slowing and the flush fading from her cheeks.

"Damn, it's freezing out here," Robert said mildly. He shook off his jacket and brought it over to Margie, settling it around her shoulders. She pulled it closer around herself, inhaling the smell of him on the fabric—soap and Brilliantine and unlit tobacco.

"I'm so sorry," she said, when the air had done its job. She had begun to shiver, but she didn't want to move just yet. The champagne giddiness had gone, replaced by a different pleasure. Above them, the stars were sharp and lustrous, and she liked the steady comfort of Robert beside her.

He was handsome in a careless way, and though he had been raised to be polite, there was something of a rake about him. He drove a sporty Monroe roadster and though he was older than she, almost twenty-five, he didn't seem to be in any rush to settle down and get married, or even work for a living. She always heard him talking about one party or another, or a trip he had taken to Atlantic City, or Boston, or New York.

Her parents had selected him to be her escort, and his parents had probably agreed for him. Yet here they were now, alone, and he didn't seem to want to be part of what was happening out in the party any more than she did. Could it be that he was like her, maybe a little shy, a little dreamy? Maybe he had been misunderstood all this time and all he needed was someone who would allow him to be himself, and he would see that in her and she would look up at him with dewy eyes, her heart pounding, and . . .

"No need to apologize," Robert said. "Your teeth are chattering—you must be frozen. Are you feeling better? Should we go back inside?"

Startled, Margie nodded, and he gestured politely for her to go in first. He closed the doors behind them, but the chill remained in the air, so Robert strode over to the fireplace, taking the match holder from the mantel and lighting the fire that had been laid there. "Have a seat," he said, gesturing toward the sofa closest to the fireplace. She settled into the cushions, sliding out of his jacket as he brought over the coverlet from the bed and tucked her in, grinning and winking at her as though they shared a secret. Margie felt the heat in her face again.

"Thank you," she said after a few moments, when she was warm again. "I don't know what came over me."

Robert shrugged. He sat down in an armchair by the fireplace, resting one foot on the opposite knee. He took the still-unlit cigar out of his mouth and set it in a large crystal ashtray on the tiny, spindly end table. "You've had quite an evening. And this party did go from amusing to outrageous rather quickly."

Margie's heart quickened again, thinking of Elsie and that man kissing passionately, of the couple in the bedroom, a flash of bare arms and legs entwined before she had closed the door. "I hear Europeans are scandalously free these days," she said, trying to sound worldly, like she went to parties like this all the time, as he apparently did.

Instead of laughing at her, Robert simply nodded. "They are. But you can't blame them. They've been through a lot. It's a miracle there's anyone left, isn't it? Between the war and the 'flu?"

"Why didn't you go?" Margie asked tentatively. "To the war?"

Instead of answering, he stared into the fire silently for a few moments. "Money," he said finally, "has all sorts of privileges. My father bought my way out."

"Oh." The idea that he had avoided service on purpose made her feel embarrassed for him. She scrambled for a conciliatory remark. "Of course you're important to the company. It's right you should have stayed home, or who would take over the business from your father if you . . ." she trailed off, realizing she was about to suggest Robert's tragic demise.

He didn't seem to notice. He was still watching the fire, and then, abruptly, he pulled himself out of his trance and slipped a hearty smile back onto his face. "Quite right, quite right. Shall I get us a drink?" he asked, but didn't wait for a reply. He pushed himself up from the chair and was out of the room before Margie could say anything.

It wasn't until he was gone that she really took in that she was sitting alone in a bedroom with a man. She'd never been in such a circumstance before, hadn't even countenanced the idea that it might happen before she was married. Was it terrible she didn't feel it was so wrong?

She knew what she should do, of course. She should leave this party and all its shocking business behind and go downstairs and get her coat from the check before it closed and her mother's fur went into whatever purgatorial limbo happened to coats in the coat check past closing time. The hotel doorman would get her a taxicab and she would say her address loudly and confidently, as if she traveled by herself in the middle of the night all the time, "3241 R Street," and she'd go home and ring the bell and her father would pay the taxi and she could be safe in her own bed in an hour, her dress hanging on the wardrobe door and this night nothing more than a beautiful dream with a queer ending.

But she didn't. She sat by the fire wrapped in the coverlet, and in a few moments Robert came back carrying a champagne bucket in one hand and a pair of glasses between his fingers. She heard a rush of music and conversation when the door opened, which stilled again when he closed it.

"I hope you like champagne. There's gin, but that's an acquired taste." He put the champagne bucket on the end table and pulled out the bottle, sweating and chilled from its ice bath, and used a napkin to gently tug out the cork. It sprang free with a sharp pop, and Margie could hear the fizz as he poured her a glass.

"I do like champagne," Margie said, although she felt sure she had been on a roller coaster of it all night and it was long past time for her to get off. Still, when he handed it to her, she took it, sipping at it gently, letting the bubbles pop against the roof of her mouth, savoring the sweetness on her tongue.

"You don't want to be out there? At the party?" she asked. Robert poured himself a drink and then, to her surprise, clinked his glass against hers as he sat down on the sofa, so close she could feel the warmth of him. Though she had touched him a dozen times that night—when he had walked her down the stairs, when they had danced, his hand against the small of her back—this felt blushingly intimate.

"Not tonight. Those girls are tiring. All they do is gossip and talk about dresses and marriage. I'd rather talk to you, Margie."

"Thank you," Margie said, dazzled by the compliment, small as it was.

"So did you enjoy the ball?"

"Very much so," Margie said with a smile, and it all came back to her. The discomfort she had felt at the shock of the party had faded, the light-headedness from the alcohol was blurring into something quieter, a buoyant contentment, and when she stretched her feet out, she could see the roses marching down the front of her dress and the toes of her pretty satin slippers. And even if Robert were simply biding his time with her, she could pretend it was something else, and no one would ever have to know.

"When do you go back to school?"

"Not for ages and ages," Margie said. She lifted her arms over her head and stretched. The fire and the champagne were making her toasty, and she let the coverlet slip down into her lap.

"I'm leaving for Europe right after the New Year."

"Oh? Is it for work?"

"God, no," Robert said, and took an enormous slug of his drink. "I am on a quest, Margie, to avoid that particular responsibility for as long as possible."

"You don't want to take over the business?"

"Not even a little bit. What about you? You aren't in some God-awful rush to get married and start popping out children and turn into your mother, are you?"

"Goodness, no," Margie said with a shudder, and took a large swig of her champagne in imitation of Robert, who laughed charmingly. "My mother is the last person I want to turn into." And then, a little ashamed of herself for speaking ill of her mother aloud, she turned to him frantically. "You won't tell her I said that, will you?"

He smiled, his teeth blindingly white, and gave her a slow, raffish wink. "Not as long as you promise not to tell my father I'd rather die than take over the helm of Walsh Shipping. Right now they're so grateful I'm not pushing up poppies in Flanders Fields, they're letting it lie, as long as I do little services like this and keep the family name clean. But eventually they'll ask, Margie. Eventually they'll demand it." He was growing sadder and more morose as he talked. "We're doomed, you know. Doomed to turn into our parents."

"No!" Margie stood up, throwing off the coverlet and stamping her foot. "I won't do it. I'm going to be different, you'll see. I'm going to be a writer, and I'm going to live in Europe, and I'm never going to get married—I'm going to fall in love again and again, and no one can stop me."

Robert looked up at her as though he were deciding something, and then he drained his own drink, stood up, and, to Margie's complete surprise, slipped his arms around her as though they were going to begin a waltz. "Of course you are," he said, and the sadness in his face was gone again, so far gone Margie wondered if she had only imagined his gloomy prophecies. "You're going to live in Paris and drink champagne from a shoe and write books like no one has ever read before," he said, and he swept her around the room as though they were back on the ballroom floor, guiding her expertly between the furniture without even seeming to look at it. Margie laughed, tilting her head back and watching the ceiling spin above her as they danced in the quiet room, the crackle of the fire and the pale thumps of the party outside their only music. "And I'm going to go to Italy and live as a marquis, and never, ever think about cargo or shipping or tariffs or any kind of freight at all." Margie laughed again, and then he abruptly spun to a stop.

"Whoops!" She was still laughing, her eyes closed. When she opened them, Robert was looking at her intently, searching her face for something.

"Margie," he said, low and quiet.

"Yes?"

He didn't say anything; he simply pulled his hand from hers where their arms had been extended and slipped it around her waist, pulling her close, far closer than they had been on the dance floor, as close as the dancers had been in the living room of the suite, the roses of her gown crushed against his stiff white vest, and then, as though she had been doing it all her life and knew what was coming, her eyes fluttered closed as he kissed her.

It seemed impossible someone else's lips could be so soft, and she wondered at so many sensations at once, at the smell of him, the warmth of his body against hers, his hands firm and strong against her back, the quiet movements of his mouth and then his tongue, at first shocking and then, when she opened her lips, both natural and incredibly arousing. Her body rose to meet his, and when he moved his mouth from hers and trailed a line of kisses down her neck, breathing in the scent of her perfume and her skin, one hand moving up, his fingers playing dangerously at the edge of her neckline, she didn't stop him, didn't want to stop him, because the voice inside her telling her she shouldn't, this wasn't something a lady, a proper girl, did, that voice belonged to her mother and this night was hers and hers alone, to do with as she wished.

They kissed until her lips were swollen and the dizziness of the champagne had been exchanged for the dizziness of desire, and they lay down on the bed together and they didn't stop kissing, and her hands were as bold on him as his were on her. They fell asleep together, their mouths close, hands claiming a confident intimacy, his body warming hers, her mind whirling with the fulfillment of all her romantic fantasies.

In the morning when she woke, the dream was over. He was gone, and she didn't see Robert Walsh again for almost five years.

three
....

MADELEINE
1999

Phillip hadn't stuck around to see how his threat had affected me. He had taken his drink and stalked off to the study. I stood in the kitchen, stunned, and then stumbled into the bedroom, grabbing for some antacids to calm my stomach.

His side of the bed had stayed empty while I tossed and turned, unable to get warm despite the extra blankets I had wrapped myself in.

Finally, I had drifted off to sleep in the gray gruel of morning, woke up groggy and disoriented. Padding across the condo, I quietly opened the door to the study, but Phillip was gone. His keys and wallet weren't by the front door. It was a weekend, but maybe he had gone to the office. Maybe he had left just to avoid me.

I had to talk to him, had to apologize, had to make it right again. No matter how much I complained, when it came down to it, I couldn't actually get divorced. I couldn't. It would be an admission that I was a failure, unlovable, that I hadn't been good enough for him after all. I would be buried by the shame. My mother would be humiliated. I couldn't.

I dialed Phillip's mobile number again and again. His office phone. Nothing.

What if he had really meant it? What if it really were over? I lifted my hand to my throat as if I could physically unstop the breath that had caught there.

And what would I do? If there were no more Phillip, who would I be? No one else would marry me. I'd have to leave the Stabler. I'd have to leave Chicago, leave the rows of art galleries in River North where I could stroll for hours and see a dozen pieces that changed everything. I'd have to go back to my hometown. Back to Magnolia, to my mother, to the Ladies Association and humid summers, to walk among my ruins and stew in my failures.

Magnolia. The fight had eclipsed my dread over my impending peacekeeping trip to see my mother, but in three hours, I was supposed to be on a plane. But I couldn't go now, could I? I had to stay and make things right with Phillip. Except he clearly didn't want to see me. Didn't want to talk to me.

But maybe if I went, maybe if I went and left Phillip alone for a while, he'd calm down. I'd just been upset the night before, drunk on the foolish idea of painting again, trapped in a too-tight dress (Phillip had been right about the cookies, he was always right), irritated by Dimpy Stockton's cheerful entitlement. And he'd calm down, just as I had. Phillip was endlessly mercurial, and horribly spoiled, and sometimes the best thing to do, I'd found, was to leave him to it. Eventually he got bored of his own drama and would emerge from it as though it had never happened. And I wouldn't say a word of it to my mother. She and Phillip adored each other, and if she knew I had screwed this up . . .

Well. I wasn't going to think about that. Because it was going to be fine. Pulling my suitcase out of my closet, I packed in silence. I'd be gone for a week and by the time I came back, everything would be fine. He'd have forgotten all about a divorce. I'd have forgotten the anger that had swollen inside me, the resentment at the way he treated me, the sick certainty I felt when he pushed at the issue of a baby. The weather would be warm in Magnolia. I could take shorts, sleeveless shirts, not that anyone wanted to see my bare, chubby arms. There would be so much pollen in the air I wouldn't be able to breathe, and my mother and I would be at each other's throats within twenty-four hours, but it wouldn't be here. I took the nearly empty bottle of antacids and ground them into a fine powder against my tongue on the way to the airport, feeling the twist in my stomach as it pulled angrily against itself.

Ostensibly, my parents had settled in Magnolia because it was in between Memphis and Little Rock, and my father had begun investing in real estate in both cities, but I think they chose it because it was equally inconvenient for both of their families to visit. My mother said she liked it because it was small, barely a city. "Memphis without all the fuss," she called it, as though Memphis were a latter-day Gotham, all crime-fighting superheroes and threatening skylines. But Magnolia was a Goldilocks city—just large enough to have the cultural amenities my mother enjoyed, just small enough that she could run its social scene with her tiny, well-moisturized fist, just Southern enough for the charm without too much culture shock for my Northern parents, just Northern enough to cool off during the winter months without doing too much damage to my mother's garden. As much as I complained about it, I'd been in no hurry to escape; it had held me in its slow, sticky thrall until Phillip and I had moved to Chicago.

I took a taxi to my mother's house, the driver listening to hypnotically aggressive sports talk radio. He left me there, standing in the circular driveway. My parents had bought this house, an old brick colonial with black shutters and a gabled roof over the front door, when they had married in 1945—my mother only twenty years old, my father a few years older, back from a thankfully bland service in the war. They had periodically remodeled the interior, but the outside looked the same as it had since I was a child. I could smell the honeysuckle and wisteria growing along the side of the house, and the summery, green scent of damp soil. The hedges surrounding the property bore tiny white buds that would explode in a few weeks and flower profusely, covering the sidewalk with sticky yellow dust, until they had sown their wild oats and retreated into orderly decency, marking the edge of the property in a military-tight formation.

My mother's house was in Briar Hill, where the enormous homes near the country club faded into family neighborhoods and trendy stores. The house next door was even older, the original farmhouse for the land that had turned into this wealthy neighborhood, and for years it had been owned by the Schulers, who were descendants of the family who had built it. My mother preferred that sort of thing, neighborhoods with history and old houses and families who had lived in them for years. The Schulers' children had already been in high school when I was born, so over the years it had seemed emptier and emptier as they moved out, and the only times it came to life were Christmas and Easter, when everyone streamed home with their own families in tow, or the occasional summer Sunday dinner, when they played croquet in the back yard and ate on the porch while the children chased fireflies in the gathering dark.

But now it looked like there was a full-on party happening over there. Standing outside my mother's silent house, I could hear conversation and laughter drifting over the fence, and people moving back and forth inside. *Maybe I should go there instead*, I thought. It sounded like much more fun.

Before I could make a break for it, the front door swung open and the familiar scent rushed up at me, dust and old books, wood polish and something floral from the arrangement on the table in the front hall, and under it all, the pale, faint traces of my father's cigars. Even though he had died soon after Phillip and I were married, it still felt painful to think of it. I took a long, slow breath, inhaling the comforting smell of him. My anger and panic had burned away during the trip and now I was left with a slow, sad burn in my stomach that made the smell of my parents' house seem comforting.

However, the person standing at the door was not my mother, but a woman about my age, her hair blown out into an appropriate bob, her makeup perfect, wearing a conservative navy suit with a white shell and pearls, straight out of the Magnolia Ladies Association Central Casting.

"Well, well, well. Madeleine Bowers. Aren't you a sight for sore eyes?"

I squinted at her suspiciously. "It's Madeleine Spencer, now, actually. Do I . . . ah . . . know you?"

She looked at me with a surprised expression and laughed. "You don't recognize me? I don't know whether to take that as a compliment or not! Honey, it's Sharon Baker. From Country Day?"

"Oh. Wow." This woman standing here with her French-manicured nails and her spotless outfit was Sharon Baker? In high school, Sharon had been the closest thing Magnolia Country Day had to a bad girl. Most of us had been together since nursery school, but Sharon had blown in at the beginning of ninth grade (the rumor, which she did nothing to dispel, was that she had been kicked out of three other private schools before she had come to ours). She smoked, and dated boys from public school, and her uniform skirt was always too short, and she had wild, loose, curly hair she never seemed to brush.

I'd always been both a little in awe and a little afraid of her, mostly because she didn't seem to care what anyone else thought. I'd sat next to her during class elections the first year, and when we were supposed to hand our ballots in, I turned to take hers and pass it down, but her hands were empty. "That shit is on the floor where it belongs," she had said. It had never even occurred to me that was an option. I had voted for Ashley Hathaway, the same way I had voted for her every year since the fifth grade.

"Hardly recognize me, huh? I went all respectable." Turning toward the mirror by the door, she shook her hair into place, needlessly tugging her jacket straight. "I know. I hardly recognize me too." She sighed, as though she were a disappointment to herself. "Don't worry," she said, turning her cheer back on. "I'm still rotten deep down at the core. How the hell are you?"

"I'm good," I said, a little timorously. I was still reeling from the great reinvention of Sharon Baker, and a little bit wondering why she was there. My mother and I had never been the best of friends, but I thought getting a new daughter seemed a bit extreme, and Sharon would have been a . . . surprising choice, even cleaned up as she was.

"And what brings you back to this shit hole?" she asked cheerfully. She was still looking in the mirror, now reapplying her lipstick, a pearlescent pink that shimmered when she popped her lips at the end. It was strange—she looked so perfect and pure, but she still had a mouth like a sailor.

"I'm just in town for a visit." I had been standing in the doorway, but I finally stepped in. "Not to be rude, but what are you doing here?"

Sharon stopped primping and turned to me, squinting slightly. "Your mother hasn't told you?"

"Hasn't told me what? Did she adopt you? Have I been disowned?"

Sharon laughed, a pleasantly rough-edged stone of a sound. Covering her lipstick, she stuck it back in her purse. "You'd better talk to Simone."

"I'm here, I'm here," my mother said, rushing downstairs. "I'm so sorry; I was terribly delayed. Have you been waiting long?" she asked Sharon solicitously, and then, noticing me, started and put her hand on her chest. "Well, goodness, Madeleine, are you arriving today?"

I looked down at myself and my luggage. "It appears I already have."

"I'm sorry, it completely slipped my mind. Your clothes are all wrinkled."

"I've been on a plane." I'm sure my mother got off planes looking fresh as a daisy, but I, like most mere mortals, was wrinkle-prone. She sighed at me as though it were a personal failing.

"Aren't you going to close the door?"

"It was on my to-do list. Nice to see you too."

"I'm sorry, I'm sorry, I'm all aflutter." She came forward and gave me a brittle hug. My mother was tiny and delicate and beautiful, like so many of the women in my life. She wore essentially the same thing every day—a pair of slacks, a cardigan, and a scarf tied around her neck. She had pearl earrings and a once-a-week hairdo and if you saw her at the grocery store you would pretty much know exactly the kind of person she was, which might be a terrible thing to say but is one hundred percent the truth.

Beauty, in my family, seems to skip a generation. I was not beautiful in the same way my grandmother hadn't been beautiful—the body that had been unpopular in the 1920s was equally unpopular now, and I don't think it ever had a heyday at any point in between. We were too tall to be average, but not tall enough to be interesting; we had broad shoulders and breasts that interfered with everyday activities and hips that belonged on a Soviet propaganda poster. When I looked in the mirror, I could see her features looking back at me—one eyebrow higher than the other, wide, milky brown eyes, a forgettable nose, a thin, poutless mouth.

But my grandmother, when I had known her, had possessed a certain elegance. She wore Chanel suits and she always had a glass of wine in her hand, and she never laughed too loud, and when she walked out of a room, you could tell she had been there from the trail of perfume she left behind, as though the room had recently been abandoned by a spirit with a preference for Shalimar. I had none of that ease: I had spent my entire life trying (and failing) to fit my uncooperative body into someone else's mold. Every ten weeks, I went to a salon where they poured chemicals over my hair to calm it into smooth submission, and in between, I regularly flat-ironed it, the smell of heat and burnt hair filling my nose. I ate as little as possible, especially in public, leaving half my anemic salad on my plate at luncheons. When I remembered all the desserts I had pushed away—the rich cheesecakes, the delicate stacks of fruit and cream, the whirls of ganache—I wanted to weep. It had worked—to an extent—I was thin, but that did not make my shoulders any smaller, my calves any less like the trunks of sturdy young trees.

My mother, on the other hand, was beautiful, a clear genetic anomaly sandwiched between my grandmother and me, with delicate features, fine bones, and hair like champagne and corn silk. She had tried to raise me in her own image, but I was never able to match her easy elegance. I sweated through my gloves at cotillion, and though I followed her instructions on hair brushing to the letter, what made her hair smooth and sleek as a thoroughbred's mane only seemed to leave mine fluffy and floating, as though I had disobeyed on purpose. I wore the clothes she bought me, though they never seemed to fit right, the shirts riding up no matter how much I tugged at them, the outfits that looked so perfect in the pages of *Seventeen* somehow losing their allure on me, making me look lumpy, as though I were smuggling packets of flour taped to my sides.

"How was your flight?" my mother asked as she released me, leaving a pale cloud of L'Air du Temps behind.

"Fine. What's going on next door? It looks like they're having a party."

"It's awful, isn't it? The Schulers sold the house and the man who bought it has turned it into a restaurant. A restaurant! In this neighborhood! Can you believe it?"

Actually, I could. My parents' neighborhood had been getting hipper and hipper for years, but my mother would have been unhappy with any change at all.

"Is it any good?"

"How would I know? They've turned my front lawn into a parking lot. I'm certainly not going to eat there."

"To be fair, it's not really your front lawn. It's his."

"It's close enough. And the noise! Trucks backing in with that dreadful beeping sound, all hours of the day and night. They've turned the Schulers' lovely back deck into a seating area and there's just the most appalling racket from the garden."

"So, like, people eating and drinking and being happy? I can see how that would be a major bummer to have around."

"Don't be sarcastic."

"Sarcasm's all I've got, Mother." I had slept on the plane, but I was tired and my emotions were still jagged and thin.

"Well, it's nice of you to come. Isn't Phillip missing you?"

I neatly sidestepped the question. "Phillip has a business trip to New York this week." This was true, but not the whole truth.

"Why didn't you go with him? You could have gone shopping while he was working! That's what I always used to do when your father had business in New York." My mother clasped her hands together joyfully, like a little girl who had been given a new doll. I should have sent her to New York with Phillip. The two of them had always liked each other better than either of them seemed to like me.

"Well, there's the fact that I hate shopping." The idea of being stuck in a store—or, even worse, a mall—for hours at a time, with nothing to do other than try on clothes made me want to gnaw my own arm off. When I'd been younger and my mother had made me go shopping for clothes, I'd always taken a book, and while she swanned around the Juniors department, I'd crawl under a clothes rack and read until she'd reached critical dressing room mass and I had to go try things on so she could criticize me in public, the way Mother Nature had intended.

"So you're staying the whole week?"

"That was the plan," I said. Unless Phillip had been serious, and we really were getting a divorce. A fist twisted my guts at the thought. But I wasn't going to get into that now. I clumsily changed the subject. "Sharon said you have something to tell me?"

"Well, I have some news." *Way-ull.* Two syllables. Though she had been born and raised in Washington, D.C., a Southern accent had grown on her like wisteria. I had excised mine when I moved, taking on the bland, regionless diction of a newscaster, tired of people, including my husband, mentally docking me two dozen IQ points whenever they heard me speak.

"What's wrong?"

"Nothing's wrong, Madeleine. You are so dramatic. I just wanted to tell you I've decided to sell the house."

Sharon had been gracefully backing away into the front room, and when I turned to her quickly, my eyes wide open, she all but bolted like a rabbit. I whirled back to my mother. "This house? Our house?"

"Of course this house. Who else's house would I sell? It's too big for me, really. Lydia Endicott has the loveliest condominium not far from here, and something like that would be so much easier to take care of."

Because my mother never admitted to any weakness, I was instantly on alert. She woke up every morning and had dry toast and coffee for breakfast, while torturing whichever housekeeper was unfortunate enough to be in her employ at that time. She dressed (perfectly), she gardened (beautifully), she went to some luncheon function (elegantly), she played bridge (competitively), she had dinner at the club with a single glass of wine (socially), and she came home and went to bed. Her skin was luminous, probably due to the truly staggering amount of money she spent on moisturizers and facials and the vague promises of rejuvenating treatments, and though she was almost seventy-five, she didn't look a day over sixty. Not even a silver hair on her head, though that may have been due to the ministrations of her hairdresser and not entirely to genetics.

"Are you okay?" I asked, bracing myself for some admission of illness.

She sighed in irritation, turned to the floral arrangement on the front table, and began to fuss with it. "Didn't I already tell you I was fine?"

"You did, it's just . . . what about . . . your garden?" I asked. It wasn't the most intelligent question, but the idea of my mother moving someplace where she couldn't have a garden was strange. She had always had a garden. Multiple gardens, in fact: the front garden, the herb garden, the rose garden, the back garden, the ornamental garden, and the side garden.

Oh, and the kitchen garden, for the growing of vegetables she never seemed to eat. And there was also what was affectionately known as "the orchard," which was actually a somewhat confusing collection of two apple trees, a pear tree, a plum tree, and a handful of raspberry bushes that had lost their way.

"There's a community garden. Lydia has a plot. And I can have window boxes and planters on the balcony, of course. I mean, I'll be left off the garden tour, but if it means I don't have to manage three floors by myself, it will be worth it. I've been run off my feet with no housekeeper since Renata left. Honestly. Who gets married during planting season? That girl doesn't have the sense God gave little green apples."

"Mother!" I said sharply, interrupting what I knew was bound to be a detailed recounting of how much work the house was to keep up and how terribly *busy* she was all the time, interspersed with (and I am not kidding here) exegeses on how hard it was to find good help these days. No normal person would consider the housekeeper's not planning her wedding around my mother's gardening schedule a selfish act, but my mother was not normal. She was the star of her own movie. "When are you selling the house?"

"That's why Sharon's here. She's a real estate agent. Her mother and I are on the Garden Society board."

The mind boggled at the idea of Sharon's having an actual job. We'd had geometry together first period sophomore year and she had regularly stumbled in late, smelling of cigarettes and coffee, asking to borrow a pencil. And now she was going to sell my mother's house?

"You can't sell it now! It's too soon!" My emotions were already off-kilter, and the idea of her selling the house struck me with dumb terror.

"Too soon for what? If you had to take care of this place all on your own, you wouldn't be saying that. Why, just last week the wiring in the living room was going absolutely haywire . . ."

My mother launched into a lengthy complaint about finding an electrician, and I tuned her out, trying to get my emotions under control. I hadn't lived in my parents' house for years. I went back to visit once a year and spent the entire time arguing with my mother and bumping into the enormous antique furniture that always seemed to be lurking around corners, waiting to surprise me. I had never had any particular feelings toward the house, but right then it seemed like the most important place in the whole world, as if it were a monument slated for demolition, to be replaced by a shopping mall.

"Mother, you've lived in this house for over fifty years! How can you sell it?"

"Don't yell, Madeleine." My mother flipped her hands into the air, her balletic fingers waving me away. "I'm right here."

"I'm not yelling," I said, even though I was.

"Sharon is here to go through the house with me, and I'd appreciate it if you'd stop with your hysterics long enough for us to do that."

"I'm hardly hysterical," I said, and that, at least, was true.

On cue, Sharon reappeared at the doorway and my mother turned to her as though she were an enormous relief, which she probably was, for all kinds of reasons. The two of them walked into the front room and I followed, mostly because I didn't have anything better to do. As my mother guided Sharon around as though they were on the Parade of Homes tour, and Sharon took pictures and made notes to herself, I looked around, trying to see the house through someone else's eyes. I could hear Sharon's tone, and I knew she was making a colossal list of things my mother was going to have to fix or change or update. I couldn't wait to hear that conversation.

My parents' house had always been a showplace, more museum and shrine to family heritage than home. As a child, I had longed to touch everything, largely because it was off-limits, but also because everything was so beautiful. There were delicate bone china teacups to use for tea parties, tiny porcelain figurines I could pose and shift around to tell the stories that were always running wild through my mind (I was an only child of older parents, and often dreadfully lonely), antique furniture to climb, silver to smudge, and perfectly ironed, handmade table linens to drape myself in for costumes—bride, sheik, Greek goddess, attendant at the queen's ball.

When I was a child, my parents had maintained a few employees—a cook, a housekeeper as well as a maid, a gardener, and the occasional backup dancer, a handyman or a builder, usually. Having "help" had always seemed old-fashioned and indulgent, but looking at the house now, I understood. It had been built for a large family and lots of guests. The furnishings were from another time, when there had been a full staff to take care of the endless dust, the silver that oxidized without any attention, the linens in need of ironing. And my mother was busy. You could make fun of ladies who lunched all you wanted—really, it was my favorite hobby—but my mother's work mattered. She had raised and contributed literally millions of dollars to charities. And that, even I had to admit, was more important than vacuuming.

I carried my suitcase upstairs and tossed it into my old bedroom, watching Sharon making another note as I did. Probably "Madeleine should put her suitcase away instead of throwing it on the floor." Duly noted.

"Can I see the attic?" Sharon asked.

"It's a little chaotic," my mother said. She pulled at the door, but it had swollen slightly in the heat and wouldn't budge.

"Let me," I said. I gave it a firm tug and it popped open, groaning to express its displeasure. The trapped air rushed out at me, stale and musty. "We're in," I said, like I was engineering a bank heist.

The stairs were so narrow I had to walk with my feet sideways so they would fit on the treads. When I was little, the attic had been one of my favorite parts of the house, a place to find a hundred mysteries and compose a hundred stories. A dress rack with plastic bags holding my mother's old clothes, including her wedding gown, yellowing delicately in the silence, and enough vintage clothing to provide me with hours of dress-up entertainment. Boxes and trunks filled with the detritus of family shipwrecks, inscrutable objects from times gone by—shrimp forks, salt cellars, rolling ink blotters, monogrammed wax seals—piles of photographs of unidentified ancestors, and the occasional piece of broken jewelry, which I would generally stick in my hair, so when I came down for dinner I looked like a magpie had built its sparkly nest on my head.

"We could advertise this as a playroom," Sharon said as she reached the top of the stairs, as though she had heard my memories. I could imagine what she was thinking—toy boxes lining the walls, a pink plastic castle, stain-resistant carpeting—and it made me feel protective of the attic's homeliness. It had always been playroom enough for me with the ancient, creaking wooden floors and dust-covered hatboxes and trunks.

While my mother and Sharon talked about air-conditioning and Pottery Barn furniture, I sat down by one of the windows and looked out over the yard, the way I had so many afternoons when I was little. I didn't remember its being so warm, but it certainly was now; sweat was already trickling down my forehead and I lifted an arm to blot it away.

Next door, the restaurant was open for lunch. I could see people sitting on the porch, the motion of servers walking back and forth. Beyond that, the entire yard had been transformed into a garden with slender paths between the beds for easy passage. It was early in the season, but the vegetables were already growing there; besides the tomato plants by the edge, I could see a small herb garden near the opposite fence, rows of strawberries, vines of squash spreading over the ground, and neat, orderly rows of lettuce, blossoming out of the earth like bridal bouquets. My stomach growled. I was definitely going there to eat sometime soon. I had never been one of those people whose appetite fell away under stress and grief. In fact, my consumption of snack cakes rose in direct proportion to my emotional turmoil.

When I turned away from the window, my mother and Sharon had disappeared back downstairs, heading for the basement. Looking around the attic, I imagined going through these things, packing them up, sending them off to auction or to the landfill, and it made me feel terribly wistful, as though I were saying goodbye to a part of myself I would never get back.

In front of me was a low, small trunk. Leaning forward, I opened it to find a stack of folded, faded fabric and a wooden box with a sliding top that turned out to be full of dark pebbles, rescued from the gentle smoothing of the water by some curious hand long ago. Below those were an accordion file full of financial paperwork, a stack of envelopes bound together so tightly the rubber band had bitten into the centers of the envelopes on both the top and the bottom, a pile of books, and a few composition books, their covers yellowed and dry. Picking one up, I flipped through the pages. It was a mishmash of things: a listing of clothing comprising a girl's wardrobe, some poetry, a draft of a letter to the aforementioned girl's mother with lots of cross-outs and exclamation points, a hastily drawn calendar, and some absentminded doodles. I looked through, smiling, thinking this could have been any girl's diary, really, from anytime. Substitute high-heeled sneakers and short overalls for petticoats and gloves and it could have been written today, but the dates sprinkled throughout the pages told me it was from 1914. I flipped back to the front cover and there, in a valiant (if failed) effort at pretty penmanship, was my grandmother's maiden name: Margaret Brooke Pearce.

Putting the notebook aside, I pulled the next one out of the trunk. This one was labeled four years later: 1918. It was more of a diary than the first notebook, though there were still occasional digressions into the mundane: pages of addition adding up to a teenage budget, a list of girls' names and where they were going to college (I felt a little surge of pleasure at this: 1918 and the entire graduating class of girls—only thirty, but still—were every one of them going to college). In February, I read this entry:

The 'flu is here, and the school is in a complete panic. They can't send us home, they say, because too many people are sick and we'd only infect them on our journeys. Instead, they're quarantining us here. Everyone is awfully disturbed, but I think it's rather romantic. Of course, I don't have it yet. I've always been healthy as a horse, as Mother says, so maybe I won't get it at all?

And a few weeks later:

Well, Lucinda's caught it. They've run out of spaces in the infirmary, so they've gone and turned the gymnasium into another infirmary. She's there now. Of course, it's not as bad as it could be—there are these awful photographs of soldiers who are down with it, just shoved into bed after bed anywhere they can find the space—churches, gymnasiums. Abbott ran out of medical staff and teachers to help long ago, and they're asking the mothers to come. The funniest part—Mother has agreed! I suppose she thinks it's war service, even though the war is practically over, or so everyone keeps saying.

Anyway, they've closed down one of the other dormitories, so I've got a new roommate now that Lucinda is gone (and good riddance to bad rubbish, says I); Ruth is only a sophomore, but she's quite droll and we get on très well. Her sister sent a pack of peanut brittle and we stayed up late last night gorging ourselves and laughing until we felt positively ill (or possibly that was due to the peanut brittle). The good news is there are only half the classes and with the weather so drab I was able to sleep it off. Mother would be furious I ate so many sweets.

To be honest, I feel a little jealous that Mother is coming up here to take care of these other girls. She's never been up to visit me, not even for Family Weekend. Part of me wishes I would get

*the 'flu, just a little case, and then she'd have to take care of me,
too. When I picture my own mother ministering to mean old
Lucinda, sitting by her bedside and dabbing at her forehead with
a cool cloth, it makes me more than a little ill with jealousy.*

It was so strange to read the entries and think of my grandmother
writing them. She had died when I was twelve, so to me she had only
been Grandmother, old and stiff and formal to a fault. It was impossible
to reconcile the woman I had known with this girl, so honest and young
and silly. It could have been my diary, with all the complaints about her
mother and the sugar overload.

My stomach growled again, hard and insistent, and I wiped a few
more beads of sweat off my forehead. Time to go, then. I'd check in with
Sharon to see if she'd strangled my mother yet, and then I'd figure out
what to do next. I started to put the notebooks and letters back into the
trunk and then paused. In my confusion that morning, I hadn't packed
a book, and these looked like a better-than-average distraction. Maybe
I'd find something my mother and I could bond over. Gathering up the
packet of letters and the pile of books and notebooks, I stacked my arms
full and headed down the stairs.

In my bedroom, I dropped the papers on the bed and went to wash
the travel stink and attic dust off my skin. Drying my hands, my engagement ring snagged on the towel, and I tugged it free, staring at it. It had
been cleaned a few months ago when I went to Tiffany's to buy a present
for one of Phillip's nieces (why a five-year-old girl needed a present from
Tiffany's was beyond me, but this was how the Spencer family worked),
and it sparkled in the light, the scratches on the metal, evidence of years
of bumps, bangs, and scrapes, barely visible.

There was a dark blue thread from the towel stuck underneath the
stone. I pulled it out, the thread breaking on either side, leaving a tiny
piece of blue fuzz underneath the prong. I picked at it for a moment, a

tide of irritation building inside me, pushing aside the sick, sinking fear that had been resting heavily in my chest. Why did Phillip get to be the wronged party? What had I done wrong, other than be honest, admit for once that I was unhappy, that there was something broken between us?

On the counter was a small china dish and I tossed the rings in there, clinking the lid back on with satisfaction. Now I wouldn't have to look at that piece of lint marring the ring's perfection. I wouldn't have to think about it at all. And I certainly wouldn't pay any attention to its bare and blinding absence on my finger.

four

MARGIE
1924

Five years after her debut, my grandmother was sitting in the parlor, twenty-four years old and generally agreed to be a spinster. She had graduated from college two years before, and now she found herself lost.

"What are you thinking on, Margie?" her mother asked. "You've done half of that in the wrong color."

Margie lifted her embroidery hoop and peered at it closely. "Oh, damn," she said. "Well, it's not as if it was any good to begin with."

"Don't swear, Margie. You'll never get a husband with a mouth like a fishwife," her mother scolded with a tired sigh. She held out her hand. "Give it here. I'll take the stitches out."

Margie crossed her eyes. There was going to be no husband. She knew it, and she guessed her mother knew it, and only said things like that to keep the fiction alive, for whose benefit she wasn't sure. Margie hadn't been keen on getting married in particular, but she had very much liked the idea of a love affair or two. There had been a time when she had been starry-eyed enough to think some man might see beyond her plainness and find the person underneath and fall madly in love. She thought maybe Robert Walsh had. Oh, but she didn't like to think of him at all.

"Mr. Chapman is coming for dinner tonight," her mother said without looking up. She was plucking out Margie's sloppy, miscolored stitches. When she handed it back, there would be tiny holes where the thread had been, and puckers in the fabric, but Margie would be expected to redo it anyway. What use were these things now? When women had the vote, when girls could go to medical school, when every day little earthquakes of change brought something new? The time of embroidery and silver polishing was ending, and another time, one Margie had only glimpsed the night of her debut, of dancing and parties and women free to do as they pleased, dress as they wanted, had begun. But not in her mother's parlor. It might as well have been 1885 in there, the décor Victorian, ornate wallpaper and dark wood and enormous, heavy, velvet-covered furniture that seemed to do nothing except produce dust. Her mother, who had been raised in a house even more dependent on rules and rigidity than the one she ran now, had gritted her teeth and barred the door against any change.

Margie wasn't really interested in the speakeasies or the liquor or the Charleston, and heaven knows the clothes wouldn't have suited her. Her interests were more creative. Upstairs in her room was a series of notebooks—some she used for journals, the others for her stories. Abbott Academy's literary magazine had published a series of poems and short stories she'd written, and Margie had been proud to bursting to see her words somewhere other than in her notebooks, and in typeface instead of her cramped, busy hand. But when she'd shown the magazine to her parents, their reaction had been condescending, a dismissive nod after skimming through. Her father had grunted. "That's nice," her mother had said, but her mother didn't think much of stories or poems in the first place. She believed reading should be edifying, and was particularly fond of publications from the Temperance League.

In college Margie had won the Mary Olivier Memorial Prize for Lyric Poetry, and the literary society had published a few of her stories in their journals. It wasn't like high school; they didn't send copies of everything home, and she didn't think her parents had ever seen those, which was a pity, as they were much better. This was what she wanted, why she longed to be able to leave the parlor and go into the world outside, to write and to publish and to talk to other people with imagination. Nowadays it wasn't like the unfortunate Brontë sisters, who'd had to publish as men to get any attention. Now women could be reporters and poets and even novelists. But how could she have anything to write about if she never left these four walls? She wanted to be out there, living!

"Again? Didn't he come last week?"

"He did," her mother said blandly. "I invited him back. I thought you two got on awfully well. And so did he, apparently. He was pleased to accept my invitation when I told him you would be at home."

"Oh, no, Mother."

"Now, Margie, he's a perfectly nice man. You said so yourself."

"I was being polite! Mother, he's twice my age! And so dreadfully dull. All that talk about government securities or exchange rates or something. I wanted to impale myself on the shrimp fork."

"Margie, do you always have to be so dramatic?" her mother asked, shaking her head in a disappointed way Margie knew well. She finished pulling the last line of thread out of the hoop, wrapped the loose floss neatly into a bundle, and handed it back to Margie. "I don't have to remind you that you are in no position to be turning down offers from eligible bachelors."

"Mother," Margie cried. She felt as if she were sixteen again, being pressed to go to a dance she had no interest in. After her season had ended, her mother had continued making arrangements for Margie to go out: to the symphony, to balls, to parties. There she was either roundly ignored and would find a quiet corner to read in (in which case she might as well have just stayed home), or she was yanked around from group to group by her mother as though she were an exotic new pet who needed showing off. Worse, lately, her mother had taken it upon herself to invite her father's single business associates over for dinner, seating them next to Margie as though to judge how they would look as a pair, so Margie was forced to make conversation. And of course all the men her own age were either married or terrible rakes (and sometimes both, she thought, thinking of Anne Dulaney's husband), so the dinner guests had skewed older and older until they had lit on Mr. Chapman, who was nearly fifty and never married, and who was perfectly genteel, but, as previously mentioned, dreadfully boring (which probably explained the never-married part).

"Mother, please don't make me." Margie sighed. She hated the way she sounded, young and spoiled, but how could she sound any other way when she was being treated like a child? This was the problem, she thought, with living in this house year after year, locked in this room with her mother, Margie embroidering while her mother tore her stitches out, having the same conversations while they both went quietly mad. She faked headaches on a regular basis so she could sneak upstairs to her room and write or read. Her mother hated how much Margie read; in addition to the frivolity of novels, she complained, squinting at those books all the time was going to ruin Margie's eyesight.

Margie wished she could run away. Women lived on their own all the time now. One of the houses at the end of the block had been turned into a boardinghouse; she saw the girls who lived there heading off to work every day in twos and threes, laughing, heads bent close, sharing the secrets of a life she could hardly imagine. Surely they had their own problems, but they also had the freedom to take whatever job they wanted and live wherever they wanted and marry whomever they wanted, and she imagined those freedoms were worth a fair amount of pain.

And she could work, couldn't she? She could work at the library— just the thought of spending her days with all those books made her giddy. She could be a writer for a magazine. She could fetch coffee or take notes, if it came to it. And as always, when she ran through this scenario in her head, she could feel her hopes rising, could *see* it as though it were already true. And then something would happen, someone would speak, and her bubble would burst and she would come back to the ground, to her mother's parlor and this crooked, rumpled embroidery, and a life full of gatherings she didn't want to go to and people she didn't want to talk to and all the obligations her mother pressed on her until she wanted to scream.

"It will be fine, Margie. He's a lovely man, and financially secure."

"I don't care about financially secure."

"You'd care a lot more about it if you hadn't lived that way all your life," her mother said.

"It doesn't matter to me, Mother. Not the way it matters to you."

"It will be all right in the end, Margie." Her mother lowered her head to her embroidery with a quiet smile, as though she had won something. "You'll see."

Though in the end, it wasn't fine. It wasn't fine at all.

After dinner that night, an endless affair in which Mr. Chapman and her father talked at length about some provision in the Howland-Barnes Act and Margie valiantly resisted falling asleep in her potatoes, her mother suggested Margie and Mr. Chapman take a walk. Margie, who had been cooped up inside all day, nearly fled for her wrap. Even a walk with Mr. Chapman was better than sitting with him and her parents for the length of coffee and polite conversation in the parlor.

They had walked for a few blocks in silence when they reached Book Hill Park and Mr. Chapman suggested they sit down. Margie had a disturbing feeling of foreboding, and thought wildly, crazily, about escaping, about simply turning and running far away, where Mr. Chapman couldn't catch her.

Instead, she sat down on the very edge of the bench, leaving a good two feet between them. "Margie," Mr. Chapman began, in a somber tone, as though he were preparing to deliver a college lecture, "I'm sure you're aware of how closely your father and I work together."

He paused, and Margie realized she was supposed to respond. "Yes?" she said, though it came out more question than confirmation.

"It's an alliance I wish to preserve at any cost. Your father is a great man, Margie. He's brought change to Washington, to the banking industry." Mr. Chapman was starting to drone. Margie wished there were a nearby plate of potatoes she could put her face in. She didn't understand a fifth of what her father did; it all sounded dreadfully boring. The most exciting thing he had, as far as she was concerned, was a partial share in the Washington Senators, the baseball team, and her mother rarely allowed her to go to the games. "The obligations of someone of your class" apparently didn't include eating peanuts, or doing anything fun, for that matter.

"I'd like to cement that relationship by marrying you, Margie," Mr. Chapman said finally, putting his hands on his thighs and sitting up straight. He wasn't looking at her; he hadn't looked at her during the entire duration of his speech. He might have been talking to someone else entirely.

Margie wanted to laugh out loud, but she was too horrified. "I'm sorry, Mr. Chapman, but are you proposing?"

He looked at her frantically and she realized, with a jolt of sympathy, that he was nervous. Could it be that in his lengthy—impossibly lengthy, she thought!—life, he had never proposed to anyone before? Or maybe he had never proposed successfully, and was afraid of being shot down yet again?

Clearing his throat, Mr. Chapman pushed his hands down his thighs again. Margie guessed his palms were sweating. "I am, yes. Margie, we should get married. Your mother is anxious for you to get married, you know."

Margie, who had read all sorts of romantic novels, had never heard of a proposal like this before. He hadn't mentioned his feelings for her; hadn't even mentioned *her*, really. Even Mr. Darcy had finally been moved to confess his emotions. She knew Mr. Chapman was older, and a pragmatic man, but what was she expected to say to this? If she'd been a different sort of girl, prettier, more graced in social niceties, she might have known how to respond, how to turn this back so he didn't feel offended (though, really, she thought with some indignation, he deserved to be offended—he couldn't even bother to *pretend* even the smallest bit of love for her?), but if she had been that sort of girl, she wouldn't have gotten a proposal like this in the first place.

So Margie did the only rational thing. Standing up from the bench, she pulled her skirts up slightly to keep from tripping over them, and she turned toward the entrance of the park and ran. She ran the entire way home, not caring what the people she passed thought of this woman tearing down the sidewalk in her dinner clothes; she ran up the stairs and into her room, locked the door, and collapsed on the bed, panting, her body overheated, her feet sore from the press of her toes on the pavement through her delicate-soled shoes, her mind spinning.

She heard a knock at the door downstairs, voices in the hall, her mother's high and anxious, her father's and Mr. Chapman's low and murmuring. The sound of her father's study door opening and closing, and then an ominous silence for a long time. Margie closed her eyes on the bed. She couldn't even think of what to do next. They were going to come up here, maybe both of them—God forbid all three of them—and her father was going to look hurt and her mother was going to be furious. She thought back to the conversation with her mother in the parlor. Her mother had known. Of course her mother had known. Mr. Chapman would have asked her father's permission, and maybe her mother had been there, maybe her parents had even pleaded with him to take her on (that thought was too humiliating to linger on for long).

Below, her father's study door opened and closed, voices in the hall, this time calmer, more conciliatory. The door closing. Her parents' voices now, just the two of them. Margie stood, unlocked her bedroom door, and then lay down on the bed again, bracing herself for their footsteps on the stairs, their disappointed arrival.

No one came.

Instead, she heard them move into the parlor, their voices becoming only the faintest sound in the still house. The maid and the cook had cleaned up after dinner, put the house to bed, gone to bed themselves. It was only her parents below, deciding her fate, and her, lying hopeless and powerless in her room, wondering what, exactly, was to become of her now.

Finally, her mother flung the door of Margie's room open. "Margaret Brooke Pearce," she thundered, and her face was so tight with fury that Margie slid backward on her bed, as though she could disappear into the wall. "You horrible, ungrateful thing. How dare you refuse Mr. Chapman?"

Margie opened her mouth, but all that came out was a squeak. "Do you think you are such a desirable property that men are lined up around the block for you? You are twenty-four and unmarried. Do you know what that means? The men who might marry you are taken. Every day you get older, and every day there are girls younger than you, prettier than you, and heaven knows more polite than you, who are making themselves available for marriage. This was your chance, Margie, and you have destroyed it."

"I didn't want to marry him," Margie said, her voice wavering on the edge of tears. "He doesn't love me. And I don't love him."

"Love. Love! I suppose you get these ideas about love from the books you are always reading. Oh, you think I don't know what you do up here with your time, Margie, but I know how you waste away the hours dreaming. Other girls are bettering themselves. They do good works, they go to Temperance League meetings, and if they do read, it's something edifying. They go to parties without complaining. And you're shut up here with your books and these notebooks and the one time you get a chance at marriage, you ruin it." Her mother's fury arced up and she raised her arm, reaching out and swiping a stack of notebooks and papers off Margie's writing table.

Leaping off the bed, Margie stood up straight, her fists clenched by her sides. "You don't care about me. You only want me to marry him because it will be good for Father's business." One of her notebooks had fluttered open on the ground and she lunged for it, closing it and clutching it to her chest.

"And what's wrong with that? Your father's business is what feeds you and clothes you. That business is what you use to buy these precious books. That business is what will pay your way when we are gone and you are old and alone and unmarried."

A sob caught in Margie's throat at her mother's harsh words. "I'm not going to get married. I will pay my own way."

"How?"

"I'm going to be a writer." Margie lifted her chin defiantly, though she didn't feel defiant. She felt like burying her face in the pillow and crying. It was all so unfair. She understood love didn't have to be like it was in novels, but was it so wrong to want there to be *something* between her and the man she would marry? Something to look forward to, other than the cool, businesslike agreement her parents had?

"A writer? A woman writer? What living would you earn doing that? Not one that could keep you in the style to which you've been accustomed, I can tell you. You are far too old for these silly, foolish dreams, Margie." She looked as though she were going to say something else and Margie braced herself, then, as abruptly as her mother had come, she turned on her heel and left the room, closing the door loudly behind her.

When her mother had gone, Margie unclenched her fists, looking at the pale moons her fingernails had carved in her palms. She felt, suddenly, very, very tired. She lay down on the bed again, staring at the ceiling, tears rolling down the sides of her face. There was no way out. She had everything, and she had nothing. She was going to spend the rest of her life like this, watching her mother pulling the threads out of her embroidery, sneaking up to her room to write stories no one would ever see, her parents bringing suitors to the table, digging closer and closer to the bottom of the barrel until there was no one left, and then Margie would be alone forever, and none of those foolish, lovely dreams would ever come true.

Margie fell asleep in her dinner dress, her shoes still on, lying there on top of the coverlet. When she woke in the morning, she drew herself a bath and sat in the water until it went cold. She pulled her hair into a simple knot at the base of her neck, dressed, faced herself in the mirror. She looked the part of the wretched spinster, she thought: pale, wearing a dark dress as though mourning the death of her own life. *Well, this is it*, she thought. *And if they want me to marry him, I won't. I just won't. I'll get a job, not even a fancy job, a typist somewhere—places are hiring female clerks more and more often now. And I'll move into one of those boardinghouses, and I'll only come over here for holidays, and we'll all sit around the dinner table and be terribly polite, and then I'll be happy because I'll be free.*

Squaring her shoulders, Margie shook her head. She marched herself downstairs and into the dining room, where her parents were eating breakfast. As usual, her father was hidden behind a newspaper. Her mother was drinking tea and did not, to Margie's surprise, throw it in her face when she slid into her chair.

"Good morning," her father said from behind his paper.

"Good morning," Margie muttered. She took a piece of toast from the toast rack and spread it with marmalade.

Her mother lifted her eyes above her teacup, saying nothing. Margie chewed her toast, the crack of the crumbs between her teeth loud as artillery fire.

Finally, her father turned the last page of his paper, folded it, and put it on the table. Margie swallowed hard, the dry toast scraping its way down her throat.

"You're going to Europe," he said. Her father had the habit of starting conversations wherever his own thought process was, which generally caused a great deal of confusion and required catching up on the part of the listener.

"I'm sorry?" she asked. Of all the possible scenarios she had imagined last night, many of them deeply melodramatic, inspired by Gothic novels and a handful of Valentino movies, being sent to Europe had not been high on the list. Hadn't been anywhere on the list, really.

"I'll book your ticket today. Your mother will take you to New York and you will leave from there."

"I don't understand." Was this supposed to feel like a punishment? A banishment? Europe. Margie had dreamed of going, of course, but it had always seemed just that—a dream.

"Your cousin Evelyn is going on her Tour." Margie's mother spoke finally. She lifted her napkin, dabbing carefully at the edges of her mouth, though there was nothing there, and Margie wished, sadly, for the millionth time, that she had been born with the tiniest amount of her mother's poise. "And she's in need of a chaperone. You're to go with her."

"But," Margie started to object, and then closed her mouth. Evelyn was eighteen and incorrigible. Margie and Evelyn, being the only two cousins close in age, had been thrust together at family gatherings for years, and Margie was ashamed to admit Evelyn had bullied her from the start. Spoiled, demanding, and domineering, Evelyn took great pleasure in ordering Margie around. In their games, Evelyn was the princess, Margie the lady-in-waiting. Evelyn was the knight, Margie was the steed. Evelyn was the brave hero, Margie the (actually fairly ineffectual) villain. Evelyn was greatly experienced in setting up situations to her best advantage, and Margie would rather have eaten broken glass than spend six months traveling with her.

Except the alternative wasn't broken glass. It was a lifetime with Mr. Chapman. And in contrast, dragging Evelyn to art galleries sounded like an absolute treat. And in Europe! London! Paris! Rome! The cobblestone streets, the cathedrals, the opera houses, the museums, the castles, the princes. Margie sighed a dreamy sigh.

Her mother, catching Margie's slip into fancy, frowned. "You'll be responsible for Evelyn, you understand. They're sending her on the Tour in hopes that she will . . . mature somewhat. And frankly, I'm hoping the same thing for you. You've proven yourself unwilling to accept any responsibility here. I pray, for your sake, Margie, that this trip teaches you the value of everything you seem to think so little of." She took a sip of her tea, but from the way her lips were pursed, she might as well have been drinking grapefruit juice.

She could have argued. But here she was, twenty-four and unmarried, and her best—well, only—prospect was someone she would marry only if he were the last eligible man on earth, and even then she would have to think hard on it. So here were her options: embrace her destiny as a maiden aunt to one of New York City's most notorious harpies, or marry Mr. Chapman and be doomed to decades of conversations about municipal bonds and tax acts.

"When do I leave?" Margie asked.

five

MADELEINE
1999

Despite my exhaustion, I had stayed up late reading my grandmother's journals, and I dreamed of flappers and debutante balls all night. When I woke in the morning, I was sleepy and disoriented. I blinked at the ceiling a few times, wondering why it was a different color, until I remembered where I was. Thought of Phillip. My mother. Sharon. Tensed, relaxed. Tensed again.

It was almost nine o'clock, which wasn't entirely surprising. I had always been a morning person, but after I had gotten married, there was no reason to get up. "It wouldn't look right for you to work. People would think I can't support you," Phillip had told me when I had started to browse the want ads, and when I said I would like to anyway, he was so irritated I had put the argument aside. At first I thought it might just be for a year, and then a year had grown into two, and then somehow the compromise I had made as a momentary peace offering had become permanent. When I had started volunteering at the Stabler, I had been desperate for the contact, the purpose, the meaning. The volunteer coordinator had told me she'd never had anyone master the entire collection of presentations so quickly, which had made me feel slightly embarrassed, but no less eager.

Downstairs, I could hear my mother moving around, a door opening and closing, her quick, efficient steps on the floor. For a moment, I imagined I was a child again, and I could run down to the kitchen and my father would be sitting with his newspapers at the table and I could steal the funny pages and we would read in silence together. It felt so real, the smudges of newsprint on my fingers, the smell of his coffee, the way he would clear his throat as he read an interesting story in the paper, that I caught my breath and held it in for a moment to keep from crying, overwhelmed with memory and confusion and loss.

And then, as if to remind me of the hierarchy of needs and nostalgia's place in it, my stomach growled loudly. The night before, my mother had gone out and all I'd had to eat was a handful of stale crackers and some cheese of questionable freshness that tasted a lot like dirt. I sighed, pushing back the covers and dragging myself out of bed. I had been sleeping in an oversized shirt and a pair of boxer shorts, which was exactly what I loved to sleep in, and exactly what Phillip would never allow, and I looked down at my rumpled self, shrugged, and headed downstairs.

My mother's refrigerator was as empty as it had been the night before. I took a swig of sweet tea from the carafe inside (sure, there was no food, but my mother clearly had her standards), wiping my mouth with the back of my hand, and prowled through the pantry and the rest of the cupboards, coming up empty.

As a last-ditch resort, I headed out into the back yard, padding barefoot through the moist grass, still damp with dew and the remnants of the morning's sprinkler run, the perfect, soft blades tickling my ankles. Summer was my favorite season in my mother's garden, when everything was exploding, wild and ripe, but it was already beautiful that spring. Early roses were opening, arching their stems as they spread their petals to the sun. The fruit trees bore pale leaves and buds extended blindly from the branches, testing the air. The herb garden held rows of low, cautious greenery, and the hedges and stones bordering the ornamental garden waited patiently for everything to bloom so they would have something to contain. Ducking under one of the apple trees, I walked over to the vegetable garden by the low fence.

It was really too early for anything to be ripe, but I pawed through the leaves, thinking nostalgically of summer afternoons when I would sneak through my mother's kitchen garden, leaves brushing against my face, and pluck a fat, warm tomato from where it lay, sleeping heavily on the ground, and eat it like an apple, wet juice and seeds and plump, yielding skin. It was months too early for tomatoes, but I found a miracle in the form of a patch of strawberry runners, bearing tiny but inarguably red fruit. I picked them greedily, two at a time, eating one while I held my shirt out to make a basket and dropped the other in there. They were firm and not as juicy as they would be in a few weeks, but they were sweet and fresh and my stomach accepted them gratefully.

When I finally rose up, my tongue stained red, my shirt containing another handful or two of berries, I looked down over the other side of the fence and saw a man crouching low underneath the leaves of a pepper plant. He blinked at me solemnly through the green.

With a startled yelp, I stepped backward into a clump of soft dirt, nearly losing my balance and dropping the strawberries.

"I'm sorry, I'm sorry." He rose, holding his hands out in surrender. He was wearing gardening gloves and holding a rubber mallet in one hand. Now that he was standing instead of crouching in the bushes like a serial killer, he looked much less threatening, even considering the mallet. His T-shirt was stretched out, with holes at the bottom, and his loose khakis had smudges of dirt all over them. His eyes were fringed with lashes I would have traded him for in a second, and his eyebrows were a little too thick, and he had shaggy brown hair and an equally shaggy beard. He looked like a large, friendly family dog. "I thought you were Mrs. Bowers."

"You were hiding from my mother in the bushes?"

He gave a sheepish shrug. A pair of headphones hung around his neck, the cord trailing down into his pocket, where a Discman pushed the line of his pants out of shape.

"Mrs. Bowers is your mother? She doesn't like me much," he said, and he sounded disappointed about it.

"Buck up. She doesn't like anybody, really. Not even me."

"I'm sure that's not true." He had a comforting drawl that marked him as a local. Tilting his head, he looked at me curiously. "You don't favor her at all." His Discman was still playing; I could hear the tinny squeal of guitars issuing from the headphones into the still air, already heavy and wet, preparing itself for the hard work of humidity ahead.

Self-consciously, I reached for my hair with one hand, patting it down. I generally woke with a spectacular case of bedhead, and I hadn't even bothered to look in the mirror before stumbling downstairs. No, at that moment I probably looked even less like my mother than usual.

"Oh, we're not related," I said. "I was hatched from a walnut shell."

To my surprise, he threw back his head and laughed, a rich, low sound that rang through the morning. "You're funny."

I blinked at him. "Nobody thinks I'm funny."

"I do," he said, looking surprised.

"Well, there's no accounting for taste, as my mother would say. Who are you, anyway?"

"I'm so sorry." He pulled his gloves off and politely extended a hand to me. I took it, and instantly regretted it—my fingers were strawberry-sticky. "I'm Henry Hamilton. And you're The Heiress Bowers."

"You can call me Madeleine. No honorific necessary. And my last name is Spencer. I'm married." I don't know why I clarified my marital status, as though he might be interested in my pajama-clad, strawberry-stained self. Not that Henry was anyone to impress, really. He was perfectly nice-looking, but in general I wanted to take a pair of clippers to him, trim back the wildness of his curls, the scruffiness of his beard. He wasn't especially tall, but he was broad-shouldered and big of hand, and at the moment, covered in dirt. My mother would have been horrified by the first impressions we were making.

"Madeleine Spencer. It's a pleasure. So now you know my hiding place. May I ask why you're creeping around in the garden?"

"My mother doesn't keep any food in the house. She survives on Melba toast and the blood of her enemies."

He barked out another laugh, his curls bouncing. "You're lucky. Those strawberries shouldn't be ripe for another two weeks."

"Yet another one of the myriad ways fortune smiles upon me. What about you? Do you work at the restaurant?"

"I own it, actually."

"Congratulations. My mother thinks you're Satan for opening it next to her house, by the way."

Henry winced. "I know. I feel awful. She's an incredible gardener. I'd hoped we might have something to talk about."

I looked over his shoulder at his garden, which was all function, long, straight rows of turned earth, tomato cages and strawberry planters standing sentry, stakes at regular intervals to separate out the crops. "Do you grow all this food for the restaurant?"

"As much as I can."

"That's amazing."

"I'd like to grow more. I wish your mother would talk to me. I have so many questions about how she gets such incredible produce, but she refuses to talk to me."

"Well, you don't have to worry about it for much longer. She's selling the house, apparently."

Henry lifted a broad fist to his chest. "*Mon Dieu!*" he said. Okay, no, he didn't, but he looked so surprised, his eyes opening wide, his hand clutching his itty-bitty sledgehammer to his heart as though he were a well-armed heroine in a Regency romance. "Oh no! Was it something I said?"

"Hmm. She does hate you a little bit."

"Yes, she's made that fairly clear. I invited everyone in the neighborhood for a private dinner before we opened. Everyone came except her. And this one other couple, but I gave them a bye because the wife was giving birth."

"Generous of you."

"I like to think of myself as a magnanimous neighborhood overlord," he said, giving a little bow and then returning the mallet to his side. "In any case, your mother marched the invitation back over to me and told me exactly what I could do with it."

"My mother? I don't think so."

"Well, there were no specific body parts suggested, but the phrase 'ruining the neighborhood' might have been involved."

"Huh. Well, if anyone could tell you in a polite way that you're ruining the neighborhood, it would be my mother."

"So I'll extend the invitation to you instead. You should come to dinner sometime. My treat."

"That's a very kind offer," I said politely, but my stomach, hearing the suggestion of food, growled again quite rudely.

"You should get back to your strawberries," he said, nodding at my impromptu basket.

"You should get back to your lurking."

"Can't lurk all day if you don't start in the morning," he said, with such genuine cheerfulness that I couldn't help but laugh. "Nice to meet you, Madeleine."

"Likewise."

Trying to keep from exposing myself in my flimsy boxer shorts, I took a few steps backward, the earth yielding gently beneath me. How long had it been since I had felt the ground beneath my bare feet? It was delicious and made me feel oddly like weeping. When Henry went back to his work, I turned and began to walk toward the house, looking up at its sprawl, the empty windows winking back at me in the sun.

It had always been my destiny to have a big house like this, filled with antiques and enough furniture for dinner parties and enough lawn space to host a fundraiser. It was what everyone I had gone to school with was doing; my mother sent me casually remonstrative pages from the *Magnolia Providence-Journal* and *Magnolia Style*, in which the girls I had once known, now women, were photographed hosting luncheons at their home with distinguished guests.

But I didn't want a house like this. I felt lost in our condo, which was not even a quarter as big, and still more than we required. I dreaded the day Phillip would announce we were going to move to the suburbs and I would have to hire a housekeeper and a gardener, a pool service. I far preferred a life I didn't need assistance to maintain.

I finished eating the strawberries and tossed the hulls in an oversized planter by the French doors leading into the living room. Inside, the house was still. "Mother?" I called.

"Good, you're awake." My mother came bustling into the kitchen, carrying her purse and a stack of papers. Of course, I was still in my pajamas with sleep in my eyes and my hair standing on end, while my mother, who had probably been up since five, had her hair and makeup perfectly done and was armored in a pair of charcoal-gray slacks, a lavender cardigan, and a scarf knotted neatly around her neck like an air hostess.

"Sentient, even."

Unlike Henry, my mother was practiced at ignoring my wit. "You should get dressed. I've got to run some errands and drop these papers off before lunch."

I braced slightly. "What lunch? I haven't even eaten breakfast."

"Well, you'll be eating lunch soon, so don't worry about it."

"No, I mean, where are we eating lunch?"

"There's a speaker at the Ladies Association. You can see all your old friends—Ashley Hathaway is introducing—I don't know why you never make the effort to see those girls when you're in town."

Ashley and I had gone to Country Day together every year since pre-kindergarten, and for every single one of those years, she had been both my friend and my nemesis. She was the daughter my mother would have preferred, and the girl I would rather have been. She was delicate and petite, with smooth blond hair as perfect in humid July as in damp December. At our debut, she'd been escorted by a third cousin of some sort, who happened to be a supporting actor on a television drama. While I can't recall her ever being mean to me, exactly, there was something about being around her that felt like sucking on a copper penny.

"What if I don't want to go?" I asked.

"That's not an option," she said.

I pictured the luncheon at the Ladies Association. I pictured the clothing I didn't want to wear and the people I didn't want to say hello to. They would ask how I had been and wonder where my handsome husband was, and I'd spend yet another meal wishing I were eating a hamburger instead of pretending I was too full for a salad.

But my mother's expression made it clear I was going. "Fine," I said. What I really wanted to do was eat strawberry jam straight out of the jar without even closing the refrigerator door, and then get back into bed and read some more of my grandmother's journals, but clearly that was not going to happen.

"It starts at eleven. You should get your skates on."

"Sure." I took the card and headed upstairs.

"And don't forget to comb your hair," my mother called after me. I rolled my eyes.

Yes, my mother was hypercritical, but I was an endless disappointment to her. She had wanted a specific kind of daughter, pretty and petite and soft-spoken, someone to shop with, to show off at Ladies Association meetings. And I had failed her on every front. When I had looked at the girls across the cotillion tables, girls my mother would have chosen over me a thousand times, my heart had ached to be one of them. And, to be completely honest, it still did. If you had told me I had three wishes, I would have spent them all turning into the woman my mother wanted me to be. The woman Phillip had thought he was marrying. Maybe then we would all be happier.

Upstairs, I flipped through everything I had brought, wondering what I had been thinking when I was packing. Finally I settled on a light wool dress in soft rose pink. I had a gray cardigan to cover the cap sleeves, and a pair of pearl earrings, and though the outfit was a little warm for the day, I thought I looked appropriately costumed, as though I might actually belong.

My mother drove us to the genteelly aging hotel where the Ladies Association met, and I chewed another batch of antacids before summoning up the strength to go inside. Despite the stream of women heading into the ballroom, Ashley Hathaway spotted me immediately. "Madeleine," she said in a breathy voice as she approached, as though my presence had literally knocked the wind out of her. "Why, I haven't seen you for ages. Don't you look just the same?"

"You look exactly the same too," I said, unsure whether either of us meant it as a compliment. Ashley was wearing a twinset and little pearl earrings to match her pearly white teeth, and her hair was a perfect pale bob, exactly like my mother's. She leaned forward and slipped her arm around me as she brushed an air kiss toward each of my cheeks. I awkwardly returned the gesture. I wasn't a good hugger. Graduating from college had been a relief for all sorts of reasons, including not having to endure the frequent hugging all my sorority sisters seemed to do on a whim, as though they had magnets implanted in their bellies and couldn't keep away from each other. Those hugs always made me feel uncomfortably large and self-aware, my hand on the back of someone like Ashley, delicate as a bird.

"Where have you been? I don't think I've seen you since your wedding! How's that handsome husband of yours?"

The mention of Phillip made me feel queasy, and I clenched my left hand with its bare fingers, sliding it behind my back. "Oh, you know," I said, which didn't really answer anything. "How are you?"

"Absolutely run off my feet. Grayson and Hunter are in fourth grade, if you can believe that! And Graham's practice is just exploding." She made a face of pretend exhaustion that made me feel exhausted for real.

"That's great!" I said, wondering why I was congratulating her on her schedule.

"So you're in town visiting your mother? Aren't you the sweetest?" I narrowed my eyes at her. What was this? Was this an act? She looked at me with those wide blue eyes, as if her entire happiness hinged on my answer.

"She's getting ready to sell the house. I thought I'd help her get it ready." I had thought no such thing until right that moment, but it made me sound altruistic, and I found I rather liked the idea. It made me feel like I had a purpose other than avoiding my own life.

"She did mention it," Ashley said, putting her hand over her heart as though the news had wounded her. Ashley had known about my mother's selling the house before I did? "Poor Simone, and she's already so busy. Well, bless your heart for coming to help. Come in and say hello! There are so many Country Day girls here!"

Following Ashley into the ballroom, I endured a series of air kisses and half hugs from women I did indeed remember from school. Of course all of them were here. Our mothers had been in the Ladies Association together, and now they were in the Ladies Association together. Their children were going to the schools we had gone to, would take piano from Mrs. Miner and ballet at Miss Patty's Academy of Dance as we had, would learn to waltz at the Magnolia Blossom Cotillion and debut at the country club, and then they would repeat the process with their own children.

Three other former classmates, Emma Fischer, Ellen O'Connor, and Audrey Alexander, followed Ashley like a sorority Secret Service, a bouquet of thirtysomething perfection in matching sweater sets. We had all been friends in school, I was sure of it, but I couldn't remember doing anything with them that felt friendly. I could picture myself at Emma's birthday party and standing behind Audrey during our debutante ball, waiting to be presented, but I couldn't remember any conversations between us, any secrets shared, any real connection. Had I spent my entire life without any real friends?

Before I had gotten married, I had seen these women all the time, been in their weddings, attended their housewarming parties, endured their baby showers. As I sat in the chilly ballroom, looking around me at the women hovering and chatting between the tables, I felt like a visitor from another planet. They had all managed to perfect the look I never could, until they were one undifferentiated mass: untanned white skin, smooth, chin-length hair, sweater sets and slim skirts. We all worked so hard to look exactly like each other, and though no one ever would have spoken the words, it was clear that anyone different—in race, religion, taste, opinion—was Not Allowed.

Being around them, I felt a little shabbier, a little chunkier, a little frizzier. This was the way it had always been with those girls and me—especially Ashley. I couldn't even blame her, or resent her, really—it was nothing she did. It was just that she was a litany of all the things I wasn't—petite and pretty and well put together and efficient and so very normal, and I had always been galumphing and sloppy and uncomfortably different. Maybe if I had gone to public school, or if my mother hadn't been so wedded to the Garden Society and the country club and all the markers of polite society, I could have been different. I could have found a group of friends whose presence didn't make me think less of myself, didn't make me ache to be someone else, coating me with a thin layer of self-loathing that made my skin greasy in the humid summers. It seemed so unfair to have been born into this life and not have been given the tools to mine it properly.

"If I can have your attention." Ashley was standing on the stage, tapping the microphone with one French-manicured finger. A spray of forsythia behind her set off her yellow sweater perfectly. "Attention, ladies. Thank you so much for coming today."

Ashley gave a smoothly polite introduction to the speaker, a local author who took the podium and droned endlessly. There's something about ballrooms that sucks the personality out of everyone at a microphone. As she spoke, the servers darted in silently with our salads, the dressing in tiny silver cups on the side, of course. I picked out the dried cranberries and contemplated flicking them at Ellen O'Connor, who was wearing an angora sweater the exact color of the berries and might not even have noticed their addition.

"Jesus, what a bunch of bullshit," Sharon whispered loudly, walking up from behind us and throwing herself into the empty chair next to mine. She tossed her purse underneath the table, making it shudder. I rescued the coffee cup I had balanced at the edge only to have it spray three tiny, perfect, milky drops across the hemline of my dress. Of course.

"Hi," I whispered back, stilling the table and putting my coffee cup back. Sharon handed me her glass of water and I dabbed some on my skirt. "I didn't know you were in the Ladies Association."

"Occupational hazard. These ladies have houses to buy and sell, and they are rich. What's your excuse? You don't even live here."

"Peer pressure."

"Yeah, well, if I were on vacation I certainly wouldn't be spending my time dealing with these bitches," Sharon said. She turned to the table of our classmates and flashed them a hundred-watt smile, as though she hadn't just called them all bitches, and then folded her arms and turned toward the speaker, slouching in her chair like we were back in geometry class and she was daring the teacher to call on her.

I looked over at the table where the women from Country Day were sitting, at Ashley and Ellen and Emma and Audrey. I'd gone to dances and on school trips with them. We'd worked on school projects together. We'd been in the same sorority in college, and after graduation we'd attended one another's weddings and met up for brunch in groups.

And now, looking at them, I felt—emotionless. I wasn't angry, I held no childhood grudges, I didn't think they were bitches. They were perfectly nice, most of them. Instead, as I watched Ashley and Audrey sip at their unsweetened iced tea and dip just the tips of their forks into the salad dressing before spearing a single, wretched lettuce leaf, I felt an unfamiliar surge of sympathy. I had always been focused on the litany of ways I didn't meet the demands being forced on me. But I had never stopped to consider that every other woman in this room was being asked to fit the same mold, and just because they made it look easy on the outside didn't say anything about how it felt on the inside.

And it broke my heart that we would never be able to talk about it, that none of us would ever be able to break through the rules and traditions and ossification in order to have an honest conversation. The thought gave me a heavy ache in my heart, and I wanted to stand up, to burst through the ballroom doors and run out into the sunlight, break free of every tender silk ribbon holding all of us prisoner to some outdated, uncomfortable set of values I couldn't imagine any of us agreeing to. But I couldn't do that. It wouldn't look right. Turning toward my own plate, I lifted my fork and dipped the tines into the dressing.

six
....

MARGIE
1924

The ship was leaving from New York City, so Margie and her mother and an unwieldy collection of luggage all took a train up and stayed at the Waldorf-Astoria for a few nights while visiting with Evelyn and her family. It had been a whirlwind few weeks, and Margie's mother had been forced to compromise on all sorts of things—the number of new dresses that could be fitted and made, the purchase of a new coat, how many books Margie was allowed to take. But Margie suspected her mother's greatest disappointment was that she hadn't had time to create an entirely different daughter before shipping her off.

Aunt Edith, Evelyn's mother, gave them a lengthy list of sites and museums to visit, though she had never actually been to Europe. Margie thought, looking at her aunt across the dinner table, her gown cut a little too low, her hair bobbed (a woman of her age, if you can imagine!), the lights of the room low to allow the candles to take over, that Aunt Edith's heart was breaking, not over saying goodbye to her daughter, but over not to be going herself, not to be nineteen again with her whole life ahead of her.

Margie, who had spent the afternoon with Evelyn, supposedly shopping for gloves but really sitting and reading in a tearoom while Evelyn smoked and talked to the ten million people who stopped by the table, wanted to tell Evelyn's mother she was welcome to go in her stead. She was feeling particularly mean about Evelyn, who, when they had come back without gloves, had lied and announced that they hadn't been able to find any because Margie's hands were so terribly large. Margie had to fight the urge to use one of her terribly large hands to land a terribly enthusiastic punch on Evelyn's terribly lying face. Perhaps the worst part of it was, Margie realized, as her mother poked her under the table repeatedly while they discussed Evelyn's beaux and plans for the trip and, upon her return, how grand her debut ball would be, that she was being sent on this trip as much to learn from Evelyn as to keep her out of trouble. And Margie wondered, given Evelyn's behavior the moment she was out of sight of any adult, how she was going to do that.

Their mothers installed them in their stateroom, the trunks and baggage having been delivered the day before by porter. Standing on the dock, staring up at the immense ship, my grandmother felt a shiver of anticipation pass through her. She didn't think about the endless, inevitable conflict with Evelyn lying ahead, and she didn't think about Mr. Chapman or the disappointment lying behind her. She was going to Europe. She was going to explore the Tower of London and write a story in a café in Paris and see the ceiling of the Sistine Chapel, and she was going to be someone different, someone adventurous and glamorous. They stood on the deck of the ship underneath a brilliant blue sky, all the promise of summer before them, all the promise of a continent filled with treasures and history and stories to be discovered, all the promise of people who didn't know dull, plain Margie Pearce, and she shivered with delight.

That delight lasted for approximately two hours. Because once they had waved goodbye to their mothers, who stood on the pier as the ship gave a long, mournful wail of its horns and a groan of its steel sidings and pulled away from the dock, two tugboats escorting them out toward the ocean like tiny bridesmaids at a wedding, Evelyn turned to Margie with a hard, mean look in her eye. Around them, most people were drifting away from the railings, some of them heading to the top deck for a better view of their departure, the city spreading out behind them, wider and wider, others heading to their staterooms to settle in, some looking for entertainment. Evelyn dug into her handbag and pulled out a cigarette, lit it, and turned her head slightly to exhale, so the smoke brushed against Margie's cheek as it drifted away. "Here's the situation, Margie. I let you come along because I knew it was the only way Mother would allow me to go to Europe. But I intend to have a truly fabulous time on this trip, and I don't want you ruining it."

Margie hadn't suffered any delusions about what her relationship with Evelyn on this trip might be like. Neither of them were the type to giggle girlishly together through castles and moors, and Margie hadn't pictured them gossiping about dates over *café crème* at Café de la Paix, but she'd thought Evelyn might be willing to compromise. Margie had imagined she'd have to drag Evelyn through the Uffizi Gallery and the Louvre, and wake her after she fell asleep during an opera at La Scala, that Evelyn would smoke and make eyes at the porters and would have to be rescued from a couple of nightclubs before the trip was over. But Margie had never predicted an open rebellion.

"So I'm going to do what I want to do, and you're going to do whatever it is you . . . do," Evelyn said, casting a doubtful glance at Margie's sturdy traveling dress, "and we'll not get in each other's way, all right?"

With that, Evelyn glanced over Margie's shoulder meaningfully, and she turned around to see a group of young people, somewhere between her age and Evelyn's, she guessed. Two women and five men. The women were sipping champagne from glasses, but two of the men had gotten hold of bottles and were drinking straight from them, as though they were common rummies. She'd known alcohol was legal on the ship, but she'd thought there might be a formality, waiting until some invisible border line were crossed. "What will I do?" Margie asked.

"Why don't you read a book or something? Isn't that what girls like you do?" Evelyn asked. She checked her reflection in a newly shined brass finial on the nearest rail, and then, without so much as saying goodbye, she slid past as though Margie were a ghost, all air and no substance, and joined the group, laughing and talking. One of the girls produced another champagne glass, but Evelyn saucily took the bottle and drank straight from it, to their cheers and applause. When had she met them? Maybe they had just known one another on sight, people like Evelyn and those other girls, beautiful and confident, made for this strange new world where women had jobs and wore short skirts to their debuts and smoked openly.

The group drifted away, and Margie stayed, alone on the deck, looking over the railing at the shipyards until they passed beyond the fingers of land that made up New York, and then, after a time, she moved to the back of the ship, looking off to the side where the Statue of Liberty stood, her torch raised high. Margie saluted her, watching the land recede into the distance. As the tugboats split off, making their slow way back to land, Margie faced the empty blue ocean ahead.

So much for glamor and adventure. Turning back, she looked at the blank space behind them that had been the city, the ship now picking up steam at an amazing rate, the smokestacks bellowing black into the air. There was a little twinge of homesickness in her belly, and her throat closed up behind a swell of tears.

"Enough," Margie said aloud. She threw her shoulders back, blinked her eyes rapidly. Homesickness. Of all things. What on earth did she have to be homesick for? Hadn't she spent years wishing for something, anything (other than Mr. Chapman) to take her out of her parents' house, to set her free? Hadn't she read a hundred novels about women having adventures and pictured herself in their stead: traveling through time, falling in love with a seemingly dastardly but actually quite charming pirate, solving thefts of art in Milan, exploring the Nile? And now here she was, with a paid ticket—a whole series of them, actually—to adventure, and she was weeping on the deck and wishing she could go back to the mother she'd been wishing to get away from. "Be a heroine, Margie," she said aloud, and strode off down the deck to explore the ship.

Somehow, the hours passed and the week went by. Margie walked on the wind-whipped open decks, and she read in a window seat in the ship's library overlooking the bow of the ship, cutting through the endless sea. At night she dressed for dinner and ate next to Evelyn's empty chair, and she made polite conversation with the older couples at the table, all of whom seemed to wonder what she was doing there but none of whom were impolite enough to ask. She went to lectures and one night walked out with the astronomy club, looking at the spray of stars across the sky, shining through the night like a lost message from centuries ago. She found an alcove in a little-used lounge where she could write undisturbed, and she took her notebooks there and filled page after page, settling into the flow of the words, never having to keep an ear cocked for the tread of her mother's feet on the stairs, prepared to jump up and shove her notebook into a drawer, to hide her ink-stained hands guiltily.

Here and there she saw Evelyn and her group. The ship, which had seemed immense the first day when she had walked it from stem to stern, going into every room and club and restaurant, admiring the gleam of the wood and the shine of the windows, now felt small and well trod. The night she had gone out with the astronomers, she had come back, her eyes sparkling with the refracted light of a thousand stars, her mind full of stories and wishes and daydreams and myths, and had passed Evelyn and the crowd of them, drunk and laughing down the hallway, here and there colliding with one of the stateroom doors, careless of the people sleeping inside.

Each night, a small ensemble played in the conservatory, and the ship's staff set up a tiny dance floor over the carpet, where the bridge tables stood during the day. One night as Margie passed through on her way to her stateroom, she saw Evelyn and one of the men in the center of the floor, dancing close and slow in the dim light. Evelyn's hands were draped casually over the man's shoulders, and she held a champagne glass loosely between her fingers, as though she had only interrupted her drink for a moment. Their friends were gathered on a cluster of chairs in the corner, leaning together like the stones of an elegant ruin, exploding occasionally with laughter. The next morning, Margie had sat there with her tea in the same chairs and tried to capture the feel of them, had leaned close to the cushions to catch the scent of the girls' perfume, but all she could smell was stale smoke and the pale memory of magic. It wasn't the room; it was the people in it. And Margie feared she held no magic in her at all.

As the ship came closer and closer to Cherbourg, Margie began to grow nervous. It was fine to let Evelyn roam around the ship with that crowd. It was a contained space, and short of falling overboard, what could happen to her? But in Europe, she would be Margie's responsibility again.

Still, when the ship docked, surely the young men and women with whom Evelyn had allied herself would take off to wherever they were bound, and she and Evelyn would be alone. And they had an itinerary. They had tickets, and their mothers had written and wired ahead for hotel reservations. It would all be fine, she told herself, quelling the nervousness in her belly.

On the morning of their arrival, Margie got up early to see the ship's docking, the comforting sight of land instead of the endless flow of ocean, the scurry of activity on the dock below, the huge ship pulling alongside the pier and the ramps being set up. Breakfast was served early, and she ate in silence with the other sleepy-eyed passengers, caught between exhaustion and excitement. She paused on the deck on the way back to the room, watching the people disembarking below, lifting their heads to smell the air, to look at the sun, the porters scurrying about, loading luggage onto trolleys to take to the train station.

Evelyn, of course, hadn't been back to the room the night before, and

Margie was feeling more and more anxious. But when she returned to the stateroom after breakfast, there was Evelyn, packing her trunk. Or, more precisely, there was Evelyn, sitting among the wreckage of her belongings, the trunk taking up nearly all the empty space on the stateroom floor, while Evelyn herself lounged on her bed in her dressing gown, flipping through a magazine. "Oh, hello." She seemed entirely unsurprised to see Margie, as though she hadn't been purposely avoiding her all week long. "Isn't packing dreadful?"

"I suppose it is, yes," Margie said tentatively, quashing her irritation, wondering if this casual conversation indicated some thaw in Evelyn's demeanor. She hoped when they got off the ship, when it was just the two of them again, Evelyn would calm down, express an interest in helping to choose the museums and monuments they were to visit. After all, how could she not be excited at what lay ahead of them? They were to spend the next two weeks in Paris, and Margie wondered how they were possibly to see it all: the museums and the boulevards, the shops and the cafés. All week long, Margie had been dreaming of the adventures they might have. And the management of the trip had been given to her— their money, their passports, their hotel reservations, and the list of educational things they were to do, not that Margie felt entirely bound to those plans. Why, if Evelyn wanted to spend an afternoon shopping, or if they decided to take a day trip to Versailles, there was no harm in it. Freedom, glorious, delicious freedom, stretched out in front of her like a promise. And even though Evelyn had expressed no interest in Paris, other than to ask in which hotel they were staying, Margie was certain she would come around once she saw it.

"It will be nice to be off the ship, won't it? It's feeling a bit claustrophobic."

"Definitely," Evelyn said. The thought seemed to cheer her, and she hopped out of bed and began to fold some dresses carelessly and put them in the trunk. "I can't wait to see Paris."

"Me too!" Margie didn't even bother to hide her glee. She was a hopeless sap, and she knew it, but how could she be expected to hold back her anticipation? She was going to Europe. She was following in the footsteps of Edith Hull and May Sinclair, Gertrude Atherton and Edith Wharton, of all the writers she had loved and admired for so long.

Evelyn lifted a dress, shook it out, and dropped it in the trunk. "I had the loveliest night last night. We went to the Captain's Ball—did you go?"

Margie shot her a look, wondering if Evelyn were being purposefully mean, knowing Margie wouldn't have had anyone to go to the ball with, but Evelyn looked wide-eyed and open. "I only stopped by," Margie said. She had walked by the ballroom after dinner and peered inside, where the evening was warming up, women luminous in their finest dresses, saved for the occasion, the orchestra playing softly, a few couples testing the dance floor. She had indeed longed to go in, to join the glittering party, to sit down at a table of those gay people and drink champagne, to take a dance with a man in a tuxedo. She had danced so much the year of her debut, and now she hardly danced at all. When she went to balls at home, she was often trapped at a table full of women older and sadder than her—true spinsters, or widows—and Margie had started taking a book and sneaking off in order to avoid that fate. But here, she didn't know anyone, and when she looked down at her dress, a beaded thing of eggplant and black crêpe georgette, it looked dull and drab and unworthy. If she went in, she would only stand by the wall and watch everyone else's good time. Instead, she had taken her notebook and gone to the conservatory, where a pianist played softly to the empty room, and she wrote a story about a girl on a ship who goes to a ball and meets a handsome man who dances with her all night, and when it was finished, she cried a few tears of resentful happiness and went to bed.

"Well, it was absolutely berries. Truly, Margie, you ought to have come. Now let's get off this ship and go to Paris. I'm dying to buy a new dress—I haven't had a thing to wear all week."

By the time Evelyn finished her haphazard packing job and dressed, there was still a stream of people flooding from the ship. A porter hurried ahead with their luggage. At the post box, Margie dropped a letter to her mother, full of pleasant lies, to go on the ship's return journey. She had invented charming dinner conversations they hadn't had, described dances she hadn't attended, and people she hadn't met. And her mother said all her dreaming would never come in handy.

On the train, Evelyn chattered inanely and endlessly until Margie had to excuse herself to go to the dining car simply to get a break. She didn't know which was worse—worrying about the trouble Evelyn was sure to land herself in if Margie left her to her own devices in a strange city, or having to stay with her. A taxicab, directed by Margie's clumsy, thick-tongued French, took them to their hotel, Margie and Evelyn pressing their noses against the windows. "Look!" Margie said as they passed, "Notre-Dame! The Place de la Concorde! The Champs-Élysées!" She laid her hand flat against the window as though she could run her fingers over every inch of Paris, touch it the way Robert Walsh had touched her that night all those years ago.

At the thought, Margie pulled back as though she had been shocked. Evelyn's face was still pressed to the window, but Margie could see the younger girl's eyes were closed. She had fallen asleep there, leaning against the cool glass.

What had made her think of Robert, after all this time? She didn't want to think of him, not here, not now. She'd had that one night, one perfect night, and there was no point in spoiling it with reality. She wanted Europe to be about romance and joy, about newness and adventure. She wanted it to be different. She didn't want her happiness spoiled by being reminded of who she had been in America.

When they had settled in their room, the porter having carried their luggage upstairs with no small amount of grumbling and ill will, at the end Margie guiltily pressing into his hand what she would realize later was an outrageously large tip (the money was so confusing), Evelyn began to go through her trunk, tossing things about until the room looked exactly as their stateroom had. She slipped out the door into the bathroom and emerged, somehow, despite the fact that the entirety of her sleep in the past twenty-four hours had been in the taxi on the way here, looking refreshed and lovely. Margie had changed her shoes and was consulting her Baedeker's *Paris and Its Environs*. It was already late afternoon, but certainly they could fit in a stroll through the Luxembourg Gardens or down to the Seine.

Evelyn picked up her bag and her wrap. "I'm going downstairs to cable Mama that we've arrived," she said. Margie sat in the room for a moment and then decided to follow her. She'd wait in the lobby while Evelyn sent her telegram, and then they could go out exploring. Her heart beat a little faster at the idea. She was eager to go, to step onto the streets where the heroes of the French Revolution had walked, to pass the cafés where the artists of Paris gathered, to squeeze every drop of joy out of this trip so when she was home again with her mother, sticking her needle into the tiny circumscribed round of an embroidery hoop and listening to the endless ticking of the clock counting off the stultifying hours, she would have an infinity of things to remember, to dream about, to write about.

But when she got down to the lobby, of course Evelyn wasn't sending a telegram. She was standing with the group from the ship, who had thrown themselves on a few of the sofas in the lobby's sitting area as though it were their own living room.

"Evelyn?" Margie asked, coming up behind her.

Evelyn whirled around, wide-eyed. The others in the group looked at Margie lazily, one of the girls pausing to whisper behind her hand to another, who giggled. Margie flushed, red and hot and pathetic, a low, sinking feeling in her chest.

"What are you doing?"

"We're going out," Evelyn said, as though this had all been arranged, as though she and Margie had spoken about it only a few moments ago.

"But . . ." Margie began, and then realized she didn't know what to say. *But what, Margie? But you had some grand vision of how Evelyn was going to become a different person between the ship and here? You had imagined yourself to be a different person now that you were in Europe, someone Evelyn wouldn't insist on leaving behind at every possibility?* And then there was a sickening sadness as she realized it had been the plan all along. That was why Evelyn had asked the name of their hotel; not because she was in any way interested in the trip, but because she was telling her friends where to come get her.

"Really, Margie. You're absolutely hopeless," Evelyn said. She turned back to her friends. "Let's go," she said, and they rose sleepily, as though she had awoken them, and the men ambled and the girls glided toward the door, leaving Margie standing there alone in the lobby, her guide book in one hand and her bag in the other, with no plan and no idea what to do.

Outside, all of Paris waited for her, but Margie felt deflated and overwhelmed. She had failed, she had been rejected, and she had no idea what she was going to tell her mother. Finally, when one of the disagreeable porters cleared his throat at her until she moved out of the center of the lobby, she headed over to the front desk to send a telegram. Her pen hovered over the paper for a long, long time until she settled on something appropriately terse: *Arrived safely. M & E.*

seven

MADELEINE
1999

My mother invited me to another luncheon the next day, but I refused to go. I couldn't sit through another afternoon of pretending and watching everyone else pretend. I was still heartsick thinking about all of us in that room together, playing our parts, and I couldn't bear to do it again.

After she left, I went down to The Row to find something to eat. At the end of my parents' street, blocks of stores and restaurants housed in low, unassuming brick buildings extended in either direction. It was an older part of the city, and when I was younger, it danced on the knife edge of respectability: boutiques where my mother bought scarves alongside a head shop and the falafel restaurant where the college students hung out. In high school, I'd gone there all the time—to pretend to be tortured and drink coffee at the coffee shop, to look at the art books at the bookstore or hang around the poetry section, hoping to meet a teenage boy with a poetic soul (FYI, based on my extensive adolescent research, I'm pretty sure they don't exist), to buy a cookie the size of my head and window shop my way along the street.

But I noticed, as I strolled down the sidewalk in search of food, that things had settled decisively in favor of upscale cool. The head shop had been replaced by a store selling locally made jewelry and art, and a microbrewery had pushed out the falafel (probably a fair exchange in the eyes of the college students). I found a new restaurant with a tiny patio surrounded by a wrought-iron fence, where I ordered eggs Benedict and coffee, and while I waited for it to come, I leaned back and closed my eyes and let the sun lie against my skin like a warm promise.

The day stretched out ahead of me, empty and open and free, and for once that space felt luxurious, instead of like time that needed to be filled.

What did I used to do, when I was single and lived on my own? It seemed like I was trying to remember a story I had once heard and barely recalled, the edges soft, the details inconsistent. Afternoons spent painting until the light faded and my eyes and fingers ached, evenings in the empty second-run cinema, my hands sticky with butter and salt from the popcorn. More than how I had spent each hour, I remembered the feeling—a giddy freedom, as though I were on an eternal summer vacation. I would look at the people around me and feel as though I were getting away with something, doing something wrong. Now I wondered why I had ever felt that way—it had been my life to do with what I wanted, after all.

"Well, well, slacking on the job, are we?" I started, my eyes flicking open. My face was growing hot from the sunlight, and there were spots in my vision where it had burned into my eyes. Blinking them away, I squinted until Sharon came into focus.

"Hi. I was just—my mother doesn't keep any food in the house . . ." I was fairly sure she was joking, but I felt ashamed at having been caught here, like a cat in a sunbeam, when I should have been doing something responsible.

"Relax, relax. I'm kidding. Can I join you?" She was wearing a dress and a blazer, but before I could say anything, she eyed the black railing surrounding the restaurant's patio, hopped up on it, and swung her legs over. A moment later she was settling herself into the empty chair across from mine, hanging her purse and jacket over the back, and looking around for the server.

I sat up from my lazily slumping position and rummaged around in my handbag until I found a pair of sunglasses that had probably been in there since the previous summer, judging by the level of smudging and scratching. My fingers brushed against my mobile phone, which was stubbornly silent. Phillip hadn't forgiven me yet, I guessed. Or maybe he was just busy in New York. He was the one who had insisted we have cellular phones long before they became popular, and that we get the newest devices the moment they were released. Phillip always had to have the best of everything.

"What are you doing here? Do you live nearby?" I asked, a little too loudly, trying to force the thought of Phillip from my head.

"Me?" Sharon barked out a little laugh. She had the same voice she'd had in high school, rough and whiskey-edged. You could hear her laugh all the way across campus. "No, I couldn't afford to live here unless I was stripping on the side. And that's not likely to happen," she said, gesturing at her body, which was short and comfortably solid. "I was actually just dropping off some fliers for another client. Betsy Lynn Chivers—do you know her? She and your mother are friends."

I shuddered at the mention of Betsy Lynn Chivers, who dressed her dogs in outfits and carried them everywhere with her, but had shouted at me repeatedly when I was little for tracking dirt onto her carpet. "Unfortunately, I do know her. She gave me nightmares when I was a kid."

"She gives me nightmares now," Sharon said, and then interrupted herself to ask for coffee and an order of pancakes when the server came by. "But she's rich and she wants me to sell her house, so, cheers!" She lifted her water glass to me in a toast and then drank.

"May it sell quickly and easily, then," I said.

"No kidding. So what are you up to? Sorry for scaring the pants off you at the house the other day. I assumed your mother would have told you."

"Yeah, well. My mother and I aren't always the best communicators. Frankly, I don't think she thought I'd care."

"And do you care?"

"Weirdly, I do. Stupid, right? I haven't lived in that house basically since I left for college."

"Eh, people get weird about real estate. Don't take it personally, though. Your mom just wants to get out of there. It's a lot of house for her to manage."

"And she's moving into an apartment building? I can't imagine it."

"It's condos. And all the Garden Society dowagers move there." Sharon's coffee arrived, and she took a stack of packets, shook them, and poured the entire pile into her coffee, rendering it ninety percent sweetener and ten percent liquid. "Betsy Lynn is moving there, too, and I am sure her neighbors are thrilled, because those dogs she has yap all the livelong day. Anyway, enough about her and her problems. I'm so glad you're in town."

"Me too," I said, surprised to find I actually meant it. My visits to my mother had always been plagued by her criticism and my desperate efforts to please her, but this time felt different. I felt like I had nothing to lose, like it was easier to shake off her complaints about my clothes, my hair, my weight, like it wasn't my problem. "What about you? Have you been here since high school?"

"Nah, I did a little bit of wandering. Followed Phish around for a couple of years, lived in San Francisco and made a lot of merry. Then I met my boyfriend when I was visiting back here and I decided to stay."

Our food arrived and we settled ourselves under our napkins, shifted our plates around, made space for the accoutrements of breakfast while I pictured Sharon dancing in muddy fields, or walking along the streets of San Francisco, a little loose and free, like a flower child twenty years too late. "I have to say, I can picture you much more easily doing those things than I can seeing you living here. This place is so . . ." I struggled for a word to describe how I had felt at the luncheon the day before, the strange combination of shame for myself and mourning for all of us, and failed.

But Sharon knew what I meant, or seemed to. "Parts of it, sure. The parts you and I grew up in. But it's not all like that. There are a million great shops and restaurants and amazing live music—my boyfriend's a musician, which is basically why I became a real estate agent. Someone's got to pay the bills, you know? He stays home with the kids."

I nearly choked on my eggs. "You have kids?" I asked, wheezing as politely as I could as I took a sip of water to recover. On our senior retreat, I'd watched Sharon carve a bong out of an apple from the dining hall and then lead a group of girls straight past the chaperones' rooms to get high in the woods. And now that girl changed diapers and rocked babies to sleep.

"Sure. Twin boys. They're almost two. Kevin is home with them during the day while I'm working." She paused between bites and shot me a wicked grin. "You're surprised? I don't strike you as the maternal type?"

"Well . . . not really. I mean, I didn't really know you well in high school, but . . ."

"Ah, don't worry about it. Most of the rumors weren't true, but the sentiment behind them was. Honestly, I was glad to have the reputation I did. Kept me an arm's distance from being caught up in the perfect circle. I don't know how you survived it."

"The perfect circle? What do you mean?"

"You know. Ashley, Ellen, Audrey, Emma, you. All those bitches with their perfect hair and their Add-A-Pearl necklaces. Not that you're a bitch. I never understood what you were doing with them anyway."

"No idea. I have never had perfect hair, and I was always losing my Add-A-Pearl necklace. I don't know why they let me hang around with them. Probably I just made them feel better about themselves." I felt a little shudder of shame saying it, as though I had been hiding the truth from myself for years. Apparently, my life's purpose was to cling desperately to people who thought they were too good for me, because I believed it too.

Sharon snorted. "It should have been the other way around. I remember your paintings from the Senior Art Show—they were amazing. Are you still an artist?"

"Not really," I said. "No. I mean, I wasn't ever an artist. I was just playing around." I had told Miss Pine the same thing, but it sounded different this time. Those were my parents' words, not mine. I hadn't been playing around. My creativity had mattered to me.

"That's too bad. You were good," she said. "Anyway, I always suspected you were cool, despite the necklace and the company you kept. Glad to know I wasn't wrong."

Pulled out of my art-soaked memories, I blinked slowly at Sharon. She had thought I was cool? She, who wore a leather jacket and Doc Martens with her uniform, who had driven her date to prom on a motorcycle, who left campus during lunch (very much against the rules) to smoke (very very much against the rules) and eat pizza with the public school boys (very very very much against the rules)—she thought I was cool? Had she really been so wrong about me? Or had I been wrong about myself?

"So," I asked, clearing my throat and changing the subject before the silence became awkwardly long, "what's it like working with my mother?"

Sharon carefully cut her pancakes, obviously considering how to respond. "Your mother is . . . intense."

"If by intense you mean overly critical and negative, then yes. She is."

"That must have been fun to grow up with."

I gave a little half smile, but I couldn't summon a laugh. It had been hard to grow up with. It was hard to live with now. My mother had always been hard on me, especially about my art and my appearance. When she thought I was spending too much time in the art studio at school, she'd signed me up for Junior Ladies Association. My last year at Country Day, the Senior Art Show had been on display for three weeks, and she'd never managed to make it in, and when I'd asked, she'd said, in a tone that had made me want to weep, "Really, Madeleine, is it so important? They're just paintings." She had monitored what I ate from the time I was six until I left for college, and had regularly informed me that I would never find someone who would marry me if I didn't take better care of my hair/stop laughing so loudly/lose some weight.

But I couldn't stop trying to please her. It was unreasonable, I knew. I'd never be able to make her happy, I knew. But she was my *mother*. What else was I supposed to do? I kept hoping that one day we could have a conversation about something that mattered without her criticizing me, I kept hoping that one day she would give me a hug without silently judging how much weight I had gained or lost, I kept hoping that one day she would say, "I love you even though you are nothing like me." Fool me a hundred times, shame on me, but she was my mother, and I knew I would keep hoping for a miracle between us until the day I died.

I couldn't explain all that to Sharon, though, so I just said, "It's complicated."

"Heeeey, Sharon!" A woman stopped on the other side of the railing. She was walking an elderly dog who sniffed at my legs eagerly. I reached through the bars to pet it and it snuffled enthusiastically at my hand. I had always wanted a dog, or at least a cat, but Phillip hated shedding and I refused to get one of those creepy hairless breeds.

"Hey, what's up?" Sharon stood up and hugged the woman over the railing. They chatted as I petted the dog with one hand and ate with the other. "Madeleine, this is Cassandra. She owns the knitting store down the street. Have you seen it? It's new since you left."

I gulped down a bite and patted my lips with my napkin in one hand as I reached out for Cassandra's hand with the other. She was tall, with long, brown braids streaked with bright purple, and a nose ring, lending her a glamor I far preferred to the stuffy elegance of the women at the Ladies Association.

"Nice to meet you."

"Hey, do you want some breakfast?" Sharon asked.

"Nah, I already ate. But I'll have some coffee." And with that, Cassandra tied her dog to the railing and hopped over like Sharon had. After pulling another table toward ours, Cassandra settled in, ordering a coffee from the waitress.

"So you own a knitting store?" I asked, trying to keep the doubt from my voice.

"Yeah. We opened last year down the street, by Java Good Day."

"They're where the fancy dog store used to be. The one that sold, like, tutus and socks for dogs. Remember?" Sharon interjected.

"Right. Thank God that place is gone. It used to creep me out."

"I know. I actually called in a woman to do a spiritual cleansing when we moved in to chase away the ghosts of all those poor dogs forced to wear doggie nail polish and bows in their fur. Totally legitimate business expense," Cassandra said. She picked up a grape from Sharon's fruit bowl and popped it in her mouth. "So how do you guys know each other?"

"We went to high school together. And now I'm selling her mom's house," Sharon explained. "She's in town to help out."

I liked that she gave me an alibi, but of course Cassandra didn't know me, couldn't have cared less why I was there, or who my mother or my husband were, or why I wasn't wearing my wedding ring. No one cared. No one cared about my clothes or what I was supposed to be doing. It was as liberating as a sprinkler in summertime, and I wanted to throw my arms back and let it wash over me.

"Cool," Cassandra said, and helped herself to another grape.

"Sharon Baker." I recognized Henry's voice and looked up. "And you said you'd never eat at another restaurant." Clearly excited to see him, Sharon jumped up from her chair and gave him a hug over the railing.

"To be fair, you don't serve breakfast," she said, releasing him and sitting back down.

Henry was wearing sunglasses, and he had a newspaper folded under one arm and a paper cup of coffee in his hand. Cassandra gave him a hug, too, and then he spotted me. "The Lady Bowers," he said, dropping me a mock courtly bow.

"Sir Gastropub," I returned.

"Nice to see you again. I didn't know you all knew each other."

"Sharon and I went to school together. Cassandra and I just met. You, on the other hand, are apparently Magnolia's best-kept social secret."

He pushed his sunglasses up into his hair, which was as messy as it had been when I'd seen him the last time, though he was less covered in dirt. His pants were baggy and worn at the knees, and his T-shirt was loose over his broad body, but to my surprise I felt a little shimmer inside when I saw him. Which was stupid, of course. I was married, and Phillip was far better-looking than Henry. I blushed anyway when I looked at his scruffy beard, thinking of how it might brush against my skin, and then stopped myself from wondering anything else at all.

"I'm pretty much the sun around which the Magnolia social scene orbits," Henry said, as if he were admitting a great burden. I snorted into my water, imagining him at the country club with Betsy Lynn Chivers and my mother and Lydia Endicott, who always looked as though she had been soaked in lemon juice.

"Henry used to be in a band with my boyfriend." Sharon gestured at Henry with her knife as she went back to her pancakes.

"A band? Well, aren't you full of hidden secrets," I said.

"It was a long time ago. And we were really atrocious."

"So why'd you quit? Atrocious sells these days, or haven't you heard?"

"I got too old for that crap. Staying out all night at clubs with kids ten years younger than me? Not my idea of a good time. Also, I found it was much more rewarding to do things I didn't suck at."

"Hey, are you doing anything for First Friday this weekend?" Cassandra looked up from her assault on Sharon's breakfast and squinted up at Henry.

"Oh, you know. The usual. Feeding hungry people. What about you?"

"There's a knitting group meeting in the store and I've got a fiber artist who's displaying some of her stuff. It's amazing—you should come check it out if you can get away."

"I should be able to," Henry said.

"What's First Friday?" I asked.

"First Friday of every month they close off the street and make it like a block party. All the stores and restaurants do something special, there's live music. You should come! It's a good time."

"They block off the whole street? My mother must hate it."

"So you'll come, then," Henry said.

"Wouldn't miss it for the world."

"And don't forget, you're invited for dinner at the restaurant. Anytime you like." He pointed his newspaper at me and I nodded obediently. "Speaking of which, I've got to bail. Nice to see you all. Cassandra, let me know if you all want refreshments for Friday. We'll work something out."

"Awesome," she said, and he waved as he turned and headed back up the hill toward my mother's house and his restaurant.

"How do you know Henry?" Sharon asked.

"We just met in the yard the other day," I said, omitting the parts about my pajamas and my strawberry feeding frenzy.

"He's a nice guy."

"My mother can't stand him."

"Well, you can't ask for better proof than that," she said, flashing me a wicked grin.

The three of us sat in the sunshine, lingering over coffee long after the waitress had cleared our dishes. I lived so much of my life in taxicabs, in climate-controlled rooms, that I had forgotten what a real neighborhood felt like, one where people lived and worked and ran into each other by coincidence instead of by engraved invitation. As we sat, people came by—people Sharon knew, people Cassandra knew, artists and musicians and store owners. Wanee, who owned the Thai restaurant down the street, stopped by long enough to say hello and invite me to lunch there. Cassandra introduced me to Kira, a sculptor who owned an art-supply store a few blocks away, and Pete, who had bought the coffee shop with his partner, and Sharon's boyfriend, Kevin, arrived with the twins in tow and dark circles under his eyes and we talked and laughed and watched the kids running around the now empty tables. I automatically reached into my purse for my antacids, and realized, with a little jolt of surprise, that my stomach didn't hurt.

Walking home, the noise of The Row fading behind me, absorbed by the trees shading the sidewalk and whispering soft blessings above my head, I couldn't stop smiling. How funny, how sad, to realize at this late date that Magnolia wasn't only the country club and Ashley Hathaway and Ladies Association literacy fundraisers. It was Cassandra and knitting groups and Kevin's band and restaurateurs and people who opened Wiccan shops on The Row and sold crystals and sage and led past-life-regression workshops.

It made me love Magnolia in a way I never had. How many First Fridays had I missed? How many meals with people whose stories could make me laugh and who made me want to sit them down and say, "Now, tell me everything about this thing you love"? How much had I missed out on because I had never thought to push the boundaries of what I knew? And who was I doing this for? The hair, the clothes, the right committees, the perfect husband who wasn't the perfect husband for me—I certainly didn't care about any of those things, and I didn't like most of the people who did. So why did it matter to me?

My mother's house, which had always seemed so big, seemed so small as I turned up the walk toward the front door. Looking to the side, I saw the restaurant's parking lot was empty, but I could still hear sounds from inside, faint music and a clatter of pans and an occasional shouted demand. I longed to be there. I longed to be back at the table at the café down the street, greeting everyone who came by, getting to know them and this new way of seeing my hometown.

eight

MARGIE
1924

Margie sat alone at breakfast in the hotel, fuming. Evelyn hadn't come back the night before; her bed lay as still and untouched as when she had left. Margie had tried to read a novel, had tried to write, first a story and then a letter to her mother. But how could she explain the truth now, when the last letter she had sent had been lies?

She had written those things with the expectation that her relationship with Evelyn would get better—that Evelyn would *behave* better—when they were on land. But of course nothing had improved, and Margie was left with an overwhelming fear that this adventure might be over before it had truly begun, that Evelyn's behavior would mark Margie as an unsuitable chaperone, that her parents would demand she return and everything would go back to the way it was before, the musty parlor, the clock on the mantel chewing away the hours, the awkward dinners with desperate bachelors or widowers, and the endless growing sadness inside her as she realized there was no escape.

Well. Enough of this. She had been looking over her Baedeker, and she had decided she would go out on her own, Evelyn be damned. As long as she returned before dinner, she would be sure to catch Evelyn preparing for her night out, and the two of them would have a conversation. Margie would allow her this time in Paris, but when it was time to leave, it really would be just the two of them, as planned. When she pictured it in her mind, she was firm and strong, and Evelyn recognized the wisdom of it and nodded agreeably.

Outside, her confidence faded. In the hotel, most everyone had spoken at least some English. But here, on the street, she heard nothing but French. Margie panicked slightly at the sound—she had studied French in high school and college, but hadn't spoken it since, and she longed for the artificial environment of the classroom, of the single, American-accented dialect, of the slow, steady speech of her teachers and professors. She had never imagined the different accents she would need to contend with, the people who mumbled or spoke quickly, or that when she descended into the Métro station and asked a question about which platform the train might be on, she might be answered with anything other than the orderly dialogue laid out in her textbooks: *Où est le train? Le train est là.* Instead, the man at the ticket window released a torrent of rapid French, of which Margie caught only the words for "right" and "left," and, unable to remember which was which, she retreated, burying herself in a crowd of people and praying they were going where she wanted to go.

But she did find her way, unfolding the maps from her guide book and, when she got close enough, following other people who seemed to be slightly less lost than she. In the Louvre, she found herself tagging along after groups of Americans as though she belonged, attaching herself at the end, listening to the comforting width of American vowels, the drawls and sprawls of Southerners and Bostonians alike. The museum's floors creaked and groaned pleasantly beneath their feet as they moved through, and Margie found her mind wandering away from the art to the palace itself. She could picture the courtiers, the kings and queens, moving along the same floors, and she closed her eyes and tried to feel their steps beneath hers. In the larger halls, she imagined people arriving for balls in the grandest, most extreme costumes, saw herself stepping out of a carriage in a high, powdered wig, her face stylishly made up, her ball gown shimmering, and there would be a handsome man to greet her—a prince!—and he would . . .

"Pardon, mademoiselle."

Margie opened her eyes to find herself standing in a doorway while a couple, attempting to pass by, stared at her curiously. She shook her head, breaking free of her daydream's spiderweb strands, and stepped aside, offering a sheepish smile. Still, she kept looking for her prince as she moved through the rooms, her eyes dropping on one young man or another, picturing her hand in his as they strolled together, on his in a courtly dance, or resting on his face during a caress. She was awful, she knew; she should have been paying attention to the art, should have been improving herself, but her imagination always seemed to carry her away.

She walked home through the Tuileries, moving as though she were drifting, the afternoon sun falling across picnickers, strollers, young children carrying ice creams. Maybe this was why they called Paris the City of Love—its languid beauty gave her the feeling of endless summer, an eternal freedom, making love impossible to suppress. She smiled her way through the gardens, emerging to the rude insult of the traffic around the Place de la Concorde, buses and motorcars and horses and wagons all in chaos, and drifted her way dreamily back to the hotel.

It was late afternoon, and the light was strange and golden, a hint of violet in the sky and a stronger yellow where it fell across the endless rows of Haussmann buildings, their black balconies and windowsills spilling over with flowers, red and purple and blue and white. The people moved more slowly than in Washington or New York, strolling along the streets instead of hurrying, and everywhere were cafés and restaurants, people sitting at tables on the sidewalks, eating, or drinking coffee and smoking and talking. As she walked, she watched the crowds, the faces passing by, the people in the restaurants or at their own windows. The smell of food was overwhelming—mussels in butter and garlic sauce, their shells gaping open at the sky, warm bread, yeasty and steaming, the sharp snap of fresh green beans.

She felt, wandering through the city, as though she were a part of it already, as though it belonged to her now that she had seen it. When she didn't actually have to speak to anyone, she rather liked the French wafting through the air around her, the snatches of conversation she heard as she passed by a café, the occasional sharp shout like an arrow—a mother calling out the window to a child, or a workman barking a warning. And being alone felt strange and new. Had she ever been alone this much before? Even when she locked herself away in her room, feeling very much like Emily Dickinson as she scribbled out her stories, she was not alone. She could hear her mother and the maid moving around the house, the clatter of dinner being prepared in the kitchen below, or, while she read at night, the murmur of her parents' voices in the parlor. Here, too, she was surrounded by people, yet separate from them. She felt pleasantly anonymous, isolated by language and culture but mostly by choice, and she moved through the city streets as though she were held in a globe of glass. She ate an early dinner in a café, she drank a rich, red wine, she finished with crème brûlée, heedless of her waistline, and walked home to the hotel in a pleasant sugar haze.

Margie had lingered over dinner, and when she returned to the hotel, she could see Evelyn had come and gone already; the mess was slightly disturbed, and the air smelled of Evelyn's perfumes and lotions, of lemon and rose and lavender. She might have gone to look for Evelyn, but where would she begin? The city was wide and busy, opening itself to the night, and her cousin could be anywhere. As the evening fell, the cafés came alive, the streets, which had gone quiet for a time, filled again. In the other buildings windows glittered in the fading light, blank faces hiding their secrets, and Evelyn could have been behind any one.

Across the street, music drifted up from a basement, and Margie saw people descending the stairs to enter. A nightclub, then, though the people going inside looked utterly normal, far unlike the degenerates she had always been warned about. She could go, couldn't she? No one was stopping her. But the stories she had been told froze her there, the pleasure of independence she had felt a few hours ago swallowed by the habit of fear. What if she went out and were mugged? Or mistaken for a lady of the evening? What if, once they were inside, those utterly normal people turned into angry, violent drunkards? But oh, that music. She'd heard so little jazz—her parents certainly didn't listen to it at home, nor was it played at any of the parties she went to. But didn't it make you want to dance? Margie leaned against the window, looking down, her feet moving sadly on their own, wishing she had the courage to go out and be part of things.

That was how it went. Evelyn came and went when Margie wasn't there, and Margie began to suspect more and more that Evelyn was avoiding their inevitable confrontation. Margie woke early, walking through the streets when they were still quiet, the trash men and the bakers about their business, the rest of the city stirring sleepily. She went to the places she had read about, had dreamed about—she walked through the Luxembourg Gardens, envious of the lovers who lingered there between the statues, who kissed underneath the shade of the trees, making her blush and look away as she hurried past. She climbed the endless stairs to Sacre-Coeur and sat on the steps with a hundred other people, watching the sunset, all of Paris spread out below her like an offering. She walked across the Pont Saint-Michel, waving to the boatmen who passed below, and lingered in the tiny shops on the Île de la Cité and then disappeared into its crooked, ancient streets, so quiet it was as though the entire town had paused around her and was holding its breath. She fell a little bit in love with every young man she saw, and she sat on the steps of the Panthéon, its columns soaring majestically behind her, and wrote imaginary love letters and lines of poetry to try to capture the ache of emotion in her heart. She never wanted to leave.

In this way, a week went by, and then one night when she went back to the hotel, scurrying home as the city turned into the night version of itself, the darker side that still made her so afraid, she found Evelyn waiting for her in their room. To her surprise, Evelyn was packed, though they weren't due to leave Paris for another week.

"Hello," Margie said tentatively. Closing the door behind her, she let her hand linger on the knob, as though she might need to make a quick escape.

Evelyn was dressed to go out, and Margie, who had been, as usual, floating along in her own daydream in which she was as beautiful and stylish as any of the women she passed on the street, felt suddenly sad and dowdy. Evelyn was wearing white, sheer and gauzy, like a fairy's dress, covered with beads of starlight. Her white wrap was trimmed with ermine, and though Margie's mother would have raised an eyebrow at wearing fur so close to summer, Margie thought it added to her glamor. Evelyn looked like one of the lost Russian princesses, like a creature formed of snow, all magic and sparkle and the promise of dreams to come.

"Hello," Evelyn replied. Her eyes flicked impatiently up and down, evaluating Margie and, clearly, finding her lacking. Margie hunched her shoulders, wishing she hadn't worn this dress, these shoes, wondering if her stockings were bagging around her ankles, her face red, her hair messy.

"Have you been having a nice time in Paris?" Margie asked politely, and immediately hated herself for the question. There was so much she ought to have said, and yet she couldn't seem to summon the nerve to say it.

"Look, Margie," Evelyn said, her mouth set tight, "I'm leaving. I just came by to pick up my things and get my spending money."

"Leaving?" Margie asked weakly. The cheese she had eaten for lunch, a pleasant picnic by the Medici Fountain in the Luxembourg Gardens, which had seemed such a romantic idea at the time, churned in her stomach. "Are you going home? Are you ill?" She felt herself still clutching the doorknob, her hand wound into a claw, and she forced herself to let go, to step forward.

Evelyn shook her head. "I'm not ill, Margie. I'm leaving Paris. And you," she added, as if to make things clear. "Now, if you'll give me my share of the money, I'll be on my way."

"Wait, where are you going?"

"Nowhere that matters to you."

"Of course it matters! I'm responsible for you. Your mother would never have let you come if it weren't for me. We were supposed to travel together." She sounded wretched, she knew, whining, as though she were in the wrong. She stood in the middle of the room, fists balled up by her sides, her knees shaking a little underneath her dress. This was not how it was supposed to go. She had been giving Evelyn a little freedom, that's all, and then when she had gotten this silliness out of her system, they would begin the trip their mothers had sent them on. The trip Margie had been dreaming of, with rich paintings and nights at the opera and handsome unexpected princes in castle gardens.

"I'm not a child," Evelyn said, and now she was whining too, though Margie didn't want to point it out. "I don't need a chaperone. And I certainly don't need you, with all your guide books and your boring history. You may be an old maid, but I'm still young, and I want to enjoy it. I don't want to see a bunch of fusty old castles or museums. I want to see what matters *now.*"

But all those things did matter now, didn't they? Margie wanted to ask. She thought of how she had spent her days, wandering around those fusty museums and lingering in the gardens of Le Palais Royal, looking for the romantic ghosts of nobles past, and she felt ashamed. Oh, she was boring, wasn't she? She and Evelyn were never going to get along. Any change she had hoped for she now saw clearly was her own imagination, yet another unfulfilled daydream.

"I'm not an old maid," she said, finally, miserably.

Evelyn stood. Shrugging her wrap onto her shoulders with a sigh, she shook her head, her bobbed hair moving slightly, then falling perfectly back into place. "I'm not staying with you one minute longer, Margie. Can't you take a hint? You're like a puppy following me around, and I don't want you. Now give me my money and let me go."

"What should I tell your mother?"

"Tell her whatever you want. What's she going to do? Come over here to fetch me? She's too scared even to leave New York. I'm not going to be her. I'm not going to live my entire life wishing I had done things—I'm going to do them. And I'm not going to drag you around with me. You're deadweight."

Margie thought of the plans, the telegrams, the letters written, the hotel arrangements, the itinerary, the list of places she was never going to see now. She thought of the promise this trip had offered her, the relief, and she thought of getting on the ship alone to go home, now weighed down not only by the future that awaited her but by the heaviness of this failure, her inability to control one silly, spoiled girl. Anger welled up inside her, resentment toward Evelyn for her selfishness, her childishness, her ungratefulness for all she had been given, for how easy it had been for her, how luminous and golden her future was, how she was sure it was okay to do anything she wanted, while Margie's own future looked dark and uncertain as a wave.

To her own surprise, her anger roiled out of her, her voice and her hands shaking in equal measure. "You're spoiled, Evelyn. You're spoiled and selfish and cruel, and you always have been. Go on, go on to your silly parties with your silly friends. But I'm not lying for you, and I'm not protecting you. I'm writing our mothers in the morning and I'm going to tell them the whole story, and you can go right ahead and deal with it yourself."

Evelyn huffed in a breath as though she were about to respond, and then clamped her jaw shut so strongly Margie could hear the click of her teeth. Her own heart was pounding so loudly she was sure the entire hotel could hear it, and the furious blood rushed in her ears in waves that sounded like the buzzing of bees. She felt a little faint. Had she ever spoken so plainly before? Ever stood up for herself before? She couldn't remember a time. "Agreeable," people had always said. "Dreamy." Too lost in her own fantasies to make a fuss. But here she was, making an absolutely enormous fuss.

Apparently Evelyn was equally shocked. Her delicate nostrils flared so she looked uncharacteristically unattractive and bull-like, and her eyes were hard and angry. Margie braced herself for a torrent of abuse, but Evelyn finally simply reached out, grabbing for Margie's bag. She shook it out onto Margie's neatly made bed, picking up her passport and the wad of money Margie had carried so carefully, so safely until now, turned on her heel, and stalked off. She put her hand on the door handle and then turned back. The last of the light fell through the window, making her skin glow, her dress glitter. Evelyn always knew how to make the most theatrical presentation. "Go home, Margie. Paris isn't for someone like you." And then she opened the door and let it slam shut behind her.

Margie stood there, her heartbeat slowing, her anger abating, Evelyn's words ringing in her head. It wasn't true. It wasn't. Paris had opened its arms to her over the past week. It was far more her city than it was Evelyn's. And now it didn't matter at all, she thought bitterly. Because without Evelyn, she had no reason to stay. She was going to have to go home, and she would never see Paris again, and she would never, ever be the woman she had known Paris would let her become.

nine

MADELEINE
1999

When I thought of Chicago, I could picture only its gleam—the glare of the sun on the water, and the thousands of windows in the skyscrapers, nothing but brilliant glass, reflecting and refracting the light back in an infinite loop. It seemed white in my memory, its brilliance blinding.

The seasons were short there, except for winter. It always seemed to be cold, to be frozen, so far north it might as well have been a city of ice, rather than glass and steel. It was the ice I remembered more than the snow. Fall came and went in a moment, the trees turning brilliant overnight, a hopeful blast of color, spring in reverse, and then, just as rapidly, winter would come, and ice would cover the city, nature adding its own glimmer to those shining silos of glass lining the streets. The ice coated the pavement in thick sheets, alluring and dangerous, before the leaves had been swept away, so walking down the street you were likely to see them frozen there, the burgundy and gold of fall overlaid with the cold blue of winter, like an insect trapped in amber, a curiosity from a foreign and forgotten time.

And it was winter for so long. When I got into bed at night, I piled blankets and quilts on myself, the weight as comforting as the warmth. The thermostat might have claimed the temperature was just fine, but the cold sat deep in my bones, where I could feel it even if I was sweating.

And then spring came in a burst, overnight the ice melting, giving way to a damp chill that the buds of trees fought through nonetheless, revealing their hopeful promise, white-green and palest yellow clearing away the coating of frost on the branches. Water ran in the gutters, the river's banks bloomed high and full, and the city's residents emerged, blinking and shaken, eyes wide open to the miracle of spring. But spring, like fall, does not last. Summer would come in a brief gasp, as though the other seasons had been holding it underwater, and it could raise its head only long enough to exhale the delicious heat, the pressure of the sun, the long, luxurious hours of daylight, before it gasped and went under again.

And even though Magnolia has a winter of its own, I could only imagine its summer. In the depths of winter, when I pictured Magnolia, I could only remember wet, humid days, the air lying on my skin, a soft, damp caress. I thought of how the underside of my hair was always damp, my face always flushed and pink. I thought of my mother's gardens, an explosion of greenery in soft fronds, long spikes, the pale undersides of leaves, the seductive petals of flowers, coyly hiding their hearts until the sun coaxed them open—roses of butter yellow, peonies pink like ballet slippers, stalks of gladiolus in royal purple, marching up the back fence, dahlia and amaryllis in violent, brazen red. I thought of ice cream cones melting onto my hands, and long, lazy sunsets, and the smell of chlorine and the way the light lay, as though it had been filtered through a golden sieve, on everyone and everything, making the world seem bright and vulnerable and just a little bit more perfect.

And though it wasn't summer in Magnolia yet, I felt something awakening in me very much like it, the fingers of the sun finding their way into the parts of my heart that had frozen solid, the slow drip of melting in my belly. I stayed up late with my grandmother's journals, reading about her fear of facing Paris alone, her embrace of it, and Evelyn's betrayal. It made me think of the pain of not being beautiful, and the wonder of a kiss, and the excitement of discovery, and it made me cry a little for the girls we had been. I wished I had known her.

My own debut had been a disappointment. I had waited for it for years, sat through endless hours of cotillion and deportment classes, thinking the ball would be the brass ring at the end of it all. I'd be a caterpillar turned into a butterfly, an ugly duckling turned into a swan. I'd been part of that existence since I was born, but I had never felt I belonged. My friends and classmates had never gone through an awkward stage. Their hair was smooth and straight, while mine was wavy and disobedient. They were slender and delicate, while I was thick and swimmer-shouldered.

No one was overtly unkind to me. We were all vaguely friends in the way you must all be friends if your entire graduating class numbers a total of eighty girls, but I was never fully included, always on the edge. Most weekend nights I spent alone, painting or reading, or going to a movie with my childhood best friend, Amanda, who had switched to public school and therefore might as well not have existed. During the week, I went to school and then swimming, or to one of the various preparatory functions our mothers set up for us, cotillion or piano lessons, or some fresh hell like the Junior Ladies Association. We were thoroughbreds, led around a ring and told to leap over fences until we learned the skills by heart.

Other girls went to dances, had boyfriends, but as they had been to my grandmother, to me, boys were as mysterious and foreign a substance as radium. There was a boy I saw sometimes at the bookstore, all angles and loose limbs and sleepy eyes that, in retrospect, were probably drug-induced, but at the time simply made him look thoughtful and romantic. Once I dropped my scarf and he picked it up and handed it to me and I blushed. It turned out he went to school with Amanda, but I never asked her to find out more, never told her I was interested in him, never told her I daydreamed of kissing him, of running along River Street with him down to the water, never told her sometimes I looked forward to seeing him, to brushing past him in the fiction section, all week long.

Looking through my high school yearbooks, I pored over photos from parties and dances I hadn't gone to, looking at my classmates' pretty Laura Ashley dresses, their wide, bright smiles, their dates. The girls in those pictures were confident and poised, and I was awkward of voice and nervous of stomach. Some nights I lay in bed and the thought of what they had, what I knew, even then, I would never be, made me ache.

At first I thought college would be my moment. I rushed Chi Gamma Delta because my mother insisted, and I was admitted because I was a legacy. They liked me fine, but in the chapter photos, I was always standing in the back row, somehow never managing to smile when the shutter clicked, my face red, my shirt wrinkled, looking like someone who had wandered into the picture accidentally instead of someone who belonged there just as much as anybody else.

My debutante ball had been my last hope, but at my first dress fitting, I knew it was all wrong. I had dreamed for years of an off-the-shoulder dress, had pictured it all, how perfect I would look, like Scarlett O'Hara or Princess Di. When my mother took me shopping, I practically grabbed a dress off the rack, exactly what I had pictured, a perfect white with an off-the-shoulder neckline and a full skirt. But when I had slipped it on and looked at myself in the mirror, my mother and the saleswoman waiting outside, the former imperiously, the latter obsequiously, my heart broke for a last and final time. I leaned my forehead against the cool mirror, closed my eyes, and cried. The neckline I had dreamed of for so many years was unflattering, the folds of fabric on my upper arms made my shoulders look even wider, and the dropped waist hit the center of my hips before billowing out, making me look like a sausage being pushed into its casing. Crying made my face and my chest blotchy. "Come out, Madeleine," my mother trilled, and I clomped out of the dressing room.

"Oh, my," the saleswoman said, looking at me in my dream dress.

"That is a disaster," my mother said. "Certainly we can do better," she said to the saleswoman, who nodded and practically fled back out onto the floor to find some alternatives. When we were alone, my mother looked at me. "Don't cry. We'll find something suitable. Now take that off. Please," she said, and her voice was almost pleading. We found a dress, of course, but it wasn't the one. It wasn't the one I had dreamed of. Nothing ever seemed to be the way I had dreamed it.

I spent my morning cleaning the kitchen while my mother flitted in and out, sitting down at my father's desk to make phone calls (apparently this was Serious Business and needed to be conducted in the office, because every other phone call I'd ever known her to make had been in the kitchen or the living room), and then dashing out to a meeting or to sort donations for the Collegiate Women's Society rummage sale. Next door at the restaurant, they served lunch and then dinner, and I heard the sounds of laughter from the back yard as I worked my grim way through the house. I had grown so used to the condo, to living on one level, that each trip up and down the stairs seemed exhausting. No wonder my mother wanted to sell that place; everything seemed to take ten minutes longer than it should have.

A little after eight, my mother out at another dinner that I had politely refused to attend, my cell phone finally rang. I had to rush madly for it, scrambling for my purse on the front table, as it trilled robotically at me once, twice, three times. The blossoms in the flower arrangement on the front table were fading, and a few petals had fallen onto my bag while it sat there. They fluttered to the floor while I finally pulled out the phone.

"Hello?"

"Hello," Phillip said.

My stomach sank a little, but why? A few days ago, hadn't I been calling him, praying for him to answer, to tell me it was all a mistake?

"Hello," I said again, because I wasn't sure what to say next.

"I'm home from New York."

I wasn't sure what the appropriate response to that was. "Congratulations?" I said finally.

He didn't laugh. "I was calling to check when your flight arrives on Saturday." All business. Of course. He wasn't calling because he missed me. It was as impersonal as scheduling a doctor's appointment. And there was no forgiveness—and no apology.

"I don't know," I said. "I'll have to check." There was a touch of defensiveness in my tone. Hadn't I come here to wear a hairshirt, to wait for him to forgive me? But I hadn't been doing that. I'd been imagining what it might be like to live here, what it might feel like to have Cassandra and Sharon and Henry as my friends, how I could forge a life that didn't include the Chicago Women's Club or the Magnolia Ladies Association, and I realized none of those thoughts had included him.

"There's a dinner with one of the investors on Saturday night. You'll be expected to be there."

Another dinner. I thought of the last one, of Dimpy Stockton's braying laugh, the conversations about the cost of vacations and jewelry that could have funded a charity for a month, the endless one-upmanship, and was flooded with the painful desire not to have to go to that dinner, not to have to go to a dinner like that ever again. "Look, I don't know if I'll be back on Saturday." I tensed, waiting for his response.

"You have to. The dinner is on Saturday night," Phillip repeated, but he didn't sound angry, only irritated, as though I were keeping him from something he'd rather be doing.

"That's the thing. Mother has decided to sell the house, and she needs help getting it ready." I made myself sound busy, sound confident. He couldn't be mad at me for helping my mother, right?

"Can't someone else do it?" Phillip asked peevishly. I felt my own ire rising in response.

"Well, I'm an only child," I said, explaining it as though he and I had never met, as though I hadn't ever told him how I'd longed for a sibling, how disappointed I was that his sisters and I hadn't grown close. "And yes, she can pay someone, but there are things to go through. Family things."

"But the dinner is this Saturday. What do you expect me to tell them?" His voice was reedy and querulous. I could picture him standing in the living room, looking out over the lake. There would be takeout containers on the island in the kitchen (he had never learned to cook, and whenever I was away I came back to find a trash can full of plastic forks and Phillip complaining about the weight he'd put on in his stomach, as though it were my fault), and there would be a growing pile of dress shirts on my side of the bed because he thought he was too busy to go to the dry cleaner himself.

"I don't know," I said honestly. It felt so far from being my problem.

"You're not even close. When did you start caring about your mother?" he asked.

His words stung. How many times had I complained to him about my mother, wished aloud that we were more alike, that I wasn't such a disappointment to her? How many times had I groaned and procrastinated about packing before going to visit her?

I knew what I should do. I should tell him that of course I was coming home. Getting him to forget about divorce, to realize he missed me had been the whole point—give him a little space, come back and smooth everything over. Except shouldn't it have been different? Shouldn't he have apologized? Shouldn't he want me to come back?

And shouldn't I want to go back?

Because I knew now I didn't want that. I didn't want that at all.

"I'm not leaving her to do this on her own," I said. I was still hiding behind my mother, who needed me there about as much as she needed a chocolate teapot, but it was all I had.

"You're so selfish. I need you at this dinner. We're supposed to be married, Madeleine. Remember that?"

"And you said we should get a divorce. Remember that?" I spat the last word.

"Don't be stupid," he said, with an enormous, exhausted sigh, as though divorce hadn't been his idea in the first place, as though I were making it up. And I felt foolish for ever believing he would actually follow through. Saying we should get a divorce had been nothing but a way for him to win the fight, a reminder of how lucky I was and how easily he could take it all away. "You don't know how good you have it. Do you know how many women would be happy to be married to me?"

He said this as though he were the greatest prize anyone could have had, an end worthy of justifying the means. And, I thought guiltily, hadn't I thought of it the same way myself at the beginning? Hadn't that been what had encouraged me to push away all the warning signs, the glaring lights and bells worthy of a carnival midway, all of them shouting the same thing: "Don't do this!"

"I don't want to talk any more right now," I said, and my voice was empty and tired. The fact that he would rather crush me, rather hold me to him cruelly than let me go, forced me to face everything I had refused to see about the man he was. And if he didn't see how wrong this all was, I didn't even know how to begin to go about explaining it to him.

"Well, that's great. Because I don't want to talk to you anymore either, Madeleine," he said icily, stretching my name into three precise syllables. I pulled the phone away from my ear and stared at it, wishing for a good old-fashioned rotary phone, where you could slam down the receiver satisfactorily. Instead, I shoved some of the flowers in the vase to the side and dropped the phone in the water and walked away, feeling both triumphant and terrified.

ten

MARGIE
1924

The morning after Evelyn's departure, Margie sat at Les Deux Magots, a pretty little café on a corner across the street from the Saint-Germain-des-Prés church. But Margie wasn't much in the mood for sightseeing. She had written a letter to her mother, a truthful one this time, reporting the situation with Evelyn and her own now tragic finances, and asking for advice. It would have been more appropriate to send a telegram, she knew. This was, after all, urgent. But she hoped the letter would delay things a little. The hotel was paid up for another week, and Margie had a little more money she had tucked away here and there in her luggage—not enough to live extravagantly, but enough for a few things—admission to a few of the less dear sites or museums, and her *café complet* here—a large cup of coffee with cream, and a roll with butter. Surely she could manage on such little food if it meant she could stay in Paris a little longer.

No one seemed to mind if you stayed in a café for ages, and so she was, sitting at a table outside, as the morning geared up like a rusty calliope. She had sealed the letter and, to wipe away the bitter taste of the envelope, was writing a story about a girl who became tragically ill on a trip to Europe and was forced to return home, which sounded much more romantic and less depressing than her own situation, even if the end result were the same. At a table nearby sat a young man she was considering writing into the story as the French suitor of the tragically ill girl. He was unbelievably handsome, with long blond hair, though the fashion was for it to be short and slicked back, and strong bones in his face that made him look as though he had been chiseled. A pen and an open notebook lay on his table while he leaned back, fingers laced behind his neck, his head tilted up toward the sunshine. His eyes were closed and a light smile played on his face.

He opened his eyes and caught Margie looking at him. She started, horrified to have been caught, but before she looked away, he gave her a long, slow wink. Flushing a hot scarlet, Margie lowered her head to her writing again. No, she couldn't put him in her story. He might catch her at that, too.

It was such a pleasure, though, to see a young man like him, to see any of the young men in Paris, lively and healthy. The war had rendered men of a certain age glaring in their absence, left behind on fields in France, in Italy, in Germany, their presence now limited to the mothers still wearing black mourning crêpe. A group of young men who looked to be about her age passed by and then came into the café, and she wondered at the luck, the miracle of them, young and healthy and enthusiastic. They piled into the chairs around the table, and there seemed to be so many of them, so many limbs in motion, so much noise and bluster, she thought surely there wouldn't be enough room. But of course there was, and then there was a flurry again as they ordered and coffee was brought and they settled in with their cups and their cigarettes, some of them leaning forward, hands on the table, conversing vehemently, others leaning back, watching the people go by as she was, and it all felt so *right*, as if this had all been planned, them and the other young man and her, as if they had all been born just to be here in this moment.

She paused, putting down her pen and flexing her fingers, pulling on them one at a time to make her knuckles pop. Her mother hated the habit; she said it made Margie look like a baseball player, and wondered if she would take up smoking cigars next. Mentally, Margie stuck her tongue out at her mother, but she must have done it actually, too, because a woman sitting at a table nearby gave her a queer expression, and Margie sighed, clamping her tongue inside the prison of her teeth.

"*Bonjour*," a man said, and Margie looked up to see the young man with the blond hair who had winked at her now standing in front of her table, his cup and saucer in his hand, his notebook tucked underneath his arm.

"*Bonjour?*" Margie replied. She had been practicing her French over the past few days, but it still felt graceless and uncomfortable on her tongue, and it sounded dreadfully American to her ears.

"May I sit with you?" he asked, in perfect English, turned into something more beautiful by his decidedly French accent. Before she could demur—she had thought it was unseemly enough initially for a young woman to be sitting at a café on her own, let alone to take company with a strange man—he was putting down his things and pulling out the other chair at the table, sitting down as though she had been waiting for him all along. "You are a writer?" he asked.

Margie looked down at her notebook and blushed, closed the cover to hide her messy scrawl and the messier emotions it exposed. "Not really. I would like to be a writer, but right now I am—well, I don't know what I am. I'm just playing, I guess."

"You look like a writer," he said, fixing her with a sharp stare. "You are writing, *oui?*" His eyes were a brilliant green she had never seen before, at least not on a person. She had seen it on summer fields, in the sparkle of an emerald ring, but his eyes made the color elsewhere seem shoddy and false.

"Just writing doesn't make you a writer. Not a real writer, like one who writes books or something."

"Well, how do you think the writers who write books began?" he asked, gesturing at her notebook. "They wrote in cafés in Paris, like you."

"Maybe," Margie said doubtfully, but she had to suppress a little smile at the thought of someone thinking her a real writer.

"Not maybe. Definitely." He broke into a wide smile. He had a full mouth and broad, white teeth. "Do you mind if I sit here?" he asked, despite clearly having already made himself at home. He reached into his jacket pocket and produced a pack of cigarettes and a box of matches, though he made no move to smoke them, only putting them on the table as though he were settling in for a workday.

"No, it's fine."

"Are you American?" His accent twisted his vowels and made the consonants scrape against the roof of his mouth in a delicious way.

"*Oui.* Er, yes." She coughed. Did she look so obviously American? She certainly didn't think she looked Parisian. The Parisian women were delicate under their loose dresses, their ankles slender, their cheekbones high under cloche hats. They wore their coats slipping slightly off their shoulders, as though they were always arriving, about to sit down and stay for a while, or always ready to leave, heading off on another adventure. Margie felt solid and indelicate next to them and their easy elegance. Even the men had a certain panache to them; the young man talking to her had a scarf loosely knotted around his neck in a casual way she knew it would take hours to reproduce, and his hair fell impishly into his face, a caramel blond that set off his eyes.

"Everyone in Paris is American now. Except for me. I am French. *Je m'appelle Sebastien.* And you?"

"Margie," she said, and then she caught herself, changed her mind, though she wasn't sure why. "Margaret."

"*Marguerite,*" he repeated, turning what she had always thought of as a dull, workaday name into something new and elegant. In French class at school, they had simply pronounced her nickname with an accent—*Mar-ZHEE*, which had sounded dull and leaden, as it did in English. But *Marguerite*. Marguerite was someone different. Marguerite wouldn't be abandoned by anyone to go to a party—she would be invited to the party, would be the life of it. Marguerite would sit in cafés and flirt with strangers and maybe even drink wine and dance sometimes. With a sudden, swelling ache, Margie wanted to be Marguerite more than anything else.

Sebastien lifted his cup and clinked it against hers. "*Enchanté*," he said, and he winked again.

Margie sipped at her coffee. Her secret was that she didn't really like coffee, but she had learned to order it with cream instead of milk, and with extra sugar, which she dropped in until the coffee could no longer absorb it all and the last few sips left her with a pale, sweet sludge at the bottom of the cup, a deliciously wasteful extravagance after the war. "So are you a writer?" she asked.

"*Non, non*," Sebastien scoffed. "Only Americans are writers." He gave her a little wink and she couldn't resist smiling back. She didn't know why he had chosen to sit with her, but his good mood was infectious, and she was happy to have a little cheer around her. If she only had a week left in the city, she might as well spend her time enjoying things rather than moping around. "No, I am an artist. Frenchmen, we are painters." He flipped his notebook open, showing her the sketches that covered the pages, sometimes only tiny pieces jumbled together on a single page— the Eiffel Tower rendered in crosshatches, a quickly sketched coffee cup, a woman's ear, delicate as a seashell—and sometimes a drawing spreading across both pages, a bridge across the Seine viewed from the water, an explosion of flowers in a garden. He paged through rapidly, as though he were making a moving picture, and then closed the notebook when he came to the blank pages at the end. Margie wanted to take it from him, open it again, let its secrets unfold in front of her. She was a dreadful artist herself, capable mostly of childish stick figures and landscapes—square houses, stiffly symmetrical trees—and she envied people who could draw.

"Those are lovely," she breathed.

Waving his hand as though he could dismiss the air that held the compliment, Sebastien took another sip of coffee. "Not so. They are only things I draw to remind me of what to paint later. Like making a note for a story, *oui?*"

"*Oui,*" Margie said, and this time she didn't correct herself, because Marguerite felt like someone who would say *oui* instead of yes, even if she was American.

"So what are you doing in Paris all alone?"

Margie sighed. "I was here with my cousin. I was supposed to be her chaperone."

"Where is she?" Sebastien looked around. For once, Margie was grateful Evelyn wasn't there. If Sebastien saw her, it would be, "So long, Margie." It had always been that way: when Evelyn was around, Margie might as well have been invisible—and not only to young men, but to waiters, or porters, or shop clerks. She'd actually had to snap her fingers in front of the face of the porter when they were getting off the ship, he had been so entranced. She had once seen a man walk into a lamp post on the street because he had been so busy watching Evelyn. It had sounded with a loud *bong,* and the poor fellow had seemed so surprised, and had looked at the lamp post with such personal offense that Margie had to smother a laugh in her hand.

"She met some friends on the ship when we came over, and now she's run off with them."

"Run off?"

"You know. Left me to spend time with them."

"I see." Sebastien frowned, piecing the story together in his mind. His English was impeccable, but Margie wasn't sure how much of what she said was clear. She had never thought so much about idioms, about the way they crept into your language and became untranslatable. She remembered, years ago in high school, missing a meeting with her French teacher, who had then accused Margie of putting a rabbit on her—"*Tu m'a posé un lapin!*" What a silly thing to say, Margie had thought, but in the end, was it any sillier than saying, "You stood me up!" What did that even mean?

"So she is gone, but you are still here."

"*Oui.*"

Sebastien broke into another smile then, wide and disarming. "So this is better, then! Now you have all of Paris and none of her." He spread his arms wide, as if to take in the entirety of the city and offer it to Margie.

"No, no," Margie said. "I . . ." She tried to think of how to explain it. "You see, I was only here to be with her. I was meant to take care of her. And now I must go home."

At this, Sebastien looked so horrified that Margie almost laughed aloud. "Leave Paris?" He spread his hand over his chest, as though Margie had wounded him. "You have just arrived!"

With a shrug, Margie tried to ignore the tug at her own heart. She knew. Oh, how she knew. For every word she had written to her mother, she had composed ten in her heart illuminating how unfair the whole thing was. "I know. But I can't stay here alone. It wouldn't be appropriate."

"Is this a . . ." He snapped his fingers in the air and squinted at the sky, looking for the word. He really was terribly attractive, Margie thought, so attractive she forgot to question why he was sitting there talking to her. She had originally thought his hair was the color of burnt caramel, but as he moved his head in the sunlight, it lit up a dozen different colors—strands of corn silk, of strawberry blond, of deep chestnut—and his eyes blazed green, the lashes around them unfairly dark and thick. He had slim hands with long fingers, and when he moved them in the air when he spoke, she watched, transfixed, picturing herself capturing one of his hands and holding it against her face, just for a moment, just to feel how real he was.

"A punishment? Is this a punishment?" He looked pleased at himself for having found the word.

"I suppose it is," she said, and the thought made her blue. "My mother . . ." she began, unable to bring herself to finish. Margie's feelings about her mother were too complicated to explain.

A woman with a small child had arrived and was sitting on a bench outside the church. She had given the child a baguette, and he toddled around, alternately pursuing and pursued by the pigeons as he tossed crumbs in the air. At another table in the café, a man with a mustache sat, nursing a drink and writing in his own notebook, his meaty hands so large they nearly eclipsed the paper. Beside him were two French women, their heads bent together as though they were telling the most important of secrets. It was punishment to take her away from the sights she had not seen—*la tour Eiffel!* Napoleon's tomb!—but it was punishment of a harsher sort to take her away from this, from the simple pleasures of Paris, from this place where she could sit alone in a café without anyone speculating on her virtue, where she could write for hours without being interrupted by her mother's criticisms, where she could watch the parade going by, this brave new world that had such people in't.

"Well," she said, pulling herself out of her own sulk, "I've written my mother and told her Evelyn is gone. She'll write back and send me money to come home." She left out the parts she didn't want to think about— her mother's fury, her own disappointment, the storm awaiting her when she got back to Washington. And, she thought, as she was pushing those thoughts to the back of her mind, her parents' anger wouldn't be the worst part of going home. It would be Mr. Chapman. Because this had been her chance at escape, and she had ruined it. And now she had no more excuses. Mr. Chapman waited at the other end of the journey like a thin-faced executioner. She wanted to drop her head on the table and weep.

Leaning forward, Sebastien lifted the envelope Margie had set aside, facedown. He looked at her questioningly, and she nodded. He lifted it between two fingers and read the address written in Margie's sloppy scrawl and then, as though it answered some question, nodded.

"And what if you do not go home?" he asked, turning the envelope slowly. She could hear the crinkle of the paper against his skin.

"Oh. I couldn't do that. It wouldn't be appropriate," she started.

"You said this already."

Flustered, Margie continued. "Well, Evelyn took most of our money. And I don't know anyone here. The hotel is already paid for one more week. After that I don't have anywhere to stay, and I don't have enough money to live on."

With a sigh, Sebastien dropped the envelope, lit a cigarette, shook out the match with his hand and dropped it in an ashtray on the neighboring table. He exhaled, squinting at her through the smoke. "You could find work. And Paris is cheap for you. So many Americans are here because it costs them so little. You can live in Paris no problem." He snapped his fingers again and she looked at his hands.

"Who are you?" she asked, suddenly self-conscious that she was sitting here, confessing her worries to a stranger, a handsome young man who would not have found anything in her worth looking at if she had been at home.

He grinned at her again, took a slow puff off the cigarette and let the smoke draw a lazy haze in the air before he replied. *"Je m'appelle Sebastien."*

"No, no. I know your name. But who are you? What do you do? Why are you talking to me?"

"Ah." Sebastien tapped his cigarette end in the ashtray, rolling it around so the tobacco formed a pointed tip. "I am a painter, which I told you already. And I am talking to you because you look like you need someone to talk to."

"Oh." Margie deflated a little. Well, what had she thought? There might be about her something particularly appealing to French men? But would that be so wrong? Would it be so awful, once in her life, for someone to tell her she was beautiful? She had been told she was clever, even brilliant. But she wanted to be beautiful, wanted someone to say it. She thought she had been beautiful once, the night of her debut, that there had been some magic in her dress and in the night, blown in on the cold, cold air. But in the morning, the magic had gone, evaporated in the sunshine, and whatever beauty there had been had gone with it, and the only proof she had of it was the memory of Robert's kiss. "Well, thank you."

Sebastien leaned back, lowering his eyes in thought, smoking silently. "I have a solution," he said finally.

"For what?"

"For you, of course. You must stay in Paris. I know a place where all the American girls who come here live. You will live there too. We will tear up this letter and you will write to your mother and tell her you are staying." He picked up the letter again and then let it fall from his fingers, as though it were as worthless as sand.

"I can't stay, Sebastien." In her heart, she was already saying *au revoir* to all the things she might have done when she was here, watching the sun rise on the Pont des Arts over the Seine, walking the narrow back streets of the Left Bank, eating *pain au chocolat* whenever she wanted, drinking wine and writing in cafés, beside the artists and writers who had made Paris the place to be.

"You must! Leaving would be a waste. A waste!" He stubbed out his cigarette, leaned forward, looked into her eyes with his brilliant green ones, placed his hand on hers, soft, the fingernails edged with tiny moons of paint. She looked down at his hand on hers, the quiet pressure. "What is waiting for you in America that you must hurry back?"

What was waiting for her? Nothing. Nothing she wanted. Her parents' disappointment. Closed, stuffy parlors and embroidery. Ladies' benevolent societies. Mr. Chapman. She looked past Sebastien's face, both serious and pleading at the same time, out the window again. The bell in the church tower was calling out the noon hour. The child had distributed the bread to the pigeons and was now sitting with his mother on the bench, insistently bending her ear about some issue of crucial small-child importance. Across the street, a vendor had arrived and was carefully hanging bits of fabric over the church's fence as though it were a display case, and a flower-seller was happily accosting people, thrusting bouquets at them as they alit from the Métro. She didn't want to leave this, didn't want to break the promise she had made to herself without even giving it a try. She didn't want to go home yet.

Her parents would be furious. And they would refuse to support her. She had—what, a few hundred francs? And then it would all be gone. But he had said Paris was cheap. And she could work, and her French would get better. She would be independent, like those girls in the boardinghouse. She'd have her own money, her own job, her own life, and there would be no one to criticize how she spent her time or what books she read or who she was.

Sebastien was still holding her hand, keeping her in place as though she were a rare and precious bird who might fly away. She thought of Mr. Chapman's dry, nervous hands, his chapped lips. She thought of everything she had yet to explore—the grand cathedral at Chartres, Versailles, the open-air markets.

Margie took a long breath, as though she were raising her arms in the air to dive into deep water. "All right," she said. "Where is this place you say I should stay?"

eleven

MADELEINE
1999

When I dragged downstairs the morning after my argument with Phillip, my mother was already dressed (including full lipstick) and sitting in my father's office making phone calls. A yellow legal pad sat in front of her, covered with notes written in her perfect penmanship, and as I came in, she hung up the phone and made another note.

"You haven't brushed your hair," she said, looking up at me.

"That was an actual life choice." I'd woken up with it looking not half bad, and I'd been afraid to touch it. Of course it had gone into its natural curl, which my mother regarded as a failing on the same level of magnitude as, say, becoming a heroin addict, but I couldn't do anything about that.

My mother glanced back at me, looking as though she had stepped in something. I lifted my voice and changed the subject. "So what are you working on?" I asked, too loudly.

"Don't shout, I'm right here. I've been calling some appraisers."

"Doesn't Sharon do that?"

"Not for the house, for the contents. I know you think everything in here is ancient and worthless, but much of it is quite valuable."

"Wait, where did you get that idea? I don't think these things are worthless."

"I've seen your house. It's very . . . modern." She said the word as though even having it on her tongue disgusted her.

"That wasn't my choice! It was like that when we moved in. You remember my place here? Before Phillip and I got married? That wasn't modern." I felt a pang of sadness when I remembered my apartment in Magnolia, where I had lived after college and before Phillip. I'd almost forgotten I'd once had a home that was wholly mine, and I felt the loss of it with a surprising ferocity.

It had been in one of the older buildings downtown, with gorgeous original parquet floors and French doors opening up on a balcony so charmingly tiny it was unusable. There were three bedrooms, one of which was a guest room no one ever used, one of which was mine, and the master, which I had repurposed as an art studio. My not using the master to sleep in had made my mother absolutely batty, which made me love it even more. My father had disapproved, had wanted to buy me a condo in a newer building, with a doorman and a business center and a more prestigious address. But all that had sounded so complicated, and I had wanted something of my own. And now I hated that I hadn't known how wonderful it was when I had it.

"Well, if you want anything, you need to let me know before the appraiser comes."

There were a dozen things I would have loved to have—things I remembered from childhood, pieces my mother had told me the stories of—but where would I put them? I thought of the condo in Chicago, austere and elegant and cold, and shivered.

"Okay," I said. Scarlett-like, I would think about it tomorrow. "Is that Sharon's list? What do we need to do next?"

My mother fixed me with the precise tractor beam of her gaze, the same look that had caught me a hundred times over in my childhood, pinning me in place and pulling the truth from me. "Why do you keep saying 'we'? What's going on? Is everything all right with Phillip?"

Oh, dear. That was such a very, very large question. There were so many things that were not all right with Phillip, and even more things that were not all right with Phillip and me. And perhaps an even longer list of things that were not all right with me individually. But I had no interest in exploring those subjects with my mother. Or, more likely, at all.

"He's fine," I said. And wasn't that true? Phillip was always fine. And Phillip would always be fine, because to Phillip, there was absolutely nothing wrong with him. Any problem, any difficulty, any flaw belonged to someone else. "I just want to make sure you're taken care of."

She looked at me for another long moment, coolly appraising. "Is there something you want to talk to me about?" Leaning back in the chair, she put down her pen and crossed her arms on her chest. The chair squeaked and another rush of sadness came over me as I was reminded of my father's absence. I'd had a hundred conversations with him in his office, just like this. Him sitting in his chair behind his desk, leaning back so it squeaked, me sitting in one of the chairs across from him, as if I were one of his clients and not his daughter, though it had never felt that way.

Between my parents, my father had been the soft touch. He had always talked to me as if I were an adult, and when I had been in trouble, I'd always gone to him first, and we'd work out some solution, and then he'd offer me a piece of candy from the jar on his desk, walk me to the door, and send me back out to play.

I opened and closed my mouth a few times. "It's complicated." I couldn't imagine saying to her that Phillip and I were miserable, that he had threatened to divorce me, and even though he had backpedaled, in the meantime I had become half convinced it was a good idea. I didn't know how she would respond. My mother and I had never been that honest with each other.

"Marriage is difficult, you know," she said, and her voice was unusually sentimental. My mother would needle at me and pick at me and criticize my hair and make exhaustive lists of all the things I was doing wrong, but she was still my mother, which meant there was an eternal flame lit inside me in honor of the moments when she didn't see me as something broken to fix. My heart lifted slightly. Maybe I could tell her. We could actually have this conversation, and she would help me figure it out.

"I know it's difficult." But I imagined it was a lot easier when you married the right person in the first place.

"I'm sure you'll work things out," she said, and the smile on her face went smooth and plastic, and the brief hope I'd held flickered and then died. There was going to be no Hollywood ending where we embraced each other and cried while an emotionally manipulative song played in the background. Things are never like that in real life. At least not in mine.

And maybe Phillip and I would work things out. Maybe I did belong there after all.

Because people in my family didn't get divorced. My parents' marriage hadn't been any great love story, but they had stuck it out together. I couldn't think of anyone who had gotten divorced. The apocryphal stories I had heard always involved some dramatic circumstance—a mistress, a secret bank account in the Cayman Islands, a gambling addiction, alcoholism. No one else gets to upend their entire life just because they are unhappy. Why should I?

Anyway, I didn't know where I would go if I left. It would be better, I thought, to stay with him, to have him leave the bathroom scale pointedly in the middle of the floor when I let myself slip, to continue to wear the disguise of the perfect society wife I had put on to impress him. It would be better than whatever lonely uncertainty lay out there.

After all, it had been my choice to marry him. It had been my choice even though my reasons weren't the best: because I was tired of being lonely, because I wanted to please my parents, because life looked like a gigantic game of musical chairs and I was sure the music would stop at any moment and everyone would see I didn't have a partner.

And, at least at the beginning, I had seen so many other advantages to marrying Phillip. For instance, I had always wanted a sister. So when

Phillip told me he had two sisters, I was absolutely over the moon. Here it was. Here was my family. Here were my sisters. Unfortunately, it didn't work out that way. Phillip's sisters were cool-weather versions of the women I knew in Magnolia, the same frozen hair, in black instead of blond, the same sleeveless shift dresses, in muted solid colors, not summer prints, and they knew I was not one of them.

There was a bond among the three Spencer siblings that felt like a force field; whenever I tried to approach it, I was thrown back. They followed their mother's example in doting on Phillip to distraction, and there was a sibling connection that I, as an only child, would never understand; the three of them were best friends, so close it would have been impossible to separate them. At the engagement party with Phillip's family (there were two of everything except the wedding, which meant many, many presents and many, many thank-you notes), a sister clung to each of his arms, accepting the congratulations on my behalf, laughing with the relatives and friends I should have been meeting, basking in the warmth of the family I knew, with growing certainty, I would never fully be able to join. For my part, I spent the majority of that party, ostensibly held in my honor, hiding from Phillip's mother, drinking far too much red wine, and making sweet, sweet love to a garlicky plate of hummus. But I got to keep all the presents, so I guess I won?

After the wedding, when the photographer's proofs arrived, there was a whole series of Phillip and his sisters cuddled together in an armchair, laughing, a matched set of dark-haired beauty. Somehow, his sisters' dresses had remained perfectly unwrinkled. Personally, I had been so terrified of crushing my own dress that from the moment I had put it on, I had refused to sit down, and I had nearly fainted during the receiving line from keeping my knees locked for such a long time.

"When did you take these?" I asked him when we looked at the pictures, running my finger along the edge of the page, as though I could join them by touch.

Phillip leaned over and peered at the page. "In the groom's room. Before the ceremony."

"Oh," I said. At the moment Phillip and his sisters had taken this picture, I was standing silently in the bride's room, my dress stiff and uncomfortable, my hair pulled back too tightly, the combs of the tiara pressing against my scalp, my mother looking at me critically, the rest of the bridesmaids gathered in a corner drinking a bottle of champagne and laughing.

Phillip clearly had no problem playing his part. During the reception, he strutted around the room, circulating among the tables at dinner without me, accepting the congratulations and best wishes of people who adored him. I only knew half the people there, so after I made a few tentative forays to greet them, I retreated to the head table to eat my dinner alone. It would have been kind of him . . . well, why not say it as it was? He should have taken me with him. He should have introduced me to the people I didn't know, held me beside him as his wife. But that was not the way Phillip worked. Before the wedding, it had been all about my mother, who had planned the entire thing, right down to the personalized tulle bundles of Jordan almonds and the napkins that matched the bridesmaids' dresses. And then on the day itself, it was all about Phillip. I wondered how I had lost my place at my own wedding, feeling more and more kinship with the tiny plastic bride sitting on top of the wedding cake, nothing more than a part of the set dressing in The Phillip Show.

Every night on our honeymoon, I slipped into sleep and he went down to the hotel bar and drank until the stars faded, chatting with the patrons, accepting their congratulations on his own, again. I would wake and find him gone, the room empty except for the cold company of the moonlight, and I lay awake, staring into the silvery darkness until the door creaked open and he settled into bed beside me. I never said anything, and he never intimated he thought there was anything wrong with the arrangement. And there wasn't anyone I could ask. There are a hundred etiquette guides for weddings, and not a single one for marriage.

I had made an awful mistake. And the stupid thing was, I had known. Standing in the vestibule of the church outside the sanctuary, I had looked at the scene inside—that's what it had felt like, a scene. A red carpet ran down the center aisle from the altar to the door, lolling like an obscene and thirsty red tongue. Walking down the aisle, I had been uncomfortably aware of the audience. *Should I be smiling? Or should I be solemn? Should I look at Phillip? Or at the guests?*

Looking at the photos, I had been horrified to see my own expression. There was not a single photo in which I looked happy. Instead, I stood, unsmiling, eyes wide and frozen. It was the expression of a woman who had done something terrible and had no idea how she might get out of it.

Phillip didn't notice. He was entranced by his own appearance. His bachelor weekend had been by the pools in Las Vegas, and he had been slightly, gorgeously tan for the wedding, sun-kissed and healthy. Already unforgivingly pale, I had been encouraged (and by encouraged, I mean forced) into a dress of pure, icy white that washed me out, turning me as frozen and blue as though I were winter itself, even though our wedding had been in June. Phillip didn't seem to notice. "Look at me," he had crowed, turning page after page, while I grew more and more shocked and horrified by my appearance in each photo. "I look so tan. These are great pictures," he said, running a finger along his own face in a portrait of both of our families.

I looked at him, the narcissistic man I had married, so in love with his own reflection he could not see me at all. Beside him in those pictures, I looked like a ghost, as though it was a mourning photograph taken long ago, a family gathered together around the body of a cold, dead bride.

That night, as I looked at myself in the mirror, I had seen the same wide-eyed terror that I had seen in the photos. "What have I done?" I whispered to myself, reaching out a tentative, trembling hand to the woman reflected back at me. "What have I done?"

twelve
··················

MARGIE
1924

Margie's parents, as she had known they would be, were furious. Even if cables weren't written in all capital letters, she swore she would have been able to hear them yelling from clear across the Atlantic.

LETTER UNACCEPTABLE STOP

PASSAGE BOOKED CHERBOURG 5/22 FOR NYC STOP

AUNT EDITH HEARTBROKEN STOP FATHER FURIOUS STOP

COME HOME IMMEDIATELY STOP

She hadn't even bothered to reply to the last one, because the only answer she could think of was no. No, she wasn't leaving Paris. No, she wasn't coming home. Not now, and maybe not ever.

Because in the meantime, my grandmother had fallen hopelessly in love with Paris, with the city that had had enough of war and sadness and had promised itself it had reached *la der des ders*—that the Great War would be the last war, and they would not think on their grief and the empty bellies and the wounded and lost husbands and fathers and brothers. They would rebuild from the rubble and drink and celebrate. Margie went to the top of the Eiffel Tower and looked at the city spread out beneath her feet, and she walked endless miles along the sidewalks, past lovers, past arguments, past families, past drunks reeling their crooked way home, past joy and heartbreak and rages and passions that would not be denied. She went to Napoleon's tomb, which she found both ghastly and awe-inspiring, and she went to see the *Panthéon de la Guerre*, a panoramic painting which she knew she ought to object to, as it went against all her pacifistic beliefs, but was so wonderful she couldn't contain herself from weeping a little bit, for the glory and pain of war and its endless bitter romance. She walked along streets of worn stones, and she stumbled into silent churches full of dust and the flicker of candles she never saw anyone light, and she walked through the galleries at the Jeu de Paume, thinking of when it wasn't a museum and instead was where Napoleon played tennis, and she wrote a story about an art theft and a daring girl detective and fell asleep in the Tuileries under a tree and when she awoke there was a guard shooing her away, and she ate a *crêpe noisette et chocolat* on the steps of the Hôtel de Ville and licked her sticky fingers as she walked back home.

She never, never wanted to leave.

The place Sebastien had suggested she stay was the American Girls' Club, a large building sprawling lazily down a side street off the Boulevard du Montparnasse. When she turned off the wide boulevard and saw it sitting there on the narrow street, leaning forward as though it were eager to make her acquaintance, she wanted to gasp and clasp her hands together in joy, like a character in a Gilbert & Sullivan operetta. The buildings on the street were old and whitewashed, rather than the creamy gold of so much of the city, beautiful but exhaustingly repetitive, and the Club had green shutters and flower boxes filled with an explosion of purple and pink and blue. It looked more like a country cottage than a building only steps from one of the busiest streets in Paris.

She knocked but there was no answer, and when she turned the handle, the door swung open easily. She stepped into the foyer, deliciously dark and cool after the brightness of the day outside. A woman sat in an office, a window open to the foyer, and Margie stepped over, waiting politely for her to take a break in her typing and notice Margie was there.

When the woman finally looked up and saw Margie, her expression hardly changed. "Yes?" she boomed.

Margie jumped. "Ah, yes?" she echoed, and then felt silly. "Er, *bonjour?*" Wait, she was in the American Girls' Club. Why was she speaking French? "I mean, hello?"

"Yes?" the woman asked again impatiently.

"Yes, you see, I'm Margie, and I'm American, you see." She offered a quick smile in case her nationality might buy her a little kindness. The woman continued to look at her with a grimly determined expression, as though Margie were merely an obstacle to be mowed over in pursuit of her work, which, truth be told, is exactly what she was. "Someone said I might be able to stay here?" There was a little squeak in her voice and she swallowed hard.

"We rent rooms, yes. You have an American passport?"

"Well, yes," Margie said. "I'm American?"

Margie seemed to have spoken the magic words, because the woman began bustling about in her little office, picking up forms from various cubbyholes and bringing a notebook to the ledge that stood between her and Margie.

As she gathered her papers, the woman rattled off information about the Club's accommodations (single or shared rooms, shared bathrooms), rules (no gentlemen or liquor in the rooms, no Marcel irons in the bathrooms), and costs.

Though she gulped when she heard the price for the only available room, a single on the third floor, Margie took a deep breath and nodded. However foolish it was, she was actually carrying all her remaining money with her. Her mother had warned her, regularly and loudly, before departure, of the insidiousness of pickpockets in Europe, but also of thieving chambermaids and usurious hotel owners. To Margie's mother, Europe looked like one of those medieval maps, where the cartographer had filled in the unknown spaces with fear: *Here be dragons.* And as much as Margie didn't want to believe her mother's anxieties, she seemed to have absorbed them anyway, so every departure from her hotel room was fraught with decision: should she take her valuables with her and risk a pickpocket, or leave them to the mercies of a thieving chambermaid? In the end, she took them with her most days, taking comfort in the knowledge that the French didn't even seem to have a word for pickpocket; they'd had to borrow it from English. With shaking hands, she opened her bag and pulled out her money, slowly counting out 125 francs, the price for the first week. It was quite a bargain, and yet it felt like the greatest extravagance she had ever experienced, especially when she looked at the anemic amount of money she had left. As the woman counted the money, Margie carefully filled out the card the woman had handed her. She was doing this. She was actually doing this.

When she had finished, the woman behind the desk called for a girl to take Margie upstairs. Her guide turned out to be a somewhat swaggering girl named Helen, from Ohio, who took Margie through the Club's narrow hallways and up to her room. The building was U-shaped, with a center courtyard where a half-dozen girls were sitting in the sun, a few of them reading, a few talking. In the corner was a spigot that might have been connected to a well at some point, the stone grown mossy and cracked from disuse, and at the back of the courtyard lay a rose garden, blooms opening, fat and fragrant, to the sun. Sebastien had said the Club (or more specifically, its eponymous girls) had somewhat of a reputation, and Margie was prepared for scandal around every corner, but nothing seemed amiss, which was slightly disappointing.

Helen led her up a hysterically pitched flight of stairs to the second floor, where there was a sun room above the foyer, as bright and clean as the floor below was dark and cool, and through a rabbit warren of hallways, then up more stairs to the third floor. It was quieter up here, and the air was still and hot despite the open dormers in the hall. As they walked, Helen rattled off a list of additional rules and instructions, which Margie was following with one ear while looking around every corner with the other, trying to memorize the building's twists and turns. In her head, the drumbeat of her disobedience and the surety of her mother's disapproval played on, but she felt no shame. The stairs didn't make her feel anxious or tired. There was only the excitement of everything to come. She would be like those girls in the boardinghouse down the street from her parents' house in Washington, walking out confidently every morning to her job, she would be like those writers she saw in the cafés, head bent down, scribbling furiously in her notebook, she would be like Sebastien or Evelyn, bold and unafraid.

Finally they arrived at a door, and Helen handed her a key with a flourish. "Your room." They were at the end of the hall, and Margie opened the door tentatively to find a light-filled room, bright and swaying with dust in the sunbeams falling in through the two dormer windows. "Two windows," Helen said. "Lucky." She peered into the room and then shrugged. "See you around."

Margie stepped inside, her hands held open beside her as though she were absorbing the air, letting this place fall into her. She opened the window facing the backs of the houses on the street behind the Club, looking down at laundry drying on the lines, a rabbit eating from a vegetable garden in the corner of a yard. As the air rushed in, she ran to the other window, pushing it open too, looking out into the courtyard, the girls below still lazing in the sun, the roses sending their sweetness up to Margie on the air.

Inside, the floors were a bright blond wood that made the room practically glow despite the scuffs and cracks from years of use; the white walls were freshly painted. A bed with a metal frame, a mattress, a pillow, and a stack of sheets on top, a dresser, a chair. That was it. And

Margie, who had grown up in a home with so much wealth, stuffed with furniture and antiques and all the money anyone could have wanted, nearly wept at the simplicity of it. This room was hers, Paris was hers, this life was hers, at last, her life was hers.

The morning after she moved in, Margie approached the woman at the front desk about a job. The woman sized her up, finally producing a card with an address on it. "The American Library in Paris called yesterday. They're looking for someone."

Margie took the card with shaking fingers. A job at a library! In Paris! It was as though it had all been made for her. She put on the new French hat she had found after days of searching for something large enough—French women seemed to have tiny heads and somewhat less enthusiastic hair than Margie—and her best shoes, and headed off to 10 rue de l'Élysée.

The library wasn't a library like she had imagined, not like her library at home. Down a wide side street near the Jardins des Champs-Élysées, she matched the address to a stately town house, wide and tall, with a huge, imposing front door and silent windows. Next door, a window washer stood on one of the balconies, and the glass he had left behind sparkled in the sun. The street was lined with similar houses, and it was so quiet Margie would have sworn no one lived there at all. Across the street, a high wall topped with a wrought-iron fence surrounded the Élysée Palace, where the president lived, and a couple of *gendarmes* stepped down the street, looking askance at Margie as she hesitated on the sidewalk.

Their attentions made her self-conscious, so she pushed herself to approach the door and lifted the heavy brass knocker, letting it fall twice. In the quiet street, the sound seemed enormous, but no one came. She knocked again, and when there was still no answer, she turned the knob and stepped inside.

The once grand house was now clearly in need of love. A wide marble floor spread out in front of her, checked in enormous squares of black and white, looking dusty and dull. An empty desk stood in the center of the foyer. She walked forward, looking left, then right. Rooms opened to either side with wooden floors scuffed and dark, the Oriental carpets faded from hundreds of feet. They were filled with shelves of books and a haphazard collection of tables and chairs. In the room to the right, under a chandelier that promised it might glitter again if only it were given a good cleaning, a small, slender man with heavy, round glasses sat writing at a table, a handful of books spread in front of him. In the room to the left, their faces gone warm and golden in the sun flooding in through the windows, two women sat reading. Margie stood in the foyer, inhaling the smell of books and old wood and dust, and smiled happily.

"Can I help you?" A woman came from one of the rooms at the back, her heels clicking efficiently across the floor.

"I'm here about the job? The American Girls' Club sent me?" Margie said. The woman came up to her, putting out her hand, which Margie shook.

"Excellent. I'm Mary Parsons, the director. And you are?"

"Margie Pearce." Miss Parsons was smooth and elegant, like a Parisian, but her accent was clearly American. She wore a blue dress, belted in at her slender waist. Her hair was held at the back of her neck in a loose bun that somehow still allowed her to look young and chic. Margie touched her own hair self-consciously, tied back in the prim Victorian knot she had always worn, unfashionably demure.

"I'm so glad you've come. They sent another girl, but she was an absolute disaster. You're not an absolute disaster, are you, Margie?" She tossed this statement over her shoulder as she walked back to the desk in the center of the foyer, and Margie stood for a moment, and then, realizing she was supposed to follow, hurried along behind.

"No?" Margie said. She meant it to come out confidently, but it ended up sounding as though she weren't sure whether or not she was an absolute disaster. Living in Paris was so strange—at times she felt as if she were growing at home here, could find her tongue and ask for a baguette or order an omelet or buy a tomato from the lovely man on the corner without being reduced to a quivering aspic herself, could navigate the Métro and walk confidently along the streets without consulting her map like a tourist. Yet here she was, fumbling for words in this outpost of her own country. "I mean, no, I'm not a disaster," Margie said, finding a firmness in her voice she didn't entirely feel.

"Do you know anything about the Libe?" Miss Parsons asked. Margie had assumed she was a Miss; there was no wedding ring on her finger, though she was a good ten years older than Margie. She was confident and pretty and efficient, and modern without being inappropriate, and Margie wanted to sit down and sigh for the longing of wanting to be like her.

"Not really," Margie admitted. Should she? Libraries were glorious places that gave you all the books you ever could read. What else was there to know?

"*Atrum post bellum, ex libris lux,*" Miss Parsons said, as though it were an incantation. Margie, who had fallen asleep in Latin class more than she had stayed awake, wondered if it were. "Do you speak Latin?"

"I'm afraid not." Margie mentally kicked herself for snoozing through Miss Tappan's lessons on declension. It was just that the grammar had been so exhausting, and she had never thought she would need it, not really.

Miss Parsons didn't seem to mind. "'After the darkness of war, the light of books.' That's our motto. The American Library in Paris," she said, settling a stack of papers in front of her and stamping them firmly as she spoke, "was founded in 1920 to house the one-point-three million volumes sent by the Library War Service for the U.S. troops in France. Our purposes are to memorialize the American Expeditionary Force in France, to promote understanding and knowledge of America, and to provide an example of American library methods to the librarians of Europe." Miss Parsons had delivered this entire speech without even looking at Margie, who had perched herself on the edge of one of the chairs in front of the desk, but here she interrupted her paperwork and looked up. "Do you know anything about library methods?" she asked, with rather more interest and hope than she had expressed in Margie's Latin skills.

Margie, who was more and more certain she was failing this interview—was it an interview?—miserably, shook her head. "I was an English major," she said, and then, with genuine enthusiasm, "I really love books!" as though that might make up for her failings.

Miss Parsons only smiled kindly at her. "That's a good start. In any case, we've now got hundreds of members, and while it looks quiet at the moment, it rarely is. We're open twelve hours a day on weekdays and eight hours on Sundays, and just taking care of the people who come in to use the facilities can be a full-time job, let alone cataloging and managing the collection. Your position"—she said this so casually, as though Margie's hiring were a sure thing, and Margie's heart rose a little bit—"is a temporary one, funded by a grant from one of our more generous patrons. It's meant to be focused on some projects we have in the archives, but we're always short-handed, so you'd be doing all kinds of work. The archives, certainly, and working the circulation and reference desk"— she paused her stamping again to pat the desk at which she sat—"and doing whatever needs to be done. We're rather all hands on deck here."

In her mind, Margie was already sitting behind that desk, stamping papers with the same practiced, efficient hand as Miss Parsons, offering the same confident, gentle smile to patrons, helping the man at the table in the one room locate some reference materials and recommending new novels to the two women reading in the other. She was discovering treasures in the archives, presenting them proudly to Miss Parsons, "Look, a first edition of Twain," she might say, or "Do you suppose this is a letter from Emily Dickinson?" She was walking confidently down the street toward the library in her new hat, and her clothes looked much more flattering in her mind than they ever had in reality.

"Is that all right, Margie?"

Margie blinked, pulling herself out of the fantasy in her mind. "I'm sorry, Miss Parsons, could you repeat the question?" she asked.

"Might I ask what you are doing in Paris?" Miss Parsons asked.

"Well, I was supposed to be over here with a cousin of mine, but she has decided to travel alone. And I couldn't bear to leave Paris after only a few days." It sounded more than plausible, and Margie was half tempted to believe it herself. It had the unfortunate side effect of making Evelyn look better, but it also made Margie look less tragic. Miss Parsons put down her stamp and shuffled the papers into an orderly pile. Then she crossed her arms on the desk and leaned forward, looking at Margie more carefully now, taking in her old-fashioned hair underneath the new hat, her wide eyes and too-round cheeks, her dress, which had been sewn for her but, like all Margie's clothes, had turned out ill-fitting anyway. Finally, as though she had seen something that she approved of, Miss Parsons clapped her hands together lightly.

"And how does your family feel about your being here alone?" she asked.

Margie hesitated, only for a moment, yet long enough for Miss Parsons to nod slightly, as though confirming something in her mind. "They'd prefer I come home, but I just couldn't leave, Miss Parsons. I just got here! And there is so much to explore."

"Well, please tell your parents when you write that I will anoint myself your official chaperone and make sure no harm comes to you." She folded her hands as though her pronouncement had settled the matter. "Now, the salary is only five hundred francs a month, I know that's not much, but I presume your family will help support you?"

Margie swallowed hard. Five hundred francs would cover her room and board at the Club, but she would have to be so very careful. Still, it was worth it. It might be romantic, even, living so close to the bone. "I'll get by," she said.

"Fantastic," Miss Parsons said. "Working here is an opportunity to be part of something great. You said you like to read, don't you? You'll meet all the great American writers in Paris—Edith Wharton is one of our founding trustees, you know, and there are writers in and out of here all the time."

Margie, who had read all of Edith Wharton's books with an eye both sympathetic and deeply envious, could have broken out into applause. "That's fine, Miss Parsons. When can I start?"

"How about tomorrow?" she asked. "Oh, here's Dorothy. You'll be working together." A young woman, a few years older than Margie, had come down the stairs, and Miss Parsons waved her over. As frumpy as Margie had felt next to Miss Parsons, it was nothing compared to how she felt next to Dorothy, who was not only tall and slender and chicly dressed, but even more beautiful than Evelyn, though hopefully far less self-involved.

Miss Parsons introduced them and excused herself, hurrying up the stairs, and Dorothy sat down in Miss Parsons' place, leaning forward and resting her head gracefully on her hand. "So what brings you to the Libe?"

"I need a job," Margie said, and then added hurriedly, in case she sounded too desperate, "and I love to read."

"Me too!" Dorothy said, with a level of excitement usually reserved for discovering that what you had in common was an amusingly drinky relation, or a rare allergy, instead of a passion for books. "You'll love working here. We're run off our feet, but being able to get your mitts on any book you like is fabulous. Have you read anything good lately?"

Margie, sure this was a test, hesitated. She ought to name something serious, oughtn't she? Something to impress Dorothy, who probably read terribly complicated things and discussed them with terribly complicated people. *"The Decline of the West?"* She'd seen her father reading it. It had come in two volumes and looked completely exhausting.

"Oh." Dorothy sounded disappointed. "I'm afraid my tastes are a little more lowbrow. I've just finished *Flaming Youth*. I know, I'm so behind, but it's delicious. As scandalous as everyone says."

"I loved *Flaming Youth!*" Margie exclaimed, rather too loudly for a library. She'd absolutely devoured the book from cover to cover in a single afternoon, hiding between the stacks of her library back home. It had seemed so unfair not to have anyone to talk about it with—her mother would have been shocked to find out Margie had read something about girls so fast and forward. She might have been shocked to know anyone would even write such a thing. And all the women Margie knew would only admit to reading instructive, improving books. Being able to talk to someone about the books she actually cared about, the stories she loved, filled Margie with a frothy giddiness that made her shake a little inside. She leaned forward. "Have you read *The Sheik?*"

Dorothy sighed dreamily. "I have. I saw the movie first, and was picturing Valentino the whole time. Though I'll admit, I never thought they'd have a happily ever after."

"Why not?"

"They were so different. And she was so stubborn, at least at first. Personally, I wouldn't mind being kidnapped by a sheik and living out in the desert in the lap of luxury. So exotic. I might even trade Paris for it."

"But they had to end up together," Margie said, somewhat confused. "It was true love. And true love conquers all, doesn't it?"

Dorothy looked at her thoughtfully, as though she had said something deeply controversial. Finally, when Margie was about to start babbling to fill the awkward silence, Dorothy spoke. "I suppose it does."

thirteen

MADELEINE
1999

What had my grandmother done when her life hadn't suited her? When she saw the road ahead of her and realized she didn't want to be on it? She'd gone to Paris. And what was I doing? Lying in my childhood bed, eating a stash of stale Christmas candy I had found in a drawer downstairs, and avoiding my life.

I looked out the window of my bedroom, a dormer, like the ones my grandmother had in Paris, except hers had held a view of the Eiffel Tower and mine a view of the Hoopers' back yard. I was sitting on my bed, pillows stacked behind me, my knees drawn up to hold the notebook for easy reading. If I closed my eyes and inhaled, I could smell my mother's rose garden, and I could almost imagine it was the scent of the roses in the garden at the American Girls' Club, and I was my grandmother, seventy-five years ago, the thrill of adventure and freedom and youth beating in my chest.

Okay, so I wasn't going to go to Paris in the next few hours, but I had endangered my marriage in order to stay here. Was this really the best I could do?

Reading my grandmother's description of Sebastien's hands, I remembered the smudge of paint on Miss Pine's finger, and how, long ago, my own fingernails always had a thin U of paint around the cuticles, no matter how much I scrubbed. There was always paint somewhere on me—a smudge of yellow gluing a lock of my hair together, a drop of blue below my eyes like an errant beauty mark, a stray stroke on my skin where I had let the brush fall as I stepped back to look at the canvas. It was as though art had claimed me, made me its own, and I would bear witness to that passion whether I wanted to or not.

But now I could hardly remember the last time I had painted something. Though I could feel the weight of a brush in my hand, smell the slick, soapy scent of the paint, recall the ache in my muscles when I worked for hours, the strange feeling of time disappearing in a slow, slippery drawl as I slid into the picture, I couldn't remember the last time I had actually done it. My interest in art was charming to Phillip insofar as it made him look more cultured, but when we had first been married, I had mentioned making some space in the condo to paint, and he had refused. Phillip would have objected to the mess, the smell, the distraction. There was no place for my easel, my canvases, he had said.

But here, there was plenty of room.

I padded down the hallway barefoot. My mother was out in her garden, the contractors working up in the attic, and the house was quiet around me as I moved down the stairs, the memory of which ones squeaked coming back to me, as though I were a teenager again, insomnia-struck, sneaking down to the basement to paint. In my adolescent dreams, when I grew up I would have a light-filled studio, dazzling white, like my grandmother's room in Paris, full of air and light to illuminate my paintings, bring a brilliance to them that I never could in the basement of my parents' house. Somewhere along the way, that dream had disappeared.

How is it possible things that are so important to us when we are young somehow fade away? If you had asked me when I was in high school to give up painting, I would have laughed. It would have been like surrendering my heart. And yet I had given it up. There had been no grand ceremony, no renunciation, but it had happened nonetheless, in a small, sad way, a gradual distancing, until one day you might have asked me to stop painting and I would have been struck by its absence. All these things we hold close when we are young, when our emotions roar so loudly the only way to make it through is to live in the voices of other people's hearts, in music loud enough to drown out the wail of our own confusion, in art painted on canvases large enough to capture the whirl of chaos inside us or small enough to fill with the infinite details that explain us, in dance, in poetry, in theater, in art, how do we lose them? Why?

But as I opened the door to the basement and the smell of it rushed up to meet me, filled with more memories than a thousand Parisian rose gardens, something cracked open inside me and I felt young and wild and aching again.

The stairs were the same: wooden and creaking under my weight, with black rubber treads on each step, rough against my bare feet. Nothing had changed in the basement for years; I wondered if my mother ever even came down here. There was a shed in the back for her gardening tools, and most anything valuable was kept in the attic, and all that was here was what had been here for as long as I could remember: two armchairs and a sofa, all in need of reupholstering, old wooden tennis rackets in frames, a croquet set, stacks of cardboard boxes that looked as though they had been packed for a move and then never been opened, now sagging under each other's weight.

And there, in the corner, between two windows that spread shafts of light across the floor like pathways, was my easel. This was where I had painted during high school and college, and when I had moved out, I had bought all new things and left these here. The walls were cinder block, and I had made an attempt to paint a mural on them at some point, which was barely visible now, faded in the damp. Leaning against those walls were a dozen canvases, a few blank, most of them painted. What had happened to the rest of my paintings, my drawings? I must have produced hundreds of them. I had a vague memory of bringing some things down here for storage before I got married, but this couldn't be all of them. Had I simply thrown them away, confident there would always be more, I would always make more?

I flipped through the canvases against the wall. A still life, where I had clearly been trying to master the play of light and the prismatic translucence of a jug of water; a landscape, where I had taught myself perspective. Neither of them exactly good, neither total disasters either. An abstract painting in red and yellow, blocky stripes made with a wide, flat brush, trailing out like vapor toward the edges of the canvas as the paint had run out. I peered at that one for a while, trying to remember what I had wanted to capture. I had never been any good at abstract art, not even when I had learned to understand it, to read it.

Finally, two canvases I remembered, that worked—one, a painting of a corner of my parents' attic. A desk pushed against a window with an ancient typewriter set in the center of it, one of the keys permanently pressed down, a paper slipped over the roll, as though someone had only stepped away for a moment, mid-thought, and would return to finish what they were writing. Whatever I had been searching for in that jug of water I had found here; outside the clear glass of the window there was the colorful blur of my mother's garden, and the sunbeams fell across the floor, illuminating the dust in the air. A spill of photographs spread across the table like a hand of cards, a small box sat on its corner waiting to be opened. Even as I looked at it, I felt the urge to rush upstairs and explore the attic, to look for more of my grandmother's books, to find photos of her when she had been young and in Paris, before she had married my grandfather, to look for more notebooks to see if she had kept writing after she had gotten married, to find the person she had wanted to be underneath the person she had become.

Instead, I flipped to the last painting. It was a self-portrait, me in my debutante dress, sitting in a window seat at the country club, looking out into the night. Behind me, there was a full dance floor, a blur of tuxedos and ball gowns. Ahead of me, there was only the silent night, and I was caught in between. It was a frank portrait, so honest I was surprised I had had the stomach to draw it, my hair beginning to fall and escape its tight and elegant updo, a fold of flesh on my side pressing out against the white silk, my face blank and plain in the dim light, away from the brilliance of the room behind me. I had titled it *Escape,* and as I looked at it, I felt a little hitch in my chest, the quiet threat of tears. I had failed that girl. I hadn't escaped at all. I'd had the chance for freedom, and instead I had run straight into the arms of the life I had known was not for me.

Letting the paintings fall back against the wall, I walked over to a stool in the corner, where the paint-splattered boom box I had listened to all those hours when I painted was still sitting. I flipped it on and pressed Play on the tape deck, and music exploded out of the speakers in a jangle of guitars. At first I laughed, covered my mouth, as though I had unearthed a treasure, and then I wanted to cry, remembering how much these songs had meant to me, how I had spent hours painting to these tapes, not the music they played at school dances, or that the other girls listened to, but music that meant something to me, music that was dark and haunting and beautiful and made everything around me seem more intense, the moon brighter and the night darker and the hours elastic and full of promises they couldn't keep.

I picked up one of the blank canvases, peeled the plastic off it, ran my hand over the surface. It was smooth, the frame still straight, and I lifted it and set it on the easel, admiring its freshness, the emptiness of it. To me, this had always been the best part of starting a painting: the moment before I did anything, the moment before the paint went onto the canvas and began to shape it into something, the moment when the magic of it was all possible, the emotion in my heart and the image in my mind perfectly aligned, before I spoiled it all by actually touching my brush to the fabric.

Under the easel was the tackle box I had kept my paints in. Kneeling down, I began to pull out the tubes. Most of them were acrylic, half used and now dried up, fossils from another age. But at the bottom were three tubes of oil paint, unopened, that still yielded when I pressed on them. I unscrewed the tops and squeezed until I had three small pools of paint on my palette, found some brushes in the utility sink and rinsed them until they were pliable again, and then I stood in front of the easel, looking at that blank canvas, letting an image form in my mind, and I began to paint.

I don't know how much time passed, only that the tape had auto-reversed to play the other side and then, when it had finished, started again, twice over. I sang as I worked, the lyrics as clear in my mind as if I had heard the songs only the day before, like muscle memory, an unforgettable pattern. I was sixteen again and spending Friday night down here alone, I was twenty-one and painting out my fear about the future, I was twelve and learning how to pour my heart onto paper, and I was thirty-four and tired and scared and I put all those things on the canvas in front of me.

"Madeleine? Are you down here?"

Startled, I yanked my brush away from the canvas, bumped into the stool where I had rested the palette, and knocked it onto the floor, where it clattered on the concrete, landing facedown. Of course.

"Yeah," I called back, rescuing the palette from the floor. Well, I thought, looking down at the smears of paint on the concrete floor, it hadn't been the first time. I walked over to the stairs, looking up at my mother.

"What are you doing down there? I've never heard such noise."

"What, the music? I used to listen to this all the time."

"Well, it's terrible. What are you doing?"

"Painting," I said, and a smile pulled across my face, uncontrollable.

"Oh, I forgot you left all those things down there. We should clear them out. Sharon wants the basement empty so it looks like there's more storage."

And there was the sum total of my mother's interest in my painting. Had I expected anything different? My parents had always disapproved of my art. They had said art school was going to be a waste of time and money, because what would I do with that degree? Marry an artist?

Become a painter? There were no artists in my parents' circles. There were only practical, appropriate professions: doctors, teachers, lawyers, investment bankers. Oh, and wives.

So I had gone to college and gotten some quiet, dull degree, and I had wished I were one of the art students, walking across campus in paint-splattered clothes, tiny rocks of clay hardening in my hair. And after graduation I had gotten a quiet, dull job, but I had chosen an apartment with perfect light, where I spent hours alone, painting, as happy as I had ever been.

And then I had gotten married.

"Did you need something?" I asked.

"Yes, I just wanted to tell you I'm going to the library board meeting."

"Godspeed," I said, lifting my paintbrush to my forehead and sketching a salute.

After she closed the door, I walked slowly back over to the easel. It was getting dark, the sun disappearing outside, leaving the basement in shadow. In high school, I had ferreted out some old lamps and set them around my painting area, but when I tried to turn a couple of them on, the bulbs lit and then snapped off immediately, the sound of the filaments breaking sharp in the silence.

The thing was, I thought, giving up on the light and cleaning the brushes and my hands, going through the motions precisely as I had years ago, I didn't want to get rid of anything—not the canvases or the easel or the old brushes. If anything, I wanted more. I wanted to find an art store and come home with a bouquet of fresh, bright oil paints, a fresh new sketch pad, an oversized Filbert brush to paint a hundred wide blue skies. I wanted to feel the way I had when I was painting all the time.

Ever since I had arrived in Magnolia, the heaviness I carried around inside me like a stone had been lifting. It felt, for the first time in a very, very long time, like I was starting to know who I was, instead of who everyone else expected me to be.

fourteen
....

MARGIE
1924

Like my mother and me, Margie and her mother had never been close. And like my mother and me, Margie had always felt a thin thread of disappointment running through their interactions, a knowledge that Margie was not *enough* of anything for her mother's satisfaction. Not pretty enough or ladylike enough or obedient enough. And sometimes outright cruelty isn't necessary. Sometimes all it takes is a lifetime of disapproving glances, of disappointed sighs, of frustrated hopes.

So when she got her mother's reply to her announcement that she was staying in Paris, she couldn't even hope the news would be good.

Reading it, she was only grateful her mother wasn't able to deliver the scathing message in person. Despite her mother's perfect penmanship, Margie could see how hard the pen had been held to the paper, the depressions of the letters and tiny rips signs of the fury behind the words. Margie was disobedient and ungrateful. She was a child who didn't understand the value of security and family. She was unworthy of trust. Margie sat down on the bed in her room, her hands shaking as she read.

Margie didn't think she was being selfish. And she didn't understand her mother's anger. She was supporting herself, wasn't she? Not asking for anything from them. She threw herself back on the bed, draping her elbow over her eyes. "It's so unfair," she said to herself, and she cried a little. She should go home, she thought. Make it all go away. Smooth her mother's ruffled feathers.

"No," she said aloud, sitting up again, wiping the tears from her eyes. The evening sun poured into her room through the windows. This was her adventure. This was her city. And she was here, weeping in this room with the beautiful warm light of Paris on her, while outside the city went on, all the people she had said she wanted to know, the writers and artists, at cafés drinking and talking, making the future happen. Outside, only a few steps down the Boulevard du Montparnasse, were three of the city's most famous cafés—Café du Dôme, Le Select, and La Coupole. Upon hearing Margie was living at the Club, Dorothy had told her those cafés might as well have been the center of art scene in Paris, that people flitted between them, spreading conversation and ideas, and all of that was happening while Margie sat there, alone in her room, feeling sorry for herself. It seemed she had spent so much time locked away alone in her room, missing out on something.

Well, she wasn't going to sit there any longer, she decided. She changed out of her work clothes, hanging her skirt and her jacket carefully. She had only a few suitable outfits for the Libe, and no money to buy any more, so she was trying to be as neat with them as she could so as to keep everyone there from thinking she was the Little Match Girl.

Margie reached up to unclip her hair, letting it fall over her back. Her hair had always been a source of contention between her and her mother. It was like her father's—wavy and heavy—and had to be pressed into submission with hair tonic and a comb at regular intervals throughout the day. Her mother's hair was fine and silky and straight, and it fell cooperatively into any style her mother asked it to, though she rarely asked for anything other than the tidy Victorian knot she had been wearing for as long as Margie could remember. Margie's hair was too thick for regular combs, and the waves had their own ideas about how they wanted to curl and refused the assistance of curling tongs, and it was too heavy to dress up without dozens of hairpins and the liberal application of hair wax. Margie herself had never mastered the talent of wrestling her own hair into submission, and Nellie only tried under duress. When Margie's mother attempted it herself, she would triumph through sheer force of will, at least for a while. And then halfway through dinner, the coif would begin to fail: wisps of curls popping out of the smooth waves her mother had designed, the weight of it slipping backward, as though it were sliding off her head, collapsing into a luxurious pool at the base of her neck.

And now, the weight of it seemed wrong, too much. That hair belonged to the old Margie Pearce, the one Evelyn had called "deadweight" and an "old maid," the one whose only marriage prospects were men as old as her father, the one who lived in her parents' house while outside the world changed and other women had jobs and lives and fell in love. And suddenly Margie wished, wanted, fervently, to be rid of the hair as much as she wanted to be rid of that destiny.

The hotel had delivered her trunk, and Margie rummaged through it until she found a pair of scissors. They were on the small side and designed more for everyday sewing repairs than for cutting off six inches of heavy hair, but they would have to do. Facing herself in the mirror, she pulled her hair back into a ponytail with one hand and began to cut with the other. It was laborious, slow work, and she had to take a break a few times just to put her arms down, her shoulders aching from the awkward position, the scissors doing more gnawing than cutting. When she finished, she shook her head and it was done. She looked dumbly down at the switch of hair in her hand, the strands catching the light as she turned it back and forth, marveling at its size, and then up at herself in the mirror.

It wasn't the neatest of haircuts, she would have been the first to admit, but neither was it the worst. Freed from its own weight, her hair lifted up, curling loosely around her face. Her eyes looked wider and shinier, the curve of her cheeks more cherubic and less chubby. Shaking her head again, letting a few loose, abandoned strands float down onto her shoulders, Margie wondered at the lightness of it, at the way it changed her face. She was going to have to get someone else to even out the back—a hairdresser, or one of the girls in the sun room, but it wasn't half bad. She looked, she thought, still staring at herself in the mirror, almost pretty.

The area immediately around the Club was full of houses and apartments and families, with shops scattered here and there on the ground floor, so when she left that evening, the sidewalks were relatively quiet. People had gone home already, were eating their evening meals with their families, centered around the fresh loaves of bread she saw so many people buying on her walk home from the Libe. Margie strode confidently up to the Boulevard du Montparnasse until she saw the fluttering awning of Café du Dôme. There, she hesitated. She had chatted with a few of the girls at the Club, but hadn't gotten to know any of them, really. Some of them might be here, at one of these cafés, but she wouldn't know them well enough to pull up a chair at a table. And while it was common for people to dine or drink or sit and write at cafés, sometimes for hours during the day, at night the place was much more convivial.

As if reading her mind, a group of young men brushed past her, shouting in conversation as they did. One of them bumped squarely into her from behind, and she took a long step forward to keep from falling. "*Pardon, pardon,*" he said, stopping and turning to check on her, and then, "Marguerite?"

Margie, who had been looking at the sidewalk she had been fairly certain she was going to be pushed into, looked up into the startlingly green eyes of Sebastien. "Oh!" she said, and she blushed a little. Other girls, prettier girls, were used to good-looking men talking to them, she supposed, didn't go silly and red the way she did, weren't flustered and tongue-tied at the tiniest of attentions paid. "*Bonsoir.*"

"*Bonsoir,*" he replied. His friends had paused up ahead, and one of them called out to him in French, which, to her surprise, Margie understood.

"What are you doing there, eh? Leave the pretty girl alone."

"Go on," Sebastien called back. "I'll catch up with you." And Margie felt as though a light had gone on above her, holding her in a comforting glow. She had understood everything they had said, through their accents, through the casual, informal words. It was a miracle.

"What are you doing here?" she asked him.

"I live not far away. That's how I knew about the Club," Sebastien said. "What are you doing here?"

"I live here too."

Sebastien grinned. "*Ah, bien!*" he exclaimed. "You have taken a room at the Club. I knew you would stay. You are meant for Paris. Where are you going now? We are going to Le Dôme—would you like to join us? These are my friends. Some of the most brilliant artists in Paris today. You should meet them, if you are going to be a writer."

If only he hadn't said that, Margie thought. The idea of her sitting at a table with brilliant artists was ridiculous. The idea of her being a writer was ridiculous. If only she hadn't told him. It had been the beautiful day, it had been the child with the bread and the pigeons in the square, the church bells and the flower vendors outside the Métro. Now he would expect her to act in some particular way, some way real writers acted. Not that she would have the faintest idea of what that was—she didn't know any real writers.

But wasn't this what she had wanted? The real Paris, the Paris they wrote about in magazines Margie had gotten hold of at the library at home and devoured, right there in the reading room, where her mother wouldn't be able to ask what sort of trash she was reading. The artists who were making this city the place to be, the place to run to after the sad endlessness of the war, or the simple drudgery of a heavy, empty existence.

Noting her hesitation, Sebastien reached down for her hand. "Come on, then," he said.

Margie, who had held hands with men only in the context of dancing at highly chaperoned affairs, looked down at it doubtfully, then slipped her fingers into his and followed him.

"Your hair looks pretty," he said as they stood, waiting to cross the street.

Reaching up, Margie patted the curls emerging from under her hat, as though they might have been bruised. The feeling of them, light and soft underneath her fingers, reminded her of how she had looked in the mirror, shorn and bare and someone new and lovely, and she smiled as she said, "Thank you."

"So Paris has turned you into a flapper?"

"Oh!" She laughed at the thought of herself as a flapper, lounging around the courtyard with the girls at the Club in one of those flimsy little dresses, a cigarette in one hand and a flask of gin in the other. "No, not a flapper. I just didn't want to have long hair anymore." It was a good enough explanation.

"It suits you," he said.

She blushed a little at the compliment. "Thank you." They crossed the street to Le Dôme, Sebastien's hand still warm and solid around hers, and ducked under the awning where his friends were settling in, pushing tables and chairs together, absorbing people they knew from other tables into the group, taking off their jackets and hats, someone producing ashtrays and distributing glasses. As Margie and Sebastien joined them, a waiter appeared, bearing bottles of wine. Two of the men took the bottles from him and began pouring, and Sebastien pressed a glass into Margie's hand as they sat down.

"This is Marguerite." He spoke in French, introducing her to those who were paying attention and pointing out and naming the others who were already distracted by their own conversations. She listened to the brief biographies he sketched of them, feeling anxious and envious, wondering how these men and women had done so much already. They seemed to be so accomplished—ones who had exhibited at galleries or prominent shows, others who had studied with masters, and all of them doing something exciting, something brave and new, making space for themselves without waiting for an invitation.

A curious mix of people sat at the table, some Americans, some French, an Englishman, and two Russian girls. The blur of languages was ridiculous; the common tongues were French and English, but there were a dozen accents, and the Russians spoke in asides to each other, and at the end of the collection of tables a woman and a man were having an enthusiastic conversation in what sounded like Spanish. Their names were a blur, their faces complex and glamorous in a way Margie couldn't yet distinguish. One of the men was so blond his skin looked like parchment, his eyes a unique and intensely pale blue. One of the Russian women had cheekbones like knives, sharp slashes across her face, and arms so slender Margie could have encircled them with her fingers.

"Sebastien, Sebastien." One of the men across the table, René, snapped his fingers at him. Three of them had their heads bent together over a notebook. "*Écoutez*," he demanded. "*Si vous aimez l'amour, vous aimerez le Surréalisme.*" He spoke these words like a grand proclamation, and then collapsed back in his chair and took a large gulp of wine as though the act had exhausted him.

"*Bon, bon*," Sebastien said, with a little applause, and then, in English to Margie, "Did you understand?"

"If you like love, you'll love Surrealism?" Margie asked. She had read articles about these art movements in Paris without entirely understanding them. They described things incomprehensible to her—Margie shared none of the Surrealists' anxiety about their art, none of their desperate need to make meaning of things by taking all the meaning from them. She had read a piece by a Surrealist writer that she hadn't understood at all; it just seemed like words strung together. Margie, who liked stories about people who found the love she longed for herself, stories about people who were broken and then made themselves whole again, had read that and felt a strong desire to lie down.

"*Oui!*" Sebastien said, and he looked so pleased by her tiny feat of translation she was almost embarrassed, and made an immediate vow to work more on her French. She would spend her lunch hours reading *Le Temps*, the newspaper, with her dictionary by her side, and eavesdrop as much as possible in cafés. "They are opening a center for Surrealism, and René is creating these cards they will spread all over Paris, inviting people to come into the center and share their dreams."

"We believe," René said, leaning forward again and stroking his mustache with his thumb and forefinger—he was speaking French, and Margie braced herself, but he spoke slowly, thoughtfully, giving her time to catch up, "that dreams are the only place where the mind is truly honest. In our dreams we can find all our unexpressed desires, and our collective wisdom."

"I see?" Margie said, imagining René, who was handsome but still had the soft cheeks of a boy, sitting attentively at a desk with a pen and ledger, while people sat across from him, relating their dreams, ". . . and then there was this giant flying mouse with the face of my husband, except it wasn't my husband's face, but I know it was him, you see . . ." But she didn't know why this would be useful. She could barely understand her own dreams; she had no idea why anyone else would be interested in them.

"*Écoutez, écoutez,*" one of the men sitting next to René said, abruptly sitting forward as though he had simply been observing and had suddenly decided to join the conversation. Margie thought Sebastien might have called him Georges. His hair fell forward into his face like Sebastien's, though this seemed to be more from a general lack of combing than from any stylistic decision, and he wore a monocle, as though he were one of Margie's disapproving great-uncles. She suspected he might not need the monocle, that he simply thought it made him look smarter, though Margie thought it only made him look nearsighted. *"Le Surréalisme, c'est l'écriture niée,"* he said, holding his hands out in front of him as though laying each word in place.

"Ahhh," his companions sighed, and applauded for him. Sebastien nodded, leaning back and lifting his glass of wine. Everything he did was so smooth, his long fingers and long limbs graceful as a dancer.

"C'est vrai, c'est vrai," René said sadly—it's true, it's true—as though his friend had just pronounced the wisdom of the ages.

"What does *niée* mean?" Margie whispered to Sebastien.

"It is something not permitted. Denied?" he asked.

Surrealism is writing denied? Now they were really making no sense at all. Margie felt as though she were in the library again, poring over that Gertrude Stein piece and wanting to weep for a good love story. Georges and René had bent their heads together again over the notebook and were fashioning some other impenetrable sentence. She supposed it was a clever idea. Handing out these business cards would definitely make people wonder what on earth they meant, but she doubted people would seek out the office in particular to inquire. Then again, people did all sorts of silly things to pass the time. And while part of her felt as though she should be ashamed of herself in comparison to their limitless imaginations, another part of her saw how much they were the same. The Surrealists were dreamers, just like she was.

"How is your English so good?" she asked Sebastien, instead of pursuing the meaning of another Surrealist proclamation.

"My father is English. And of course I studied it in school. And now look how helpful it is—I can talk to American girls all the time!" He laughed, this rich, inviting sound that made Margie want to curl up inside him, if only to be so close to such happiness. The Russian women at the end of the table looked annoyed by the noise, and she was half tempted to stick her tongue out at them. She didn't want people who thought happiness was something to be sneered at polluting the party. Because here she was. Sitting in a café in Paris with bobbed hair, drinking wine with actual artists, talking about Surrealism, with a good-looking man by her side. If only Evelyn could see her now. If only Lucinda from Abbott Academy who had said she was too quiet, a dud, could see her now. If only her mother . . . well, she'd prefer her mother not see her now, she wouldn't understand, but still.

"Do you always talk to American girls?"

"There are so many of you," Sebastien said. "You are difficult to avoid." She could tell he was teasing, the little light in his eyes, the way his eyebrow was raised ever so slightly. And he was right, after all—they were everywhere. Even if she ignored the fact that she lived at the Club and worked at an American library, she heard American accents around her all the time; drawling their way through transactions at shops and cafés, chatting as they walked down streets, the inimitable casual loudness that marked her people.

"Why are so many Americans here now?" she asked him.

"Why are you here?"

Margie shrugged her shoulders, self-conscious. "Freedom, I suppose. It's so far away from everything. And it's, you know, Paris."

"Well." Sebastien spread his arms slightly, his wine glass tilting, as if to indicate the entirety of the city.

"I know. But we can't all possibly have something to run from, can we? Some people must be happy just to stay where they are."

"No, no. That is not human nature. We are all trying to escape something. Some people do it by moving to Paris. Some of us do it through our art." He gestured here to the Surrealists, who had apparently come up with a cracking good joke and were laughing and clapping each other on the back over it. "Some of us do it through wine, or money. No matter how, we're all trying to escape something."

"Ourselves," Margie said. She could see herself reflected in the plate-glass window of Le Dôme, behind the Surrealists. Her hair was new, her hat was new, and there was a look in her eyes that felt new as well, a brightness she had never seen before. Had Paris made her someone different? Or was she the same old Margie, disguised with a new hat and a glass of wine in her hand, pretending to be someone she could never hope to be? "We are all trying to escape ourselves."

fifteen

MADELEINE
1999

After painting until my fingers ached, I stood in the driveway, listening to the quiet of the neighborhood, the brush of wind through the trees, the shush of a car passing by on the street. Next door, I could see dinner was winding down; the parking lot was half deserted, the noise floating over the hedges emptier somehow. But they were definitely still open. And I was starving. And the fact that my patronizing Henry's restaurant would upset my mother made the idea of dinner there even more appealing. Well, she had driven me to it. I hadn't gone to the grocery store, so there was still nothing to eat in her house, and my strawberries-and-crackers diet book would sell exactly zero copies.

I went back inside and grabbed my purse and, after a moment's hesitation, one of my grandmother's notebooks. My father, a devoted bookworm, had carried *The Wall Street Journal* with him everywhere he went, and had more than once been nabbed by my mother hiding out at a party (and occasionally during the symphony) behind its pages. "Never be caught without something to read," he had admonished me from the time I was a child. And so I toted books with me everywhere, especially places where I learned I might need a little distraction: *The Story of Ferdinand* to Christmas Eve services at church, Nancy Drew to the doctor's office, novels to cotillion teas, where I learned to hide the paperbacks carefully under the edge of the tablecloth so I could read and pretend to be paying attention at the same time. That skill had served me well all through high school and at the Junior Ladies Association functions, where the other girls tried to imitate their mothers' bizarre fascination with committee meetings and I worked my way through Jane Austen, sneezing to cover up my snickering. For years, everyone thought I had a severe allergy problem.

Despite my mother's newfound romanticization of them as the apogee of neighbors, the Schulers hadn't taken great care of the house. For years, she had tutted over the wood in need of repainting, the yard that was never kept to her satisfaction, the brick front walk that could have used a good acquaintance with a mason. Now I could see, as I walked over the path by the new parking lot, that Henry had changed all that. The house had been repainted, the hedges and grass were neatly clipped, the bricks on the walk had been removed and replaced with smooth, even flagstones. A subtle sign hung above the front porch steps, painted in elegant script: *The Kitchen*. The front porch, now empty, was filled with small clusters of wicker furniture, where people could wait for a table. I opened the front door, which had been repainted an inviting red, and stepped inside.

"Whoa, are you here for dinner?" A young man stood behind the host desk, though I thought he might have felt more at home on a surfboard. His hair was gelled into crisp spikes and he had wide, round eyes that made him look as though life were handing him a series of unbelievable surprises.

"Erm, yes?" I said, unsure how to respond to such a greeting.

"It's kind of late," he said doubtfully.

"I'm aware of that. Are you still serving dinner?"

"Yeah!" He brightened. "Would you like a table?"

"I would."

"For two?" he asked, peering around me as though someone might be hiding behind me, ready to engage him in a game of peekaboo.

"No," I said slowly, because I was beginning to guess that's the speed at which he best operated. "Just the one."

As he processed this new information, a waitress walked by carrying a tray full of food, including a cheeseburger piled so high with fixings that it wore the top half of its bun like a jaunty beret. The smell of it exploded as she moved, the food held high in the air like an offering, and it smelled so rich and delicious I would have fallen to my knees and begged for it if it would have made a difference.

Fortunately, it wasn't necessary. "Follow me," he said, picking up a menu and turning toward a side room.

I remembered the layout of the Schulers' house immediately—over there would have been the dining room, and we were passing through the hallway toward the back, where the living room had been. A bar, made of dark wood gone shiny from use, had been built in the front room, where there were a couple of small tables looking over the front porch, and as we passed by the staircase, a server came running down with an empty tray. Had the Schulers known, I wondered, what was going to happen to their house when they sold it? Or, like my mother, had they pictured another happy family taking over, another line of generations stretching into the future, raised between these walls, playing in the yard, family dinners on the back porch during summer as night fell and the fireflies gave chase around the grass? I wondered if anyone had told them the house had become The Kitchen. Antique photos marched along the walls, other people's lives now designated as decoration for ours.

As we passed by the kitchen, the door swung open and Henry came out. Distracted by looking at the fresh paint and the photographs of someone's abandoned ancestors on the wall, I walked right into him.

"Oof," I said.

"Oof," he said, and then in recognition, after we had bounced off each other like human pinballs, "Hey! How are you?"

"Hungry."

"She's kind of late for dinner," the host said. It had taken him a half-dozen steps to realize I wasn't following him, and he was already standing beyond the archway leading to the living room on one side and what had been the study on the other.

"Austin, we serve until eleven. People can eat whenever they want," Henry said. He strode over and gently took the menu from the boy's hands. "Would you please go back to the host stand and check to see if anyone's waiting, and then finish bringing up the glasses?"

"Hey, okay!" Austin said, as though this were a brilliant idea, and trotted back past us toward the front of the house.

"I'm sorry about him. I had a couple of servers call in sick, so we're a little short-handed. He's actually a bar-back, and a good one, but as a host, he's . . . problematic."

"Give me a cheeseburger and all will be forgiven. I've been painting for hours."

"You've got a little paint right here," Henry said, tapping his thumb on his cheek and I reached up, embarrassed, to scrape it away with my fingernails. "Are you painting to get the house ready?"

"No, no. Painting like art."

"You're a painter, your mother's a gardener. Art runs in the family, I guess," he said, making a "Come on" wave with the menu. I was surprised—I'd never made the connection between my mother's gardening and my painting, but hadn't I learned about color from gladiolus and phlox, about repetition of form from ornamental cabbages, about texture from lamb's ear and dill? Maybe I owed more to her than I thought.

Henry led me back into what had been the Schulers' living room, now cozily filled with tables, most of them empty by now. In one corner, a couple leaned together, their conversation tense and low. Across from them, a table of four was finishing up their desserts, leaning back in their chairs in satisfaction. It looked like they had demolished something chocolate, and I restrained myself from grabbing the plate and licking it.

Note to self: Buy some damn groceries. "How's this?" We had arrived at a table in the corner of the back room.

"This is great, actually," I said. Henry pulled out a chair and I slid into it.

"I'll get a cheeseburger going for you pronto. Medium? You want a salad while you wait?"

"Please and thank you."

He clicked his heels together like a butler and headed off toward the kitchen. A few minutes later, a waitress, a little wisp of a girl, pale and delicate in her all-black uniform, came by bearing a water glass and a salad. I had barely finished it when the burger arrived, and it was as amazing as it had smelled, so high I had to smash it down to get it into my mouth, a perfect balance of salt and crisp vegetables and a sweet-and-sour spread on the bun that puckered my tongue. I was fairly sure I could have eaten another one.

By the time I finished the burger, the room had emptied. I dragged the last of the French fries lazily through ketchup with one hand as I wiped off the other and used it to open my grandmother's notebook, disappearing back into her story.

I had just finished reading my grandmother's report on her evening with the Surrealists when Henry arrived. "Mind if I join you?" he asked, and then, without waiting for my answer, spread his hands on the table and slid into the chair opposite mine with an audible sigh of relief. "What a night. How was your dinner?"

Pulling myself out of the Jazz Age and into the present, I refocused, looking over at my plate, now entirely empty except for a few crumbs and the thin remnants of a pool of ketchup. "Horrible," I said.

"Clearly. You want some dessert? There's a really great apple cobbler with homemade vanilla ice cream, or a moist chocolate lava cake, with this fabulous chocolate sauce in the center that oozes all over the place when you put your spoon into it."

In my head, my mother admonished me not to eat dessert, pointing out how easily I gained weight, and that it wasn't appropriate to eat dessert in front of a man.

I told my mother I was having a tough time of it and a little chocolate would help.

My mother informed me that this was eating my feelings.

Yes, I agreed. Yes, it was.

"I want that chocolate thing, with the moist and the ooze," I said.

Henry nodded. "An excellent choice. Ava," he said, raising his hand to call over the waitress who had brought me the salad. "Would you please bring us a chocolate lava cake?"

"On it," she said, and disappeared again.

"So what are you reading?"

I flipped back to the cover, as though to show him the title, but of course there was only the blank front of the notebook. "It's interesting, actually. These are some of my grandmother's journals. I'm reading about this trip she took to Paris in 1924."

"Paris in 1924? Like, F. Scott Fitzgerald Paris? Hemingway Paris?"

"I don't think she was hanging with Hemingway exactly. At least not that she's mentioned. But she was definitely enjoying herself. Before, she was this quiet, bookish wallflower, and now she's hanging out at cafés with artists and bobbing her hair."

"Maybe she changed."

"Maybe," I said slowly, closing the notebook and running my finger along the edge, as if to seal the words inside. And then she must have changed again, because the grandmother I knew hadn't been like this at all. My grandmother had been like my mother—stiff and formal, judgmental and proper. What had happened to her? Why had she come back from Paris? And how had she turned from this fun-loving girl who drank with Surrealists and loved books and writing and couldn't bear committee meetings into . . . well, into my mother?

"It's been funny reading these, getting this look inside her. I mean, I'm sure she was different when she was younger. And these were her journals, so she was pretty unguarded. You don't get to see that kind of honesty often."

"Or ever," Henry said. "Does it make you feel guilty? Reading her private thoughts?"

"I guess I hadn't really thought about it. Now I do feel guilty. Thanks a lot."

Henry laughed. "I don't think you have to. Is she still alive? Your grandmother?"

"Oh, no. She died when I was in junior high—I didn't really know her well."

"So this is a way of connecting with her."

"I guess. It is changing the way I think about her. It feels like a novel, reading it. Living in those times. Going to Paris, for heaven's sake. In 1924! Who does that?"

"Well, the aforementioned Hemingway, for one." Leaning back, Henry clasped his fingers together behind his neck. His arms were broad, with wide tendons that flexed when he moved, and I had to pull my eyes away.

"Not Hemingway people. Real people."

"She was lucky. I would love to have been in Paris then. I'd love to be in Paris now."

"You and me both, my friend. Anyway, she's met this artist who sounds really charming."

"Maybe she'll have a wild affair. That would be romantic."

"I guess so. I don't know how that would work out—she married my grandfather in 1924, and my mother was born in 1925. So something happened."

"1925, huh? You must have been a late baby."

"I was. My mother was forty when I was born, which was crazy uncommon back then. My parents had given up on having kids and then"—I shot my hands in the air and wiggled my fingers like a magician—"ta-da!"

"I was a surprise too," Henry said. "At the opposite end. My parents were in high school. Ta-da!" He waved his hands back at me and I had to laugh.

"Still, you seem to have turned out all right."

He shrugged. "They were lucky. They had a lot of support from their parents, and they happened to stay in love. I've got five younger siblings."

"I'm jealous. I always wanted brothers and sisters. Well, sisters, mostly. But I would have taken either."

"They're pretty great. But there were times being an only child would have been great."

"Ugh. Why do people with brothers and sisters always say that? Being an only child is boring. And lonely."

"Being one of six has its own issues, trust me. Grass is always greener," Henry said, and then looked up as Ava arrived at the table. She set a wide, shallow bowl in front of me with the promised dessert, and I could feel the rush of warm, chocolate-scented steam rise up toward me. It was beautiful, a perfect tiny cake with fluted edges and a dark pool of melted chocolate, a shade darker, in the center. The ice cream, flecked with specks of vanilla beans, sat off to the side, melting daintily around the edges of the cake.

"Oh. My. God. I just want to go face-first into this thing."

"Exactly the compliment a chef likes to hear," Henry said.

"And this is for you." Ava put a large and impolitely full glass of red wine down in front of Henry.

"Bless you, my child," he said, lifting the glass carefully to avoid spilling it, and taking a sip while she refilled my water.

"Anything else?" she asked.

"That's it. Thank you. As you were."

She nodded and walked back toward the kitchen while I stared at the cake, mesmerized. Taking the first bite, I closed my eyes and moaned in pleasure. The cake was sweet, the center ever so slightly bitter, and together they melted luxuriously on my tongue.

"Good?" Henry asked, smiling behind his wine glass.

"Amazing. Has anyone ever said you should do this for a living?"

"Once or twice. But you can tell me again."

I sighed, took another bite of cake, scooping up some of the ice cream on the tip of the spoon and swallowing, closing my eyes again to enjoy it. I was going to have a terrible sugar hangover the next day, and it was going to be worth every second. "You should do this for a living."

"I'll think about it."

Pausing between bites, I put the head of the spoon into the cake and looked up at Henry. He looked tired, like he'd been working since the crack of dawn, which he probably had. I'd never worked in a restaurant, but I had always thought it would be so exhausting—the physical back and forth, the bending and lifting, juggling orders, constantly making and remaking schedules, prioritizing and reprioritizing, remembering drink and dish instructions, birthday wishes, and special requests.

Because of that, I was an overly generous tipper. Phillip was a stingy one—"If they wanted to make good money, they should have stayed in school," he would say, which I always found infuriating, as though it weren't a perfectly important and necessary occupation—who, after all, would bring him his Caesar salad if everyone went to law school?—and I had been known to sneak back to the table as we were leaving a restaurant under the guise of having forgotten a scarf or my gloves in order to give a larger tip.

"Am I keeping you from working?" I asked.

"Nah, it's nice to have a break. I like talking to you. You're funny. And you're interesting."

I peered at him suspiciously, licking my spoon. "Me? I'm not interesting."

"Sure you are. You're an artist, and you eat strawberries straight out of the garden for breakfast, and other than the art, you're so different from your mother you might as well be from different planets. I like being around interesting people. Keeps me creative."

"Me too," I said.

Henry sipped his wine, looking at me thoughtfully. I went back to the lava cake to avoid his gaze. "How long are you staying?"

"I don't know." I didn't want to think about leaving, honestly. I wanted to be here, with Sharon and Cassandra and Wanee and their friends. I wanted to be with Henry, who had fed me dinner and now the best dessert I'd ever had, and who talked to me like I mattered. And I liked talking to him. He made me laugh, and he got my jokes. In most of my life, I felt as though I were following a script, like I couldn't say any of the things I wanted to say. I couldn't even say them to Phillip.

"I wish I could help," he said.

"You have helped." I had finished the dessert and was casting longing glances at the plate. "You gave me really amazing food in my hour of need."

"They do have grocery stores in Magnolia now, you know," Henry said. He put down his wine glass and leaned back in the chair, slipping his hands into his pockets and stretching his feet out to the side of the table.

"I hear. And also indoor plumbing. My, how things have changed since my day." I pretended to flutter my eyelashes.

"You're welcome to eat every meal here, but as Sharon pointed out, we don't serve breakfast."

"I could eat this for breakfast," I said, pointing at the remnants of my lava cake.

"Fair enough. The Kitchen Gastropub, now open for lunch, dinner, Sunday brunch, and diabetic comas."

"That's catchy."

"Thank you. Doesn't your mother feed you anything?"

"Ugh, it's a long story." I wasn't about to spoil the mood and the sweetness on my tongue by launching into a long recounting of my mother's and Phillip's endless efforts to control what I ate, and my own chocolate-fueled rebellions. "It's just nice to eat something real."

"My pleasure."

"I should get going," I said, reluctantly pushing myself away from the table. "Should I pay Ava?"

"Nope. It's on the house, remember? I invited you."

"No, I couldn't! You have to work next door to my mother; the least I can do is pay for the hamburger."

"Don't be silly. We're neighbors. I told you, it's on me. Come on, I'll walk you out. I'm going to stay and help them finish closing up."

Before I could object again, he had crossed the room in three quick, long strides and was standing by the entry to the hallway. I left a tip on the table for Ava, picked up my things, and hurried after him. "The restaurant really looks amazing," I said. The rest of the rooms were empty, and I could hear singing and laughter and the sounds of cleaning from the kitchen as we passed by. "You did an incredible job."

"Thank you," he said. "But it's not just me. A whole lot of people have worked their tails off to make it happen." He held the front door open for me, and we stepped out onto the porch. Ava was wiping down the chairs and tables here, and I gave her a little wave.

"Well. Thank you for dinner. I owe you a favor, I guess."

"Not necessary. And if you can't make it to the grocery store, I'll whip up a breakfast lava cake for you anytime you like."

"It's a deal. It was a pleasure," I said, and I stuck out my hand for him to shake.

He took it, closing his hand warmly over mine. "The pleasure was all mine, Madam Spencer," he replied, sketching a slight bow.

I giggled and gave an awkward little wave, and managed to make it down the front steps without tripping. A burger with Henry wasn't exactly the same as wine with Surrealists at a Parisian café, but somehow I thought my grandmother might approve. Pausing on the sidewalk under an oak with a thick trunk obscuring the view of my mother's house, I let myself linger for a moment, the darkness making me feel as though I was hovering between two places, floating in space.

The thing was, though, my grandmother hadn't stayed in Paris. At some point she had given up and gone home, married Robert Walsh and become a mother instead of having affairs with delicious French men and writing stories in Paris, though I didn't know why. Was that what I was going to have to do? The thought made the air feel thick and I pushed my hands against my stomach as though I could force my breath through. The Kitchen wasn't a Parisian café, and my mother's basement wasn't a Parisian studio, but it felt closer to that kind of freedom than I had known in a long, long time, and I couldn't bear to imagine I would come so close only to have it disappear when I tried to close my hand around it.

sixteen

MARGIE
1924

In Margie's opinion, the Libe was really the most fantastic place to work. Her coworkers were fascinating: there was Miss Parsons, of course, who had been a nurse during the war and now practically ran the place. And then there was Dorothy, who had cleaned up the messy edges of Margie's haircut and told her she looked positively dishy, just like Zelda Fitzgerald, which had made Margie blush with pleasure. In her letters to her parents, Margie had made sure to mention that Dorothy's uncle was the president of Cornell and her father was a professor at Princeton, but she didn't mention how beautiful Dorothy was, or that she went out with a different man every night of the week, it seemed. Every time Margie saw her, she felt surprised anew that Dorothy spent her day here shelving books that had been passed around the hospitals and barracks and trenches during the war, and talking to Margie and the patrons, as though she weren't something rare and lovely and altogether different. There was Olav, a Russian prince who seemed to have lost his way and his fortune, and one of the board of directors, Mr. Alsop, who was always in meetings and terribly busy, and who called Margie "Mary," which she decided was close enough.

Sometimes, when she was putting a book on the shelves, Margie imagined the people who had held it before. A handsome young soldier who had died before his time. A war-weary general, looking for respite from the stress of his job in the pages of Zane Grey. A fierce-minded young nurse like Miss Parsons, who had joined the war effort because she wanted to contribute, and found herself exhausted and haunted by the things it had asked of her. Sometimes Margie put those imaginary people in scenarios together, the general and the young soldier facing off over a matter of honor, the nurse tending to the soldier before his death. And sometimes she just let them be, and she imagined all the times the book she held had told its story, and she put it on the shelf where it could fall into someone else's hands and tell it once more.

The library had been an effort to manage the enormous number of volumes that had been collected by the Library War Service, once there was no longer a war. They collected three volumes of each book that had been sent out, but more boxes arrived each day, as though people were still sorting through the rubble and saying, "What's this here? More books? Better send them to Paris!" And it seemed some days even the boxes and boxes of unpacked books, to say nothing of all the ones on the shelves, would never be enough. The library had hundreds of members, and though it had been quiet the day Margie had first gone in, as Miss Parsons had predicted, she had never seen it that way since. The Libe was something of a social club for expatriates in the city, a place where they could shut out their differences for a while and luxuriate in their own language. There were writers, of course, some of whom frequented both Sylvia Beach's Shakespeare & Company bookstore and the library. And there were academics, university students desperate for answers they could find without resorting to their *Petit Larousse* for awkward translations, and there were readers, the ones Margie liked best of all, who simply came in, hungry for book after book after book, who sometimes wanted to talk about what they had read, or ask for recommendations, and Margie, who had never had anyone to talk to about all the books she read, so many books she couldn't remember them all if she tried, was in heaven.

One Saturday it was only her and Dorothy together when they closed down for the night, and Dorothy said, "Hey, let's go have a little dinner, what do you say?"

Margie, who was dressed in a simple shirtwaist and skirt and a pair of stockings with a run in them (she'd tried to hide it by turning that part to the inside, but she felt it every time she walked), looked down at herself. "I'm not really dressed to go out, am I?" she asked.

"Neither am I." But of course Dorothy looked gorgeous, wearing a fashionable green dress that set off her eyes and didn't show a speck of dirt, as though she hadn't been working with the same dusty old books as Margie all day. "But we can stop by your place if you'd like to change," she offered, taking in Margie's stricken expression.

"That would be better," Margie said. And though she usually walked home to save the carfare, she was too embarrassed to admit it to Dorothy. They took the tram, as Dorothy said the Métro was too slow for her, to the Club, and Dorothy waited in the courtyard, smoking and talking with some of the girls there as though she'd known them for years, while Margie changed into her good blue crêpe de chine dress.

She picked Dorothy up from the courtyard and they headed down the street to Rosalie's. Everyone talked about Rosalie's, a tiny restaurant in the basement of a corner building only a few blocks from the Club, but Margie had never been, and when they arrived, she was torn between being thrilled they had and wishing they hadn't. The place was filthy—the floor covered with undiscovered countries of spills, some of which sucked at her feet as they made their way between the tables. When they sat down, Dorothy, who looked so out of place in the dark and dirty room, like a firefly glowing in a dustbin, took a handkerchief from her bag and carefully wiped the previous diners' crumbs from the table.

Despite the grimy appearance, it was an exciting, lively place to be— the men next to her with paint splatters on their shirt cuffs, two of the Surrealists from the café having dinner with two other men, their heads bent together conspiratorially, a gaggle of young girls in fashionable dresses, edged with shimmers of beads and tassels, making it seem as though they were endlessly in motion, laughing loud and wild in the corner. As was always the case in Paris, everyone here seemed to know everybody else, people coming in stopping to greet friends with shouts of pleasure, as though they hadn't seen each other in years, though Margie guessed, given how small Montparnasse—and Paris in general—seemed to be, it might have been twenty-four hours at the most. There were long tables and benches, and when a newcomer decided to join his friends, everyone would shuffle agreeably to one side or another, the shape and form of the groups shifting, expanding and contracting, the pulse of the evening like a giant beating heart.

The menu was written on a chalkboard on the wall, dinner for two francs, which was ridiculously cheap, even for Paris, and was delivered by Rosalie herself, a short, stout woman with heavily accented French. The food was achingly good, and when they finished, Margie felt like she had been part of the real Paris again, and, more important, was almost full.

Ever since she had gotten to Paris, she had been hungry constantly. It was all the walking, she thought, much more than she was used to at home, where her mother insisted on taxicabs to carry them anywhere more than a few blocks in the city, due to her bad feet. And certainly it was the student portions on which she lived, trying to save money, eating what was cheap—bread her body ran through in moments, and inexpensive vegetable soup. She had walked by a café one day and seen a man dining on a sausage covered with mustard so spicy just the scent of it made her mouth water, and drinking a beer, and Margie, who didn't even like beer, had almost wept with desire. Her savings meant she could splash out on a meal here and there, but there was an asceticism to her diet she found attractive, the constant rumble in her stomach a metaphor for her appetite for the city and all she wanted to draw from it, and she preferred to leave herself slightly hungry.

"So," Dorothy said, when they had finished dinner and were drinking the last of the cheap wine that had come with it. It was sweet and slightly vinegary, but Margie was thirsty and it left a pleasant blur in her head that she wanted to hang on to. It made her love everyone in the room, these strangers with their theatrical greetings, their intense conversations, the laughter exploding and then disappearing into the crush of bodies, even the room itself despite—or because of—its dungeon-like air. "What are you doing in Paris?"

Margie hesitated, unsure of how to answer. Dorothy leaned forward over the table, as though she were expecting some thrilling confession, and Margie hated to disappoint her. In the dim light, she practically glowed, and Margie had seen half the men in the place looking over at her. Dorothy, of course, ignored the attention, or worse, didn't seem to notice. That was always the way with beautiful girls. "I'm working at the Libe."

Rolling her eyes, Dorothy pressed her hands flat on the table and leaned even closer, as though proximity could pull Margie's nonexistent secrets out of her. "I don't mean that. I mean why are you here to begin with? Why did you come?"

"I guess . . . I wanted an adventure?"

This answer seemed to satisfy Dorothy. She sat back up and slapped the table with her open palms, as if to say, "I knew it."

"Me too," she said. "I was going to go crazy at home. My parents want me to get married, but I wasn't ready to settle down. They said I could come over here for a year. It's been two already and I'm still not ready to leave."

"They don't mind?" Margie asked. Was there some secret to managing one's disapproving parents she hadn't yet learned?

"Of course they mind." Dorothy threw her head back and laughed gaily. One of the painters sitting by them glanced at the tender skin of Dorothy's throat with a hot flash of desire that made Margie's stomach flip. Imagine having someone look at you that way, she thought. Imagine having *everyone* look at you that way. "But what can they do? They can't make me come home. I've got my inheritance and my salary at the Libe. Besides, there's no one to marry at home. All the interesting men are in Paris anyway, don't you think?"

"When do you think you'll get married, then?" Margie asked. Because you had to get married eventually, didn't you? For all her talk, she knew everyone did get married, even if it was to someone like Mr. Chapman, who was old and stodgy and didn't love her any more than she loved him, which was not at all.

"Someday," Dorothy said with a breezy wave. It was the tone of a woman who knew she would always have plenty of opportunities to get married, who might not stay young but would always be beautiful and rich and smart and funny and charming, while Margie was only a few of those things and, it seemed, the ones that didn't really matter. "What about you?"

"I don't know," Margie said, trying to match Dorothy's casual tone. She wasn't about to confess to beautiful, confident Dorothy that her best odds of getting married were to a short, nervous business associate of her father's who was nearly old enough to be her father himself.

"I'm not getting married unless I'm really in love. Like in an Ethel M. Dell novel. Have you read her books? So romantic!"

"Yes!" Margie said. "She's one of my favorites."

"I just adore a good love story." Dorothy rested her elbow on the table despite its stickiness and put her head in her hand, her eyes gone soft and dreamy. "Don't you?"

"I do," Margie said, and as much as the two of them had chatted about the books they had read and loved or hated, saying this aloud still felt like a confession. "My mother always said they were silly. I mean, she thinks all novels are silly. If it's not 'edifying,' it's a waste of time to her. Love stories especially. I feel so wicked when I read them, like I should be reading something better."

Dorothy shook her head so her curls bounced prettily. "What's better than a love story?"

"You know what I mean. Not better as in more fun to read. Better as in more important." Margie ran her fingers along the edge of the table until she encountered something sticky, and then withdrew her hands and put them in her lap.

"That's what I mean too. What's more important than love? What's silly about Paris and Helen of Troy? Or Romeo and Juliet? Or Orpheus and Eurydice? Or Troilus and Cressida?"

"Nothing, I suppose," Margie said. When Dorothy put it that way, it didn't make any sense, the way she'd hidden what she was reading inside something weightier (and infinitely duller), the way she had read entire books in the dustiest, most ignored corner of the library to avoid taking them home and risking her mother's judgment, the faint but persistent shade of shame she'd felt every time she'd written a love story of her own. What was the difference between the love stories she wrote and the ones Dorothy had named, other than the patina of age giving everything a brassy air of respectability? What was so wrong with stories about the greatest emotion any of us would ever know?

"So." Dorothy widened her eyes and leaned forward again. "What shall we do tonight? Go to Harry's? Or La Rotonde? Or maybe Zelli's?"

"I don't mind." Margie shrugged. She had never been to any of those places. She had never even been in a nightclub. She had always thought they were dangerous, dark and smoky places, where people were drunk, drunker than you could get on wine at a café, or even in a bar.

"Where have you been? Let's go somewhere you haven't gone before."

"I've hardly been anywhere. Cafés, mostly. Le Dôme, Deux Magots. I went to the Ritz, but the bar was closed."

Dorothy's eyes went wide, as though Margie had confessed something deeply scandalous. "You've hardly seen Paris at all!" she protested. "Come on. Let's get out of here. We have so much catching up to do."

On the Boulevard du Montparnasse, the light had turned from the golden glow of the afternoon into the soft grays and lavenders of evening, the whitewashed buildings, untouched by Haussmann's strict hand, glowing softly. Dorothy practically skipped down the street, Margie following behind her. When they reached the door she had been looking for, Dorothy waited for Margie to catch up, and then pulled the handle hard, letting out a rush of noise, of laughter and the cheerful undercurrent of clinking glass, and they stepped inside. "This is the Dingo. Absolutely everyone goes here. Come on."

She began to thread her way through the crowd, and Margie followed. People seemed to part to allow Dorothy to pass, while Margie felt as though she were struggling through mud, awkwardly pushing people aside while trying not to be rude. "*Pardon*," she said, again and again, though she was fairly sure she was shoving her way through piles of Americans. "*Pardon*." Finally she broke through the press of bodies and found Dorothy already sitting at a table, half on the lap of a young man who had a cigarette in one hand and a drink in the other and was therefore reduced (happily, Margie suspected) to nuzzling Dorothy's neck with his lips.

"Margie, Margie!" Dorothy called out as though Margie had been tragically lost and finally found, instead of having been bare seconds behind her the whole time. "Come sit with us. This is Arturo," she said, pointing at the man who was too busy kissing her arm to do anything more than raise his eyebrows in greeting, "and Pierre and Lila and Mimi," she introduced the others who sat around the table, two women and another man. One of the women was looking furiously at Dorothy, and Margie suspected there was a date going on, or at least there had been before Dorothy had arrived. No one offered Margie a chair.

"I'll stand," Margie said. A girl from the Club passed behind her. What was her name? She felt guilty until the girl looked at her as though she had never seen Margie, despite their having sat at breakfast together twice in the last week. Margie took a deep breath instead and looked away.

At some point, someone arrived with a tray full of drinks, and Margie took the one that was offered to her, though she hadn't ordered it and didn't know what it was. At the table, Dorothy and her beau continued to canoodle. The other man and the two girls got into a dramatic conversation, and Margie drank her drink and then stood there awkwardly with the empty glass in her hand, jostled each time someone passed behind her. It was hot inside and she really wished she had something to read. There was a man at the bar reading a book, despite the noise of the crowd around him, and she seriously considered stepping over behind him to read over his shoulder, but the book, she could see from the cover, was in French. In high school they had read *The Hunchback of Notre-Dame* in the original French, and it had taken her a half hour to get through each painful page.

She was still looking longingly at the man's book when Dorothy sprang up from the table. "Come on! We're going to Zelli's."

The group of them, along with two other people they somehow picked up along the way, left the bar and disappeared down into the darkness of the Métro. When they came up again, they were in Montmartre, the hills spreading up above them. Despite the hour, the streets were busy, cafés overflowing with people talking over a bottle of wine, sidewalks crowded as couples and groups headed to another party, some of them laughing and singing as though they were in a show.

Margie followed the group down the streets, until they stopped in front of a building with a crowd outside. There was an astonishing blur of languages, shouts and laughter and bursts of song in English, French, Russian, Portuguese, Italian. In contrast to the cafés in Montparnasse, where the artists had an air—and more often than that, an actuality—of studied scruffiness, the men here wore suits, were smartly turned out and fashionable. The women's dresses were stylish and new, and Margie felt dowdy and lost. She thought longingly of the café the other night, of Sebastien's disheveled artist friends, their silly Surrealist sayings, the passionate argument over whether one of them had betrayed the movement by taking a portrait commission (Margie's opinion: no, as things like eating and having a place to live were important).

"Come on, Margie!" Dorothy called over her shoulder, and Margie rushed forward as the crowd parted for them, catching the end of their wake, and then they were inside.

By the entrance was a balcony overlooking the entire club, the dance floor already crowded. On the lower level was the altar of the stage, where a full orchestra was hurtling itself at popular songs, all the musicians so deep into the sound they were transported, the tendons on their fingers pulling music from their instruments, sweat standing out on their foreheads, half dancing themselves as they played. The floor was crowded, men in tuxedos and suits, women in dresses so filmy and silky they made Margie's more modest dress look heavy as a duvet, packed together on the floor. From above it looked like a jittering, bustling beehive. Here and there, waiters darted along the edges of the dancers, barely averting one disaster after another, trays of drinks held above their heads, which they delivered to one of the dozens of tables lining the floor and ducked under the balconies above. Champagne buckets gleamed on tables, where people leaned their heads close together to talk.

Looking everywhere, taking in the dizzy glamor, the elegance, the energy that bubbled and fizzed like a thousand popping champagne bottles, Margie felt as though she might go off like a cork herself. Outside, she had felt frumpy and plain, the same Margie Pearce who had plodded through so much of her life, who had been given a single night of magic at her debut and had thought she would never have another, but in here she felt part of something exciting and exotic, and its refracted magic fell on her, illuminating the beads on her dress, making her skin glow in the dim light.

"Well, well, if it isn't Sebastien's American girl," a man's voice said in her ear, close and so intimate that Margie jumped back, her head narrowly missing clocking Georges in the face. He was cleaner than he had been the other night, wearing a tuxedo, even, his hair combed back instead of falling forward over his eyes. Alas, he was still sporting that silly monocle as though he might be asked to examine a document or a diamond before the night was through.

"Oh, *bonjour*," she said, placing her hand over her heart to calm the beating. The noise and music buzzed around them, and she had to raise her voice to be heard, even as close as he was. His hand rested on her lower back.

"*Bonsoir*," he corrected her with a smile. "What are you doing here, Sebastien's American girl?"

"I'm not . . ." Margie began to object to being called Sebastien's American girl, but when she stopped to think about it, she decided she actually liked it a little bit. "I'm Marguerite," she said, reminding him, and feeling a little thrill of using her French name, which was so much fancier than boring old Margie.

"What are you doing here, Marguerite?" he asked. He guided her away from the balcony as more people pressed in behind them, greeting the owner, checking their coats. It seemed impossible that more people could fit into the club, yet they kept coming, slipping into the boxes upstairs, women sitting on men's laps by the table, the tiny spaces on the dance floor filling in, couples pressing tightly to one another, glad for the excuse, and above it all, the band was still playing, the screech of trumpets wailing and the dance floor jumping right along with them.

"I came with some friends," Margie said, though as she looked around, she didn't see Dorothy or Arturo or any of the other people they had come in with, just an undifferentiated mass of celebration. She had grown to think how small a town Paris was, when she saw some of the same people again and again, the writers she saw at the Libe and then writing or arguing over a bottle of wine at La Closerie des Lilas, the girls from the Club she saw flirting with young men in bar windows, but here Paris felt infinite, like she would never see it all or know it all or meet the people in it, which was neither strange nor terrifying, only joyful, as though she had been given a gift with no end.

"Come drink with us instead," Georges said. They reached the stairs and he offered her his arm and they walked down.

The Surrealists and a handful of other artists she didn't recognize had taken over two tables in the back. Margie didn't even have time to sit, because René saw her arrive and rose, bent to kiss her hand, and whisked her onto the dance floor without offering a formal invitation or waiting for her reply.

Men were so rare these days: Margie had read a newspaper story asserting that after the war, young women in Europe had only a one-in-ten chance of getting married, which she thought was probably exaggerated but nonetheless dreadfully sad, especially those who had offered their bodies as comfort for soldiers on leave and, when the soldier had been killed in action, been left with a squalling, hungry memory they would raise alone. But the Surrealists were all men, the core of artists Sebastien knew, and Margie, who had so often been sequestered among women, felt gloriously feminine and desired. She had never been much of a dancer, and had never even tried to shimmy or do the Toddle before, but the floor was so tightly packed it didn't matter. She slid along on her toes, René gripping her hands, bumping into everyone else on the floor who was bumping right back, and when she was sweaty and breathless, they ran over to the tables and Georges poured her a glass of champagne, and then one of the other artists took her hand and swept her onto the floor for a slow dance, until the band exploded again and the floor erupted as though it were shaking, and they did the entire thing all over again.

Margie, who would have sworn her idea of a good time was staying at home with a book, far from exactly this sort of noise and crowd, was exhilarated. They danced for hours until she felt dizzy from the excitement and the champagne and the lack of sleep. People came and went along the table, and she ran into Dorothy dancing in the center of the dance floor and the two of them Charlestoned for a moment until their partners pulled them back and Dorothy gave Margie a huge wink over her man's shoulder and Margie, to her own surprise, winked right back. Just think, on the ship on the way over, she had been too shy, too scared, to go into the ball, and here she was, dancing as though it came naturally.

She had always thought she wasn't the sort of girl men wanted to dance with. She had always thought she was lesser somehow, that she would never have the things other girls had. But maybe the problem hadn't been her. Maybe it hadn't ever been her. Maybe it had been the place, and her mother's unforgiving expectations, and the way everything expected of her was tight and ill-fitting, and had never allowed her to breathe properly, never allowed her to see anything properly, not even herself.

When it began to grow light outside and the crowd had thinned, people stumbling out into the pale early morning, the waiters arrived with breakfast, fruit and croissants and pots of yogurt. Margie ate some berries, but her stomach was too light to hold anything, so she found Dorothy and the two of them went home, Margie floating the whole way. It hadn't been her at all. She hadn't been the one who was wrong, who didn't fit. She had been this girl all along. It had been the place that was wrong. And now, here, in Paris, she could see herself clearly. She could see who she had been meant to be, now that Paris was hers.

seventeen

MADELEINE
1999

"Go through and pack up whatever you want," my mother had told me. When I had gone to her with each piece to ask for permission, she waved me away. "It's fine," she said each time. "It's fine."

"Don't you want some of these things?"

She shook her head. "There's more than enough."

And really, there was. My mother and grandmother had both been only children, so they had inherited all the family flotsam and jetsam. I supposed I should have been grateful I wasn't going to be expected to take everything with me, as they had. Instead, I chose the things I had loved as a child. I packed boxes of hand-painted china, so thin you could see your fingers behind it if you held it up to the light, boxes of silver, monogrammed and tarnished and entirely impractical for anything. I wrapped photographs and paintings without wondering where they might find a place to rest in the modern wasteland of my condo. I rolled up my favorite carpet and moved my father's chair out of the sitting room. I piled my treasures in the dining room until I realized I was rapidly running out of space.

"What are you going to do with all this stuff, anyway?" I asked the crowded room. The furniture stared back at me, silent and stoic. It was okay. I knew the answer, even if I wasn't willing to admit it. I was furnishing my house. Not the condo I lived in with Phillip. Some mythical, imaginary place, like my old apartment in Magnolia. A home decorated with furniture and rugs worn to a comfortable shabbiness, warmed by the memories of people who had lived there before. Rooms where the decorations held stories and histories, and where I could leave a teacup on the coffee table or a book on the sofa without its looking like a violation.

When Phillip and I had moved into the condo, I had donated all my books to the library. He said they ruined the look of the shelves, the gorgeous, wall-to-wall shelves in the living room that clearly called out for rows and rows of books and instead held the oddest objets d'art: a silver sphere woven out of twigs with a tendency to shed spray-painted bark onto the carpet, empty vases covered in mirrored glass, so every time you touched them you left fingerprints as though you were creating a crime scene, a pair of white papier-mâché masks I found so disturbing I had finally turned them to face the wall, a sculpture made of menacingly twisted railroad spikes, and a set of metal leaves that looked as though they had been plucked from a forest near Chernobyl. Despite his faith in my artistic knowledge, whenever I complained about them, Phillip insisted the decorator had known what she was doing.

I would have rather looked at a shelf full of books.

"You have to move these things," my mother announced, sweeping into the dining room with the grandeur of a duchess arriving for dinner at Buckingham Palace.

"I'm realizing that." I put my hands on two boxes and carefully—and clumsily—clambered out from between them. Pulling a chair out from the dining room table, I collapsed into it. I had been on my feet nearly nonstop, either painting or packing or carrying boxes up from the basement for my mother to sort through, and the exhaustion hit me, sudden and strong. Upstairs, a carpenter moved from room to room, fixing the molding, the comforting buzz of a saw and the intermittent thwack of a hammer punctuating my thoughts.

My mother was still standing with her hands on her hips, as though she expected me to magic the boxes away.

"I'll put them in the basement. I've cleared out half the stuff down there and once you look at what's left and decide what you want to keep, I'll call someone to haul the rest away."

"You can't. Remember? Sharon says it has to look like there is a lot of storage space downstairs."

"There is a lot of storage space downstairs."

"Yes, but it has to *look* like it."

Leaning forward, I pushed the chair at the head of the table out for her. "Have a seat, Mother. Take a load off."

With a movement somehow both reluctant and grateful, she sank down into the chair as well, looking as happy to be off her feet as I was, though she most emphatically would never have referred to it as "taking a load off." My mother was always in motion, on the phone or writing letters or rushing off to a meeting or a fundraiser or a function. I had never even thought my mother had the capacity to be tired or stressed, and yet here she was. Despite her makeup, I could see shadows under her eyes, and there was a slump to her shoulders that made her seem even smaller than she was.

"I shouldn't be sitting. There's so much to do," she said. She folded and refolded her hands in her lap.

"There's less than yesterday," I said. Above us, the carpenter's saw bit into a piece of wood. There was a clatter, then silence again.

"Did you need something?"

"We can't just talk?"

"Well," my mother said, as though that were an answer.

I nodded over at one of my grandmother's notebooks, sitting on the edge of the table. "Grandmother wanted to be a writer. Did you know that?"

"Did she?" My mother's interest was polite.

"She had some stories and poems published, in high school and college. The literary magazines. I've read them. They're pretty good."

"Where did you find those?"

"Up in the attic. You've never read them?"

"There's so much junk in the attic—who knows what's up there?"

"Did she write? I mean, do you remember her being a writer?"

My mother looked at me as though I were simple. "She didn't have time. She practically ran the Collegiate Women's Society in Washington, and she was on the boards of the symphony and the library, and they needed to entertain because of my father's work. If you're having senators and diplomats over for dinner, there's not a lot of time for scribbling."

It broke my heart a little to hear my mother call my grandmother's writing "scribbling." She sounded like my great-grandmother, Margie's mother. I thought about telling her what I had read, about Margie's trip to Paris, about her daydreams and her friendship with Sebastien, about her writing, but I kept my mouth shut. Telling Henry hadn't bothered me at all, but telling my mother seemed like a betrayal. I knew she wouldn't approve, and I wondered again how the woman in those journals had raised this woman, how the woman in those journals had become the Grandmother I knew, stiff and formal and reserved. She had been so happy in Paris—what had taken that from her? What had made her stop writing? What had changed?

"We could arrange to have these things shipped home to you," my mother said, smoothly changing the subject. "Instead of taking them down to the basement just to bring them back up in a few days."

The casual nature of the offer made me freeze, my stomach tensing. "What do you mean, a few days?"

"When you leave. You've been helpful, but don't you need to be getting back to Phillip?"

There was a pause, heavy and expectant, between us. We hadn't spoken about Phillip, or about me, or about anything serious, really, since our conversation the other day, and the idea of arguing with her made my chest feel tight. "I'm thinking about it," I said. Though I wasn't, really. It was odd how little I thought of him, how comfortable I felt without him.

"He called here, you know. He said you weren't answering your cellular phone."

"I . . . lost it," I said. I should have felt better that he was calling, but that part of my heart felt dark and shriveled and unforgiving. He wasn't reaching out. Not really. All he wanted, I suspected, was to berate me more, to put me back into the box I was breaking out of.

"Is there something you aren't telling me?" my mother asked. She was hesitant, and a momentary shard of hope rose inside me, as it had the other day when I had thought she might be opening to me. "Has Phillip—mistreated you in some way?"

I paused, equally hesitant. We were wandering the edge of undiscovered emotional territory—honesty. Reality. "No," I sighed. He would never hurt me, not the way she was asking about, anyway. As small and mean as he could be, he had never raised a hand to me, and as far as I knew, he hadn't slept with anyone else.

"Maybe you're disconnected. That happens in a marriage sometimes . . . things get busy . . ." She trailed off, hopefully, and I realized she was waiting for me to jump in and agree, to put her at ease, to end this awkward conversation.

"Maybe," was the best I could give her.

"Madeleine," my mother began, then interrupted herself to reach over and pat my hand. Her fingers were slender and cool. "You can't just sit here and let it all fade away. Call him back at least. Talk to him. If there's no real problem between you, then you have to give it another chance."

I leaned back in my chair, lifted my hands to the ceiling, then let them fall back in my lap. I could feel myself starting to cry, and I didn't want to cry. My mother never cried. My sorority sisters cried, but those were pretty, delicate tears, energetic enough to evoke sympathy, but not enough to cause mascara to run or redden their noses under their foundation. When I cried, it was loud and messy and ugly, my eyes pink and swollen, my nose red and stuffy. I didn't want to cry in front of my mother for all kinds of reasons, including the fact that it made me so unlovely, and I already felt unlovable.

"You know why he married me, Mother. Did you really think it was going to last?"

"He married you because you were in love," she said, with the strength of conviction of someone who refuses to see anything they don't want to.

I fast-blinked away the tears hovering at the edges of my eyes, blurring the dining room into a soft wash of green and blue, like a Monet painting. "Well, I may have loved him, but he didn't love me. I probably even knew it at the time, a little bit. Why was a man like Phillip going to marry someone like me? You thought that, Mother. I know you did. Everyone did. I know it's all anyone at the wedding was thinking about." My self-pity was coming to a rapid boil, and I couldn't hold back the tears anymore, angrily wiping them away with my forearm. "He married me because I was malleable, because I'd let him walk all over me. And he does. He married me because I was pretending to be someone else, someone who would make him look good. He married me because he wanted Dad to invest in his company. He didn't marry me for me. He doesn't even like me. He doesn't even know me."

"Madeleine, stop talking like that right now. Your poor father—what a horrible thing to imply." My mother was flustered, which never happened. Maybe because we were having an honest conversation for once in our lives, because she was trapped here with me and couldn't invent some excuse for hanging up the phone, a pile of correspondence she just had to deal with or remembering the roses needed deadheading or there was a committee meeting she was late to.

"I never would have married him if you hadn't pressured me so hard." I was pushing back tears, raw and ugly, and I wanted to hurt her, to break her perfect facade, to make her cry with me.

"I'm sorry, are you saying this is my fault?" my mother asked.

"You were the one who wanted me to get married! You were the one who was so embarrassed I wasn't! I married him because I didn't want to disappoint you anymore."

"Don't put your unhappiness on me, Madeleine," my mother said, and the disdain in her voice only made me feel smaller and less worthy. "You were the one who accepted his proposal. You made the vows. I didn't force you to do anything."

She was right. And yet she wasn't. I had spent so much time wishing someone would love me, and she had underscored that desire in a million ways, from every time she had told me I would never find a husband at art school to every date she had set me up on. And when she had met Phillip for the first time, before we got engaged, I could practically see the hunger in her eyes. She had wanted that for me so badly. The first time we had dinner together, she had dug her sharp elbow into my side repeatedly whenever I veered onto some unapproved conversational topic, and when Phillip had proposed, she almost collapsed in gratitude.

She was my mother. If she thought I was capable of withstanding the buffeting winds of her opinions, she was wrong.

"What is all this really about?" my mother asked. I suppose she was trying to be sympathetic, but there was too much between us for me to be able to accept it, and I was too angry and bitter to even really hear it.

"I just don't think Phillip and I should be married anymore, that's all."

There was a pause. "I see."

We sat there, the tick of the grandfather clock in the foyer echoing emptily, the floors above us squeaking as the carpenter moved back and forth.

Finally my mother stood up, placed her fingertips on the table like a CEO about to make an announcement of quarterly earnings. "I don't know why you're so determined to feel sorry for yourself, but I won't be a part of it. Everyone has difficult times, Madeleine. But if you're going to insist on wrapping yourself up in your own victimhood, I can't stand to listen to it." Turning, she walked out of the room and down the hall, and a moment later, I heard the firm sound of the door to my father's office closing.

Numb, I climbed the stairs and walked down the hall to my bedroom, where I sat on the bed, bringing my knees up to my chest, curling in on myself like a pill bug.

What I had said to my mother I hadn't said to anyone, not even to myself. Phillip and I shouldn't be married anymore. Should never have gotten married. Phillip had been right—we should get a divorce.

I felt myself starting to cry again, and pushed the tears back down. My grandmother's journals were stacked by my bed, and to distract myself, I picked up the one I had been reading.

I blamed Phillip for my decision to stop painting, but I had let it happen. I just had nothing to say. My ideas, my emotions had dried up, the flood of ideas that used to rush through me now a still, shallow lake. But as I turned the pages of my grandmother's notebooks, sat with her in the cloistered, oppressive parlor of her parents' house, walked the streets of Paris with her, both alone and terrified and thrilled to be on her own, I felt something inside me shifting, felt the emotions that had frozen inside me with each successive winter thawing.

I often looked at the women around me and wondered if any of them had dreams. Of course they did—it wasn't fair of me to continue to assume they didn't just because of how they looked on the outside. It's so easy for those dreams to get run over by other people's ideas about what we should do, or to be eroded, little by little, by the day-to-day drudgery of living, or to lose heart when faced with the long, hopeless struggle between where we are and who we want to be. But I didn't want to succumb. I wanted to not go gentle into that good night, I wanted to sound my barbaric yawp, I wanted to live deliberately. And I wanted to know why my grandmother, after all she had done in Paris, hadn't.

"I heard you had a good time at Zelli's," Sebastien said. He had been waiting outside the Libe, leaning on the wall across the street, below the high fence guarding the president's residence. When Margie appeared, he crushed his cigarette under his toe and sauntered toward her.

"News travels fast," Margie said. She pretended she wasn't pleased to see him, continuing to slide on her coat, smoothing down her hair, then slipping on her hat.

"Paris is a small town." She loved the way he said *Paris*, with precisely the right rush over the *r* and the gentle softening of the end—*Paree*, not *Pear-is*. She loved the way he said everything, really. He had a slow drawl, so different from the rush of the Parisian accent, and Margie imagined if he were American, he might be from Georgia, all peach trees and slow-moving air. "Did you have a good time?"

Unable to keep a smile from her face, Margie grinned. "I did. I'd never thought I would enjoy going to a nightclub, but I danced all night long. It was absolutely worth the awful blisters I have."

Sebastien grinned back at her. Without discussing it, they had begun walking, turning away from the rue du Faubourg Saint-Honoré and passing the other way, until they were in the park. The glass roof of the Grand Palais glowed ahead of them, as though it held fire inside. Moving into the evening, Margie marveled at how the light changed, growing dimmer and softer as the hour grew later, the city inhaling its inhabitants back into their homes and then exhaling them onto the streets again for the evening, for strolls, or dinner at restaurants with tables filling the sidewalks so people had to walk down the middle of the street for blocks at a time.

They walked without discussing their destination, talking about Zelli's, and the Libe, and Paris, and the future and the past, the city unfurling beneath their feet. They stopped on the Pont Neuf, the oldest bridge in Paris, made of pale stone with bastions like Juliet's balcony, and they looked out over the water, the boats passing by, the people walking on the banks, some of them in a hurry to get home, others walking slowly, enjoying the water and the warmth of the fading sun on their faces. Crossing over to the Left Bank, they passed the Saint-Michel fountain, children dancing under its eager spray, behind them Notre-Dame laid out against the sky, the stained-glass windows glowing from the inside, and Margie thought Paris would never look so beautiful again. She had thought they might walk toward home, but Sebastien led her a different way, along some streets leading diagonally to a neighborhood close to her first hotel in Saint-Germain-des-Prés.

"Where are we going?" Margie asked as they tripped down a quiet, narrow street, the storefronts lined with art dealers and antique stores.

"I'd like to show you some of my paintings," Sebastien said, with the slightest touch of shyness in his voice. It seemed so unlike him, and yet it made her like him all the more to know there was vulnerability in him after all. "Would you like to see them?"

"Of course," Margie breathed. For so long, Margie had thought of art as something that happened only in secret, a night-blooming flower, and to be invited to see his work felt as intimate as a kiss.

Sebastien stopped in front of a store, the window and door painted a radiant royal blue. Behind the main window was a sculpture, bathed in the soft light of early evening, the shape of a woman emerging from gray stone, her back arched in delicious pleasure, a cat stretching in the sunlight. Opening the door, Sebastien gestured for Margie to enter, and she stepped into the silence. He followed behind, the door closing quietly in his hands. Underneath their feet, the floors, wooden, scuffed, and ancient, squeaked in the stillness. "*C'est moi,*" Sebastien called to the empty air. "*Sebastien.*"

Someone responded from the back, a man's voice, muffled so Margie couldn't understand him. In any case, no one emerged.

"This gallery is very famous," Sebastien explained. Do you know Impressionism?"

"No." Margie shook her head, feeling ashamed. At home, she would have been considered well educated, even cultured. Here she was reminded again and again of all the things she did not know, of how much there was to learn, to know, to explore, to find.

"Come." Sebastien reached out his hand, and Margie slipped hers into his. Touching him felt so different from dancing with the other artists at the club. His hand on hers made her stomach flip in a pleasant way, and she pushed down a girlish smile. He led her to another wall, the sun falling close enough to the painting to illuminate, though not to fade it. "Come closer," he said, and they moved closer, close enough to breathe on the canvas. So near, the image was a soggy blur; the colors fading into one another as if the painting had been left out in the rain. Nevertheless, there was a warmth and a glow to it Margie found herself drawn to, the particular orange of a sunrise, a blue flowing like water.

"Do you see it?" he asked. Margie, somewhat ashamed, shook her head.

"I really don't know much about painting," she apologized, sure she was disappointing him.

Sebastien smiled. "This is the joy of art. You do not need to know it to embrace it. Step back with me."

Together, they took three long steps back, and the picture came into focus. It was as though Margie had been looking at it through a rain-spattered window and it had suddenly become sunny and clear. The orange glow was now clearly a sunrise, the blue obviously water. What had looked like smudges and darkness up close now looked like boats caught in a morning mist. "I see it! I see it!" she said, caught up in child-ish delight, as though she had solved an unsolvable puzzle, and then she was ashamed again at her silliness. It was exactly the kind of thing Eve-lyn would have been embarrassed by, pretended she didn't know Margie for. She cleared her throat and tried again. "I see the image now. The boats on the water." She pointed as she spoke. "The sunrise. That's why it's so unclear, isn't it? Because there's morning fog."

"*Oui, oui,*" Sebastien said, clearly not embarrassed by Margie's out-burst. "Painting is so much about the light. Come, here, see this one."

He took her close to a painting, this one with tiny smudges of green and white and pink and purple, as though paint had been splattered and then smeared across the canvas. But when they stepped back, Margie saw it—in the foreground, a profusion of wildflowers, stretching back, a field of grasses and flowers and trees. "It's amazing," she breathed. "It hardly looks like anything, and then it becomes so clear. Look at them." She pointed to a blur of darkness toward the back, so formless and yet so obviously two people standing amidst the greenery.

"Our eyes do much of the work." He touched his face as he spoke, gesturing to his own eye, and Margie watched his movements, those impossibly long, slender fingers, the fine bones of his face. He was like a painting himself, all perfect lines and balanced symmetry, the warmth of his skin and the gold in his hair a perfect match for the light coming through the gallery's front window. "It is a miracle, yes? The Impression-ists know precisely how to balance clarity and color so we will see some-thing that is not clear at all."

He walked her through the gallery, pointing at the paintings that had come between the Impressionists and his work, and though Margie could not have named the progression of styles, she could see it happening from one painting to the next, images blurring and then refocusing, growing clear and then unclear again in new ways. Figures grew square and folded in on themselves as though they had been caught in a broken mirror, or stayed as clear as the lines of a portrait while turning nonsensical—landscapes filled with trees covered in human eyes, a woman's ball gown with a basket beneath it like a hot-air balloon, both familiar and unsettling.

"Do you like this one?" Sebastien asked. He stopped in front of a painting of a woman dressed for a party in a pink dress, the skirt falling into uneven, loose lines at the bottom, so you could almost see it fluttering. She wore a long rope of pearls and her hair was shingled fashionably close to her head. Though she wasn't looking at the artist, it was clear she was aware of being watched, and she was used to it. She wasn't quite beautiful; her nose was too strong and her eyes too wide, and she was broad-shouldered and turned in such a way that she took up nearly the entire frame. There were none of the mind-bending mirror-folds of some of the other paintings, where it looked more like the subject had been folded and refolded like paper, but neither were her angles entirely clear, and her edges were soft, as though she were in motion. A curious feeling of jealousy settled in Margie's chest.

"I do. She's beautiful. And the painting is almost . . . alive. It's like she knows I'm looking at her, but she doesn't want to look back."

"This is mine," Sebastien said proudly. "I am glad you like it."

"This is yours?" Margie breathed, and she turned back to the painting, looking at it again, now less as a piece of art and more a link to its creator. She wondered what she could learn about Sebastien from this—who was the woman and what was their relationship that she refused to look at him? And how did he know her form so precisely, the shape of her under the dress, the way it fell on her body? Margie blushed to think of it, and then called herself silly—the woman was fully dressed, after all. And she wasn't classically beautiful, maybe Sebastien saw something in her, maybe artists saw beauty differently, maybe he saw Margie differently.

"I love it. What do you call it?"

"The title? *A Portrait of Cécile.* Come, see this one too." Stepping toward the painting beside it, he waved her over and Margie followed. He was clearly proud of his work, and she was glad she responded to it, glad she saw his talent. He was, surprisingly, her best friend in Paris, though her mother would have been scandalized that she regularly stepped out with a young man, just the two of them, but her mother wouldn't have understood anything about this place, this life. Margie hardly understood it herself. If she had told her parents about Zelli's, about the cafés and the Surrealists and the bars, they would have thought it wild. Depraved, even. And here it was all of an evening. The rules were different in Paris. The rules were different when you were free and the strange evening light of Paris worked its magic on you. Margie was different in Paris. She felt it, she saw it when she looked in the mirror or caught her own eye in a shop window as she passed. Her face looked different, her cheekbones higher, her eyes wider, her collarbone sharp and clean above the neckline of her dresses. And she felt lighter, as though whatever had tied her to the ground in America had been loosened.

"This one I call *Summer Ball.*" The canvas was wide, long, more than six feet on its side, Margie guessed, a panorama, a horizon, but instead of being filled with a landscape, there were a hundred figures as if at a dance. It was outside; Margie could see trees in the background, some well-behaved bushes, and a row of tables filled with people sitting together. She recognized the gold and the purple of a Paris summer evening. And miraculous as it was, every one of the people in the painting seemed to have his or her own story. Each pair of figures its own tableau. This one a couple who had just met, their bodies held apart, barely turning toward each other, beginning to open their secrets. This pair deeply in love, barely an inch of space between them, though there was plenty of room on the dance floor, eyes closed, cheek to cheek, as if no one else existed—Margie could almost see them swaying gently, more slowly than the music—for them the music didn't matter at all. These two a couple married for many years and unhappy, these two a couple married for many years and still very much in love. A couple being forced into marriage, a couple with a great sadness, a couple with a delightful secret to keep. She couldn't stop looking at the painting, from face to face, reading their stories. "It's like a novel," she said at last, her voice barely a breath.

"Do you think so?" Sebastien asked, and she could tell he was excited by it, glad she had seen the stories he had created.

"It is," Margie said, and she pointed out the couples as she told him what she saw, the relationships and histories and futures represented so carefully with the strokes of his brush.

And then, much to her shock, Sebastien reached out and hugged her with a delighted glee. It was over in a moment, but Margie thought she might live in that moment forever. The scratch of the fabric of his jacket against her cheek, his arms around her, the slightest roughness of his skin against her forehead, and the smell of him, coffee and paint and something wild and comforting, like sun-warmed grass. "You have made me so happy. I have been working on this painting for a year. To tell so many stories in one painting—I thought it was too difficult, but I had to try it. You are a writer, this is simple for you. It is much harder for me to have so many ideas at once and then to make them clear in a painting. But you see it."

"I see it," Margie said, and she was blushing from his hug, and she wanted to be in his arms again, but she could see he was distracted by her compliment. She knew the feeling well—she had felt it herself when her stories had been chosen for her school's literary magazines, or when her teachers had praised her work. She only envied him that his work was here, on display, in a gallery, while hers was still bound up in closed pages in her room. Someday, she thought. Someday all the things she had wanted so badly might actually be hers.

It became a habit, their walks home. She would leave at the end of the day and find Sebastien leaning against the president's fence and smoking, and he would cross the street to join her. Sometimes they went through the Jardins des Champs-Élysées, and sometimes they walked down the rue du Faubourg Saint-Honoré, looking at the storefronts of couturiers on one side and the enormous mansions on the other, and sometimes they stopped in a café half the way home, by the Théâtre du Châtelet and watched the people go by. And they talked. They talked so much Margie's jaw would hurt at the end of the night, and if they sat in a café, her voice would go attractively rough from all the cigarette smoke in the air.

Occasionally they were joined by Sebastien's artist friends, or by the Surrealists, who would be terribly serious until they had enough wine in them, at which point they would grow funny and wild, and always deeply passionate about their art. One of them cornered Margie one night and read her the entire list of the cards they had created for the Bureau of Surrealist Research, and he looked at her expectantly at the end of each one, as though he had told a particularly good joke and was waiting for her to laugh. Margie didn't have the heart to tell him that despite the great improvement in her French she still understood only half of what he was saying, so sometimes she simply nodded thoughtfully, and sometimes she smiled, and sometimes she laughed gaily, and sometimes just said, "Oooh," as though he had said something particularly thought-provoking. Though she did this in a pattern having nothing to do with the content of the messages, even the ones she technically understood (though she never could have translated them and gotten their intentionally obscure meanings quickly enough), he seemed quite pleased, and when he had reached the end of the list, he bought her a glass of cognac and proceeded to get very, very drunk and sing "California, Here I Come" with the other Surrealists, very, very badly.

And some nights they went dancing, and some nights they went to galleries to see other artists' paintings, people Sebastien knew or had heard of. Once, thrillingly, they saw a film some of Sebastien's friends had made at a remote château. The picture itself hadn't made any sense to Margie, and she suspected it didn't make any sense to anyone, but it had been terrific fun to see people she knew on a movie screen. Afterward she felt, even though she knew it was only a tiny art film, showing in a gallery with an enormous movie projector clacking away in the background, she might be stopped by people on the street as though she were walking with Buster Keaton or Clara Bow.

Later, they would gather at a café and talk, and she would listen to their thoughts and their passion and when Sebastien walked her home at the end of one of those nights, her head was spinning with ideas. Those conversations felt as though she were on a carousel and everything they were saying about art and truth and dreams and, sometimes, rather shockingly, sex, was lights and calliope music and the rise and fall of painted horses. She tried to keep up, though her French sometimes held her back, and sometimes it was only her own fear that she might say something the others thought was foolish, or even worse, obvious.

"You know more than you think," Sebastien would say to her when he walked her home, the cafés and bars alive with lights and people and conversation. Margie wondered sometimes if Washington were like this at night, so full of activity and celebration, and it was just that she had missed it. There had been times when she had stayed up to the hours she kept in Paris, but it had always been in the company of a book, or of her own writing, never out with other people. "You should open your mouth and say it. You will be surprised."

Margie wished it were that easy, but she had been editing her thoughts for so long, purposely keeping herself small and contained, she couldn't imagine speaking out so easily. These men and women Sebastien knew, they were great artists. Some of them were already known, some of them would only be known years in the future, but they were artists. They were daring and experimental. They made things happen. And they knew so much. They could talk of Expressionism and Neoclassical Cubism and *Ulysses* and Gothic literature, and Margie resented all those years she had spent reading books with no one to talk to about them, stuck in schoolrooms and surrounded by girls who had worried only about who they would marry and whether they might be chosen for some society or where they would spend the summer, when she could have been with these people, living.

In fact, Margie found herself writing more and more those days. When she was assigned to the circulation desk at the Libe, between busy spells she often dashed off a letter to her parents and then spent the rest of the time writing feverishly, trying desperately to record all the ideas in her head using the typewriter, which was so much faster than laboriously writing by hand. She wrote stories about people who met in cafés and fell in love, and she wrote stories about Americans who came to Paris, and she mined every inch of her own experience and what she saw and she composed. She felt like Mozart, hounded by the music, desperate to get it out.

The piece she returned to again and again was Sebastien's painting of the ball. She went back to the gallery on her own, finding it among the turning streets of the Quartier Latin, not even noticing how the city felt so navigable now, so much like home. She took her notebook and stood, mesmerized, and then began to record all the stories she could see—the lovers and the friends, the families and the enemies, and when she got home, she began to write the story.

She recorded it all: the lazy, heat-sodden Paris afternoon, the women's dresses growing damp with sweat, a few of the men bravely shrugging off their jackets, the sound of the music floating through the air, across the dance floor and out to the garden beyond.

And then, she wrote. She wrote the story of the couple meeting for the first time, the man asking the woman to dance, the way their bodies moved toward each other like an invitation, but the woman turned her head back away, blushing. She wrote about the way another man had come to the dance with only a few sous in his pocket, only enough for a single lemonade, and was terrified to think his girl might ask for something more expensive, but she saw the way his fingers moved on the lining of his pocket and suggested instead they buy one lemonade and share it.

She wrote the story of the couple whose inability to bear a child had fractured their marriage so irreparably, who were only there because the husband still loved his wife, loved her more for the trying, the endless months of tears and frustrations and blame, the doctors' painful cures and their families' ridiculous suggestions, and he had begged her to come with him, to go to this ball so they could simply dance and drink and laugh the way they used to—he had once thought her laugh was the most beautiful sound that had ever been, and he never heard it anymore, only heard her tears, which shattered him every time.

She wrote the story of the bartender who loved to dance, whose feet moved to the music as he poured drinks behind his counter, waltzing and foxtrotting along with the couples on the floor, and who, when the day was over, went home to the sixth floor of an old house, to an apartment that had only two rooms and a heating ring and was stifling in the summer and cool in the winter, but had the most glorious view of the Eiffel Tower, and he would pour some milk for his cat, and the cat would sit on the windowsill and drink it while he leaned on the windowsill and watched the world go by below and his restless feet continued to dance.

She wrote all these stories—of love lost and love found, of hearts broken and healed, of anger and sadness and loneliness, and joy and connection and hope. And as she did, the figures in Sebastien's paintings came alive in her mind, until the ball was real to her.

And when she gave those pages to him, presented them shyly, tied together with a length of ribbon she had found hanging over a rosebush in the courtyard at the Club, he had taken them as though she had offered him a great gift. They lay in the grass in the Champ-de-Mars, the sun touching its gentle fingers to their skin, as Sebastien read every page, and Margie stared at the tip of the Eiffel Tower against a cloudless blue sky and wondered at the miracle her life had become. When he finished, his eyes shone with tears, and he had touched his fingertips to hers and said, "This. Exactly this," and Margie knew no matter how many stories she wrote, she would never have a greater compliment.

Sometimes when Sebastien walked her home from the Libe, they would drift from the route and discover the most wonderful things. A carnival set up in the Tuileries, where Sebastien won her a toy and they rode the Ferris wheel and looked at the city spread out below them, and they went around and around until she couldn't tell the difference between the lights of the stars above them and the lights of the city below them; the way they both sparkled with such impossible magic.

Another night they found themselves in the Pigalle, up by Zelli's, and a prostitute asked Sebastien for a match, which he gave her, and they passed a few moments talking while Margie watched. She had never spoken to a prostitute before, had never even seen one as far as she could remember, and she looked greedily at the woman's seamy glamor—the stockings with the tears turned to the inside and the dress that had once been brilliant silk and was now greasy and dull, and the makeup on her face that hid the acne and the purple smudges under her eyes but also, Margie grew to understand as she looked at this woman silently, was a sort of armor that shielded who she was and let no one inside, and Margie thought that was the most beautiful and saddest thing she had ever seen.

Paris at night was a different place. After dark, lovers were on every street corner: drinking wine by the Seine, strolling hand in hand, finding the dark and shaded spots of the city—under the blessing of a tree or in the dark entrance to a building—to kiss. Sometimes there was so much passion between them it seemed as though Margie could see sparks coming from their skin when they touched, illuminating the bliss on their faces, and Margie had to avert her eyes because their heat was too much to bear. And sometimes it was dangerous, pickpockets lurking in their own dark spots, or drunks who were angry and lurching instead of happy and singing, looking for some way to vent the rage the wine had kindled in them. But mostly those people were looking for each other, criminals in search of easy marks, drunks hungry for a fight, and Sebastien would slip to the side of her closest to the danger, and take her elbow and they would walk by quickly, until whatever the threat had been disappeared and Paris was theirs again, theirs alone.

She did not write to her parents about the nights at Zelli's or the Dingo, and she did not write to them of Sebastien. On the one hand, she thought her mother might have been relieved to know there was a man interested in her at all, especially one so young and handsome. On the other, she would have hated that Sebastien was an artist, and hated even more the idea of them walking the streets together alone, Margie with her short hair and a dress she had borrowed from one of the girls at the Club, unchaperoned and alone in the city at night. How different her mother's world was from hers. How different our mothers' worlds are from all of ours. Margie wondered sometimes if her mother had ever been young, had ever been in love, had ever wanted to dance under the starlight with a young man, or if she had been born disapproving and hard. She didn't know why her mother clung so tightly to her rules. They certainly didn't seem to make her happy. And they hadn't made Margie especially happy either. Not happy like she was now. Not happy like Paris had made her.

nineteen

MADELEINE
1999

I was carrying boxes up from the basement, covered in dust and cobwebs, when the doorbell rang. My mother had gone to dinner at Lydia Endicott's, where I presumed they were planning their path to global domination: today, the Garden Society, tomorrow, the world.

Passing the mirror by the front door, I noted my appearance: capri pants smudged with dirt, a T-shirt advertising the Spring Fling from my junior year in high school (I had not attended—how I'd gotten the T-shirt, I could only guess), my hair pulled up in a loose knot on top of my head. Yup, ready for prime time.

Mostly it had been people my mother or I had hired arriving at the door lately—painters, appraisers, charity pickups. This time it was Henry. He was surprisingly cleaned up—a black-and-white-checked button-down shirt with the sleeves casually rolled up, a pair of dark blue jeans that actually fit, and his hair, though it would never sacrifice its curl, had seen a comb at some point in the relatively recent past. "Wow," I said, which was probably not the most tactful thing I could have said, but he didn't seem to mind. "You look nice."

"Sometimes I clean up okay," he said, and generously said nothing about my appearance, which was decidedly less nice. "Are you ready to go?"

"Umm . . . go where?"

"First Friday," he said, as though we'd been talking about it only a moment before, when it had been days since anyone had mentioned it. To be honest, I hadn't really thought about it. Mostly I had been thinking about my mother, and whether I wanted to go home, and what I would do if I weren't married anymore. And painting. I was thinking a lot about painting, which was an excellent avoidance strategy.

"Oh. Right. Is that now?" I looked down at my clothes and touched my hair, which was in desperate need of a blowout.

"I can wait for you to change. But you're fine like you are."

"Ha!" I said loudly. Henry only looked confused. Well. Maybe he really did think it was okay for me to be seen in public dressed that way, but I didn't, and my mother would have had an aneurysm. "You'd better come in," I said as I stepped back, opening the door fully and holding my hand out like a butler. "Enter the lair."

He started to step inside and then jumped back as though he had been shocked, and we both laughed. "Your mother isn't here, is she? Are you sure she didn't booby-trap the place in case I came by?"

"I'm pretty sure it's safe, but you might want to watch out for trip wires and buckets of water just in case."

"Thanks for the advice."

Upstairs, I took a quick sponge bath and changed into a clean pair of pants and a wrinkled denim shirt, and threw on a pearl necklace and earrings. My hair was beyond fixing, so I left it loose and curling. When I sprinted back downstairs, Henry was standing in the front room, looking into my mother's china cabinet.

"Hey, you look amazing," he said when I appeared.

"Yeah, right."

"Take a compliment."

I didn't bother to explain that I hardly knew how. "Thanks. You digging my mother's china shepherdess collection?"

"They're not so bad. A lot of these are actually beautiful."

"I loved them when I was little. That teacup in the back with the pink roses, if you look closely you'll see where we had to glue the handle back on because I played tea party with it."

"I knew you were a rebel."

"Mad, bad, and dangerous to heirloom china. Are you ready to go?"

"Sure," he said, and we headed out the door and into the night. I could hear the noise from the restaurant behind us, the crunch of cars arriving and leaving on the gravel.

"Is it okay that you're not at work?"

"Totally. I didn't leave Austin in charge this time," he said, flashing me a grin. "Actually, things are finally pretty much running like clockwork. I hate saying that out loud. It's like an invitation to drop a piano on my head."

"Why?" I ducked underneath the drooping arms of an unruly forsythia bush that was encroaching on the sidewalk. I could already hear the buzz and music from down on The Row. It was funny—I'd always avoided street festivals, fearing the noise and the crowds, but here I found myself almost dancing toward the sound, eager to be part of it. Eager to be part of something, someplace that wanted me.

"It's just such an unstable industry. Restaurants fail all the time, staff quit in the middle of a shift—it's notoriously difficult to find good help, if you'll forgive the expression."

"Don't apologize. My mother says it all the time," I laughed. "Anyway, you seem great to work for, so I'm sure they'll keep you around."

"Well, thanks. It makes it much easier to have great employees if you're a good boss. Short answer: they'll be fine for a while. What about you? How goes the great moving adventure?"

"It's going. She finally had an appraiser and an antiques dealer over, so they're clearing some things out of the house. It's incredible how much stuff there is."

"She's lived there for what, almost fifty years? That'll happen. My parents are still in the house I grew up in. We joke that when they die, we're just going to have to burn it down. It would be easier than cleaning it out."

I pictured our condo in fifty years, when it would still feel empty. Phillip had an almost clinical intolerance for clutter, or anything he thought of as clutter. More than once I had left a book or some papers on a table only to come home and find he had recycled them as if they were trash. No matter how many times that place was redecorated, it would never be anything other than clean and bare.

"It's amazing the things we've been cleaning out. I told you I found all my grandmother's journals, which are amazing, and there's a trunk full of books that have to be from the Civil War. Plus, of course, my Leif Garrett record collection, so clearly, treasures from throughout the ages."

"I sincerely hope the appraisers appreciate the value of those records."

"They'll go for millions at Sotheby's, I'm sure. Along with my vast collection of art works."

"Have you been painting again?" We reached a narrow point of the sidewalk, where a tree's roots had buckled the pavement, and he stepped back, letting me move ahead of him and then catching up a few steps later. It felt strange walking beside him—though he wasn't much taller than I was, he was broad and had a comforting presence. Phillip was a greyhound, all sleek lines and delicate bones. Henry was more like a bulldog, wide and solid and comforting.

"Yes. How can you tell? The rosy glow of artistic achievement?"

"Well, that and the paint in your hair."

"Oh," I said, embarrassed, patting at my head, feeling for a stiff spot. For all my bathroom ministrations, I might as well have been a hobo, just wandered in off the streets. "Sorry. You're always catching me looking like a slob. I don't look at myself in the mirror a lot. Am I totally covered in it?" I checked my arms and saw a smudge that looked like I'd rubbed against some wet paint after I'd wiped my brush on my apron.

"No apologies necessary. I'm just going to pretend I'm hanging out with a famous artist."

"Ah, I'm not an artist. I mean I was, years ago, I thought I would be. But I stopped."

"Why?"

"That," I said, whistling out a breath, "is the question of the day. I've been reading my grandmother's journals, you know? And she really wanted to be a writer, but her mother was dead set against it. And I don't know how much of that was the time, like women shouldn't be having careers in general, or how much of it was the arts in particular, or what, but I got that message too, that art was a waste of time. My parents were practical people."

We had reached the edge of The Row, and we stopped on the slight hill above the street to look at the scene. At the far end, near Cassandra's shop, a band was playing, and there was a crowd gathered in the street. All along the sidewalks, people milled around, some of them standing in groups and talking, others ducking in and out of the stores and restaurants. The patio where Sharon and I had eaten breakfast was packed, people sitting at tables or leaning against the railing. Through the wide, plate-glass windows of the bookstore, I could see a woman standing at a microphone doing a reading, a group perching on folding chairs in front of her.

I was struck again by how much the neighborhood had changed. The stores were less gentrified, less concerned with who they should keep out and more with inviting people in. The people had changed too—they were younger, they came in endless colors and shapes and sizes, and their hair was wildly dyed or gloriously plain, and their clothes were vintage or didn't quite match, and they called to each other in languages I didn't recognize, and I felt like I was living again instead of locked in a compound that was struggling to keep out anyone who didn't matter, surrounded by people who looked more like themselves and less like everyone else. "This place has changed," I said to Henry, and I could hear the breathless awe in my voice. It was silly to be so caught up in a stupid street fair, I knew, and at the same time, it wasn't just a street fair. It was like sitting at breakfast the other day with Sharon, talking to Henry and Cassandra and all the other people who had come along, and realizing I thought there was nothing to surprise me about Magnolia, but I hadn't known it at all.

"It has. There's been a concerted effort to revitalize The Row. I got some great funding to help make The Kitchen happen because of it."

"It just seems so strange, that this is the same neighborhood I grew up in. All these new stores, all these people I don't know. It's like an entirely new place."

"Well, let's get to know it," Henry said. He took my hand to help me down a few crumbling steps to the street and I blushed at the heat of his skin, the reassuring comfort of his broad palm covering mine. When he let go, it felt like a loss. There was a twinge in my chest as I thought of Phillip, and I pushed it away. I didn't want him in this moment.

We made our way down the center of the street, where the crowds were looser and more fluid. A group of girls slunk by, their youth dangerously beautiful, laughing and teasing each other in Spanish. A couple stood outside a pub with beers in their hands, chuffing out smoke as they laughed, and even the sharp smell of their cigarettes was romantic and comforting in the warm evening.

"So what were we talking about?" Henry asked as we stepped around a group of families in the middle of the street, plastic glasses of wine balanced in the cup holders of their strollers. "Oh, right. Art is impractical."

"One summer I said I didn't want to go to camp, I wanted to stay home and work on my painting, and my parents nearly went through the roof. And when they found out I was thinking about applying to art school instead of regular college—I never would have had the nerve to tell them; my college counselor spilled the beans—my father said he wasn't spending a dime on some so-called 'education' at art school."

"What did they want you to do?"

I looked up at the sky, which was the pleasantly indecisive mix of blue and gray and pink of a falling spring evening. "They just wanted me to get married. I don't think they really cared whether I had a career or not. Women in my parents' world . . . sometimes I wonder if they even know feminism is a thing. And they're total hypocrites—they give money to the symphony, they go to events at the art museum. But my going to art school, somehow that would have been the worst thing ever."

"I'm sorry," Henry said, and it seemed like the right thing to say, so I smiled back at him. Despite the rest of his cleaned-up appearance, it looked like he hadn't shaved for a couple of days, and he rubbed his face with his thick fingers. He seemed about to say something else, until a couple he knew spotted him and came over to say hello. He introduced me, and we chatted for a few minutes before they split off again.

"Thanks for coming out tonight," he said as we started walking again. "It's nice to be away from the restaurant on a Friday night. Feels like I'm breaking a rule."

"I'm pretty sure you are. But you said it's going well, right? You're going to be McDonald's before you know it."

"Thanks, but no thanks. I only ever really wanted the one restaurant. And I wanted it not to fail. That's an important caveat."

"What did you do before?"

"This, basically. I mean, not running the place, but working in restaurants. I knew I wanted to be a chef since the first time my mother handed me pots and pans to bang together. Graduated high school, bam, right into culinary school. I've worked at restaurants all over town. Spent a few years at resorts in the Ozarks, too, which was pretty glamorous."

"Even the name sounds glamorous. Ozark."

"Ozark would be a great name for a kid," Henry said, and he laughed, but my stomach twisted a little. I knew he was just joking, but that was a joke you made with someone you were dating. And we were definitely not dating. Even if I hadn't been married, he wasn't my type, and I was . . . well, like my grandmother, there had never been suitors lined up around the block.

"I envy that. Knowing what you want to do and then just doing it. I had no idea. Got a degree in marketing, which I really had absolutely no interest in, and had no idea what to do with when I graduated. I ended up working for the development office at my high school, which I guess is a kind of marketing, but I didn't like it much either. I would have been better off going to dental school."

"You would have been better off going to art school."

"Sure," I said, disbelieving. My parents had convinced me, I guess, because when I thought about it now, I wasn't sure I saw the point. What would I have done with an art degree? Although, to be fair, the only thing I was doing of any value was volunteering at the Stabler Museum, and my marketing degree wasn't much help there.

We were getting closer to the band, and the street was getting more crowded and the noise level was rising. We had to raise our voices to be heard, Henry leaning his head close to mine.

"I mean it. You say you had no idea what you wanted to do, but you did. You wanted to paint. Just because it was unacceptable to your family doesn't mean you didn't know what you wanted."

"Yeah, well. If it was so important to me I would have done it anyway. At least for fun. I haven't painted in years."

"I'm not sure that's the case. You got a pretty strong message it wasn't a good use of your time."

There was another little twist in my gut when I heard him rising to my defense, because he was standing up for me when he didn't know the entire story. I wasn't telling him everything. I wasn't telling him marrying Phillip had been the culmination of a hundred decisions, that it had required my putting away everything that had mattered to the person I really was in order to become the person I had always been told I should want to be, and one of the things I had sacrificed was painting. And I wasn't telling him because it would have required admitting it myself, and spoiling the illusion I had that this moment here, this time in Magnolia with him and Sharon and my easel in my mother's basement, was my life, that I had never been lonely or sad, had never married a man who criticized me for gaining weight instead of feeding me chocolate lava cake, who took me to parties and fundraisers I didn't want to go to with people I didn't care about instead of to street fairs that made me feel alive.

"Remember how Sharon said I was in a band with Kevin?"

"Yes!" This thought filled me with an inappropriately large sense of glee, and I clapped my hands together. "What kind of music? What instrument did you play?"

"Drums," Henry said, slapping out a quick rhythm in the air. "And I wouldn't call what we played music. It was mostly a lot of noise, but we categorized ourselves as hair metal."

"Please tell me there are pictures of you with long hair."

"You will never see them. I keep them locked up. Like the picture of Dorian Gray."

"I don't think that portrait was hidden out of eighties hair shame."

"But don't I look youthful?" He tossed his hair dramatically and I laughed out loud, surprised again at the sound of my own delight. "The point is I think about music sometimes, and how it was such a huge part of my existence, and how now I only think about it if I'm deciding what to play in the restaurant, or what to listen to on the way to work. And I don't think, 'That part of my life is over.' I think, 'That's not as big a part of my life right now.' So your painting, for a while, was 'not right now,' and now it's time again."

"Maybe," I said. Maybe that was it—my life had only been on hold, waiting for me to pick it up again.

We began to walk again until we came to the other end of the street.

Outside the Thai restaurant, Wanee's children joyfully danced to the music. Next door was the knitting shop, and as advertised, I could see a group of women at the back of the store, sitting in a circle, talking and laughing, colorful suns of yarn in their laps. A group of people stood by the door, drinking wine and laughing, and a server with a tray of appetizers passed back and forth in front of the window.

Inside, it was hot and close, bodies pressed together looking at the art or just chatting in groups. Cassandra stopped by to give us a hug, and we looked at the art—wall hangings, quilted or woven, impossible combinations of texture and color. The fabric made the "do not touch" rule feel even harder, and my fingers itched when I looked at the quilted swirls, the feathery explosions of angora, the hidden glimmer of silvery thread. To keep my hands busy, I swiped more than my share of appetizers off the passing trays. My mouth was still full when Henry asked if I was ready to go. Tiny beads of sweat stood out at his hairline.

"Yeth," I said around a mouthful of bruschetta.

"I'm glad you like my food," Henry said as we stepped back out onto the street, the cool air rushing up to meet us as though we were long-lost friends.

I finished chewing and, ever the lady, wiped my mouth with the back of my hand. "I like food in general. Don't get a swelled head."

"You'd never know it to look at you. You're too thin."

Shocked, I barked out a sharp laugh, loud enough to make the people around us turn and look. I covered my mouth and lowered my voice. "I guess that's meant as a compliment, but if there is one thing I am not, it is too thin."

"I'm sorry, I don't like to comment on women's bodies, but you look . . . hungry. I like to feed hungry people. And really, I like to watch anyone enjoying my food. You're welcome at The Kitchen anytime."

"Well, thanks." I resisted the urge to look at his eyes to make sure he didn't have a bad case of cataracts. I was used to either my mother's or my husband's acting as a missile defense system around my weight. If I had dessert twice in one week, Phillip was likely to go DEFCON 1 on the state of my thighs. It didn't help that I was surrounded by women who seemed to have been poured into a precise mold, whereas I looked more like the one that had overflowed the mold and somehow been shipped out to the store anyway.

"Do you want to get a drink?" Henry asked. We had taken a few steps and were outside Java Good Day.

"Sure," I said, and we stepped inside. Like most of the buildings on The Row, Java Good Day was in a renovated building, but it had survived the onslaught of modernization and the interior was exactly what a coffee shop should look like—battered wood floors, exposed brick walls, college radio playing, the last of the sun lying lazily across the tables. The smell of coffee brushed over my skin, wound itself into my hair, and I inhaled deeply. The coffee shop I'd gone to on The Row in high school hadn't been nearly this nice, and I was a little jealous of the kids who would get to come to this one. It was a much better place to wallow in adolescent angst.

"What do you want?" Henry asked.

"I'll have an Italian cream soda. Raspberry, if they have it." What the hell. I was fairly sure I'd gained ten pounds already, I might as well go for the full spare tire.

"No coffee?"

"Ugh, no. I'd be up half the night."

"Fair enough. I'll be right back."

Henry went to get in line while I wandered to the back of the shop. If I were to leave my fabulous life behind to open a coffee shop, this is exactly what I would want it to be, I thought. There was a bookshelf full of books people had abandoned, a row of tables with chessboards laid in them. A handful of college students, looking charmingly young, lounged on a pair of leather armchairs and a huge, bulky sofa.

Along the walls were photographs and paintings, and when I looked closer, each bore a tiny card with the artist's name and the work's title, along with a price. I could see an empty space where one had, presumably, sold. Henry walked up and handed me my soda, the cream tainted a pale pink from the raspberry syrup. "Thank you."

"You know, I know the owners," Henry said. He was drinking coffee; I could smell it on his breath when he leaned in beside me to look at one of the photographs.

"Yeah, I met him the other day. Pete. He's a nice guy."

"No, I mean if you wanted to sell some of your art here. I could connect you."

"Don't be silly. I don't have anything to sell. And no one would buy anything I painted anyway."

"How do you know?"

"How do *you* know? You've never seen my paintings."

Henry shrugged. "All right, so maybe they're horrendous. You could still put them up here."

"Sure," I said, somewhat sarcastically, but as we walked back outside, sipping on our drinks, the glass door closing heavily behind us, the thought stuck with me. What would it be like to have my work out in public? I was out of practice, but it turned out I had been storing up a lot of ideas over the years, and there were a million things I wanted to paint—the light of all four seasons on Lake Michigan, the glitter of snow against a skyscraper's glass, a cocktail party in which everyone was wearing elaborately feathered masks. This night—The Row alive with music and people and the promise of summer on everyone's mind. If I painted everything I wanted to, I would get better. I could take classes. I could be an artist again. I could be myself again.

We walked back down the street, Henry introducing me to people we bumped into, ducking into stores and drinking tiny glasses of wine or sampling the food we were offered. By the time we made our way back to the start of The Row again, my stomach was full and I felt a little giddy from the wine.

Henry's car was parked on the sidewalk outside my mother's house, so we said good night there, his keys jingling loosely between his fingers. There was a moment there, before I turned to go, when Henry looked as though he might say something else, a question resting on his lips, but when I paused, he just said "Good night" again and stepped out into the street, looking both ways before he opened the car door and slid inside. The engine sprang to life, a contented purr on the quiet street, and he waved as he pulled away and I walked slowly toward the house, listening to the sound of him driving away until it was gone.

Upstairs, I went into the bathroom to wash my face and paused, looking at myself in the mirror—all of me. I had rolled up my sleeves, and there was a tiny smudge of chocolate in the corner of my mouth courtesy of the samples from the chocolatier toward the end of the block. My cheeks were flushed from the wine and the walk up the hill, and my hair looked wild and loose, the curls framing my face. I looked, I thought, happy. I looked free. I looked like someone I would want to know. I looked alive. I didn't want to give that up.

twenty

MARGIE
1924

One night after a late dinner, as Margie and Sebastien were winding their slow way through Montparnasse toward the Club, the sky that was fading into darkness turned stormy. A rumble of thunder came from the distance, and then the rain was upon them, with no more warning. It had hardly rained since Margie had arrived. The rain would dare not ruin the perfect beauty of Paris, the way the sunlight fell so golden on the buildings, the shabby hopefulness of the vendors outside the Métro. Even the beggars in Paris had a consummately French style, scarves knotted around their necks, their dirty hair artfully arranged, an insouciance about the way they asked for your spare change, as though they weren't bothered one way or another whether you gave it to them, and then if you did (which Margie always did), they would half raise an eyebrow and nod in acknowledgment, and only occasionally would they say, in the most blasé way possible, "*Merci*." Margie absolutely loved it.

The rain came first with Parisian languor, fat drops with large spaces between them, and then furiously, hurling itself down toward the ground until, in a moment, Margie knew they were going to be drenched. They hurried under the awning of a café that had already closed, squeezing in with the empty tables, chairs stacked on top of them. What had been a beautifully cool evening quickly turned bitter, and Margie began to shiver. Sebastien slipped off his jacket and put it over her shoulders, but it was wet too, and only served to make her colder. A few people ran past, shoulders hunched, newspapers held above their heads, water spraying up from their heels.

As they waited, the rain fell harder, its rhythm on the awning above their heads turning from enthusiastic to threatening. Turning to her, Sebastien said, "Come with me. I live close to here."

Margie, who was cold and wet and miserable, didn't think twice. Sebastien took her hand and they ran through the rain, and she soon went from damp to completely drenched. A bus went by, throwing up a sheet of water that splashed over them, shocking and icy, and Margie began to laugh. And then they were at a door and Sebastien fumbled for a key and opened it and they were inside a courtyard, the buildings rising up around them. Above their heads a lantern sputtered in the darkness, and she could see a beautiful garden being beaten by the rain, rose petals scattered onto the stones in the courtyard. "This way," Sebastien said, and he opened the glass door to the building with another key.

Inside, the floor was perfect squares of creamy marble, and it held a quiet elegance Margie knew meant money. It was both familiar and unfamiliar—she had been surrounded by wealth her entire life, yet it had been months since she had been in a place like this. The ritziest building she had visited in Paris, not including Versailles or the Louvre, was the Libe, and its splendor had been all but swallowed by its new function and, to a larger extent, benign neglect. Surely Sebastien didn't live here. He was an artist, wasn't he? His shirts weren't going threadbare at the collar like René's, and he always seemed to have enough money for dinner and wine, but she had always thought he was flush from his new success, from the paintings he had sold.

Except, climbing the wide staircase that curved upstairs, the treads covered with plush, soft carpet that reminded her of the stairs in her parents' house, the banisters carved and gleaming with wood oil, she knew he was not relying on his paintings alone. Sebastien was rich. She didn't know how, or why he kept it a secret, but he was.

They alit at the second landing, Margie's dress heavy and wet, leaving a trail on the carpet, and Sebastien led her down the hall and opened a door at the end, turning on the light inside. "Come in, come in," Sebastien said when Margie hesitated, dripping water where she stood. Then she stepped inside, and her eyes widened.

"You *are* rich," she said as he closed the door behind her. She covered her mouth and laughed at the comparison, thinking of her tiny garret back at the Club, of struggling over the five hundred francs the Libe paid her, and he lived *here*.

Two easels stood by the window, where she imagined the light would be best, each holding a partially finished canvas, one of a Paris street, looking down, so it managed to contain both the famous Parisian rooftops and a street scene below, a market bursting with the rich colors of fresh fruits and vegetables, the awning of a café, a waiter standing to take an order from a man looking down at a menu, a couple crossing the street, a motorcar going one direction, a horse and cart heading the other way. Looking at the city from that perspective made it feel new and somehow secret, as though she were bearing witness to things she wouldn't see from the ground, an unfair glimpse into people's lives. As she had with his painting of the ball, she felt her fingers itching, a desire to dive into these people's stories: the weary set of the waiter's stance on his tired feet, the distance between the couple as they walked, a woman holding her hands close to her as she eyed a bin of bright strawberries, as though she might not be able to afford them but was only looking, avoiding temptation as she imagined the way the fruit would burst on her tongue and stain her fingers.

He had only just started the other canvas, the figure of a man standing by a window, sketched out, only the barest beginnings of color in the background, an unfamiliar blue sky. Between the easels stood a table full of metal tubes of paint and brushes, the wood carelessly spotted with a dozen different colors, a palette drying nearby, a stool.

The rest of the apartment was luxurious. Framing the window were heavy velvet curtains, the nap smooth and clean and obviously new. The rug beneath her feet was even more plush than the one in the stairwell, an Oriental carpet strewn with vines and richly woven patterns, so deep she wobbled slightly as she stood on it.

The ceilings were high, with wide molding along the edges, and the furniture was fine as well. And beyond the living room in which they stood, the apartment stretched back to other rooms, the luxury of space in a city where Margie had grown so used to folding in on herself to keep from intruding on other people, on the tram, at cafés, even in the aisles of the bookshops on rue de l'Odéon, where one errant shoulder could bring a stack of books tumbling down.

"I am not rich." He dropped his keys in a bowl on a table by the front door and stepped out of his shoes. "My family is rich. I am a poor artist."

"Hmph," Margie said. She had never stopped to think of the line between being rich and having one's family be rich. While her parents weren't technically supporting her now, she would never have been able to make it over to Europe without their largesse, and she knew when she went back—*if* she went back—they would support her again, and when they died, she would inherit what they had. Her father wouldn't leave her the business, but he would leave her more than enough to live on, and if she married, she would have her husband's money too. Yet none of it would really be hers. Which was why the five hundred francs she got from the Libe, paltry as it was, felt like a fortune—because it was hers and hers alone.

"Do your friends know?" she asked.

"*Vite, vite,*" he said, changing the subject. Quick, quick. "We must get into something warm or we will die of consumption."

"I don't think that's how you get consumption," Margie said, but her dress was clinging unpleasantly to her and leaving a large wet spot on Sebastien's carpet, so she followed him down the hall. He went into a room at the end and she almost followed him and then realized it was his bedroom and stopped, embarrassed, until her natural curiosity got the better of her and she peered around the door to see a table, a few sketchbooks and charcoal scattered on its surface, and a chair set up by a pair of wide French doors she guessed led to a balcony. At the other end of the room was an unmade bed, the sheets thrown back, the form of his body still clear upon them, so she could imagine him sleeping there, his hair tousled on the pillow, his eyelashes casting shadows on his cheeks. She caught her breath and stepped back into the hallway, both excited and ashamed of her own imagination.

He rummaged around the chest of drawers and then emerged with a pile of clothes in his hands. "Here. Wear these." He opened the door behind her to reveal another bedroom, a guest room, undisturbed and empty of personality. Taking the pile of clothes, she stepped inside and he closed the door behind her.

She changed into what he had given her, a shirt of soft cotton, a pair of loose pants. Sebastien was slender and Margie was broad, so they nearly fit her, and she felt somewhat charming and boyish, like a real flapper. The fabric was so fine and soft it made every inch of her skin feel alive, and she blushed to be naked against Sebastien's clothes.

When she opened the door, she was startled to find Sebastien standing there as though he had been waiting. He had changed as well, was wearing a sweater and a dry pair of pants, his hair brushed back from his forehead. Self-consciously, Margie put her own hand to her hair, which was, she could feel, beginning to curl wildly as it dried. "Let me take your things," Sebastien said, reaching for them, and Margie almost handed them over and then remembered her underthings and yanked the bundle back.

"I'll hang them," she said, and Sebastien simply shrugged.

"The toilet is just there." He nodded to the door behind him. "I have turned on the radiator. If you want to hang your clothes, they will dry."

She hung her clothes, and when she emerged, he had built a fire in the fireplace and moved the sofa toward the hearth. He was sitting in the center of it, leaning forward. When Margie padded into the room, he shifted to one side and patted the place next to him. "Come sit by the fire. I've made *chocolat chaud*."

Margie sat and gratefully took the cup he handed her, full of steaming hot chocolate, so thick and sweet it was like drinking a melted chocolate bar. The sugar and the heat from the fire made her feel sleepy, and she drew her feet up beneath her and curled into the cushions and sighed happily. "Thank you for inviting me in. And for the clothes."

"Of course."

"So do your friends know you're this rich?" Margie asked again, sipping at her chocolate.

Sebastien sighed exaggeratedly, and then looked over at her in the firelight and saw she was teasing him. "They do not. They know I can afford to pay the bill at cafés sometimes when they are short, but I let them believe it is because I sold a painting at the gallery. When some of them are struggling so much, it seems impolite to speak of it. And of course it would draw a line between us, if they knew. They might treat me differently. Money changes everything. Isn't that what they say in America?"

"It is," Margie said sadly. She thought of Mr. Chapman and his awkward proposal, about the hushed conversations between her mother and her aunt about her dowry versus Evelyn's. "Well, you hardly need so large a dowry with Evelyn," her mother had said to her aunt, and though Margie had known that was mostly meant to soothe her Aunt Edith, who acted richer than she actually was, it was nonetheless a slight to Margie, and it had made her feel even plainer and dowdier and more hopeless. She thought of how happy she was in Paris on only her tiny salary plus a little from her savings, how much happier than she had ever been at home, where there had been new dresses every season and invitations to the most important homes in Washington and Baltimore and New York, but she also thought of the way she felt now, safe inside an apartment with window glass solid enough to make the thunderous sound of the rain sound like nothing more than a gentle tapping, with a fireplace large enough to warm the whole room, with comfortable furniture and carpets thick as new grass, and she knew while it was exciting to think about throwing away material comforts in search of a romantic asceticism, money could be very nice indeed.

"And what does your family think of your being here?" She had finished the cup of chocolate, and reluctantly, she set it down on the table, half wanting to ask for more but knowing it was so rich she would never be able to drink it. She loved this about France, about how food was made to be more than sustenance, everything she ate was an *experience*, from the crème brûlée she had eaten at a restaurant when she had first arrived, to the simplest loaves of fresh bread. She often bought a demi-baguette from the corner boulangerie on her way home, and a bit of Brie from the cheesemonger, and if she hurried up to her room quickly enough, the bread would still be steaming when she broke it open, bits of crust falling onto her desk, so warm it would soften the cheese as she pressed them together, eating in pure, hedonistic pleasure.

Pushing his hand back through his hair, Sebastien squinted into the fire. "They think it is a phase. They believe when I have painted for a while, I will be content when I go back to Bordeaux and join the family business. My mother says I can paint the landscape there—it is beautiful enough that I would never have to see anything else."

Margie's eyes widened, thinking of the gift Sebastien had for seeing stories and telling them through his paintings. He could capture in square inches of canvas what it took her pages and pages to put onto paper. And then she tried to imagine how many stories were in a landscape, in a vineyard, in the climbing vines and the earth and the burst of ripe grapes. No matter how many, it would not be the same as the unending flow of humanity and its triumphs and tragedies as presented in a city. She tried to imagine Sebastien, who seemed to know everyone in Paris, and who, even if he didn't actually know them, had never met a stranger, living in the countryside. It seemed as unnatural as the expectations her parents had for her.

"That's so unfair," she said softly, not sure whether she was speaking of Sebastien or herself.

"And yet it is fair," Sebastien said. He had been staring thoughtfully into the fire. After the rush of the night, being out on the streets and then caught in the rain, Margie's sleepiness was beginning to catch up with her, and she saw a heaviness falling into his eyes as well. "They have always taken care of me. And when I told them I want to live in Paris, to study and to paint, they agreed. They said I could have five years here, before I go back and join them in business."

A surprisingly strong wave of relief rushed over Margie. Five years was forever. What she would give for five years in Paris! "Well that's fine, then! You can stay and paint—why, in five years who knows what will happen? They might change their minds. And in the meantime, if you keep selling your paintings, you won't have to go back."

In the firelight, Sebastien's eyes looked green and gold, the eyes of a cat. "Oh, no, no," he said sadly. "I am not beginning my five years in Paris. They are ending. And I cannot complain. I have lived more here than many people will in a lifetime. I have met people from all over the world. I have painted more than I could have imagined, and I have shown and sold my paintings. And my family has been so generous. How can I turn down their request to come home, to be a part of them, to work to repay them when they have given me so much for so long?"

Margie wanted to object, wanted to argue, but she couldn't. There was an honor and loyalty in Sebastien's words that made her like him even more. So much about Sebastien seemed clear now—his endless hunger for experiences, the way he always seemed determined to suck the marrow out of every night, fighting against sleep and good sense, his boundless energy. He was trying to live an entire life in five years.

Was this what Paris was to her as well? A moment of sunlight before she was thrust into darkness again? She had been having so much fun she hadn't stopped to think of what would come after. Her position at the Libe was funded for only three months, and it had been . . . well, it had been more than two already, hadn't it? She was shocked to realize so much time had passed, and then, thinking of Sebastien, she wondered if her own hourglass had been running the entire time as well.

"How much longer do you have?" she asked, a disquiet that was almost fear building inside her.

"Only a few weeks," Sebastien said, and she could almost touch the regret in his voice.

They looked at each other across the sofa, the firelight dancing on their faces, the chill that had driven them inside gone and replaced with warmth and the sadness of the conversation. In his face, she saw not only the way he looked in the flicker of the fire, but the way he had looked the day they had first met, leaning forward to convince her she must stay in Paris, and the way he rested his chin in his hand when he was listening, really listening, to one of his friends at a café, or the way he looked in the lamplight when they strolled the streets at night, and the memory of those things coupled with the look of him at that moment, tragic and lovely in the firelight, made him irresistible. And he must have been thinking the same thing about her, because when she leaned forward, he met her halfway and they kissed, their bodies leaning toward each other without touching, their lips the only point of contact. The wine she had drunk with dinner, the touch of his clothes on her skin, the heat of the fire, and the taste of him made Margie feel giddy and overwhelmed, as though she had drunk a bottle of champagne, and when he pulled her closer, she came to him eagerly.

They kissed until the heat of their desire coupled with the fire was too much to bear, and then Margie drew back, and slowly, staring boldly into Sebastien's eyes as though it were a dare, she pulled the shirt he had given her over her head. Underneath, she was bare, and she felt her body respond to the rush of air. For a moment, he didn't break his gaze with hers, their eyes locked together, and Margie held her breath. Would he refuse her? Then he lowered his eyes and took her in, and she could see him breathe, long and slow, and he whispered something in French as he moved across the distance to her and lowered his mouth to her breasts.

She knew she was doing something daring, something shocking, even, but she felt no shame. Instead, she felt beautiful and desirable and powerful, as though there were nothing she could do wrong. And when he pulled off the rest of her clothes and she stood there, naked in the firelight while the rain beat on outside and he knelt as if to worship her, she felt reborn.

"Marguerite," he whispered, his breath a kiss against her skin.

"Yes," she replied, and she knelt down to meet him.

twenty-one

MADELEINE
1999

My mother and I had been at a committee meeting at Ashley Hathaway's house for approximately ten thousand years, and I was starting to act like a toddler, pulling at my mother's skirt and begging for us to leave. Ashley's house was exactly what I would have imagined it to be if you had asked me to draw it in the sixth grade. When we played MASH on the school bus on field trips, Ashley inevitably ended up living in a mansion, married to Scott Baio with four kids, which was pretty much how her life had turned out. Well, not the Scott Baio part exactly, but her husband was a good-looking doctor, so that was pretty much a wash. There were family portraits everywhere, sitting on the hall table where everyone had left their handbags, lining the stairs going up to the second floor, perfect black-and-white pictures of Ashley in her little cardigans, the boys and her husband in sweater vests, as though they were passing through on a visit from the 1950s. The familiar taste of copper sat on my tongue.

"Aren't you just the sweetest to stay and help your mother for such a long time," Ashley said when my mother finally assented to leaving. She took me by the elbows and dropped air kisses on both my cheeks. I wrinkled my forehead at her. There was an insult in there somewhere.

I decided to return her backhanded compliment with one of my own. "Thanks for hosting. Your house looks exactly like the Pottery Barn catalog."

"Thank you!" Ashley said, clasping her hands together over her heart as though I had told her she had won the Miss America pageant. I should have known. Houses that look like the Pottery Barn catalog don't get that way by accident. I wanted to give her a hug and tell her it would be okay if little Grayson poured chocolate milk on the raffia carpet, or if she ate a pastry without feeling guilty about it for once. And then I wanted to hug her even more when I realized she wouldn't understand if I did.

My mother, spotting my sarcasm, changed the subject loudly. "You're doing really lovely work on this fundraiser, Ashley. I'm honored to be a part of it."

"We're honored to have you, Simone. You always make such an impact," Ashley said.

"Well, we'd better be going." I picked up my clutch, which I'd left on the table in the foyer (Pottery Barn Sophia Console Table, $799 in the winter catalog).

"You don't have to be rude," my mother said when we were outside, walking down the steep steps to the car. It was just like Ashley to buy a house on a hill, so everyone would be winded by the time they got to the front door.

"She started it." I hopped off the last step onto the sidewalk and headed to the car. My mother stepped delicately behind me and clicked open the car doors with the remote.

"How long are you staying?" she asked, settling herself behind the wheel, avoiding my eyes by pretending to adjust the rearview mirror.

"Don't tell me you've already tired of my witty banter and charming company."

"Be serious, Madeleine. You still haven't talked to Phillip, at least not that I know, and you haven't even mentioned going home."

"Maybe I don't want to go," I said sullenly, dragging my hand over the seat belt so the rough edge grated on the tender web of flesh between my thumb and my forefinger. "Maybe I'll move back here. I'll live in the high-rise with you and Lydia Endicott. Won't that be a barrel of laughs?" I bared my teeth at her in an evil grin, but she was looking at the road.

Pulling up to a stoplight, she pressed her fingers against her temples. "So you're not going back to Phillip. Is that what you're saying?"

There was a rawness and honesty to her voice that made my guilt crescendo. She didn't want me to get a divorce. Everyone would know. Everyone would know I had failed, she had failed. But I couldn't stay with him. I couldn't live that way anymore. I hardly knew how I had managed for so long.

"I guess I am."

She didn't reply. She unfolded her fingers from around the steering wheel, pressing her palms flat and spreading her fingers wide for a moment before taking hold again.

I spoke to fill the silence, to try to explain, the words tumbling out over themselves. "I was so lonely, and you wanted it so badly, and I thought—I thought it would be my only chance. I knew it was important to you, it was embarrassing I was the only one left. I know you wanted me to get married."

"It wasn't an embarrassment. I was worried about you, yes. I've always worried about you, Madeleine. You're so . . . different. And different can be painful."

I had started to cry, and I was trying hard to control it, keeping my jaw tight, blinking my eyes quickly. Being different, if she had just let me be different, if anyone had let me be different, would have been so much less painful than this, than trying to live up to some impossible standard, to become someone I literally could never be. "I was happy. I think I was happy. The only thing that made me unhappy was that I knew I was letting you down."

"You haven't let me down." She paused for a moment, flexed her hands on the wheel again. We were driving, as my mother did no matter the speed limit, at a steady thirty-five miles per hour, winding through the leafy streets. The houses, grand and quiet, problems hushed and hid away behind hedges and money, sat quietly observing us. "I just don't think you're really giving things a try, here, Madeleine. You can't just give up. You need to see Phillip again. Give things a chance."

I clenched my jaw, wishing she would listen to me, hear me for once. Clearly it was impossible for my mother to imagine what my life would be like if I divorced Phillip. The women she knew, no matter how miserable they were, didn't divorce their husbands. Which is how you ended up with someone like Betsy Lynn Chivers, who had spent so long in misery, waiting for her awful husband to die, that she honestly couldn't remember any other way to be. But I couldn't picture a different path for me either. Would I move back here, go to committee meetings at Ashley Hathaway's house, while everyone steered politely around me, giving me just enough berth to know they suspected divorce might be catching? Would I go back to work at Country Day, drafting politely guilt-inducing letters to people who received dozens of those fundraising appeals every day?

Or would I do something new? Would I dive into the Magnolia I had just discovered, this entire world that had existed beyond my peripheral vision for so long, where there were artists and musicians and people who didn't care what I looked like or whether or not I ate my dessert at lunch and wouldn't have blinked if I had told them I was going to art school and I didn't want to get married at all? Would I fall in love with someone like Henry, someone who wanted to feed me rather than starve me, someone who wanted me to paint and dance and be part of things I cared about?

That seemed like a terrifying leap to make without a net.

Because what if I were to leave Phillip, the world my mother had promised would keep me safe, and there was nothing out there? What if no one fell in love with me and I spent the rest of my life alone? What if no one wanted to look at, let alone buy, my paintings? What if painting didn't fill the hole inside me? What if, without having Sharon or Henry by my side, no one wanted to know me, and I ended up just as lonely as I had been? What if I took a risk and where I landed was no better than how I had been living?

The devil you know, my mother always used to say, is better than the devil you don't. And what I was thinking of doing was completely unknown. It was the social equivalent of closing my eyes and taking a step off a cliff. But now that I knew what it felt like to be surrounded by life, by laughter and good food and art and the people I wanted to be with, how could I go back to the way things had been, the way I had been?

Late that night, Henry and I were in my mother's back yard, on a small patch of grass between the rose garden and the orchard, the only space that had been spared from my mother's determined horticultural on-slaught. The grass beneath my back was lush and soft, and the roses released their rich, sweet scent into the air above us, testaments to my mother's gentle hand. The spring bulbs had burst into blossom in the past few weeks, and the daffodils and tulips stood in pretty bouquets in the flower garden, drowning in the smell of the hyacinths between them.

Above us, the sky was bright with ambient light, and beyond that, the infinite sparkle of stars. I had been in the back yard, lying on the cool grass, when Henry had come padding through the soft dirt of his garden and jumped over the low fence to sit beside me.

There was a nervous flutter inside me, as though we were on a first date, as though something had shifted between us, or maybe it was just my thoughts, maybe it was just that I was imagining a future with space for someone like him—maybe even him—in it.

"So can I ask you a question?" he asked. His knees were drawn up and his arms draped over them casually, and I was marveling at the size of his hands. As always, he smelled delicious—like rosemary and soap and wine, and when he moved, the scent wafted toward me and I closed my eyes and inhaled.

"Of course."

"You're married, right?"

"Right."

"But you've been here a long time. And you don't wear a wedding ring. And you never talk about your husband."

Closing the tips of my fingers around the space where my rings had rested, I felt only the skin, smooth and pale and bare. It felt vulnerable, like the tender underbelly of an animal. "Is that a question?"

"Technically, no. I guess I was just wondering what's going on. If you need to talk about it or something. If I'm prying . . ."

"No, no, it's okay. It's—things are complicated. Being here has been a break, I guess."

He nodded. "So it's a good thing, then? Taking a break?"

"Yes," I said slowly. I couldn't explain it. There was too much. I couldn't explain how leaving Chicago had felt like releasing a weight from my shoulders, how the constant thrum of anxiety in my bones had faded, how I slept better at night and didn't feel the pull of exhaustion during the day, how I didn't wake up with a feeling of dread hanging low in my chest, how the stomachaches I had grown to accept as a constant in my life had disappeared since I had come here. It was odd, that the place I had avoided for so long, this town with all its ghosts and memories of my disappointments and my failures, with my mother's presence looming over it like a threat, odd that this place would feel like a relief. Odd that because of Henry in particular I would have discovered there was so much more to this place than I had ever anticipated.

"Have you ever been married?"

Henry nodded slowly. "I was. A long time ago. Didn't last."

"What happened?"

"We were young. Too young. Young and stupid. I don't think either one of us knew what we were getting into."

"Were you in love?"

"Of course," Henry said, turning to me and giving me a confused look. "Or at least I thought I was. No, that's not fair. I was. Just because I didn't recognize the import of what I was doing doesn't mean I wasn't in love. There's different kinds of love, you know? And we were in the kind of love you can only be in when you're so young you don't know any better."

I had never been in love like that. I had never been in love before Phillip, really. I'd had tremendous crushes, but had never had a relationship last long enough to call it love. And I had always attributed it to some failing on my part, proof I wasn't lovable, but what if that hadn't been the way of it at all? What if I had pushed them away? I had known falling in love would lead to marriage, and maybe I had known I didn't want to get married. My grandmother had been the same way, hadn't she? Swearing she would live in Paris and write and have a life different from the one she had been born into. And I had thought I would be the same way. And yet, both of us had ended up with exactly what we had promised we wouldn't have. I might have avoided falling in love because I knew what would follow after.

Henry continued his story. "We got married and we both realized very quickly it wasn't what we wanted. She wanted to travel, and I wanted to work. I wanted to make a name for myself quickly, and she wanted to explore."

"Did you resent her?"

"At the time, probably a little. She certainly resented me. She said I was holding her back. But it wasn't that. Or it wasn't only that. We wanted different things."

A car drove by on the street out front, and quiet fell again. In the city, the noise was a perpetual unwelcome guest. Even in our condo, well above the street, there was an unrelenting blur of noise underlying everything. I had learned to tune it out, but if I stopped and listened, it came flooding back, and it was startling to realize how constant it was. Here I felt like I was a hundred miles from any distraction, the way the night and the stillness fell heavy and soothing around us.

"You know," Henry said thoughtfully, stroking his beard, "it took me a long time to leave her. I didn't think I had a good enough reason. I thought we needed to be fighting all the time, throwing things, crying."

"I'm pretty sure it does have to be that way if you want to get a divorce in my family. I need to have a good reason if I'm going to upset the country club register."

"It is enough. Being unhappy is enough."

"Is it? Happiness is so transitory. I could be happy today and unhappy tomorrow. And it's affected by so many things out of your control—the weather, the traffic, other people's behavior."

Henry was shaking his head. "That's not what I mean. I'm not talking about good moods or bad moods. Sure, those blow over with the weather. But whether you are happy deep down, whether you wake up and have to summon up the energy just to get out of bed, or whether you feel like every day is an opportunity, that's different. That doesn't change because of a thunderstorm or someone cutting in front of you in line."

"I guess," I said, though I was strangely unwilling to concede the point. I had been sure for so long my unhappiness didn't matter, had held it underwater for so long in an effort to drown it, that my entire life seemed like a waste of time if it actually did matter in the end.

"Well, let me ask you this. Why did you marry him?"

"My parents wanted me to." And then I paused. "And I was afraid no one else would want me."

Henry's eyes went wide, but he said nothing.

"I was living alone. I had my own job. I supported myself. But I was kind of a metaphorical burden. It was hard for my mother to tell her friends I was almost thirty and still single when all their daughters were married already, and having children, most of them. My failure to follow the plan made her look like a failure as a mother, and that was uncomfortable for her."

"You sound so forgiving."

"It's not her fault." I shrugged. "She was raised with those expectations."

Henry looked at me with those wide hazel eyes, serious and intense. "I think you're too hung up on what everyone else thinks, and you haven't given enough thought to what you think."

"Let me ask you a question," I said, bristling slightly. "Was it easy for you to leave your relationship? Did you wake up one day and decide it wasn't for you? Just walk out?"

"Of course not. I agonized for—well, frankly, for years. In hindsight I know I waited too long. I knew long before I let myself know, if that makes any sense."

"So why are you rushing me?" I asked. "And besides, just because it was right for you doesn't mean it's right for me. Maybe Phillip and I are meant to be together. Maybe I need to stop being so self-absorbed and worrying about my feelings and pull myself up by my bootstraps and recommit."

"It's possible," Henry said. "Do you love him?" he asked.

I sighed, a long and slow exhalation into the night. "I don't know," I said. It seemed disloyal to say I didn't. And how do you know if you love someone? Someone you've been with for that long? Phillip was just a fact of life.

"Did you ever?" he asked gently.

"Of course," I said with a confidence I didn't feel. It was an unfair question to ask anyone who has become disenchanted with a relationship, who is angry or sad or broken, because of course they won't be able to remember what it felt like when they were in love. Hindsight is 20/20, et cetera. I could see clearly that I had been attracted to Phillip, to the same things that attracted everyone to him—his charm and his chiseled features and his perfect hair and the way he had of offering the perfect toast for any occasion. And I knew I had felt relieved by his proposal, that part of my attraction had been gratitude, and that I had been in love with the idea of marriage and family and finally, for once, fitting in and doing what I was supposed to do rather than endlessly letting people down. But we had hardly known each other. I had loved the image he presented to me, but he had held me at arm's length, and our engagement had been short, and then, finally, when he had what he wanted, a woman with a social pedigree who would let him criticize her when he felt small and the money to rescue his family's business, and we had begun to live together and been unable to hide our true selves, I had come to realize I didn't love him, and most days I didn't even really like him, and to be brutally honest, he probably felt the same way.

That was all my fault, wasn't it? One more in a string of Madeleine-shaped failures. And why should I put my mother through that much humiliation at the Ladies Association over something as trivial as my own happiness? I thought of all the money—the money my father had given to Phillip to rescue the business, the money they had spent on the wedding. I thought of all the people who had come, all the gifts, the end-less thank-you notes, all the people who would have to be told. All the people who would say, "I knew it wouldn't last," who had looked at my plainness and Phillip's glow and raised an eyebrow, all those people who had seen the years before go by without my getting married and tutted and said of my mother, "That poor woman," as though I had been living off their largesse instead of supporting myself.

I didn't want to endure that.

"Were you ashamed? Of the divorce, I mean," I asked Henry in a small voice. That's what it was, the emotion behind everything. Shame.

Shame I had failed in this thing I had claimed I wanted, shame I had failed in this thing that mattered so much to the people around me, shame I had failed in something so public.

Henry lay back and looked up at the sky. It was a clear night, and stars speckled the darkness above us. I knew there were thousands, tens of thousands, millions more we couldn't see because of the light pollution, but it was still so much better than in the city, where the best I might be able to see were Orion's belt and the North Star, and I felt rudderless, like a lost sailor looking for direction under a cloudy sky.

"I was, a little. But more brokenhearted than ashamed. We'd been in love at one point, and it was so sad, that breaking apart of something that had once been beautiful. I knew it was the right thing to do, and it didn't make me question the decision, but I mourned it. It was something real, and I felt—I still feel, actually—a tenderness toward that relationship. At least the way it was when it was new."

"I don't feel brokenhearted. I only feel ashamed," I said. I lay back on the grass beside him. There was no funeral in my heart. If I mourned anything, it was the time I had spent with Phillip, the way I had buried myself in our marriage in order to be the person my mother needed me to be, to be the person Ashley Hathaway needed me to be, the person I had thought I had to be in order to belong.

Don't you still? something inside me asked.

I turned my head, as though my thoughts were something unpleasant I could look away from, the honesty of my conscience too much to bear. My head rested on Henry's arm. He was wearing a button-down shirt with the sleeves rolled up, his arms hairy against my skin. I wanted to roll over and bury my face in his chest, breathe in the scent of him, feel his heart beating against my cheek, feel someone solid and strong and alive.

And, I realized with a jolt, I felt attracted to him. Alive and aware and even aroused. He felt real, felt solid and imperfect, and so close, and his eyes were on me, seeing me, knowing me. We talked and I was aware of our lips moving in the darkness, aware of the smell of the flowers in my mother's garden and the vegetables in his, of the earth and the air and mostly of him, strong and solid beside me.

I bent my elbow and rested my head in my hand, looking down at him. His eyes were dark and unreadable, shining dimly in the starlight, but I felt as if something were pulling us together, and when he rolled onto his side, I felt his closeness in my entire body—an awareness of not only his eyes and his mouth but every inch of him.

I don't know who kissed whom first. I suppose it was me, but there was a point at which the kiss was inevitable, when we had moved so close together, the small space left between us filled with tension and heat and desire, it would have been impossible to draw apart again. Maybe it wasn't so much my initiative as a slow, magnetic pull, as though the earth's gravitational force wanted us together, and our lips met and we kissed, gently, softly. I had never kissed a man with a beard before, and it made the act of kissing him feel new and beautifully strange, unfamiliar and familiar at the same time. His lips were soft, his beard brushed lightly against my skin as we fell together, his arm around my waist, mine around his neck, the brush of his hair against my fingertips, the length of his body against mine. We kissed like that, and I felt a long-forgotten warmth inside me, as though I were a flower opening to the spring of him, and I wondered where this would go, whether we would make love here on the grass, under the stars, as though the night belonged only to us. Until when I moved my hand to his shirt, pulling the back up and spreading my fingers over the warmth of his skin, he pulled back and looked at me, his eyes searching mine in the darkness.

"No," he said gently, and he pulled away. "No. Not like this." He removed his hand from my waist and shifted backward, letting the night fall between us, cold and dark.

"What do you mean?" I asked.

He rolled onto his back and blew a long breath out toward the stars. "Well, for starters, you're married."

"Separated," I said, my protest feeling weak even as I made it. Even if our separation had been something formal, it wasn't an actual condition. It was a liminal state. It was the state of someone too afraid to commit, to speak her mind. A punishing fist squeezed at my stomach.

"And even if you were divorced, it's too fresh. I don't want you to get hurt, but, to be selfish, I don't want to get hurt either. Your heart—I don't know where your heart is." He spoke to the sky, as though the stars and the moon and the satellites drifting lonely through space, bleating out their lights like Morse code, could hear him.

I sank back onto the grass beside him. "I don't know where it is either," I said. Above me, the stars kept their silent watch, their glacial changes invisible to me.

I hadn't intended to kiss Henry. Hadn't admitted to myself until that night I was attracted to him. It had been the moment, the conversation, his easy smile, the way everything felt comfortable with him. Was this how it was supposed to be? I felt like I had been clenching every muscle in my body since I had met Phillip, and with Henry I felt like liquid. I felt smarter, sharper, more creative. More alive.

In the end, it didn't matter how much I liked him, or how I felt when I was with him, because he had turned me down. And I was married. What was I doing? Creating this whole fantasy life here, as though I could stay forever. I couldn't be a painter. I couldn't be friends with Sharon and Henry. Maybe that was why my grandmother had left Paris— because she knew it had to end. At some point you have to go back to reality. Nobody gets to live their dream.

twenty-two
....

MARGIE
1924

Margie and Sebastien became those lovers she had seen on the streets so often, the kind her mother would have considered completely shameful. They walked hand in hand, and often he lifted hers to his mouth and dropped a gentle kiss on her fingers or the tender skin of her open palm. He bought a bottle of wine and they sat on the banks of the Seine at night, watching the slow movement of boats up and down the river, their lights shimmering onto the dark water until it was impossible to see where the stars ended and the lanterns began. In noisy bars and busy cafés, they sat with their foreheads touching, talking endlessly about art and writing and Paris and America and all the things they knew and could not know, and when their friends rose and announced it was time to move on, to Zelli's or the Jockey or La Coupole, they nodded and rose too, but instead of following the crowd, they would slip away from the group to return to Sebastien's apartment and make love and fall asleep in his bed until the sun woke them, naked and new, in the morning.

And everything was perfect, until it wasn't.

It started with the Libe. Margie went into work one day and Miss Parsons, who was normally—frankly, oddly—cheerful, looked pale and worried.

"*Bonjour!*" Margie said happily, because she had started the day in Sebastien's arms, and what could be better than that? She hung her coat on the rack by the front door and put her bag and her hat in one of the cubbies behind the desk, preparing to take over Miss Parsons' position there.

Miss Parsons simply muttered a hello and then quickly looked away, gathering the papers she had been working on and scurrying upstairs to her office. They had been offering classes to French librarians, and for people who worked in libraries they were awfully noisy, always clomping back and forth between the two classrooms upstairs, but that day it was silent, and she heard the sound of Miss Parsons' quick, efficient steps on the floor above, the closing of her office door, and then nothing else.

Margie shrugged and sat down behind the desk, putting a piece of stationery from the Library War Service—there was reams of it, they'd be using it forever—in the typewriter and starting a letter to her parents, only to interrupt herself to write in her journal at great length about Sebastien. She considered using code, in case anyone else were ever to read it, but who would want to read her lovesick scribblings anyway? Miss Stein came in and asked for help in her usual curmudgeonly way. Margie hardly noticed, moving airily along the shelves, pulling volume after volume until at last the woman retreated, mollified. Margie answered two telephone calls and found the answers they were looking for (the height of the Eiffel Tower, 954 feet; the sixth U.S. president, John Quincy Adams). It felt as if nothing could disturb her happiness.

And when Miss Parsons called for Margie after lunch, asked her to come upstairs to her office, Margie was so happy she didn't even think something might be wrong.

"Margie, I have some bad news."

"Oh?" Margie said. She was still smiling, Miss Parsons' serious demeanor having failed to immediately crack her good mood.

"The grant we applied for didn't come through. Well, it came through, but it wasn't as much as we were hoping."

"Oh no," Margie said, with the detached, polite disappointment of someone who has just heard bad news that in no way impacts them. "How much did they give?"

"We asked for fifty thousand dollars." She stopped, hesitated. "They only gave us seven thousand."

"Goodness. That is disappointing."

"It is." Miss Parsons ran her fingertips along the edge of her desk, then put her hands in her lap. "The thing is, Margie, one of the things we had earmarked that grant money for was your salary."

The smile finally faded from Margie's face, and a slow, cracking chill spread from her feet up to her heart, like a river icing over in the winter. "What do you mean?"

Miss Parsons, to her credit, looked utterly heartbroken. "It means, Margie, I have to let you go. The Libe's funding is so tight, and you've really been absolutely invaluable. It's just . . . we simply can't afford to keep you."

"I thought there was a grant just for my position," Margie said, as if Miss Parsons might have miscalculated.

"Yes, well." Miss Parsons shifted uncomfortably in her chair. "Things have been tight, and we've borrowed against it."

"But I thought the library was doing so well. The classes for the French librarians, and the grant from the Carnegies and the membership is up quite a bit. I signed two people up myself yesterday. . . ."

Miss Parsons was shaking her head, looking at Margie with an expression somehow both guilty and sympathetic. "It's much bigger, unfortunately. Our costs are so large and our support now that the war is over is so small. And if I could keep you on, Margie, I would. I would in a heartbeat. The way you've taken to Paris, the work you've done here, your attitude—you're so helpful. We just can't afford it now. I'll give you a reference anywhere you want to go."

"Sure," Margie said dully. Over Miss Parsons' shoulder she could see out the window into the yard behind the Libe, and beyond that the grand roof of one of the mansions along the rue du Faubourg Saint-Honoré. It glittered in the sunshine, winking at her cheerfully, mindless of her tragedy.

After Miss Parsons had dismissed her, Margie dragged herself back downstairs to the desk. The letter to her parents still sat, half typed, in the typewriter, and she pulled it out, folding it and putting it into her bag. She would finish it by hand later. The cheerful clack of the keys right now would be too much to bear. Her joyous journal entry, also half finished, seemed silly and inconsequential now. She would have to leave Paris. She would have to leave Sebastien. She calculated frantically the amount of money she still had. Oh, she shouldn't have bought that new hat, she should have insisted she and Dorothy go to Rosalie's for dinner instead of having tea at Rumpelmayer's—it was far too dear.

Only what was the point of being in Paris if she hadn't enjoyed herself? And she really had been so conservative. She had gone to the Opéra Comique twice, and to the Palais Garnier to see *Parsifal* only once, though she could have lingered in that incredible building for hours, would have been delighted to go every night just to stand in the Grand Foyer, to see the spectacle of the paintings and the carving and the gilt-edged furniture and the way it shone everywhere you looked. The opera was a necessity, wasn't it? And other than that, she ate at the artists' cafés, and Sebastien bought her dinner sometimes, and when she ate on her own she stuck to bread and cheese and once, because she couldn't resist their perfection, a lovely carton of strawberries from the market on rue Mouffetard.

All the regretful accounting in the world couldn't save her now.

She finished the day, apparently so sad even grumpy Miss Stein seemed concerned, and walked home. She would still have a few more weeks of work at the Libe, but that night it already felt like the last time, and she was prematurely nostalgic for the route she had grown to love, past the Place de la Concorde and the Gare d'Orsay, along the busy

Boulevard Raspail and through the narrow alleys behind the churches and the shops, and then to the wide and welcoming quiet of Montparnasse, turning the corner by La Closerie des Lilas, impervious even to the rich smell of the lilacs that always reached out to her, welcoming her home.

Instead of turning down rue de Chevreuse to the Club, however, she kept walking until she came to Sebastien's, waiting outside until someone came out the door, and then slipping into the courtyard as it closed. She nodded to the caretaker, who was trimming back the roses reaching so eagerly up the wall toward the sun, and he paused and waved back, his shears gleaming in the sunlight.

She buzzed up to Sebastien's apartment and his voice came through the speaker, tinny and blurry. *"Allo?"* he asked, distracted.

"It's Margie," she said. She couldn't even bring herself to use his name for her, couldn't call herself Marguerite. She didn't feel much like a Marguerite just then. She felt like Margie, plucked and deflated, brought down to earth.

He buzzed her up, and she rushed up the stairs, sure seeing him would bring her some relief. But when he opened the door, he looked even worse than she did. He looked, she realized with horror, like Miss Parsons had, right before she had told Margie they would have to let her go.

"Come in, come in." He looked as though he had been painting; there was a streak of blue in his hair and he wore an old shirt with holes in the elbows and paint spattered over the buttons, but when she walked inside, mostly what she noticed was the trunk lying open in the middle of the floor, and the stack of paintings against the wall.

"What's going on?" she asked. She was still so much in shock over Miss Parsons' news she couldn't imagine anything worse, and still, the hard rock of her stomach seemed to be falling lower.

"Please, sit down," Sebastien said, taking her hands and leading her to the sofa. The same sofa where she had first kissed him, where, after they had made love for the first time on the floor, he had tenderly wrapped a blanket around them both, and they had lain together, their bodies warm, curled around each other as if they had been designed to do so, watching the fire until they fell asleep there.

Sitting, she could see down the hall to the bedroom, where another trunk had been opened, clothes laid along the edges. "Sebastien," she said, and her voice was rising into what she could clearly identify as panic, "what's going on?"

"Shh, shh," he said, stroking her hands. "It is time. I am leaving Paris—I have to go home."

"You are home!" Margie looked frantically around the apartment, as though she might have mistaken it for someplace else. No, these were the same rooms she had been in so many times. She knew the smell of it— the smell of him—paint and dust and the scent of the fire.

"Home to my family. I told you my time here was limited."

"You can say no, can't you? My parents tell me to come home all the time, but I don't listen," Margie said. She heard the futility of her own argument.

Sebastien was leaning forward, elbows resting on his thighs, head hanging low. He shook his head slowly and then looked at her. His eyes, his beautiful green eyes, the eyes she had fallen for the moment she had seen them for the first time, alive with the excitement and energy that was Sebastien, were dark and serious. "I cannot turn against my family. It is a duty."

Margie threw her hands up and rose from the couch, pacing back and forth. "Duty. Responsibility. I'm sick of hearing those words. We're young! Why should we have to settle down just because they did? Don't you want to stay in Paris, Sebastien? Don't you want to stay here and paint and see the Surrealists' Bureau open and go to the Olympic Games with me? Don't you want to paint? How can you turn your back on your art?"

"It has nothing to do with what I want. It has to do with honoring my family and what they have given me. I have had my time—I have had more time than most people do. I had my time to play and now it is time to work."

"You said we would spend Christmas together! You said we would go ice skating at the Petit Palais and see the lights on the Champs-Élysées. You promised!" Margie knelt in front of Sebastien, wrapped her hands around his, squeezing his fingers tightly, as if she could convince him, make him stay through the sheer force of her desire.

Gently, he lifted her hands to his mouth and kissed each of her fingers in turn. She loved the way he kissed her, the way he treated her, the way he cared for her. She would never find another man like this as long as she lived. He made her feel beautiful, cherished. Her. Sturdy, plain Margie Pearce. With him, she wasn't that same dull, solid girl. She was Marguerite, an American in Paris, and she spent her days with writers and diplomats, and her evenings with artists. She had been to Harry's New York Bar and the Casino, she had a lover—a lover who was a painter. She thought of all those girls at her debut, beautiful girls whose lives had seemed full of promise. Now all those beautiful girls were married, stuck on the same merry-go-round of parties and obligations as their mothers, and here she was, in Paris, kneeling at the feet of her French lover. But if he left, who would she be? Would she go back to being Margie Pearce again? She could think of nothing worse.

"Marguerite," he said softly, and she wanted to weep at the sound of her name on his lips. It would never sound the same when someone else said it. And soon, there would be no one who called her Marguerite at all. She would run out of money and she would have to go home to Washington, and she would eventually be forced to marry one of the suitable men her parents presented to her, and they would call her "Margie" or "dear" with a flat, disinterested accent, instead of calling her "Marguerite" and *"mon coeur"* with the gentle curl of a French tongue.

She would not be a writer anymore, not a real writer; she would go to Temperance League meetings with her mother and her mother's friends and all their daughters who had been roped into the same cruel joke. And then the daughters would raise their own daughters and deliver them into the same cycle. She wouldn't have time to write; she wouldn't have space to dream, and this time in Paris would become nothing more than a memory, insubstantial as smoke, something she would recall, wondering if it had ever really happened at all.

"What if we were to get married?" she asked, with a quick, wild hope, and then, "Oh," when she saw his expression turn from surprise to something like sadness. "No, I didn't mean—" she said, and shifted away, as though she were going to stand.

"Stop, stop." He pulled her back toward him. "It is not about my feelings for you. My feelings for you . . ." He paused, looked away, and she could see him swallow before he gazed at her again, and the green of his eyes, which she was so used to seeing sparkling with life, looked somber and dull. "You know how this works. My parents will have made arrangements for me to marry the daughter of a family with whom we are in business, but Margie, you must not let that happen to you. This is where you are meant to be. Here, in Paris. Writing."

It took Margie a moment to hear him, really, over the sound of her own shame, and the surety of his rejection. But of course he was right. They had talked of their families, and she knew they came from similar backgrounds. Marrying him and living with his family in Bordeaux would give her exactly the life she had run from—she would be trapped by the same duties, the same formalities as her own mother. And she had seen what happened to the husbands of girls she knew—they became buried under their work, lost themselves to their own pressures. Who said Sebastien wouldn't lose everything that made him sparkle so brilliantly to the weight of duty, just like the rest of them?

And, if she were being honest, she didn't want to marry Sebastien.

They had never said they loved each other, never talked about the future longer than a few months out. He had made no promises to her, and she had made none to him. The romantic Margie who had danced at her debutante ball years ago would have been shocked by such a pragmatic relationship, could never have conceived of passion without a grand romance, but she wasn't that Margie anymore, in so many ways.

In fact, since her debut, each month that passed without a proposal had lifted her up. She had felt as though everything around her had been hazy and was now growing clearer. And then when she had come to Paris, she had thought, *Yes, this is why. This is where I am supposed to be.*

What she knew of marriage did not fit with the way things were in Paris. Marriage was her father's staid gravity, her mother's fretful imprisonment. Marriage was rounds of required visits, of household management and parties that never seemed to be any fun. Paris was none of those things. It was bread and cheese for dinner in the Luxembourg Gardens, or a cheap plate at Rosalie's at ten o'clock at night. Paris was parties lasting until dawn, where you danced until you were breathless and drank until the world itself seemed to have become unmoored, the floor unsteady beneath your feet. Paris was sunrises and sunsets, was art and music and books and the people who made them, unstoppable around you. Paris was endless music and endless joy, and to get married, to change anything at all, would have ruined it.

Except it was being ruined anyway. It was all slipping away from her, and there was nothing she could do to stop it. Sebastien was leaving, and she thought she would not be able to endure this city without him. Every time she walked by Les Deux Magots she would remember meeting him, and the food at L'Écurie would be tasteless as sawdust if he were not smiling at her across the table, and the tiny afterthoughts of streets would lose their magic, the miracle of stumbling down an alley along the wall of a church at midnight, only to look up and see the stained-glass windows glowing softly above like a benediction, the unexpected joy of

ending a late night of dancing by standing outside the window of a boulangerie in the pale morning light, faces pressed to the glass, inhaling the
scent of the first baguettes of the day, and there would be no more joy in
being lost. Sebastien had opened the city to her and she feared she didn't
have the courage or the strength to live in it without him.

She lowered her head into his lap and wept, and he stroked her hair
and murmured to her in French, and she didn't even try to understand.
It was all ending, all falling apart, and she felt herself sliding down the
endless precipice toward the life she did not want, had never wanted, and
everything she grabbed at on the way down in a desperate attempt to
stop herself came away in her hands.

twenty-three

MADELEINE
1999

I had never thought Phillip would come for me. I had been doing my best to push him out of my mind. I knew that wasn't a mature way to deal with problems, nor an especially effective one: no matter how much I pretended he didn't exist, he stubbornly insisted on doing so.

When he arrived, I was up in the attic, shifting around the last of the boxes, covered in dust and dirt and the funk of forty thousand years, trying again and again to forget the feeling of Henry's body against mine, our kiss, the way he smelled, the way he felt. It didn't belong to me, and I didn't deserve it.

My mother was sitting downstairs in the parlor, reading the newspaper, so when the doorbell rang, she was closer, and I ignored it, until I heard the sound of talking in the foyer, filtered up two staircases.

Is it terrible to admit I didn't even recognize my husband's voice? I only heard my mother talking to a man and with a little wisp of happy hope I crushed as soon as it came to life, I thought it might be Henry (although I should have known it wasn't; my mother sounded far too pleased to see him). I lifted a box onto my hip and carried it downstairs, and there was Phillip, standing there holding my mother's hands and smiling that perfect smile at her, and I nearly dropped the box, my face flushing hot with guilt.

I had been making such an effort to put him out of my mind that the fact of him seemed completely foreign; to me, he looked less like the man I had promised, in front of God and pretty much all of Magnolia society, to love and cherish for the rest of my days only to betray him with a moonlit night and a kiss, and more like a stranger. A handsome and well-dressed stranger, but a stranger nonetheless. I didn't want to face him, I didn't want to talk to him. I felt like waving at him and going back to wrestling with the boxes. Later I might paint. At the library I'd found a book of old photos of Paris, and I wanted to try painting them, wanted to capture the light my grandmother had been so in love with. Frankly, what I really wanted to do was drop everything and actually go to Paris, but that didn't seem particularly practical.

I suppose it would make a better story to say Phillip's and my reunion was like a movie, that tear-jerking music swelled in the background and we rushed into each other's arms (politely stepping around the table so we didn't knock over the flower arrangement), and all was forgiven, even the parts we would never talk about.

But it didn't feel like a romantic moment. It felt weighted with guilt and confusion and surprise and distance. So basically I stood there in the hallway, looking at my husband curiously, as though I were an anthropologist and he were a previously undiscovered tribe, until he asked, "Aren't you going to say hello?" and I pulled myself out of my twitching mind and walked over to him (bumping into the table on the way, though it turned out the flower arrangement was way too heavy to knock over) and gave him an awkward hug, and he bent to kiss me except I was already pulling away, thinking he wasn't the last person I had kissed, so he got the edge of my mouth, and if we had been actors in a romantic movie, we would have been fired.

In retrospect, "What are you doing here?" was probably not the most welcoming thing I could have said. It wasn't meant to be accusatory. I just honestly couldn't think of why he was there, and if there was any edge to my voice, it was because it had been sharpened on my shame.

"I thought I'd come see how things are going here," he said. And then, pointedly, "You haven't been returning my calls."

I winced, thinking guiltily of the cell phone, which, as far as I knew, was still marinating in the water at the bottom of the vase, about two feet from us. "Sorry."

"And of course I wanted to check on Simone," he said, turning toward my mother and shooting her one of his patented dazzling smiles.

"Oh. Nice," I said. And oddly, the thought that floated through my mind was one of relief. *Well*, went the logic somewhere deep in my lizard-brain, *at least he's not here to see you. That takes some of the pressure off.*

But of course he was there to see me. I was the one who had married him, and here he was, charging in on his white horse to rescue me. Or, more likely, to rescue himself. That was more Phillip's style. He would never let me go, no matter how unhappy he was. It would make him look weak, or wrong, or out of control. No, he would rather maintain his image and keep me in check, even if it meant he would be stuck with me for the rest of his life.

"You're a mess. What have you been doing, cleaning the gutters?" he asked, his gaze skimming over my clothes. I looked down at my outfit, which was pretty much the same one I had been wearing when Henry had come to pick me up for First Friday, and brushed off my shirt a little.

"Moving boxes. It's dirty work," I said, and my shoulders slumped as I felt myself moving back onto the familiar battlefield that was my relationship with Phillip. This was real life. I'd been on vacation, that's what it was. That's why everything had felt so easy and free. But you don't get to stay on vacation forever. At some point, you have to go back to work.

My mother cleared her throat, surprisingly awkwardly for her. "Shall we go into the parlor?" she asked. Without waiting for an answer, she led us regally into the front room. She and Phillip ended up sitting together on the sofa while I took the chair opposite. It looked as though we were conducting an awkward job interview rather than having a family reunion. "The house looks lovely, Mother," Phillip said.

"Thank you," she preened, and I had to admit it did look good, especially without all the things we had sold, packed, or otherwise disposed of. Remembering the things I had packed away for myself, with the full knowledge there was no room in my home for them, made me feel guilty, and I rearranged my face so it wouldn't show.

"How are the preparations going for the move?" he asked, leaning slightly toward my mother and placing his hand on hers, as though she might need moral support through the difficulties of the conversation.

"It's going well. There's just so much to *do*," my mother said. She made it sound as if she were organizing an invasion of Russia instead of moving house, which, frankly, people do literally every day, but my mother had always had a tendency for the dramatic, especially around men. Just call her Scarlett. I wouldn't have been a bit surprised if she had leaned back and laid her hand over her forehead in a swoon.

Phillip looked over at my mother with kind sympathy and patted her hand. He could be so charming when he wanted to be. When we had been dating, he was one of those men who always knew when to send flowers, who told you how nice you looked when he picked you up, whose dates were elaborate as scenes from a romantic movie. It had been nice, being treated that way.

"And how are you, Phillip? How is work? And your lovely mother?"

I snorted aloud and my mother shot me a withering glare. Mrs. Spencer and my mother, despite their essentially being two peas in a pod, loathed each other. The wedding weekend they had been inseparable, cooing over everything, bending their heads together as though they were sharing secrets, and then at the breakfast the morning after the wedding, when Mrs. Spencer had left early to go to the airport, my mother had whispered to me, "I thought she'd never leave."

"My mother is well, thank you so much for asking. And work is busy. We're growing. We're going to have to move to some new offices soon or we'll all be sitting on top of each other."

"Isn't that something," my mother said with the same cheerful, if vague, lack of interest she'd always taken in my father's work. I couldn't blame her; whatever Phillip did involved the sort of inscrutable financial transactions that populate the pages of *The Wall Street Journal* and I understood it only vaguely. Amortization and deeds and all kinds of impenetrable abbreviations: REIT and GLA and TPTI. It wasn't that it was uninteresting . . . no, actually, it was uninteresting.

The conversation had ground to a screeching halt. "It's so nice of you to come," my mother said. "Isn't it nice of him?"

"Yes . . ." I said cautiously. Her question felt like a trap. "How long are you staying?"

"Just a day. I've got to get back to the office. I figured I'd come and help you pack up. We've got tickets on the noon flight home tomorrow."

The warmth that had been growing inside me froze. "But my mother . . ." I started.

She cut me off. "I can manage things around here."

"There's still so much to do . . ." I said weakly.

"I'd hate to keep you from Phillip any longer." The smile on my mother's face had steel underneath it. I was going.

"So it's settled, then," he said, and I saw the unfriendly resolve in his eyes when he turned to smile at me, in triumph, not in warmth. As much as I didn't want the shame and discomfort of a divorce, my mother and Phillip wanted it even less. I heard the "lock" of wedlock clicking shut.

And what did it matter? Henry had turned me away. I could see only two vague images of what my life might look like without Phillip, and both were terrifyingly empty. Either it would look exactly like my life in Chicago, only with bonus ostracism, or it would be an unsure world in which I would have to make my own way. I couldn't predict my future based on a couple of outings with Sharon and Henry, who had their own lives and were in no way bound to be my guides through anything. And Henry—well, Henry wasn't interested anyway. What was I even thinking? I had a husband and a life. A perfectly good life. A life a lot of people would have been terribly envious of. Just because it wasn't the right life for me didn't give me license to throw it away.

"Well. We should all go out to dinner tonight to celebrate. I mean, after Madeleine takes a shower, of course." Phillip's eyes flicked over me again. I folded my arms, trying to disguise the bulge at my waist where the chocolate lava cake and strawberry jam and raspberry Italian sodas were making themselves known. "I saw there's a new restaurant next door—shall we try it?"

My mother looked as though Phillip had suggested we all have slugs for afternoon tea. "Never. We'll have dinner at the hotel when we drop off Madeleine's bags."

"Not any good?" Phillip asked.

"It's excellent." I didn't want to go there either, not with their critical eyes keeping me from eating what I wanted to eat, and definitely not with Phillip and Henry in the same room. I could hardly let them both occupy space in my head.

"It's been a nightmare ever since they moved in. Can you imagine having a restaurant as a neighbor? I haven't slept in months."

"You're exaggerating," I said, but I felt embarrassed defending the restaurant in front of Phillip. Putting my loyalties with Henry made me feel as though I had been cheating.

Had I been cheating? I mean yes, I had kissed him. It had only been a kiss, but maybe it had meant more than that, maybe it had been—no. I stopped myself. My husband was here now. And though I hadn't been thrilled to see him, I saw how it would be. His threat of divorce hadn't been real. His mother wouldn't stand for the scandal, he wouldn't stand for the appearance of failure. We had existed in a peaceful détente up until now. Surely I could do it again.

Phillip left to go check into the hotel, and I told him I would pack while he was gone. I had a ticket. I was out of excuses. My mother didn't need me to stay, and I had no reason to. Henry and Sharon and everyone else in this city would go on just as they had, as if I had never come. I had made no difference in their lives. I had hardly made a difference in my own. And it would be the right thing to do. I had signed up for this, had married Phillip, had chosen to become the woman I was. What right did I have to back out now? Especially when I had nothing sure laid out in front of me?

When I was packing in my room, marveling at how after only a few weeks I had turned it back into a teenage lair, all crumpled food wrappers and dirty plates and clothes discarded on the floor, my mother knocked gently on the door. "May I come in?" she asked.

I flinched, bracing for the criticism about the state of my room, and then remembered I was an adult and didn't live here anymore and didn't have to put up with complaints about my messiness or questions about whether or not my homework was done. "Sure," I said, sweeping a pile of dirty shirts off the chair. Instead of sitting, she stood in the doorway, hands folded neatly in front of her like a chorister. I balled up the shirts and stuffed them into my suitcase.

"Aren't you going to fold those?"

"They're dirty. I'm just going to wash them when I get home." My purse was on the floor and I picked it up, rummaging through until I found a roll of antacid tablets and tossed four in my mouth, chewing grimly. My stomach felt as though someone had gripped it in a tight, bony fist.

My mother cleared her throat. "I'm glad you and Phillip are getting along."

Getting along. Was this the standard we aspired to in our marriages in this family? "We were never not 'getting along,' Mother. It's not that easy." It would have been easier on some levels if we hadn't gotten along. Hadn't I wished for that? For big blowout fights, with plates hurled at each other's head, complaints from the neighbors about the noise? Wouldn't that have made it so much easier to say, "I am unhappy. I want a divorce"?

"Did you tell him to come here?" I asked.

"No, I didn't. But I did talk to him a few times."

"That's great. Thanks for going behind my back."

My mother was flustered, patting her hair and then tugging at her sleeves as though anything about her would dare to be in a state of disarray. "I didn't know what to do. You're here, and he's calling, and really, Madeleine, he is so charming. I've never understood why you can't be grateful for what you have. It wasn't like there were men lining up down the block to marry you."

I slammed the lid of my suitcase, which, given that it only flopped limply on top of my dirty clothes, was tremendously unsatisfying. "And why do I have to be grateful for that? You act like he rescued me by marrying me, like not being married was a fate worse than death. Why is that the most important thing I could have done with my life? What if we hadn't gotten married and I had—I don't know, moved to India and worked with lepers or something?"

"You aren't really the type."

"Ugh! That's not the point!" I threw my hands up in the air and sat down on my bed, nearly sliding off the clothes still piled there as I dug out another handful of antacids. I looked at my mother, standing there, perfectly coiffed, her posture stiff and straight, as though she were a rocket ship about to take flight.

"You've always been a romantic, Madeleine. But life isn't romantic. Most of the time, it's rather mundane. There are things that must be done, bills to be paid, obligations to be met, people to mollify, choices to make. You've got this silly idea your life should be all rainbows and sunshine."

"You're making me sound like a child."

She sighed, turning her gaze from me and looking out the window. "In some ways you are a child. You clearly don't value Phillip, or anything that has been given you."

"It's not fair to say that. You don't know what things are like between Phillip and me. You don't know what goes on in someone else's marriage, or someone else's house."

"You can't tell me he's some monster. He's well raised and a good businessman and he's polite. And so handsome."

I shot her a look from beneath lowered eyebrows. "Handsome is not a personality trait."

She shrugged, crossed her arms in front of her chest. "I'm saying you should be happy with what you have. You're wasting your time. Do you know how long your father and I waited for you? You could have had your children by now, and instead you're holding out for some perfect dream of a life that just doesn't happen!"

I had never seen my mother so emotional. In the scheme of things, of course, she wasn't emotional at all. But for her to raise her voice was highly uncommon. It just wasn't something she did. Even when I had been a child, my parents had spoken to me calmly and reasonably. When I was a teenager, prone to attempting fits of drama and picking fights, it was seriously disappointing to shout and slam doors only to have them respond in quiet, measured voices I couldn't rail against.

"Don't you want more for me, Mother? Don't you want me to be happy?"

"The thing that's holding you back from being happy isn't your situation, Madeleine. It never has been. It's *you*."

I opened my mouth to respond and then clamped it shut again as what she said sank in.

It was true that I had always been restless, always uncomfortable, always chafing against the things everyone around me seemed so happy with. And I'd tried so hard to fit in. I'd had my hair straightened, eaten bean sprouts and crackers and cottage cheese until I wasn't the fattest girl in the yearbook photo, learned what to talk about at fundraising lunches, pledged a sorority and memorized the bylaws, greetings, and songs. I had joined the organizations I was supposed to join, gone to the parties I was supposed to go to, donated to the charities I was supposed to support, married the man I was supposed to marry. And I was still miserable. But everyone around me was happy. So maybe it was me. Maybe it had been me all along.

"I'm not going to be a shield for you to hide behind. Now, my suggestion is that you go back and commit yourself to Phillip and your life there, instead of lying around here moaning about how difficult everything is when you have it more than easy." My mother stood up and nodded, as though she had finally said what she had come here to say, and turned and walked out of the room, leaving me certain, yet again, that I was in the wrong and everyone else must be right.

They say the definition of insanity is doing the same thing over and over again and expecting different results. So despite having done exactly what my mother suggested—gritting my teeth and diving into the fray—more times than I could remember, I decided to do it again.

I swore this time would be different. This time it would work. I would really enjoy my charity work. I would go out with Phillip to the places he wanted to go. I'd host dinner parties for his colleagues and I wouldn't doze off when they were talking about gold bricks or pork bellies or whatever it was they talked about. (Really, I had only fallen asleep the once, and only because I had already been having trouble sleeping—it turned out Terrence Mather's explanation of the future of mutual funds had done the trick.) Maybe if I were more like the person I had been when Phillip and I got married, he would be more like he had been then too—charming, romantic, complimentary.

I could do this. I could be the woman my mother had always wanted me to be, the woman Phillip wanted me to be, the woman I wanted to be. Because that woman wasn't constantly torn up inside, thinking of the way things might be different. She just took what she was given—and really, hadn't I been given so very much?—and she learned to like it. And it wouldn't matter anyway. I didn't have anything better to turn to. I didn't have Paris, I didn't have Sebastien, and even my grandmother hadn't kept those things. I had the life I had chosen, the life I deserved, and I might as well start living it.

twenty-four
....

MARGIE
1924

At first Margie thought she might get another job. She told herself she could stay even if Sebastien left. Paris was hers now, and she couldn't bear the thought of leaving it, even if he wasn't there.

She asked Miss Parsons if there were other places an American girl might find a job, summoned up the courage to inquire at the front desk of the Club if there were any new jobs. But there were so many American girls, and Margie knew she looked so heavyhearted, so flat and broken, when she went to inquire about the few open positions, and so she was unsurprised when she was not hired.

And she must have a job if she were to stay. Her parents would not send her any money, unless it were for passage home, and even then she could feel the strings attached to that generosity pulling at her, even from so far away.

In the end, it didn't matter. Because Margie got terribly, terribly sick.

There are gaps in her journals then, and I can only piece together the story through her parents' frantic letters and telegrams, and then Robert Walsh's responses, calm and orderly, confident and soothing.

Margie spent her days walking through Paris. She had thought she and Sebastien could say goodbye to Paris together, but she hadn't seen him since the night he had told her he was leaving. What would be the point? What was the use of a grand goodbye, when, after all, it was still goodbye? Instead, she prepared to leave Paris on her own, in a quiet way. She said goodbye to the Libe, and the Place de la Concorde, and the art gallery where she had seen Sebastien's work, and the streets where they had walked and talked of nothing and of everything. At the end of each day, she bought some bread and an apple and a hunk of good cheese and she took them up to her room and she ate as she wrote in her journal. And then she went to bed.

For days, Margie had been feeling exhausted and she had developed a rough cough, but she had chalked it up to shock, to too much news, to the pain in her heart when she thought of leaving. She ignored both the physical symptoms and her emotions. She had made no plans, had not inquired about train timetables or sailing times or tickets. She could live for the rest of the month on her salary, and then she would have a few more weeks with her savings, but on some level she seemed to have decided that if she refused to think of it, it might not happen.

When she went to bed one Sunday night, struck with a more intense fatigue than she had felt before, she knew she could no longer deny that she was sick. She slept through the night, feverish and uncomfortable, turning again and again so the sheets twisted around her legs. A deep, raw feeling settled in her chest, and she woke herself coughing. Leaving her bed to use the toilet, her vision was blurry and indistinct, and she had to lean on the wall halfway to the bathroom to rest. She sat in the stall, pressing her face against the cool tile wall, until someone knocked on the door, and she started awake and stumbled back to her room.

She slept that way, woozy and fitful, the pain in her chest when she coughed growing sharper, for a day, and on Tuesday, when she didn't show up for work, Miss Parsons called the Club. The woman at the front desk agreed to check on Margie, and found her still in bed, dehydrated and near delirious, her skin so flushed with fever she looked like she had been sunburned. Her cough had an unpleasant rattle to it, and though her skin burned to the touch, she was racked with chills. The matron called Miss Parsons, who called a doctor, who protested at having to climb all the stairs, and examined her. After the Spanish flu pandemic, most people had been anxious to the point of hysteria about illnesses, but he seemed unimpressed. "Pneumonia," he said. "She needs sea air. There is a fresh-air colony at Cavalaire-sur-Mer on the Côte d'Azur."

Miss Parsons was certain a stay in the south of France would do wonders for Margie, but who would take her there? And who would pay? She sent a telegram to Margie's parents with the news, and they sent a panicked telegram back, pleading for more information. But how much information can one give in a telegram? The limits of communication that had given Margie so much time to spread her wings, to put her parents' inquiries off again and again, to distract them with stories of markets and museums and her detailed description of the interior of Sainte-Chapelle, were now an enemy.

On top of Margie's inability to eat, the fever and endless coughing fits left her exhausted. Dorothy piled pillows on the bed so Margie could sleep without drowning in the fluid in her chest. She dozed, waking only to cough, her body shaking with the effort, wheezing for breath, silent tears on her cheeks from the knife-edged pains in her chest. Sometimes she stayed awake, staring glassy-eyed at the ceiling, until whoever was sitting with her was so scared they would call the doctor, who only said she would be fine with a little rest and sea air and gave them another packet of pills.

It was only by coincidence that Robert Walsh, her escort from that long-ago debutante ball, was coming through Paris. He had been in Europe for five years, a trip his parents had continued to fund in hopes it might give him some level of gravitas. And he had changed, grown older and more thoughtful, though he had also spent a fair amount of time drinking and wooing Italian and Czechoslovakian girls.

But his parents had tired of funding his exploits and demanded he return home. He booked a ticket home through Cherbourg, and arranged for one last stay in Paris, and when he arrived, he found a telegram from Margie's parents, pleading with him to bring her home. And so he did. He got dispensation to go to her room on the third floor, setting off piles of charmed, pretending-to-be-offended squeals when the other girls saw him there, and placed her journals and her notebooks in a trunk—the same trunk in which I would find them almost seventy-five years later. He packed up her dresses and her shoes and her new Parisian hat. He hired a driver to carry her things downstairs and then take them to the train station, and then, when it was time to go, he half carried her down the narrow staircase himself.

Robert took her to Cherbourg, buying a sleeping car for the short journey on the train, and they boarded the ship together. He took her to see the ship's doctor, who refused to keep her in the infirmary for fear of contagion, so Robert took her back to the stateroom. There had been no more rooms available, so he had simply bought her a ticket in his. Her parents would never know, and he could take better care of her there.

The journey was a week long, but to Margie it might have been only a few minutes, or a few years. The doctor had been right, at least, that the sea air and being away from the dirt and smoke of Paris would ease the irritation in her lungs. One day she was well enough to bathe and wash her hair, and then to go up to the deck and sit outside, wrapped in three rugs, pulled back toward the wall to shelter her from the wind, but the next she was so exhausted she only wanted to sleep, Robert sitting by her side, putting warm, wet cloths over her nose and mouth to loosen the remaining mucus in her lungs.

The roll of the ship in the deepest waters, pushing through the summer storms, kept her nauseated and unbalanced, and she pushed away the soup Robert had sent down. When she was awake, she turned her face to the wall, memorizing the whorls and flecks of the wood. He had unpacked some of her books and he read to her for hours at a time.

The words passed over her like water, but the sound of his voice and the motion of the ship lulled her to sleep in quiet calm. He left the books on her night table for her to read herself, but she did not touch them, and one particularly rocky night they flew across the room and hit Robert in the head while he was sleeping. He kept them in the drawer afterward.

That week on the ship, taking care of Margie, sickly and silent, changed Robert. He went to the lounge to play cards and found he could not concentrate. He dressed for dinner but left the table before dessert to check on her, he nodded absently at the women who flirted with him, not even bothering to make promises he wouldn't keep, avoiding the balls and parties each night where he would have been endlessly fawned over and fêted, instead spending the night in the cabin with Margie, reading to her as she closed her eyes and braced her stomach against the movement of the ship on the waves, finding stewards to bring endless hot water for compresses on her chest and cool water to soothe her when she felt feverish, hanging up his tuxedo and spending nearly all his time in his flannels.

Watching her sleep, he remembered the way they had talked at her debut, how they had both been so young and romantic and foolish, thinking the world could belong to them without consequence. She had been honest and optimistic, different from the girls he knew, all talons and agenda. And now she was so vulnerable, and he was awash with guilt for taking her away from the place she had told him she dreamed of being.

When they arrived in America, her parents whisked her away and Robert went home alone, arriving on his family's doorstep exhausted, stacks of luggage on the street behind him, an unpleasant tangle of emotions inside him—shame and regret and disappointment for the years that had disappeared with so little to show for them, trepidation about what might lie ahead now that he must face it, and a curious feeling of loneliness that stemmed, he realized as he was bundled inside and made much of by his mother and the household staff alike, from missing Margie.

For her part, Margie rode home on the train without speaking, and walked slowly up the stairs to her old bedroom, the effort leaving her winded and rattling out the last of her cough. Shutting the door, she closed her eyes and pretended to sleep for days until she could think of everything she had lost and everything she now had to do. Paris was already receding into a memory, the precise color of the afternoon sun on the buildings hovering tantalizingly out of reach, the calls of the flower sellers and the rag-and-bone men faint and muffled, the feeling of lightness, of freedom, she had experienced there distant and unbelievable as a mirage. It had been only a few months, but she felt new and raw, plunged too soon into the darkness of her parents' house, wondering how she would go on, wondering what could possibly lie ahead.

Oddly, it was being so sick that made Margie's feelings toward her mother change. Weak and empty, Margie watched her mother bustling back and forth, in and out of her room, calling the cook for some toast and broth, or stewed fruit, heavy and sweet. She longed for the fresh fruit she had eaten in Paris, the color and flavor still bright. Her mother did not read to Margie as Robert had, and Margie found she missed the low, steady sound of his voice, an anchor against the constant rocking of the ocean, the close, small space of the stateroom. But when the house had gone quiet at night, her mother came into Margie's room and simply sat by the bed, holding her limp, damp hand in the small, dry palm of her own.

Margie thought back to school, when her mother had come to Abbott to care for her roommate, Lucinda. Had her mother only been waiting for a moment of vulnerability, an excuse to care for her? It was the first time she could remember in years that they weren't at war.

The pneumonia faded, but she still felt frail and tired. She slept often, though she knew it was partly avoidance and escape. In her dreams, she was still in Paris, walking down the slender, cobblestoned alleys of the Latin Quarter with Sebastien, finding the city's secrets and cracking them open for their own pleasure. In her dreams, she could smell the flowers in the Tuileries and the garbage in the passageways behind the buildings and the sweat and perfume of Zelli's and the buttery rise of croissants at the boulangerie when she came home particularly late. In her dreams, jazz played in nightclubs and there were concerts in the gardens, and endless conversations in the cafés, and she drifted through it all, both in the world and not of it. In her dreams, her feet were never sore, though she walked and danced her way through the city. In her dreams, conversation still swirled around her, and every nerve ending in her body was alert and awake, and she could write for hours without her fingers cramping, capturing every scent, every taste, every sound, every emotion. When she woke, she would try to push herself back down into sleep, and if it would not come, she sometimes cried thin tears of frustration that entrance to Paris was denied to her even in her dreams.

"What will I do now?" she asked herself when she was alone in her room. Her voice only echoed emptily off the walls.

As she grew stronger, she realized she had a larger problem than being away from Paris. Though her lungs healed and her fever abated, and she began to take walks around the square, she was still fatigued, and the smell of food often made her feel ill. There was a taste of metal in her mouth no matter what she ate, and though she had lost even more weight during her illness, her breasts were oddly full and tender.

Though she had been raised at a time when such things were not discussed, Margie was a reader, and she had listened, at college and at the Club, to the conversations around her, and she knew exactly what was happening. Margie was pregnant, the father was literally across an ocean and promised to someone else, and her life was going to be over when her parents found out.

twenty-five

MADELEINE
1999

The city had thawed while I was gone. I could walk along the beach without my breath being taken away, my cheeks at the end pink from exertion and not the frosty weather. Spring had painted everything hopeful and green. Flowers appeared in people's window boxes as they brought their plants out from hibernation. College students hurried to class in shorts and short-sleeved shirts, their skin tender and raw against the air, as though they could bring summer weather by pretending it was already here. Women wore dresses with floral prints instead of the muted grays of winter, and the sky hovered, wide and blue, dotted with clouds, above us.

I told myself it was my best option to try to make things better with Phillip. But when it came down to it, I seemed unable to force myself into anything more than politeness, as though we were overly solicitous acquaintances who happened to be living together. I had become strangely modest, dressing in the bathroom, sleeping in heavy winter pajamas. The distance and alienation between us had not melted with the warmer weather.

Sometimes I watched him, eating dinner or cursing at a game on the television, and wondered who he was, who he *really* was. For a long time I had assumed I was the only one with a deeper heart I kept hidden, the only one with private wishes. But of course we all have secrets. If I had not known that before, my grandmother's diaries had illuminated it for me. Imagine carrying the secret she had—her child belonged to a man other than her husband. I had a million questions I wanted to ask, and no one to ask them to. Why had Robert Walsh agreed to raise my mother as his own? Had my grandmother ever told Sebastien? Did my own mother know? I didn't know how to bring up the topic. What if she really didn't know? She'd said she hadn't read my grandmother's journals, and given their chilly relationship, I wasn't surprised. And I wasn't going to be the one to break the news to her.

I buried my questions and my confusion and the endless rounds of self-doubt in work. I doubled my hours at the Stabler Museum, working in the gift shop as well as leading tours. I went to committee meetings and when I caught myself doodling in the margins of my notes, I would force myself to raise my hand and volunteer for something, which was how I ended up on the registration committee for the library's annual fundraiser and responsible for finding speakers for the next three Women's Club meetings. At first I felt proud of those jobs, and I understood why my mother loved what she did. I had a purpose, a reason to get out of bed in the morning.

While I surprised myself with my own efficiency, my own competence, all of those tasks didn't solve my problems. So I dug in harder, I laughed louder at Phillip's colleagues' jokes, and I pasted a smile on my face when I worked the registration desk at the Stabler auction, handing out name tags and bidding numbers with such aggressive cheer I think I scared a few people.

And none of it made me feel any better. I ate antacids like candy, lining up the empty containers in a kitchen cabinet where they stared at me accusatorily every time I went to get a plate.

I tried to remember a time when I had been wholly happy, outside of those few weeks in Magnolia. A time when I had felt connected to what I was doing, and was heartbroken to think of how few of those there were. Volunteering at the Stabler. Living alone in Magnolia before I was married.

And before that, in school. I had painted sets and cut backdrops, watching something emerge from nothing, and then seeing the magic of theater transform it into something different altogether. I had made signs for Ashley's elections, lettering her name over and over again until I knew it better than my own. I had helped make the mosaic that spread its broken, glittering way across the school's front hall, pressing glass and tiny ceramic squares into plaster again and again until calluses formed on the tips of my fingers and my hands were sticky with mortar. I had helped lay out the art and literary magazine, bent carefully over the pages with a knife sharp as a scalpel to cut away the wayward edges, flipping through the order again, looking for the story it told. I had done things that felt like a part of me, not like wearing a Halloween mask that made it hot and hard to breathe underneath.

One afternoon, when the sun had shone high and bright in the sky long enough to warm the entire city, people carrying their coats instead of wearing them, turning their faces toward the sky as they walked, blinking into the light like moles, unsure and slightly fearful, as though they had never seen it before, I found myself wandering through a street full of warehouses in Bucktown, a questionable neighborhood teetering on trendy. In a clean window on the bottom floor of a wide, low, brick building was a sign reading: *Artist's Studio for Rent.*

I remembered Miss Pine's invitation to the painting class, and wondered if this was the same place. And something inside me made me stop, made me press my hand against the new glass doors and push my way inside.

Inside, the building was bright, the wood floors pale and scuffed, sunlight striking across them in wide, cheerful squares. The muffled sounds of a radio and voices floated down from upstairs, and the floors groaned gently as people moved somewhere in the building. Beyond the entrance, which was being used as a gallery, the walls hung with photographs, was a long hallway of doors I presumed were studios. One of them was labeled *Office*, and when I knocked, a man poked his head out, keeping the door mostly closed as though he were afraid I might attack him.

"Yes?" he asked. I couldn't help thinking of the man at the gates to the Emerald City in *The Wizard of Oz*, and had to cover my mouth briefly to hide my smile.

"I saw the sign? About the studio for rent?" I had no idea why I was talking like a teenager, full of half questions and knock-kneed nervousness.

"Yeah. It's on the third floor. You want to look?"

"Sure." Was he not wearing any pants, and that's why he'd only stick his head out?

He disappeared for a moment, closing the door fully, and then reappeared, thrusting his arm out and dropping a key into my hand. "Number 314. Stairs are that way." He pointed to the opposite end of the hall. "Bring the key back when you're done." And then he closed the door again, but not before I caught a solid view of a pair of khakis. Whatever his secret was, it wasn't pantslessness.

Passing down the hall, I peered through a door with a large glass window in it to see a classroom. This must have been the place. It was almost as I had pictured it—light and airy, easels and stools waiting, a raised platform at the far end where a teacher or a model could stand. Putting my hand against the window, I leaned in, my breath forming a hot circle on the glass. I pictured Miss Pine jingling her way through the room. I pictured myself sitting on the edge of a stool, my feet hooked under one of the bars, my brush moving over a canvas, filling in the emptiness with everything I saw and didn't see. There might be music as we painted, and bursts of conversation and laughter to punctuate the silence of creation, and I would feel a part of something in a way I never did no matter how many people surrounded me.

Finally, I pushed myself away and found the stairs. As I climbed, they clanged underneath my feet, the sound of music growing louder as I approached the second floor, and then fading again as I reached the third. It was warmer up here, the sun trapped by the windows deliciously greenhouse-hot, as though I were back in Magnolia. I heard people working as I walked to the far end of the hall—I passed the steady whir of a potter's wheel and the rich, sharp smell of wet clay, and through another door I heard someone humming along with a series of steady, slow taps I couldn't identify. And finally, I slipped the key into the lock of 314.

The warehouse had clearly been an open floor that had now been subdivided into these smaller studios, and this one was tiny—if I stood in the middle, I could have touched both walls with my arms. But the back wall was taken up by a wide, clean window, and though the light had faded, it would be bright and sunny in the mornings, and there was enough room for a table and a cabinet for supplies, and an easel or two. I imagined myself coming here early, closing the door to keep the blur and buzz of the city outside, sipping orange juice while I laid out brushes like a surgeon's tools, letting the light paint the canvas and show me where to draw. Virginia Woolf had said writers needed a room of their own, and maybe artists needed them too. Maybe everyone needs a room of one's own where there are no expectations, and no compromises, and you can be the person you know yourself to be.

The music coming muffled or tinny through the walls, the smell of clay and paint and charcoal, all that meant it was possible. All these people were making the things they wanted happen. I wasn't the only one. I didn't have to be afraid. My grandfather had been a painter, my grandmother, a writer. My creativity wasn't a fluke. It was my destiny.

By the time I got home, I was late, I suppose, but we had never really had a dinner time. Phillip often ate at the office or out with clients, and I pieced together meals from bits and pieces I found in the refrigerator—yogurt and two small pieces of steak left over from a dinner Phillip had gone to, and a handful of macadamia nuts and a pickle. Except apparently that night he had expected my arrival, had been planning, bringing things home from work, and he was angry at being delayed.

"Where have you been?" he asked.

I didn't want to tell him. He would not see my wanting to paint again as the compromise I needed to make to stay here, as the reward for enduring all the things I did not want to do. But I was done with lying. I had tried it his way, my mother's way, and it had never worked. I couldn't go on like this forever, not now that I knew there was the possibility of something more. "I was looking at an artist's studio."

"An artist's studio?" He said this as though I had told him I had been hunting one-legged unicorns. "What for?" His confusion was understandable. I don't think he knew any women who had hobbies, other than shopping and complaining about their daughters-in-law. And the only hobbies any of the men he knew had were golf and infidelity. I was fairly sure he hadn't taken up either, but it was only a matter of time.

"You know. For making art."

"Like painting?"

"Yes, painting. And drawing. And, I don't know, collage. Whatever I feel like."

"Who's going to pay for that?" he asked sharply, and now I knew he was angry. He never questioned the way I spent money—probably because I hardly spent any. My joy began to fade and the room grew darker around me. Phillip paid the bills. If he didn't want to pay for it, he didn't have to, and who was I to object? *This is why women should have their own jobs, their own money*, I thought. *This is why I want my own. Like my grandmother had.*

"I don't mind working," I said quietly. "I wanted to work. You were the one who didn't want me to." I could have argued a dozen things, compared myself to the women I knew who shopped their boredom and their pain away. But this wasn't a financial reckoning. This wasn't about fair. This was about control.

He didn't respond. Instead, he looked around the kitchen and said, "I've been waiting. I'm starving. You should call if you're going to be late."

"Wait, what are you talking about? Did we have plans? How am I late?"

He sighed in frustration, as though I were asking for clarification on some basic tenet of our relationship. "Past dinner time."

"I'm sorry?" I wasn't entirely sure what I was apologizing for. I sat down on the arm of the sofa, as though I were only staying a moment.

"If you're not going to try, Madeleine, I don't know why I'm bothering."

"Try what?" I asked. I was becoming genuinely confused. It was as though Phillip were having an entirely different conversation and not letting me in on it.

"This." He lifted his hands in frustration. He was standing behind the island in the kitchen. A bottle of wine, a half-empty glass, the opener, and the cork were lined up beside him in a tidy row. Everything about Phillip was so neat. It was fascinating, in a way, as though he had been molded from plastic. When we were first married, I had watched him endlessly, wondering at the way his hair fell perfectly into place as soon as he brushed it and stayed that way the entire day, how his suit jackets remained unwrinkled, even at the insides of the elbows, and how he never seemed to spill anything when he ate, whereas my every encounter with food was a battle in which my clothing was likely to end up as collateral damage. "Us. This relationship. You can't go running off to—I don't know, move in with your mother or become a painter or whatever every time you have a bad day."

"It's not just a bad day. It's every day."

"That's my Madeleine. Always complaining about something."

"Phillip, you don't even like me. Why did you marry me?"

"Of course I like you," he said, scoffing. He spun the corkscrew on the counter and it made an irritating rattle. "You're my wife."

"Those two things don't have to go together, you know. I know tons of married people who hate each other."

"I don't hate you."

"Well, that's great." What a ringing endorsement this was for our marriage. So far he'd told me he liked me and he didn't hate me. When I was younger, boyfriendless and hopeless, I had dreamed of the relationship I wanted, of the man I would fall in love with. I'd pictured someone with whom I would truly share a life. He would be a writer and he would sit at his typewriter and compose brilliant poems or novels while I sat in a large, comfortable leather chair by a sun-lit window and sketched. Our life together would be rich and joyous—we would laugh, and cook dinner, and read to each other by a fire at night. Our passion would be legendary, our desire a constant, smoldering fire that would need only a single glance to flare into brilliant, burning flame. We would have no secrets, and he would accept me completely, would tell me I was beautiful, would *believe* I was beautiful, would find my perpetual messiness glamorously artistic, my sarcasm hilarious, and we would create our own little nation of two, and the only people to whom we would issue visas would be people who loved us as well as we loved each other.

At some point, I had stopped believing in those romantic dreams. My imaginary husband and the steady clack of his typewriter and the messiness of his hair and his imperfect hands on my face had evaporated, and I had let the dream go, float away and disappear into the sky like a child's balloon, with as much chance of reclaiming it. Instead, I had chosen the easy path, the love that resembled the love around me—formal and real and designed to look better on the outside than it felt on the inside. I pictured my sixteen-year-old self, painting in that cool, damp basement by the inconsistent light of a dozen lamps, the way everything had looked possible and real to her, and it broke my heart that I had betrayed her for such a small, inconsequential prize. Instead of a husband who was per-fect for me, I had taken a husband who looked perfect to everyone else. Instead of the love that made my heart sing and brought out the best in me, I had chosen . . . well, that was it, wasn't it? I didn't love him. He didn't love me. And I didn't want to pretend anymore.

You might think realizing you don't love your husband would be cause for panic, a little hysterical weeping, but that wasn't the case for me. Instead, a heavy peace descended on me, a feeling of calm so still and strong I could not mistake it for anything other than what it was: a cer-tainty, at long last, that I knew what I wanted, that I knew what was right.

"I want a divorce," I said to my husband.

I hadn't known I was going to say those words before I did, and in some way I had known I would say them since the moment I had agreed to marry him. I felt no alarm at the way they sounded when spoken aloud, at their sudden, serious weight. Outside, the city continued apace; traffic hummed by, the quiet tides of Lake Michigan slapped their lazy way against the shore, people walked and worked and laughed and ate and drank and fought and loved, and nothing changed except every-thing.

Phillip did not look surprised, and for some reason his lack of surprise didn't surprise me either. "Don't be ridiculous, Madeleine. We can't get a divorce." I tilted my head at him curiously, wondering at his words. Not "I don't want a divorce," or "We shouldn't get a divorce," but "We can't."

"Why not?" I asked. "We're adults. And I don't want anything from you. Your money. This place. You can have it all."

Now Phillip looked exasperated. "We can't get a divorce," he repeated. "Think of how it would look. Think about my family. Think about my mother. Think about your mother!"

I had struggled against that same thought for so long, but it all seemed clear to me now. It was a chance I had to take. "This isn't about my mother, or yours. We don't have to stay together just because of how it looks. In fact, we shouldn't. We should be happy. And if we stay together, neither one of us will ever be happy. Not really."

"So that's it. You're divorcing me."

"I guess so."

There was a small silence, and then his face twisted bitterly, a sneer raising his lip. "You're never going to find someone else to marry you," he said. "You're fat, and you have the strangest sense of humor, and you can't even make conversation at a party, for God's sake."

And there it was.

Silence hung between us for a moment, and then I spoke.

"Thank you," I said, and Phillip stared at me. More evidence of my strangeness, he was thinking, but to me his words had been a gift. If I ever harbored any doubts about my decision, I could remember that moment, the hardness in his eyes, and I would know I had done the right thing. I would not dwell on his viciousness, but I would remember all the times it had been there, and if we stayed together, it would have kept coming out, in larger and larger ways, until my misery turned to despair, until anything good and happy inside me had been destroyed completely.

"You're not staying here tonight. And I'm not giving you a dime."

"All right," I said calmly. And standing up, I walked into the bedroom, packed my suitcase for the second time in a month, and walked out the door into the night air and uncertainty.

twenty-six

MARGIE
1924

A few weeks after they had arrived back in Washington, Robert Walsh came to see my grandmother. She could barely remember his coming to her rescue in Paris, and her memories of him on the ship home were distorted by exhaustion and illness and grief. But when she was brought down to see him in the parlor, she was shocked by his appearance. He looked pale and drawn, with dark circles under his eyes. His suit hung loosely on his body.

When she came into the room, he rose quickly and came over to her, kissing her on the cheek as the maid withdrew, leaving the door open just enough for respectability. "Margie," he said. "I'm so glad to see you looking so well. I was so worried about you. How are you feeling?"

She accepted the kiss and sat down gently, slowly in the chair he led her to. How different she felt now. A handsome man was in this room with her, a man who a few years ago she had been so swayed by, and now she felt calm and cool, almost emotionless.

"Better, thank you. And thank you so much for coming to my rescue. I'm sorry to say I was too ill to notice, but it seems you were my knight in shining armor."

Robert smiled, a thin, heartless thing. He sat down in the chair fac-

THE LIGHT OF PARIS

ing her. "It was only good luck I was passing through Paris when you were ill. I'm glad to have been able to help."

"Good luck," Margie echoed, though she wasn't sure it was true. Maybe if she had stayed, she would have been able to find another job eventually. Maybe Sebastien would have changed his mind. Maybe . . . With effort, she pulled herself back to the conversation. "So how are you finding Washington after all this time?"

Robert's eyes fluttered closed for a moment, as though he were marshaling his strength. "It's different, isn't it? How long were you in Paris?" he asked.

"Three months," Margie said. *Three months, five days, and twelve hours*, she thought. *Forever*, she thought. *Not long enough*, she thought.

"So you had a little time to get acquainted with the European style of things. It's all so different than here, isn't it? The war changed them. Everything over there is freer. It seems so contained here by comparison."

Looking around the dark parlor, the same heavy furniture, the same ugly, flocked wallpaper, the same fireplace—which was lit, despite the warmth of the day outside; the house always seemed chilly—Margie nodded. "It does."

They sat in silence for a moment, and Margie imagined they were both mourning what they had lost in Europe, both wishing they were back there. "So what will you do now?" she asked.

He cleared his throat. "I've been invited to join the family business."

"Invited?"

An expression crossed his face and he closed his eyes again. Leaning forward slightly, he lowered his voice. "Margie, we've known each other a long time."

"Years," Margie said. Her voice sounded so hollow. Would it always be like this? She wondered what she should do. Could she go back to Paris? To have the baby there, to have a life there. It was so cheap; she wouldn't need much. She couldn't live at the Club with a child, but she could find someplace like it, a similarly small, sunny room, and they could live there, the two of them. *On what?* her conscience asked meanly. *And where would the baby go when you were working?* The tiny flame of hope inside her that had sputtered to life died under the harsh wind of reality.

"So let's be honest with each other. Can we?"

Margie looked at him, expressionless. "Of course." Why not? What was the use of all these charades? Any taste she'd had for the rules and limitations of polite society had disappeared in Paris, had been crushed under the enthusiastic swell of the people she had met, the artists whose emotions overflowed every conversation they had, who could argue passionately about Surrealism and dreams and the messages of Cubism, who saw through different eyes. What was the point of pretending things you didn't feel?

"My parents have told me that if I don't join the business, if I don't settle down, I'm cut off. They said I've played for far too long, that it's time for me to grow up."

The maid came in, carrying a tray with tea and thick, tasteless cookies no one had asked for, and Robert leaned back in his chair quickly. "May I pour?" she asked.

"No, thank you," Margie said, and the maid nodded and disappeared. When the door had closed—almost—again, Margie turned to Robert. "I've been issued a similar ultimatum. What are you going to do?"

Robert shot her a quick, soulless smile. "I'm going to join the family business and settle down, of course."

"Is that what you want?"

He raised his hand to his head and needlessly smoothed down his hair. He had missed a spot when he was shaving; Margie could see a bit of stubble at his jawline, and it made him softer to her, reminded her that underneath his bravado, he was only a person. A person who had been kind to her. It was hard to see through her own pain and fear; her misery covered everything in a gauzy dimness. Light refracted back at her, illuminating the cracks in her own heart instead of allowing her to see anyone else's.

"No," he said. "But it's fair, isn't it? They've supported me, let me do as I pleased for years, in exchange for only a few requests, like acting as an escort for the season." He nodded at Margie and she smiled quickly, a perfunctory recognition of the night he had served as her escort. His words sounded so much like Sebastien's. Duty. A debt to be paid.

"And my sister, Eliza—you went to school with her, didn't you?"

Margie nodded.

"Well, she's going to be getting married soon. And my father's getting older."

"You sound like someone else I know." She thought of Sebastien, who had worn the same look of resignation on his face, his eyes tired, yet determined. How alike they had all been, how many dreams, how much hope. And yet now they were, all three of them, bowing to the duties they had once sworn they would not take on.

"I don't think mine is a new story," Robert said, without humor.

"Did you come here just to tell me this?" Margie was suddenly tired. The tea sat untouched between them, growing cold, and it might have settled her stomach, but she couldn't even bring herself to reach forward to pour it.

"No." Robert shifted, stiffening his spine, tugging his pants straight at his knees, setting his jacket neatly over his shoulders. "My parents have another requirement they have set out for me."

"Oh?" Margie leaned forward, plucking a sugar cube from the bowl and putting it on her tongue, letting it melt there, a little sweetness in a life that had become so very bitter.

"They want me to get married."

"Of course they do." That's what all their parents wanted, didn't they? Their children were nothing more than pawns in an endless chess match they were playing with each other. So it had always been, and so, if no one stopped it, it would always be. Margie knew it was only a matter of time before she married Mr. Chapman—or someone exactly like him, it didn't matter—succumbed in the way of all the girls who had gone before her. That is, if she could figure out a way to include her little friend in her dowry. "Bully for you. Who's the lucky girl?" Her voice came out hard, and she regretted it, because she felt no anger toward him. It was only that her heart was drained and bleak and hard, like a shell of ice, frozen around nothing but air.

"Well, Margie," Robert said, leaning forward again and gently taking her hand in his, "I was hoping it would be you."

twenty-seven

MADELEINE
1999

I allowed myself to watch my mother carefully, in a way I never had before, the delicate flutter of her fingers, the glittering green of her eyes, so unlike mine, her high cheekbones, the tilt of her head. Every move she made, I wondered where it had come from, which echo of the past was ringing out in her—was the way she drank her coffee the way Sebastien had taken his? What about her gift for gardening? Her cool, calm way of handling crises and public speaking? The way she walked with tiny, quick steps, almost on her tiptoes? My mother had always been inscrutable to me, but this added an entirely new layer of mystery.

How could I not have seen it before? I pictured my grandmother, who looked almost exactly like me, with broad shoulders and heavy thighs and uncooperative hair, and my grandfather, who was tall and rangy and had black eyes. And there was my mother, blonde and slender and small, just the way my grandmother had described Sebastien.

Finding out Sebastien was my grandfather had not shaken my foundations the way it might have if I had discovered I had a different father. But it had made me see my mother differently, and recast the chain of connection—my grandmother, my mother, me.

She had been reading the newspaper and it was spread out over the sofa beside her, open to the society pages. I could see Ashley Hathaway's toothy smile in one of the larger photographs, a choker with pearls the size of marbles around her neck like a collar. "So you're back."

"I am." I'd shown up on her doorstep, unannounced, with rather more suitcases than my last visit, and she'd taken one look at me and nodded and stepped aside, opening the door without ever inviting me in. I suppose it's not so much "Home is the place where, when you have to go there, they have to take you in," but "Home is the place where, when you have to go there, they have to take you in, but they don't have to be happy about it."

"And what does this mean? How long are you staying?"

"As long as you'll have me. And I think you know what it means. I've left Phillip."

My mother let out a long, slow sigh, as though she had been holding a century of air. "I see."

"That's it?" I asked. I had been bracing for an onslaught. Her response seemed underwhelming.

"What would you prefer I say? Shall I jump up and down for joy? Throw you a parade?"

I winced at her sarcasm. She was right, I supposed. What is the culturally appropriate thing to say to someone when they tell you they're getting a divorce? "I'm sorry"? "Congratulations"?

"Don't be mean, Mother."

"I'm not being mean," she said, though she was. "I just don't know what you expect me to say. Am I supposed to be excited about your divorce?"

"You could be supportive. I wouldn't be doing it if it weren't the right thing."

"So you're sure, then."

"I'm sure." I was sure of very little just then, the future opening in front of me like a hungry maw. The one thing I was sure of was my future had no place for Phillip in it, and it would be so much the better because of that.

"Well, I'm sorry. I don't know how to behave. No one in our family has ever gotten a divorce before."

"That's what you're worried about? That I'm the first person in our family to get a divorce? Don't you care about my happiness? Or do you only care about how you look at the Ladies Association?"

My mother's eyes flashed at me, hard and brilliant green. "Of course I care about your happiness. You're my daughter."

"Then why have you spent your entire life criticizing me? Making me miserable?" Tears caught in my throat, and I hated them, tried to push them down. I hated the way they made me feel weak, out of control, like a child. I hadn't cried when I had left Phillip. Any emotion I had invested in him had been gone so long ago it would have been stranger to cry than not. But my mother—I had never been able to protect my heart from her. No matter how many times she had shut me down, I had never stopped wanting her approval.

"I have tried to keep you safe. I have tried to keep you from making choices that would only end up in disappointment. I have tried to save you from pain. I have never, ever, ever tried to make you unhappy."

"You have. You always have." I shuddered in a long, slow breath. "You didn't want me to paint. You wanted me to go to cotillion, even though I hated it. You wanted me to go to college, when I only wanted to go to art school. You wanted me to stay with Phillip when I wanted a divorce. You wanted me to be *you* and I can only be myself no matter how messy and inconvenient and broken I am."

My mother's normally smooth brow was wrinkled, and she looked genuinely pained. "I wanted you to have an easy life, Madeleine. All the paths you wanted to take were only going to leave you heartbroken."

"How can you know? How can you know unless you let me try? It's exactly like Grandmother," I said, shaking my head. I snatched a tissue out of the box on the end table and blew my nose, loud, ugly, unconcerned with being ladylike or attractive. I was done with that. I was done with the performance of fragility, done pretending to be beautiful, or delicate, or any of the things I was not and didn't care to be.

"What do you mean?"

"She wanted to be in Paris. She wanted to write. She wanted to live abroad, and she didn't want to get married or have children. And she didn't get to do any of those things. She ended up doing what her mother wanted anyway."

"And wasn't that for the best, in the end? Wasn't she better off married to your grandfather, with a good life and a stable home and never having to worry about where her next meal was coming from? She made herself miserable wanting things she couldn't have, and all I wanted was to save you from that."

"And all I wanted was the chance to choose for myself."

Folding her hands in her lap, my mother stared down for a moment. "I see that," she said. "I can't apologize for wanting to keep you safe. I can't apologize for wanting to protect you from failure. But I see that."

And for the first time, I felt like my mother heard me.

My tears were slowing and I blew my nose again, long and loud and unattractive, until I could breathe again. "I'm sorry. I'm sorry I've disappointed you. I'm sorry I'm not the daughter you wanted. I'm sorry I'm not Ashley Hathaway. I'm sorry I don't like the things you like."

My mother looked up at me, surprised. "You do like the things I like."

"What are you talking about? Fundraising committees make me want to slit my wrists with a butter knife." I blew my noise again, loudly. My eyes were hot and swollen and I was unexpectedly exhausted, as though I could have lain down and slept as long as a princess in a fairy tale.

"Not that," my mother said, waving her slim hand dismissively. "We love reading, and art. We love to make beautiful things. My garden, your pictures. We are like my father, both of us."

I furrowed my brow, thinking of my grandfather, who, like my own father, was always hidden behind some dreadfully boring financial newspaper and thought savings bonds were a good gift for children. "I'm nothing like Grandfather."

"Not Grandfather," my mother said softly. "My father."

My eyes widened and my breath caught sharp in my chest. "You knew?" I asked, the words carried out on a breath.

"Of course I knew. I read the journals and the letters."

"You said you didn't."

"It's so hard to talk about."

The questions boiled up inside me. "Did you ever ask her? Did you ever talk to her about it?"

My mother shook her head. "I didn't. I didn't think I could, really. My mother and I—we were never close. But I understood why after I read the journals. I think I reminded her of him."

So it ran in the family, then, this estrangement. There was a sadness in my mother's eyes I had never seen before, and it made my heart ache for her, and for myself. How had we spent our entire lives lying to each other? How had she denied herself to me—her real self—for so long? Why did the women in my family work so hard to make themselves emotionless, to shellac down their hair and close off their feelings, to stay aloof and frozen? The only time my mother ever dug in was when she was gardening. Turning my head, I looked out the window at it and saw it for what it was—my mother's art. Her gardens were her paintings—color and form and order, experimentation and creation, dirt and birth and success and failure. "You reminded her of Sebastien?"

"Yes."

"And you never got a chance to meet him?"

"He died in the Second World War. He was living in Bordeaux when the Germans occupied it. And I didn't know until after then."

"I'm so sorry," I said. I was thinking of my own father, of his comforting presence and how I missed the sound of his voice. But at least I had known him. My mother had never even known her own father. "Have you seen a photograph?" I asked. My mother nodded. She went to one of the shelves by the windows and pulled down a photo album. I remembered paging through it as a child, looking at the nameless faces of ancestors past, their funny clothes and stiff poses, the old cars and the quiet skylines and horizons behind them, but I had never before connected them to me, had never understood the way we were all linked.

The photo had been taken at a café. Sebastien—*my grandfather*, I thought—was sitting in a chair, leaning back, legs stretched out long before him. He held a cigarette in one hand, and he was smiling slightly at the camera. Off to one side I could see a woman's legs beneath the table, her ankles crossed, a pair of T-strap shoes on her feet. She had turned away while the photograph was being taken and I could see only the edge of her jaw and the line of her neck. Her hat covered her hair. It could have been my grandmother.

He was tall and slender, his features drawn as sharply as a model's. His hair was light and unfashionably long, flopping into his eyes. I looked at him, memorizing his face, though I felt as though I had already painted it in my mind a thousand times over the last few weeks. Looking up at my mother, I was shocked to see exactly how much she looked like him—not only her build and her slender fingers, but the sharpness of her cheekbones and the slight raise of her eyebrows, which I had always thought of as an expression of superiority, but on Sebastien looked like perennial amusement.

"You look exactly like him," I said.

"I know. It broke her heart." Leaving me with the album, she walked back to the sofa and sat down on the edge, leaning forward and crossing her forearms precisely.

"I'm so sorry," I said, though I wasn't sure what I was sorry for—her distance from her mother, never knowing her father, the distance between us. Maybe all those things.

"Don't be." She smoothed her skirt over her knees, straightened her shoulders. "As far as I'm concerned, my father was Robert Walsh, the man who raised me. He took me on as his own, after all, when he didn't have to. And I never had the slightest sense he treated me any differently from how he would have if I'd been his biological daughter. That's fatherhood."

"Don't you wish you could have known him?"

My mother looked out the window into her garden. The trees were in full leaf, spreading warm shadow over parts of the yard, and there were flowers everywhere. She was right—we were the same in that way. Except she had found a socially acceptable way to pursue her art and I had just . . . given up? I'd blamed my parents and Phillip for quitting painting, but I could have resisted their pressure. I could have kept going. I'd blamed my mother for forcing me into marrying Phillip, but I could have said no. A stronger woman would have. The woman I wanted to be would have. The woman I was going to be would.

Because that was the point, wasn't it? To learn from the past, to learn from my mistakes, the mistakes of my mother and my grandmother. Both of them had lived the lives that were expected of them. I didn't resent my grandmother for her choices. She had done what she had to do. I just hated that she had to do it at all. And my mother had spent so much time and energy holding me back, holding herself back. Imagine what she could have been if she had only let go and embraced who she was. Imagine what I could have been. Imagine what could happen if we all had the heart to be who we truly are.

"I wish I could have known him because it might have brought me closer to my mother. I wish I could have known him because—well, because there's something about knowing where you come from, isn't there?" I looked around at the china cabinets, which, though they had been emptied, were still full of generations of Walsh and Bowers memories. Someday it would be my job to keep these things safe, to remember the stories of the hand-painted plates my grandfather had brought back from a trip to China, to polish the silver someone claimed had been buried in the garden during the Civil War (but really, everyone said that—if it had been true, shame on the Union Army for not figuring it out).

"I can't believe you never told me," I said, and I was surprised by how bitter it sounded. I wasn't angry so much as . . . well, what was it? Disappointed? Maybe if she had told me the truth before, we might have been closer. Maybe keeping this secret from me was part of what had kept us apart.

"It never seemed to be the right time."

"I guess there never is a right time for that news." Except it had been the right time, finally. It had been the right time to know I wasn't a failure in a long line of feminine perfection. It had been the right time to know about my grandmother's dreams, and to see what giving them up would do to you, would do to your daughter, would do to your granddaughter. She wasn't wrong to have made the choice she had, but it would have been wrong for me to keep making it when I had nothing other than my own shame and fear at stake.

"Did she ever see him again?"

My mother shook her head, the light falling across her face, illuminating the lines on her skin. "I don't think she did."

So no tearful, romantic reunion then. No train station rendezvous, no lost Parisian weekend. A few weeks ago, that might have deflated me, but I had learned something from my grandmother about romance and reality, and how they had to fit together.

"Are you sure this is what you want? Are you certain it's for the best?" she asked. To my surprise, there was no rebuke left in her tone. Only sadness.

"I don't want to be married to him." I remembered Phillip's harsh words when I had told him I wanted a divorce, and a little shiver went up the back of my neck. It had been there all along, that sharpness. And if I hadn't brought it out by asking for a divorce, who knew when it might have appeared. It was for the best. My mother might never understand, but it was.

"And what are you going to do now?"

I could have named a thousand things I wasn't going to do. I wasn't going to put on a twinset and go to any meetings at Ashley Hathaway's house. I wasn't going to straighten my hair anymore or pretend I wasn't hungry. But what was I going to do? That was much harder.

I thought of my mother, of her endless charities and duties, of the organizations she supported and all the thousands of ways she had made herself matter in a culture that had devalued her because she was only a woman. I thought of how her mother had kept her at a distance because the memories were too much, and how unfair that was, and I thought of how my mother had kept me at a distance because she didn't know any different, and because she didn't want me to be unhappy, and how it had only made me unhappy anyway. And I thought of how my grandmother and I had both married men for reasons other than love—fear and duty and responsibility and loneliness, and how it had left both of us resigned and unhappy. I thought of my grandmother in Paris and how she described the light there, the way it fell, beautiful and terrible and romantic, and I thought of how little joy there can be in this world and how much I wished we should all grab it whenever it flew by, like the light of a shooting star.

I thought of my grandmother, and what she might have made of this buffet of choice I had before me, of the freedom seventy-five years of progress had given to me, as a woman, and I knew she wouldn't have been able to imagine it. I had a little bit of money, I had time, I had a passport. Really, there was only one thing to do.

"I think I'm going to Paris," I said.

twenty-eight
....

MARGIE
1924

Dear Mother and Father,

I wish to thank you so very much for such a lovely wedding. Though I have been to so many, this was truly the most splendid of them all, despite how quickly it was organized. Robert and I feel lucky to have had such a sendoff into our new life together. Thank you so much for inviting such a large and impressive group of people to celebrate with us. I do hope you are pleased.

Robert and I expect to return to Washington on Tuesday, as he must be at the office on Wednesday, and we will be pleased to have you to dinner at the new house as soon as possible afterward. It will be such a pleasure having you nearby, and I only regret our many obligations will keep us from seeing each other as often as we might like.

Thank you so much for hosting such a beautiful wedding. I am sure Washington will be talking of it the entire season.

Yours sincerely,
Margaret Pearce Walsh

twenty-nine

MADELEINE
1999

August, and the air lay wet and hot around us as we sat on the back porch of The Kitchen, the occasional quick wind more of an unpleasantly hot exhale than a relief. As was my habit lately, I had thrown my hair up into a messy knot, and the curls that sprang free pressed damply against my bare neck.

"Where are you sitting?" Sharon asked, attempting to insert a cranky toddler into a high chair at the end of the table. I had babysat the twins a few nights so Sharon and Kevin could go out, but I was embarrassed to say I still couldn't tell the boys apart. They were one gloriously sticky, flailing, kissable, undifferentiated mess. This one kept arching his back every time Sharon tried to slip his legs underneath the tray, so I leaned forward and tickled him, which made him collapse into giggles so she could catch him unawares and get him settled. "Thanks."

"I'll sit over here," I said, moving down to find an empty chair and plopping into it, setting my beer down on a napkin.

"I'll sit next to you. Kevin! Come feed your children." Kevin loped over and kissed Sharon's forehead, taking the other squirming twin and sitting down with him in his lap. Sharon left him cutting avocado and chicken for the boys and collapsed into the chair beside mine. "I am pooped. Vacation cannot come soon enough."

"When are you leaving?" Kevin's mother had a beach house on the Outer Banks in North Carolina, and they were all going for a week. There was nothing like late summer in Magnolia to make you long for water and an ocean breeze.

"Next week. I am totally planning on leaving all child care to Grandma while I sit on the sand and read a book. And drink," she said, reaching for my glass, which was sweating the napkin underneath it into wet shreds, and draining half of the beer in one long swallow. "God, this is so good."

"Henry, can you bring me another beer, please?" I called out across the porch. There were well over a dozen people there—Sharon and Kevin and the boys, Wanee and her family, Cassandra, Pete and Arthur, the owners of Java Good Day, and their daughter, Caitlin, Kira, my boss from the art supply store, and Henry and me. It was Monday night and The Kitchen was closed, the rooms strangely empty and echoing when I walked inside to go to the bathroom.

"You drank the whole thing already? You lush!" he called back, pulling a chilled glass out of the cooler behind the outside bar and slipping it under the tap, letting the caramel liquid pour out, a thin foam settling on the top. I had never liked beer, but Henry made a cream ale that tasted of vanilla and sugar and I couldn't get enough of it.

"No, Sharon stole mine," I said, as he handed me the fresh glass, so cold it felt like it would burn my fingers. "Thank you."

"You can have your own, you know," he said to Sharon.

"It tastes so much better when it's stolen." Sharon drained the rest and held the empty glass out to him. "More, please," she said, and then let loose a monumental belch.

"Well, when you put it like that." Henry took the glass and headed back to the bar.

"Charming," I said. "Really. You do that at the Ladies Association lunches?"

"I save it just for you," Sharon said sweetly. "Speaking of which, I haven't seen you there in a while."

"I've been working. My landlord is a total nightmare if I'm late on rent," I said, and Sharon punched me in the arm. My mother's house had sold days after it had gone on the market, and when it looked like I would be staying in Magnolia for a while, I had moved into the carriage house on Sharon and Kevin's property. It was tiny and the bathroom and closet doors banged into each other and the stove was the size of a toddler's play set and it had a terrible spider problem, and I loved it. There was only one large room, with an antique iron bed against one wall, the kitchen in one corner, and the living area, which I had filled with an easel and canvases and tables covered with brushes and tubes of paint and rags sprayed with color. Every morning when I woke up, the first thing I saw was a spill of sunlight across the painting I was working on, and I could smell the grass and the garden outside and hear the twins laughing, and it always made me smile.

"Well, you've been missed. Ellen O'Connor asked about you just the other day."

"Oh yeah? How's she doing?"

Sharon shrugged. "I have no idea. I can't read those people."

"Yeah, well, they don't want you to be able to."

"I told her you were working at the art store and she said she might come by."

"Really? That would be nice. She and I took art together in high school. She was good, actually. I wonder if she still draws."

"I doubt she has time, what with all her playing maidservant to Ashley Hathaway."

"Don't be mean," I said mildly. I hadn't forgotten I had been equally mean about Ellen and Ashley and all the rest of them, but I also hadn't forgotten how difficult it was to be anything other than what everyone else expected you to be.

In the end, leaving hadn't been as painful as I had feared, or as easy as I might have wished. Phillip and I hadn't spoken since the night I had left—he communicated everything through his lawyer and I mostly agreed, because I wanted it to end, because I didn't care about the money and there wasn't anything else there that mattered to me, including him, and mostly what I thought about now was how sad it was I had ever agreed to live that way.

My mother had moved into her condo, and we had dinner together there once a week, because the one time she had been to the carriage house she had nearly broken into hives at the sight of the spiders and the dust. She was too much in the habit of criticizing and complaining to stop, so I had decided to get out of the habit of taking it personally. I could see my mother's words were my grandmother's legacy of disappointment, and the best I could do was to live in a way that would break the cycle. I hadn't been to the Ladies Association meetings, but I had signed up to work at the Collegiate Women's Society rummage sale, and the Garden Society fundraiser. Just because I didn't want to feel constrained by that world didn't mean I couldn't see all the good they did, and I wanted to be a part of that. On my terms.

But I spent most of my time working at Kira's store, where I was surrounded by the smell of wood and paint and the sharp, clean aroma of new paper, and I always tried extra hard to talk to the kids who came in, especially the teenagers, with their shaggy hair and sharp, defensive edges, their cash wadded up in their pockets, their fingertips dark with pencil lead. I wanted to grab their hands as they took their purchases and tell them, "Do this forever. If this makes you happy, do this forever. Do the thing that feeds your soul and don't let anyone else tell you that you are broken because of it."

I never did. Instead, I sent them out the door with fresh charcoal and new watercolor sets and I waved and said, "Come back soon," and hoped it would be enough of a benediction to carry them through.

"Dinner!" Wanee called, bouncing the screen door open and stepping out onto the porch, carrying a tray laden with food. Her husband followed with a similar tray, and then Henry and Pete, and everyone found their seats as we unloaded the serving dishes onto the table until it was so full there was hardly room for our plates, and we shuffled drinks and silverware and sacrificed our own elbow room for the sake of the meal. We had met at The Kitchen so we could eat outside—although, feeling the damp blanket of air on my arms, I wondered why—but Wanee had cooked. There were plates of fish cakes, fried golden-brown, and pyramids of summer rolls, sprigs of green Thai basil peeking out from the edges of the rice paper. In front of me was a platter of salad, cucumbers with frilled edges, fat red tomato slices from Henry's garden, translucent onion, sprinkled with crushed peanuts and marinating in a dressing that smelled both sharp and sweet. There were endive cups filled with chicken and carrots, and homemade noodles and curries, and Henry set pitchers of lemonade and ice water and sweet tea in the middle of the table, and the sight of so much plenty made me both overwhelmed and grateful.

The night before, Henry and I had gone to see Kevin's band play at a club where the music was too loud and the beer was too bitter, but we had stayed out until the early morning anyway, and I had slept in and spent the afternoon painting until I had noticed the time and rushed over for dinner, the last to arrive. I was wearing a loose blue-and-white-checked shirt and cutoff jeans shorts and there was paint all over my bare legs, and no one seemed to care. Henry had kissed me on the cheek when I walked in, and said I looked beautiful, even though I had gained another ten pounds since I had moved back to Magnolia, and I smelled like linseed oil and newsprint.

"Can I sit here?" Henry asked, plopping down in the chair on the other side of me and running his hands through his hair so the curls stood charmingly on end. He looked, as he always did, both happy and exhausted by the blissful chaos of taking care of everyone around him.

"Please do," I said, passing him the plate of summer rolls. I remembered my first impression of Henry when he had been working in his garden, how I had wanted to take a pair of hedge clippers to him, scrub the dirt off his face, put him in a pair of pants that fit. I didn't think any of those things now. I liked his messy, curly hair, and the half beard he ought to have shaved three days ago. I liked his faded band T-shirt and his jeans with the holes in the heels where he had stepped through them. I thought he looked comfortable, warm. I thought he looked like someplace I wanted to be.

When I had gone back to Phillip, I had done my best not to think of Henry. I had wanted to be sure I wasn't leaving Phillip for Henry, or because there was the possibility of Henry, if there were indeed the possibility of him. I wanted to have left Phillip because I never should have married him, and Henry only confused the issue, with his kindness, and the broadness of his hands, and the way his beard had tickled my face when he kissed me, with the way he could coax food from the ground and the way the people who worked for him looked at him with respect and pleasure instead of irritation or fear, and the way he brought people together just for the joy of it. In the end, I hadn't needed Henry as an excuse to leave, and when I had come back to Magnolia, it was as though we were starting over, as though Henry were, like everything in my life now, fresh and new and full of possibilities.

"Wanee, this is amazing, thank you," I said, swallowing a bite of the summer roll, all crisp vegetables and soft rice noodles and the fresh, bright taste of the garden, and everyone else agreed around mouthfuls of food.

"You're welcome."

"Typical, right? It's Wanee's and Henry's day off and they're feeding us," Arthur said, winking at Henry.

"Hey, I am not feeding anyone. I am just getting you all drunk," Henry said, raising his glass and taking a sip.

Everyone laughed, and Caitlin stood up in her chair and applauded, and then grinned shyly and plopped back down when everyone laughed again.

"So when are you leaving, Madeleine?" Cassandra asked, spooning some red curry over rice onto her plate and then passing the bowl on to Kira.

"Two weeks," I said. "I'll be gone for a month."

"Ugh, you are so lucky. I wish I could just take off and go to Paris and paint for a month," Pete said.

"You can't sit still long enough to draw a stick figure. You'd go crazy in a month," Arthur said. "Ooof." Caitlin had jumped from her chair into his lap, and he kissed her as she snuggled in.

"I think I could handle it if Paris were involved," Pete said. "I mean, I'd struggle through somehow."

"Well, don't be too jealous. I'm going to be completely broke when I come back," I said.

"But you'll be rich in art," Kira said dramatically, and everyone laughed again.

"Why Paris?" Wanee's husband, Pat, asked.

"My grandmother spent some time there. And, you know, it's Paris," I said. I couldn't explain it all, how I had always felt I didn't belong in my family, but reading my grandmother's journals was like reading my own thoughts, and I wanted to connect to her, how I felt my grandmother had left something unfinished there and I had the chance to finish it for her, how going abroad by myself signified a bravery I had never even considered I might possess.

"Maybe you'll end up falling in love with it and never coming back," Cassandra said.

"Hey, now. No fair trying to get rid of me. I just got here."

"I'd like to propose a toast." Henry leaned forward in his chair and raised his glass again. "To Paris."

The others put down their forks and fumbled for their glasses, raising them high. "To Paris," we all repeated, and we clinked our glasses together and the sound rang out clear and cheerful in the softness of the evening. I looked at what lay around me—the food, and the kind and happy faces of the people I had grown to love, and the bloom of the trees and the garden, the promise of Paris and the rest of my future beyond me, unknowable but mine to own, and I thought, *This*. This life where I had the space to find the things that were important to me instead of the things I was forced to do. This life where I was surrounded by friends who believed in art and food and community and who believed, fiercely, in me. This life with the endless, terrifying, happiness of possibility before me, and the light of Paris guiding me home.

ACKNOWLEDGMENTS

······················

I am so grateful to:

Elizabeth Winick Rubinstein, for your faith and encouragement.

Everyone at McIntosh & Otis, especially Alecia Douglas.

Chris Pepe, for your guidance, enthusiasm, and kindness.

The team at Putnam and Penguin Random House, for your unflagging support, especially Ivan Held, Lauren Lopinto, Christine Ball, Alexis Welby, Karen Fink, Ashley McClay, Anna Romig, and Tom Benton. Thanks to Ploy Siripant for the cover design, Lauren Kolm for the interior design, and Ivy McFadden for copyediting.

My international publishers, for bringing *The Weird Sisters* and *The Light of Paris* to readers around the world.

Erin Blakemore, Ellen Brown, and Kelly O'Connor McNees: Thank you for your wisdom and your unconditional love.

Steve Almond, Elizabeth Gilbert, Paula McLain, Sarah Pekkanen, and Kathy Trocheck, and all my writer friends and allies who have been so generous and supportive along the way. Special thanks to Joanne Levy, Samuel Park, and Kyran Pittman.

The community at Lighthouse Writers Workshop, especially Andrea Dupree and Bill Henderson.

The team at Tattered Cover Book Store, especially Cathy Langer.

Everyone at Barnes & Noble, especially Sessalee Hensley and Miwa Messer.

Lisa Casper and the staff of Douglas County Libraries, especially Amy Pfeiffer and Pam Harbert.

My CrossFit and CrossFit Modig families, especially David Goodenberger and Corey Townsend, and the Coffee Crew.

The Denver Debutante Ball Committee and Joanne Davidson.

Chris, for never letting go.

The writers at The Writers' Table. It's an honor to be part of your creative process, and a pleasure to write and think and laugh with you.

The booksellers and librarians who love and champion books and reading, and who so generously placed *The Weird Sisters* in readers' hands again and again.

And most of all, to you, for reading.

AUTHOR'S NOTE

In 1923, when my maternal grandmother was twenty-two, she went on a trip to Europe. The itinerary was planned—England, France, Italy, home. But when she arrived in Paris, my grandmother did something quite shocking for a young woman of her social class in those days—she decided to stay.

She found a job, working at the American Library, and threw herself into the pleasures of the City of Light in the Jazz Age—dancing at Zelli's until dawn, touring the Musée Rodin's gardens, and exploring the lively Latin Quarter with her friends.

My grandmother passed away when I was young, and I never really knew her. But a few years ago, my parents mentioned that not only had she lived in Paris, they had the letters she'd written to her family when she was there.

Reading those letters, I met the young woman my grandmother had been—bookish but lively, cocky but naïve, and full of delight in the life she had been bold enough to create for herself.

Although my grandmother loved books, it wasn't realistic for her to dream of being a writer. In one letter, she says that when she returns from Paris, she'll either take a secretarial course or get married—her only options.

Almost a century later, I feel lucky to live with freedoms my grandmother could have only dreamed of. This story is in honor of her and all the grandmothers who came before us, to celebrate the brave choices they made so we can be the women we want to be.

ABOUT THE AUTHOR

....

Eleanor Brown is the *New York Times*–bestselling author of *The Weird Sisters*, which was an Indie Next pick, an Amazon Best Book of the Month, and a Barnes & Noble Book of the Month and a Discover selection. Her writing has also appeared in anthologies, newspapers, and magazines, including *The Washington Post, CrossFit Journal*, and *Publishers Weekly*, and she teaches at conferences and writing centers around the country. She lives in Colorado.

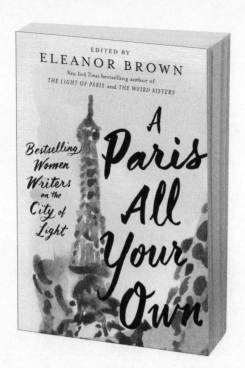

A collection of eighteen all-new essays written by some of the biggest names in women's fiction, edited by Eleanor Brown, the *New York Times*–bestselling author of *The Weird Sisters* and *The Light of Paris*.

With contributions from Paula McLain, Susan Vreeland, J. Courtney Sullivan, Therese Fowler, and many more, this collection is perfect for both armchair travelers and veterans of Parisian pilgrimages.

PUTNAM
EST. 1838

Penguin
Random
House